Books by Eric L. Harry

Arc Light
Society of the Mind
Protect and Defend
Invasion

Pandora: Outbreak

Eric L. Harry

REBEL BASE BOOKS
Kensington Publishing Corp.
www.kensingtonbooks.com

Rebel Base Books are published by
Kensington Publishing Corp. 119 West 40th Street New York, NY 10018

All Kensington titles, imprints, and distributed lines are available at special quantity discounts for bulk purchases for sales promotion, premiums, fundraising, and educational or institutional use.

To the extent that the image or images on the cover of this book depict a person or persons, such person or persons are merely models, and are not intended to portray any character or characters featured in the book.

Special book excerpts or customized printings can also be created to fit specific needs. For details, write or phone the office of the Kensington Special Sales Manager:
Kensington Publishing Corp.
119 West 40th Street
New York, NY 10018
Attn. Special Sales Department. Phone: 1-800-221-2647.

Kensington Reg. U.S. Pat. & TM Off.
REBEL BASE Reg. U.S. Pat. & TM Off.
The RB logo is a trademark of Kensington Publishing Corp.

First Electronic Edition: January 2018
eISBN-13: 978-1-63573-014-2
eISBN-10: 1-63573-014-7

First Print Edition: January 2018
ISBN-13: 1978-1-63573-017-3
ISBN-10: -63573-017-1

Printed in the United States of America

I dedicate this book to my lovely and beautiful daughter, Jessica.

Author's Note

Every breath you take, you inhale thousands of viruses. With every dip in the sea, you swallow billions. Half of those will only infect amoebae. Most of the rest are harmless as well. Some, however, are dangerous, and a few are deadly. Every day, somewhere, a virus mutates or the habitat in which it has lain dormant is disturbed, slowly swelling the ranks of the potentially fatal. This story attempts to depict plausibly the emergence of The Next Big One. May God have mercy on us all.

"O, what a world of unseen visions and heard silences, this insubstantial country of the mind . . . where each of us reigns reclusively alone, questioning what we will, commanding what we can . . . An introcosm that is more myself than anything I can find in a mirror. This consciousness that is myself of selves, that is everything, and yet nothing at all—what is it? And where did it come from? And why?"

—Julian Jaynes, *The Origin of Consciousness in the Breakdown of the Bicameral Mind*

Chapter 1

CHUKOTKA AUTONOMOUS OKRUG, SIBERIA
Infection Date 7, 1500 GMT (3:00 a.m. Local)

The sound of the zipper on Emma Miller's tent woke her with a start. Cold air flooded in. Backlit in dim starlight she saw a man, his breath fogged. Her heart raced as she fumbled for her flashlight . . . and found her pistol. "Who's there?" She flicked the light on. It was the blond Russian soldier who had saved her life hours earlier. His pupils were black and unresponsive. "Stop!" He said nothing. She kicked at him. "Stop-*stop!*" He crawled atop her. She dropped the flashlight while flicking the pistol's safety off.

Bam! In the flash, his head rocked back with a hole in his brow.

Sgt. Sergei Travkin collapsed heavily onto Emma's shins. "Oh-my-*God!*"

A knife stabbed her tent and sliced it open. Men hoisted Emma— whimpering before she thought to hold her breath—into the shockingly cold air. The ever sober young scientist loosed an animal sound. "*Nooo! No!*" Someone wrenched from her grip the pistol Travkin had given her after being infected. The pistol with which she had killed him.

Emma's sobs merged with her shivering. Anonymous men clad in personal protective equipment unzipped her blue jeans and yanked. Goosebumps sprang from bare thighs. A bright lantern blinded her. Her jeans snagged at each ankle. "Stoooop!" she screamed. "P-Please!" Buttons popped off her blouse. "Wait!" An ugly knife sliced through the front of her bra. She covered her breasts. Gloved fingers found the elastic of her panties. She clamped her knees together and stooped in a futile attempt at modesty. Her teeth clenched against an overpowering chatter. She shook from the cold, from the shock of killing a man and from the incapacitating terror at what may lie ahead.

"Would . . . somebody . . . ?" Frigid spray stung her midriff. She doubled over with a grunt. Three men in gowns, hoods, boots, and gloves sprayed disinfectant through a wand, pumped a cylinder like an exterminator, and scrubbed her roughly with a brush at the end of a telescoping pole. She willed herself to stand upright, raising quivering arms and turning circles in place, as soldiers rolled Emma's tent into a single biohazard bundle.

Travkin's dilated pupils hadn't contracted even in the brilliance of her flashlight. *Did he infect me?* Noxious liquid burned her eyes and fouled her mouth. Despite its awful taste, she swished, gargled, and spat. The pool brush scraped at her hair. She grabbed it and used it to scrub her head and face herself. "He wouldn't stop!" she shouted before coughing and spitting. *He never got closer than my knees. Maybe I'm okay?*

Soldiers hoisted the impermeable crimson bag, covered in prickly black biohazard symbols, by loops at its corners and carried away her tent, parka, and backpack along with Travkin's remains. The faint rays of her flashlight shone blood-red through its plastic.

Buckets of cold water cascaded over her head. "*Jee*-zus!" One after another. "Aaaaw!" Her chest seized so tight she couldn't even breathe.

A tall French medic extended a blanket at the end of the pole. She wrapped herself in it but could force no words past locked jaws. The medic draped a second blanket over her head and waved away Russian soldiers' rifles. In the distance—and upwind—the World Health Organization's Surge Team One, and her own Surge Team Two, which had arrived just that day, watched in grim silence. From the shadows all witnessed their worst fears materialize as the grip of rigid infection control protocols seized a colleague.

"Hang tough, Emma!" "You can do it!" "You can *beat* it!" Their accents were varied, but their theme was consistent. "*Farewell, Emma Miller.*" She cried as she stumbled barefoot across hard ground, her feet already numb. The medic kept his distance but illuminated her path with a lantern. Emma heard disturbing noises with each jarring misstep that must have emanated from her.

She asked where they were going. The French medic replied, "Quarantine." Her destiny was now binary. Either she'd contracted the new disease, whatever the hell it was, or not. Like a prisoner in a Roman coliseum, Emma awaited her thumbs up or thumbs down.

Whirring sounds grew louder—air pumps at quick-erect isolation shelters. Travkin had been hustled into one after fighting off the suicidal attack on their landing zone. Emma had watched from a distance and upwind as he, too, had been stripped and scrubbed. But the shelters had been off-limits when she'd come to thank him. Seven hours later, eyes black, it had been Travkin who visited Emma.

The isolation shelters reminded Emma of the bouncy house her brother rented for her nephew's twelfth birthday. Emma and her twin sister, tipsy from the wine at the grown-ups' table, had giggled and jumped like schoolgirls. But those playpens maintained their shape by positive pressure. Isolation shelters were the opposite—held up by poles as their tainted miasma was sucked out through HEPA filters, removing micron-sized particles one hundred air changes an hour. Negative pressure kept germs from escaping the openings.

"What about the other guy?" she asked in vibrato, shivering. "I don't wanta catch it from him."

"Corp. Leskov died," the medic replied.

Oh, God! Please! I'll be good. Please! Okay. Focus. Concentrate. Science.

"Blown pupils," she said, "c-c-can be from intracranial pressure." Her sister Isabel, a neuroscientist, had once told her about that phenomenon. "How'd Travkin get out?"

"He attacked my medical team," replied a new man, also with a French accent, also in PPE, who arrived to escort them the last few meters to the bouncy houses. "Fractured my doctor's windpipe." The open-air site of the mobile isolation ward was brightly lit. "Eye gouging and asphyxiation for one medic." Emma lay on a gurney, as bidden. "Broken neck for the other." They peeled away her blankets. Emma reflexively covered her breasts and pubis. Gas heaters bathed her in blessed warmth. "You're lucky to be alive." Emma scoffed at any mention of her good fortune, emitting a puff of fogged breath.

A wireless blood pressure cuff squeezed her biceps. A thermometer was clamped to her fingertip. The prick of an IV needle caused her to jump. A drip bag flowed cold into her arm. "Antibiotics," the doctor said.

"Cipro?" He snorted. Better. Last-ditch. Kept out of use to prevent resistance. A doomsday-stopper. But oh, the things epidemiology professors know. Statistically, the new disease was probably a virus—not a bacterium—as impervious to antibiotics as fungi, protists, prions, protozoans, and worms, other tiny predators that ate their prey from the inside.

When she'd asked others on her team earlier how bad the new illness was, it had strangely been a big secret. But she asked again, and as a professional courtesy, or as required by the Hippocratic oath, the French doctor seemed to reply honestly. "Until we get the pathogen's taxonomy done and ICD assigns it a name, we're calling the illness SED: severe encephalopathic disease."

"Severe?" Emma asked. "So, a high initial-case fatality rate?"

"Fifty percent," the doctor replied. *Christ!* An incubation period rivaling cholera. First symptoms around two hours. An even shorter latency period. People are contagious before first symptoms, which are gastroenteritis, chills, nausea, vomiting, respiratory distress, joint pain, high fever peaking at hour four in convulsions and acute intracranial pain. The medic laid a third blanket onto Emma, but it did nothing to stop her trembling. "Direct mortality is between four and six hours of exposure. But survivors then report feeling no discomfort at all."

"Whatta you mean, *direct* mortality?" she barely forced out.

"Well," he explained, "Travkin's death wasn't direct."

"*Oh.*" *Jeeze!* "So, if you survive, what th-then? What does it do?"

The doctor glanced at a nearby unit, different from the others in that its vinyl walls were opaque, not clear. Bright light leaked through the zippered seals of its single doorway. "We don't know a lot yet." Just outside the unit lay the unzipped empty body bag from which protruded the remains of Emma's tent. Her flashlight still shone inside.

"You're doing an autopsy?" Emma said. "Of Travkin?"

"You made a mess of his cranium," the doctor replied in tacit confirmation.

"What's the pathogen's vector?" Emma asked.

"It's not zoonotic. It didn't mutate and leap species. The Russians were drilling for oil when a mud logger caught it. Apparently, as an early test for hydrocarbons before the spectrographic analysis is done, old-timers *taste* the rock cuttings. Our guess is the pathogen was frozen a few dozen meters under the permafrost 30 to 40 thousand years ago. The crew, fifty-one, mostly men, all got sick. The Russians called Geneva. As soon as Surge Team One was assembled here, they declared a sudden-onset emergency and called for your Surge Team Two."

"Fifty-one people?" The other isolation shelters were empty. "Where are they?"

"The half that survived the acute phase. . . . Well, you ran into a few of them when your helicopter landed. The Russians are rounding up the others in the forest."

Jesus! Emma thought. "So, *Encephalopathic*? It causes . . . b-brain damage?"

In a terrifyingly sympathetic tone, he replied, "To the cerebral cortex," and laid a hand on her shoulder.

"Is the damage reversible?"

He shook his head.

"So, p-permanent brain damage?"

"Structural alterations. In every victim we've studied. I'm sorry."

Oh-God-oh-God-oh-God! Get a grip. Get a grip! But she couldn't. *Science!* "What," she said, choking on her fears, "what does the damage do?"

"Did you note Travkin's lack of emotional responsiveness?" He again put his hand on her now-quaking shoulder. "And they can be very, *very* violent."

The tall medic plunged a syringe into the injection port on Emma's IV.

"What's thaaah—" Emma started to ask just before tumbling into a calm and comfy bliss. She smiled at arriving Russian soldiers, armed and in camouflaged protective gear, so unlike the solid green worn by the *très chic* French. *Change of procedure after Travkin?* she wondered, barely clinging to reality against the undertow.

Emma drifted on a river of euphoria. She was Dr. Miller, epidemiology professor, yeah, Johns Hopkins, on assignment, *for* . . . for the *NIH*, that's it, and the WHO! That took a lot out of her, so she relaxed into the current. She was Emmy of sunny days playing tennis and swimming, and languid evenings gossiping and flirting. A life in a world-within-a-world, her family's Greenwich country club, in a galaxy far, far away.

In summers, she ventured out of that bubble only for sailing lessons on the Sound, which were the highlights of her poor, poor sister's week. Emma had sports teammates; clubs masquerading as charities for college applications; and boyfriends one after the other, scandalously overlapping. Her identical twin sister, Isabel, in contrast, had mom and *dad*. The three would binge-watch television series and movies, *together*—one of Dad's John Wayne movies or whatever for each of Izzy's romantic comedies. They thus ruined Isabel's scant chance for a social life by providing her refuge from some awkward years.

Both twins, now thirty-two, were five-foot-four, both 110 pounds, both fit, both pretty for God's sake. Both were groomed, educated, and well-raised in a wealthy, high-achieving family. Both had light brown hair that turned blond in summers. But Emma's was cut short for convenience on these grown-up scientific adventures. The tips of her hair now felt frozen and her arm cold as she twirled a strand. It had once been long and lustrous like Isabel's still was. Emma felt envious. A medic placed her arm back under the blanket.

Emma raised her wobbly head. Someone was dissecting Travkin's brain in the opaque bouncy house. Was hers next? She had to warn her siblings. "I wasn't told 'bout the risks."

"You were here," the doctor replied, "to determine whether there were any wildlife hosts or amplifiers. You weren't supposed to be on this side of the isolation barrier."

"Then I got *attacked!* Oops! We're sure it's transmiss'ble human-to-human?" A nod. "Also rel'vant. Listen. You *owe* me. You gotta warn my sister and brother."

"I'm sorry," the doctor replied. "I can't do that. We have strict orders to keep this totally secret." He raised a tablet. "For my report, where did you get the pistol?"

"From Travkin! He knew they turn violent? So he gave me his gun? He was . . . protective. I thought, you know, he liked me? Pro'lly wanted to make sure I was okay."

The distracted doctor said, "Or he came to rape you. Both women on the rig's catering crew were infected during sexual assaults." He gave orders in French to his staff. Among the uninfected, life went on. A medic read something off a monitor. The doctor typed something on his tablet. But in Emma's world, all was ending. She tried to focus. HEPA filtration. "It's airborne?" The doctor's silence chilled her worse than the Siberian air. "If it passes that easily, just from *breathing*, everyone is . . . *doomed!* The whole fracking world!" The doctor, medics, and armed Russian soldiers were all listening now.

They helped Emma rise and ushered her to her very own clear plastic cube. The tall medic held the drip bag over her head. The short medic held out earbuds, "To talk." The doctor held out a hand, muttering about needing visual observation. They wanted to watch her change into what Travkin had become. She gave him her blankets and covered herself with her hand and forearm. Her skin was streaked red from scrubbing. The doctor droned on and on about ensuring her a high quality of care. In a small act of defiance, Emma turned away to uncover herself and inserted her earbuds. In the silence that followed, however, her fears quickly overcame her defenses.

A lucky near miss, death or brain damage? Buy a ticket and spin the wheel.

In the cube, a medic hung the bag from a hook beside a bare, metal-framed cot and plugged more tubes into Emma's plumbing before leaving her alone. She then curled up on the plastic floor in the fetal position. *Breathe. Just breathe.* She was trembling. *Science. Science.* On the uninfected side of the transparent walls, they worked in the open. Air would dilute the pathogen, reducing its concentration and the risk of infection.

Emma considered whether the two Russian soldiers who stood outside would shoot if she ran for it, and concluded they would. But would they also shoot her even if she didn't bolt? Should she make a break now before she grew too ill? But to where? Naked in frozen northeastern Siberia? Hunted like the rest of her kind? She tried to focus. *Science.*

"Can I have a clock?" When asked if she wanted local, GMT or time since exposure, she chose the last. *Lab time.* Who cares about local, GMT or time back home?

Which was where? Her sister had fretted endlessly about rootlessness when their parents died in a car wreck their sophomore year of college. After the funeral, they had packed all their belongings into storage units. A month later, their childhood home was sold, and the three siblings were set adrift. No more shrine to childhood memories. No parents celebrating academic accomplishments or consoling broken hearts. Her sister Isabel had spent her next few summers with their big brother, Noah, and his young wife, clinging to family. Emma got a string of jobs—and boyfriends—to fill her school breaks. But now she wasn't at home in her apartment in Maryland or in any of the various guys' places she frequented or in nearby Virginia where Noah lived. Emma had people but no place, she thought, as her incomplete life possibly neared its end.

On the laptop screen, a digital clock counted up past 0:31:43.

A new, tall man arrived in full PPE. "Hello?" he said through a mic into her earbuds. "It's Hermann Lange." He pronounced his name in German fashion—"Err-mahn Lang-uh"—even though he was *French* Swiss. Emma did her best to cover herself. He took his hood off briefly to don a headset and extracted files and a laptop from his satchel.

"Thank God," she said, glad to see a familiar face. Everything had been a blur. The mobilization call the day before. Throwing cold weather gear into a bag she kept packed for the jungles of Africa, Asia, or the Amazon—nature's laboratories—where spillovers usually occurred. The huge US military transport, empty save for its crew and its cargo, Emma, departed Joint Base Andrews, refueled in Alaska, and met up with her team, from all around the globe, at a remote Siberian airport.

During their short helicopter flight, Travkin snuck glances at her. Emma couldn't imagine why, bundled up as she was. When they descended toward the tall oil derrick, Emma should have sensed danger. Apprehensive soldiers loaded rifles. Travkin kissed the Orthodox cross he wore on his gold chain. *I killed him!* She jammed her eyes shut.

After landing with a thud, Emma had climbed out, shielding her eyes against soil churned up by the rotors. As the engine wound down, she heard shouts. A half dozen men charged them at the dead run. Full-auto rips from three Kalashnikovs ended the lives of all but one. Soldiers swung their rifles but couldn't shoot through the scattering scientists. Leskov tackled the attacker fifteen meters from Emma. Travkin stabbed him. Neither were wearing protective gear. A single fountain of blood spurted from his chest. Emma had followed fleeing colleagues. But looking back over her shoulder she was struck by the man's spooky eyes, wide as the last bit of life drained from him, pupils totally fucking black like Travkin's.

"Feel like talking?" asked Hermann. He was a social anthropologist on Surge Team One who studied behaviors that caused diseases to spread, like shaking hands, unprotected sex, or ritual preparation of the dead; or that inhibited their spread like handwashing and social isolation. He was in his late thirties and handsome enough. He had twice hit on Emma, and twice failed. Too much alcohol and pot on his first try, and on the second neither had showered for days in The Congo during a now prosaic seeming Ebola outbreak. Happier times. Would he soon watch her writhe naked in this plastic cage as some parasite, now rapidly reproducing inside her, gnawed away on her brain?

"*Love* to chat," she replied. The haze of narcotics was lifting. "SED has to be more contagious than any pathogen we've ever seen. Infection without coughing, sneezing mucal catastrophes? Droplet nuclei in distal airways? Sub-five microns? So it's viral?"

"It's archaic, and we think it was probably highly evolved back when it was frozen," Hermann said. "It didn't randomly mutate, spill over into us from some distant species and barely survive. It *thrives* in us. If you ask me, it evolved *specifically* to infect humans. It's perfectly adapted to us. It just needed contact, which it got when the permafrost was disrupted, and *boom*. It's off and running."

Oh God, oh God, she thought. But she mustered the strength to shout, "So if it *had* no animal reservoir, why the fuck am I even *here?*"

"We collected wildlife specimens for you to examine," Hermann explained. "Just to be certain. If it turns out there aren't any intermediate hosts or transmission amplifiers—if humans are the only reservoir—we may still beat this one, like smallpox or polio."

"What's the R-nought?" Emma asked.

R_0, pronounced "R-nought," was a disease's basic reproduction rate. How many people in a susceptible population, on average, will one sick person infect? An R_0 of less than one meant the pathogen was not very infectious and its outbreaks should burn out. But an R_0 greater than one was an epidemic threat, and the higher the R_0, the more infectious. Touch a door knob a few minutes after a high-R_0 carrier, then rub your eye or brush a crumb from your lips and you auto-inoculate, injecting the pathogen into yourself.

But Travkin had only breathed on Emma, briefly, from a few feet away.

"What's the R-nought, Hermann?" she persisted.

"High. Higher than the Black Death, smallpox, the Spanish Flu, polio, AIDS. We may have found The Next Big One."

Oh-my-God! Heavy chains bound Emma to a dreadful fate. She again curled into a fetal ball. "Or The Next Big One found us," she muttered.

At his laptop, Hermann asked, "Emma, could you list the emotions you're feeling?"

"Emotions? Seriously? Uhm, well, scared out of my fucking *wits* would be number one on my list."

"Anything else?" he asked.

"Really!" Emma sat up. "You're *interviewing* me?" That really pissed her off! She shook the thermometer from her finger and yanked the blood pressure cuff off. The soldiers at the hatch raised their rifles. The short medic radioed the doctor, who burst out of the autopsy lab as Emma carefully removed her IV just ahead of a rush of euphoria. They had injected a sedative remotely into the tube that led into her veins, but she'd been too quick. Her head spun only once. "What the *fuck?*" she shouted. "You tried to knock me *out?*"

"Dr. Miller," the French doctor replied, "you need that IV."

"Bullshit!" Emma snapped. "If antibiotics worked, we wouldn't be here."

"You're also getting antivirals, antiprotozoals, and fluids." Emma stared with sudden clarity through the walls' distorted optics like at survivors of some post-apocalyptic hell. *She* was free. It was the people outside her plastic shelter, from those garbed head-to-toe in PPE, to everyone on Earth beyond, who now needed to cower in fear – not her.

Emma knew the feeling of spending hours in personal protective equipment. Knock headgear aside, you're dead. Prick a finger capping a syringe, dead. Tear gloves disrobing, dead. You get antsy. It's the *un*infected who were visitors to this hostile new world.

"So Hermann," she said, "parasites follow Darwin's law. What adaptive advantage do big black pupils give SED's pathogen?"

"It could allow the infected to identify each other," Hermann ventured. He'd obviously already thought that one up.

"Why? So they,"—*or is it we?*—"can . . . build human pyramids to top our walls?"

"Natural selection doesn't have a purpose, only results."

"Good one. Level with me, Hermann. Did I catch it? I can't wait hours."

"It may be sooner. Leskov had a head cold. His immune system was weakened. His fever appeared at forty-four minutes. Have *you* been sick recently?"

"No." So Hermann wasn't there as a friend. He'd been with the others too. Interviewed them too. "How can it *possibly* reproduce so quickly?" she asked.

"A high reproductive rate is one reason SED seems highly evolved *and* perfectly adapted to humans. I'm telling you. It evolved to use us, its hosts, to aid its spread. This brain damage isn't random, it's . . ." The doctor chided him in French, pointing at Emma, who cried and shivered in fear. "I'm sorry, Emma," Hermann said. "I'm very sorry. If you'd allow monitoring, you'd know sooner."

"Would you even *tell* me if the readouts show a temperature spike?" Before he could protest, Emma asked, "What was it like when Travkin went through it?"

"When you turn, you'll get. . . . He got very ill." Hermann's verbal misstep hit Emma like a body blow. She closed her eyes. She *was* infected. Of *course* she was. *Look at how they're fucking treating me!* "Physical distress, memory deficits, possibly anterograde amnesia. Deficits in social cognition." Then he again said, "Sooo, I've got some *questions?*"

"What, fill in bubbles with a No. 2 pencil? 'On a scale of one to five, how much do you wanta murder me right now?' Then some ghoul in there saws open my cranium and takes cross-sections!"

"Emma, the pathologist in there is Pieter Groenewalt," pronouncing it, "Gryoo-neh-vahl-t" with a hard German "t" even though the South African Anglicized his name. "You remember him and his wife. He's bitching that he isn't allowed on this side of the isolation barrier to see the infected—alive. But all the data is being rigidly compartmentalized."

Emma no longer cared about Groenewalt, his petty frustrations or their mission's data security rules, or felt any part of Hermann's world. She was Shrödinger's freakin' cat—maybe dead, maybe demented. Over the next hour and a half, as Emma monitored every sensation she felt plus many more imagined, Hermann talked a lot, adding small scary details to the important terrifying facts about SED. She spoke very little, mostly silently recalling the milestones of her too short life to date.

The clock passed two hours. Nothing. But a few minutes later, her head swam as if the world rotated beneath her, then it was gone. Not so the panic. Her chest clutched at her breath, forcing her to inhale deeply to break its hold. A prickly sweat burst out all over. But that was the anxiety. *Wait. Wait. Wait.*

Emma threw up without warning. It shocked her. The short medic entered—keeping his distance, eyeing her warily—and cleaned up the mess with a sprayer/vacuum on his pool-boy pole. Emma was shivering.

They raised the thermostat. Minutes later, she was sweating. They lowered it. Tears of the inevitable flowed. She was sick. *Mommy? Daddy?* Help *me!*

"Emma? Can I ask you a few . . .?"

"*Why?*" she finally shouted, pounding the plastic flooring with both fists. She had tried to deny her churning stomach, waves of dizziness, and deep fatigue. But at 2:13:25, she admitted the worst. Flushed and clammy, she broke down and sobbed.

"Let us help," the doctor pled. The tall medic sank to his knees and crossed himself.

"Bring it all back," Emma mumbled. The medics entered and reinserted the IV and reattached the blood pressure cuff and thermometer. "I have a brother," Emma said to Hermann as they worked on her. "Noah Miller, a lawyer in McLean, Virginia. And a twin sister, Isabel, a professor at UCSB. I want them notified." Hermann suggested she relax and keep calm. "I want them *warned!* You tell them what's coming and to get ready, get *ready*, you *understand*, and I'll answer anything. I'll cooperate. Noah and Isabel Miller!" Emma shouted, sobbing. "They're all I've got! They're all I've . . ."

Hermann gave her a single nod, unnoticed by the others. She didn't trust him, but it would have to do. Calmness flowed into her veins. She closed her throbbing eyes.

"We're all in this together," Hermann had the gall to say.

"*Spare* me!" Emma replied. But on reflection, he was fucking right. This thing was incredibly rapacious. *You can run, Hermann, but you can't hide.* Stomach cramps elicited a grunt. Hermann asked if she needed more painkillers. "Yes!" she replied. A wave of peace followed. *Let's just get this over with. Come on you little piece of shit virus! Give it your best shot!*

The doctor returned from the opaque morgue. Emma latched onto the spinning Earth, sat up, and asked him for news. "Groenewalt found brain damage unrelated to the trauma from the gunshot. Bleeding. Loss of neuronal mass, particularly in Travkin's right hemisphere. The damage was remarkably similar to the earlier victims."

Emma pressed on her eyelids as pain split her forehead. *It's happening! I was kidding! Please stop!*

"Emma?" she heard Hermann say. "Can you look up at the camera?" She stared into the bullet-shaped cylinder. "Thanks. So, these questions might sound odd, but humor me, okay? When we were in The Congo last year, you told me about having lunch at your country club after tennis, and the busboy was one of your classmates?" Emma was too tired to fight him and nodded. "You remember how you told me you felt?"

"Embarr'ssed," Emma said, slurring.

"Right," Hermann replied. "And do you know *why* you were embarrassed?"

"'Cause I was rich. And when he bussed our table, I was whispering to a girl and she laughed. He thought I'd said something about him. Izzy, my sister, said I'd been rude. But we weren't talking about the boy. I'd invited Izzy along to play doubles 'cause she didn't have any friends and our parents made me. We were laughing about Isabel dying a virgin 'cause she was so uptight. She pro'lly knew, and that was why she got mad."

"The busboy was poor and had to work cleaning tables," Hermann said, clarifying his point for the record. "And you were rich and playing tennis over the school break. That fact made you feel embarrassed in front of your classmate?" She nodded. "And forgive me, but when you shot Sgt. Travkin, the man who'd saved your life, how did you feel?"

That burned through the painkilling haze. "*Fuck* you! He wouldn't stop!" Tears welled up. She began to cry, but Hermann persisted. "I felt terr'ble! *Okay?*"

Before she drifted off, Hermann asked, "Why'd you feel terrible killing Travkin?"

"Why the hell do you *think?* He saved my life, then I shot him . . . with his own *gun!* He gave me his . . . his . . ." She drifted in and out of consciousness. "Remember our deal!" was the last thing she recalled saying. "Remember . . . !"

* * * *

"Emma? Emma? Emma?"

A penlight streaked across her vision, leaving red smears in her view of the French doctor holding it. Her wrists and ankles were zip-tied to her cot's frame. Coiled plastic IV tubing and her blood pressure cuff and thermometer lay in a pile. When two armed soldiers entered the unit, her heart raced and the plastic ties cut into her skin.

The doctor argued with a Russian officer in English. "She's American! W-H-O! I don't care about your orders! We take full responsibility!" Everyone turned toward the sound of a gunshot outside. Emma's tensed muscles began to quiver.

The doctor said to Emma. "We have to go. Feel up to it?" Another gunshot.

She rose, naked, when cut free. Five men, two armed, stood between her and freedom, and she felt dizzy and unsteady on her feet. The tall medic handed her an impermeable coverall, which she held until he directed her to step into it. He put plastic booties on her feet, latex gloves on her hands, a mask and goggles on her face, and a hood over her wet hair. He then taped her sleeves to her gloves and her pants cuffs to her boots. A heavy, gray wool overcoat was hung on her shoulders. It smelled of body odor.

Outside, she climbed into a huge, open vehicle. Single shots were drowned out by its big engine rumbling to life. Only Hermann sat beside Emma. The doctor, two medics, and two Russian soldiers, one at the front and one by the open rear door, lined the opposite wall. *Jump out!* Her pulse pounded.

As the slow, bumpy ride began, Hermann asked, "Emma, how do you feel?" Tree branches scraped across high metal sides, distracting a guard. A flood of frigid air drenched the benches lining the walls of the open compartment. "How do you feel?" he repeated.

"Fine," came from memory. "How are *you?*" seemed like the thing to say.

Emma couldn't read Hermann's expression. "Well, I sure wish I'd left on the helicopter with Pieter."

The doctor said something in French, shouted, stood, and banged on the metal bulkhead. The vehicle halted. The doctor exited at the rear. Hermann peered out a side hatch and gasped. "*Mein Gott!*" Emma followed his gaze. Oil workers knelt, eyes dilated, and removed hardhats on a command given in Russian. An officer raised a pistol to one man's forehead—*bang! "Mon dieu!"* Hermann cried. Although the workers bore signs of fighting—bloody faces and limbs, torn clothing—they were serene and composed, staring up at the muzzle unflinching as each was shot in turn.

Hermann jumped at each *bang*, muttering in French, his face contorted.

The Russian soldiers on the opposite bench stared at Emma from behind respirators. They would be distracted if their headgear were knocked askew. Deep breathing helped her resist the impulse to lunge, prematurely, for their rifles.

Outside, the French doctor shouted, "Murderers!" in English, at the Russians.

"Do you remember our deal, Emma?" Hermann asked. She nodded. A medic raised a camera. Hermann said, "Subject, Dr. Emma Miller, epidemiology professor, Johns Hopkins University, contracted SED six hours ago." Date, time, location. "Dr. Pieter Groenewalt departed for Geneva two hours ago with eleven brain specimens. We are evacuating to Anadyr in an open-air vehicle to lessen infection risk. Russians are killing all SED survivors except Subject. Repeating questions one and two, Event Log Twelve."

Dive across the aisle between the two soldiers and maybe neither would fire. Claw the face shield loose and yank the rifle from one soldier's lap. If the other hesitated, she could fire first and kill them all. But if the second guard was heedless of harming his comrades and opened fire inside the packed vehicle, she would surely die. Plus, there were all the soldiers outside. It took all her willpower not to obey the intense instinct she felt to flail at the men who threatened her life.

Hermann still flinched at each report from the Russian officer's pistol. "Emma, you told me about," *bang*, "about a lunch at your club after tennis. The busboy was a classmate." The rear door remained open. *Bang.* A headfirst dive outside. The woods were thick. "Do you remember how you felt when he came to your table?"

"Embarrassed," she replied from memory, uncertain what that word actually meant.

"Yes," Hermann typed—*bang!*—and flinched. "*Why* were you embarrassed?"

"Because . . . Because . . ." She was too fatigued to compose an answer. *Bang!*

The soldier by the rear door checked his safety. It was on the left, beside the trigger. "Were you embarrassed because he was handsome and you were sweaty?"

It had been a cool day. The boy had bad acne. "No."

"Maybe," Hermann ventured, "you were embarrassed because you were rich and played tennis all summer, but he was poor and cleaned tables on his vacation. Is that it?"

She had a trust fund that would pay her millions in a few years. The boy must have been working because he needed money. But . . . "No," she replied.

Significant looks were exchanged. *Take the scissors protruding from the tall medic's pouch. Jab them through the soldier's face shield. Grab his rifle. Flick the safety to "Fire." Kill everyone.* Too many steps. The second soldier would certainly fire first.

"One more question," Hermann said. "When you shot Sgt. Travkin, the man infected while saving your life yesterday, with his own gun, how did that make you feel?"

"Terrible."

"Okay. Do you know *why* you felt terrible?"

"Because . . ." She couldn't even recall what feeling terrible meant, and tried to recreate the feeling. He entered the tent. She shot him in the face. There was nothing "terrible" or anything else about it.

The doctor climbed aboard, cursing in French. The rear door slammed shut. The vehicle slowly passed the site of the ongoing slaughter. The French doctor, medics, and armed Russian guards swayed as the vehicle's treads ground across the terrain, and ducked as sticks and leaves rained down from low branches. *Now?* Emma smelled smoke.

Everyone's attention was drawn through hatches to the growing pile of burning bodies. *Now?* In the distance beyond the pyre, a small floatplane rose into the pale blue sky. *Now?* But no one other than Emma seemed to notice the departing aircraft as more bodies were tossed into the crackling flames. *Now?*

Chapter 2

WASHINGTON, D.C.
Infection Date 8, 1400 GMT (10:00 a.m. Local)

Isabel Miller had never been to the White House. Her high school trip had been canceled due to a terrorism scare. An unsmiling Patricia Maldonado, "Special-Assistant-to-the-President," she said, escorted her onto an elevator that went down, not up. In her early forties, the aide was about ten years older than Isabel, trim like a runner, with limp black hair that needed both body and a wash. Her gray wool skirt and matching, form-fitting jacket added to her already chilly, buttoned-up demeanor.

"The Secret Service wouldn't tell me anything," Isabel said. "What's this about?"

"There are some formalities first," Maldonado non-replied without looking up from her phone. The elevator opened onto a corridor of shiny cinder block walls. A Marine stood stiffly beside a closed door, hands at his back, in blue trousers with a red stripe, a white hat, and a ceremonial white holster from which poked a very real-looking black pistol.

The two women sat in silence and waited.

Isabel had been asleep in her Santa Barbara apartment when Name Unavailable rang her home and cell phones repeatedly. She ignored everything until she heard loud knocking. "Dr. Miller?" one of two buzz cut men in dark suits had said. Both had held out gold badges—"US Secret Service, Special Agent, Est. 1865." Curly wires had risen from crisp white collars to earphones. "Please pack an overnight bag and come with us."

"Have I done anything wrong?"

"Your presence is requested at the White House," was all the agent would say.

His answer had hit Isabel like a double espresso. She focused on her checklist as she packed. No husband. No boyfriend. No pets. Not even a close friend with whom to share the excitement of this mysterious invitation to the White House. Her only class that semester was Freshman Intro, and those grades had been turned in. She had only to notify the dean of her absence. The lead agent politely asked to read her text before allowing her to hit Send, then had taken her phone for safekeeping. Their SUV had driven straight to the wing of a waiting Air Force business jet, whose engines were already running.

"Are you sure you've got the right person?" she'd asked as she buckled up. "Dr. Isabel Miller?" The lead agent had nodded. "Can I maybe have my phone back and make a quick call to my sister? She lives in the D.C. area. Bethesda." Nope. That was it.

Isabel managed only fitful sleep on the cross-country flight, none after she looked in her bag. She had packed only jeans and T-shirts. *What the hell was I thinking!*

But this was undeniably exciting. She couldn't wait to tell Emma. Isabel had been in a rut lately, if she were honest with herself. Each school term had begun to feel like the last. She no longer got the sense she was going anywhere. The department head never raised the prospect of tenure even though she got rave reviews from her undergrads. Her paper on qualia inversion had been well received, but no one at UCSB ever even mentioned it. She was okay leading a solitary life, although she had thought about getting a cat. But still, she had noticed, about half of the marriageable male faculty now were younger than Isabel and preferred the easy prey of coeds on drunken college larks. Her parents had started a family. Her brother had started a family. She wanted to do the same. *But how?*

The Marine clicked his heels to attention as the door beside Isabel burst open to reveal a buzz of subterranean activity. Harried civilian and military officials emerged from a dismal, windowless room, ignoring her. "Dr. Miller?" said a tall, bespectacled man, who trailed them. Isabel stuck out her hand. He eyed it before shaking. "Dr. Rakesh Aggarwal, director of the National Institutes of Health." Emma had told Isabel about meeting the man when she had first volunteered for field assignments.

"Hi. You can call me Izzy." Dr. Aggarwal didn't seem to know what to make of her offer. "Or Iz." Isabel silently kicked herself for saying the wrong things, or saying anything at all for that matter.

Aggarwal handed her a Non-Disclosure Agreement. "What's going on?" she asked.

"You have to sign for me to answer," he replied. Maldonado held out a pen.

"Shouldn't I read it first?" Isabel asked.

"If you want," Aggarwal said. "But be quick. The president is waiting."

What? Isabel pretended to scan the contract as her mind reeled and heart thumped. Lots of redundant language about not saying anything to anyone ever. References to federal statutes, regulations, potential prison sentences. She signed it against the rough wall.

Aggarwal and Maldonado headed into the conference room.

"Wait! *Now* can you tell me why I'm here?"

Dr. Aggarwal glanced through the doorway at a glowing screen. There was a lone red dot on a map of northeastern Siberia. The bags under Aggarwal's evasive red eyes attested to sleepless nights. "There's been an outbreak." A frozen pathogen, he explained, had thawed and infected a Russian drilling crew.

"Oh," Isabel said, disappointed and embarrassed. "I'm afraid you've made a mistake. My twin sister, Dr. *Emma* Miller, is the epidemiologist. I'm a neuroscientist."

He nodded. "Research professor, Department of Psychological and Brain Sciences, University of California, Santa Barbara. I'm afraid I have bad news. Your sister was infected in Siberia while on assignment for us."

Isabel sank back into her chair. "Oh. My God. How is she?"

"She's . . . stable," he replied, looking anywhere but at her. "We need your help."

"How? What can *I* do?"

"You can help us assess your sister's . . . condition."

"Her *medical* condition?" Isabel asked.

"The disease—SED—kills half its victims. So in one sense your sister was lucky."

"Jesus," Isabel mumbled. She had worried about something like this since Emma first chose fieldwork. "Wait, you said, 'in *one* sense' my sister is lucky. But she's alive?"

Aggarwal took another moment. What the *hell?* "Y-yes."

"What does SED stand for?" Isabel asked.

The scientist seemed very ill at ease. "Severe Encephalopathic Disease."

"So, *severe*, I think I understand. And it causes encephalopathy?"

"SED causes . . . neurological deficits. We want you to assist us in analyzing them. You presumably know your sister better than anyone else. And, with your background in brain science, and being an identical twin, we couldn't have gotten any luckier." Maldonado looked up from her phone and skewered him with her gaze. "I'm sorry," he said. "I know this is tragic news." *Tragic*, was the only word that registered. "Your sister

was doing invaluable work." *Was?* "We were all very upset to learn about
. . ." He faltered.

Maldonado jumped in. "Your sister's got brain damage, like all SED
survivors. Hers doesn't seem as bad as the worst, but it's serious."

"How serious?" Isabel asked in a whisper. "What kind of . .
. brain damage?"

Dr. Aggarwal said, "We don't know. That's why we need you." With
that, Isabel was swept, unprepared, into a brightly lit room dominated
by a single long table covered in a sprawl of briefing books and laptops.
She recognized cabinet secretaries, and at the table's head—at the hub
of the room's activity—sat Bill Stoddard, president of the United States,
surrounded by waiting supplicants. Isabel had voted for the man, but wasn't
particularly political and recalled little about him other than that he had a
dog, and a family. His hair was grayer than she remembered, but his face
still looked youthful.

Maldonado and Isabel took the only two open seats along the wall
behind Dr. Aggarwal. Isabel was instantly captivated by the drama.

"If those R-nought estimates are correct, Mr. President," a briefer said,
"they're way north of measles, which is very high at around eighteen."

"And what does *that* suggest, Dr. Stavros?" the president
inquired impatiently.

"Peter Stavros," Maldonado whispered. "Director of the Centers for
Disease Control and Prevention." Like Aggarwal, he was in his fifties.
Like all the other people in the room, other than the soldiers, he wore a
dark suit. Isabel was in jeans and a T-shirt.

Stavros looked worried. "Each case of measles infects, on average,
eighteen people. For SED, the R-nought may be thirty plus. That's unheard
of infectiousness. Its RE, or its *effective* rate of reproduction under actual
conditions, should fall as we implement countermeasures, but we won't
know how far till we get more data from WHO field teams. It's possible
there's preexisting natural immunity in the population, like the 10 percent
of Northern Europeans naturally immune to HIV. And we could develop a
vaccine, but that won't protect offspring. So natural immunity is the only
infinite-time solution. Without it or a vaccine, the RE won't fall far, and
this will be a . . . a runaway outbreak, sir."

"I thought it was contained?" President Stoddard said. "That the
Russians . . . ?"

"We can hope, sir. If it is, we're lucky it emerged in such a remote place."

"And in a place," said a new, deep voice, raspy as if from a life spent yelling at people, "where the authorities were willing to undertake extreme measures."

"General Browner," said Maldonado. "Chairman of the Joint Chiefs." Lesser officers hovered about the heavyset Marine with a chest full of ribbons. "Watch out for him."

Isabel turned to the aide. *What the hell does* that *mean?* she wondered.

"Might I remind everyone," President Stoddard said, "that we've overcome epidemics in the past without committing atrocities. Does anyone remember Ebola?"

"Sir," Dr. Stavros said, "the R-nought of Ebola is two, the same as Hep C. AIDS has an R-nought of four. This pathogen is many, many times as contagious as that."

"Meaning *what*, exactly?" the president asked, sounding increasingly perturbed.

"Airborne human-to-human transmission," Dr. Aggarwal replied, "is what separates a local outbreak from a global pandemic. Physicists modelled what happens if the Russians don't nip this in the bud." Aggarwal motioned toward an airman at a laptop.

The projected image zoomed in on the single dot in northeastern Siberia, which expanded into three red splotches. The smallest, set off from the other two, was labeled Gazprom Drill Site. The largest some distance away read: Anadyr, Pop. 14,326. A third, encompassing an airport across a narrow neck of water from Anadyr, read: Ugolnye Kopi, Pop. 3,666.

"Moscow claims," General Browner intoned as heads turned to him, "that they're taking 'extraordinary measures.'" *Like quarantine?* Isabel wondered. Browner was in his sixties. The bristles on his head were gray. His neck was thick. He'd probably been an athlete once, but now just carried vestigial bulk. "'Whatever it takes,' I was assured by the chief of the main operations directorate of the Russian army's general staff."

"But that's," the president said, studying the map, "eighteen thousand people!"

"As I said," Browner replied, his tone low, "we got lucky it broke out there."

"I thought they stopped this out at the drilling site," objected President Stoddard.

Aggarwal jumped in. "We all did. But apparently a very important, very connected Gazprom executive conducting the company's investigation got away on his own floatplane and landed at the Ugolnye Kopi airport. The Russians are looking for him, but it's really too late. It just took one infected carrier to break containment, and in roughly," he looked at his watch, "seventeen hours, they have three clusters and thousands of carriers to deal with."

The president took a deep breath before nodding for the NIH director to continue.

But it was the CDC's Dr. Stavros who explained the graphic on the screen. "It turns out, sir, that reaction-diffusion equations, which describe how ripples expand outward across a pond, also model pandemic spreads. The principal vector of human-borne disease is global flight patterns. Two cities could be close geographically, but through flight connections outbreak sites may be more closely connected to distant nodes, so the model computes an 'effective distance' based on air travel. The cities with the closest effective distance will get the first waves of infection, not surrounding but unconnected rural areas."

The airman put on the screen a new, circular map. The bull's eye was the red dot on "Anadyr, Russia." A spider web of lines radiated outward to a ring of additional cities—Egvekinot, Keperveryem, Lavrentiya, Markovo, Pevek, Provideniya, Khabarovsk, and Moscow—forming a circle around Anadyr. A second concentric ring at the end of yet more lines, primarily emanating from Moscow but also from Khabarovsk, connected to the next tier of outbreaks—London, Amsterdam, Milan, Paris, Seoul, and Tokyo.

"Traditional maps," Stavros explained, "don't reveal the pattern. Biogeographers created this map showing SED ripple outward from Anadyr. The same thing happened with the Black Death. It emerged in China in 1340, followed the Silk Road west to Crimea and arrived in the Mediterranean in 1347. By 1400, it had killed a quarter of all Europeans, but parts of Asia just hundreds of miles from its source never had an outbreak because there was no travel to infected areas. Now, disease moves by jet, not caravan. SARS emerged in mainland China in November, 2002, but didn't go far until a doctor carried it to Hong Kong for a wedding in February, 2003. Two days later, it was in Vietnam. In three weeks, it was in Taiwan, Singapore, and Canada, all connected via air-travel patterns with China, where the initial outbreak had been halted. And the R-nought of SARS is only four, sir."

"Bottom line?" Stoddard said. "If they can't stop it, how long until it gets here?"

The map pulled out to reveal a third ring—New York, L.A., Chicago, Houston, San Francisco, Dallas, Atlanta, Miami, Charlotte, Las Vegas, Phoenix, and Seattle. "It arrives here in the third wave, sir," Stavros said. "SED will be impossible to stop if it reaches an active global air hub.

And for a highly connected country like ours, it can come at us from any number of directions."

"How long till it gets here?" the president repeated.

"Weeks, Mr. President. Maybe four to six weeks from now."

The room registered shock. Papers stilled. The murmur of side conversations died.

"Shut down air travel," a man said. "Phillip Struthers, DHS," the aide whispered.

Stavros said, "We modeled that. In a third of the stochastic, randomized Monte Carlo simulations, halting air travel actually *accelerated* the arrival of SED. People panic instantly and head home any way they can. Trains, boats, cars, *feet*."

The Homeland Security secretary said, "Shut down everything. *All* travel."

Stavros described the costs. "The University of Chicago estimates US GDP will fall 10 percent in one *week* once people learn about the disease, on its way toward a thirty percent drop by the end of a month. There's massive hoarding, dissaving, and hyperinflation. People spend soon-to-be-worthless dollars bidding up prices of soon-to-be-last bullets. There's widespread violence over dwindling supplies. We could see deaths from starvation *here*, in the US, before SED even arrives. Every day we put off panic is another day of life for thousands, at least until . . ."

The president said, "*Now* I hope you all see why the Security Council brokered the agreement to go to extraordinary lengths to keep SED under wraps."

"But word will get out, sir," Dr. Aggarwal braved. "It's impossible to keep it quiet."

"Every day," Stoddard said, "that our factories run, our labs work on a vaccine, and people aren't murdering each other over boxes of breakfast cereal is a win. *When* word gets out, we'll deal with it. But I've enunciated three top national security goals—keep SED quiet to avoid panic, develop a vaccine, and do what we can to keep it from reaching our shores. Now, what happens if it *does* get here?"

There was silence until the reply came not from a scientist, but the gravel-voiced Marine general. "We fight, sir," Browner said. "We fight like hell, to the last man."

The room was tomblike. *Fight whom?* Isabel wanted someone to ask, but they all seemed to know the answer. There wasn't a sound until Dr. Aggarwal cleared his throat. "I'd, *uhm*, like to introduce Dr. Isabel Miller." *What the fuck!* Heads turned. She smiled and waved, feeling like a spectator at a stadium who noticed the camera is on them.

"Dr. Miller," the president said, rounding the table. "We are *so* sorry about your sister." She half rose and bobbed her head in sort of a curtsey. "She was doing vital work." Isabel sat just as he took her hand in both of his. "Our sympathies go out to you." His hands were warm; hers must've felt like ice. "And thank you for helping with this study," he said on returning to his seat.

Isabel's heart pumped strangely, as if it had forgotten the proper contractions. Fear dizzied her. *What happened to Emmy? Is she disfigured? Did they amputate something?* She blinked at the tears. *Noah warned you this could happen!* Their brother had assumed the role of head of the family after their parents died. Emma never accepted it, but Isabel tried. Last Thanksgiving, their traditional, wine-fueled dispute had turned hot when Noah begged Emma to quit fieldwork. Both turned to Isabel. It's *science,* Emma appealed. It's *dangerous,* argued Noah. Isabel just shrugged. But if she'd said anything, she knew, it would've been on Emma's side of the argument. Science was their thing, not Noah's.

Hushed condolences poured in from all around. Maldonado patted Isabel's arm in a cursory display of shared sympathy. "What's wrong with her?" Isabel whispered.

Maldonado, lips pinched, shook her head and nodded at the new speaker as if to chide Isabel for not paying attention, then promptly returned to reading her texts.

"Surely it isn't as bad as that," objected a civilian and the only man in shirt sleeves.

"Chief of staff," Maldonado supplied before going back on her phone.

Dr. Stavros rose to answer. "Ladies and gentlemen, we're facing a pandemic worse than the 1918 Spanish flu, which overnight lowered life expectancy in the US from fifty-one to thirty-nine years. To speak frankly, I'm afraid this disease is worse than any mankind has seen since the mid-fourteenth century, and it may be far, far worse even than that."

"But we identified the outbreak quickly," argued the chief of staff. "You told us the early warning and response system was critical. Or was it just critical at budget time?"

Stoddard rested a hand on the arm of his subordinate.

"We found it early *because* of its virulence," NIH Director Aggarwal replied. "We probably wouldn't have detected the emergence of an ordinary pathogen for months."

"So what are we doing about it?" the president asked.

Dr. Stavros said, "The latest we've heard is that the CIRMF . . ."

"The *what?*" General Browner interrupted.

"The *Centre Internationale de Recherches Medicales de Franceville*."
Stavros's proper French pronunciation drew eye rolls from some of the
uniformed jock types. "It's a highly respected institute in Gabon. They
called in Dr. Pieter Groenewalt, perhaps the world's preeminent emergent
disease field pathologist, who deployed to Siberia with the first WHO
surge team and found nearly identical brain damage in ten members of
the drilling crew and one soldier. Their brains are on the way to Geneva
for a full autopsy, but the WHO suggests that the damage may provide a
physiological explanation for the aberrant behavior that's been observed,
like impulsive-reactive aggression."

Isabel closed her eyes. *Dear God, please!* A tear ran down her face.
The room fell silent. Through blurry vision Isabel saw that everyone was
looking at her. As if on Isabel's behalf, the president asked Stavros what
parts of the brain were damaged.

She dried her face when the attention left her. "Two preliminary
observations," Stavros said, "from the field work are damage to the
orbitofrontal cortex and the secondary somatosensory regions of the
parietal cortices. Dr. Miller, what might that damage do?"

Isabel flashed a what-me look before venturing an answer. General
Browner told her to speak up. She cleared her throat and started over. "The
orbitofrontal cortex sends inhibitory signals to the medial amygdala. If it
doesn't receive those signals, it would stimulate the thalamus erratically
and trigger unregulated adrenal responses."

"Is that adrenal, as in adrenaline?" President Stoddard asked. She nodded.

General Browner said, "And could that result in violence?"

Emma, violent? "Adrenaline triggers the fight-or-flight response—a
sequence of nerve-cell firing and chemical releases that prepares us to
face life-or-death threats. Most behavior is like software, but fight-or-
flight is hardwired into our primitive crocodile brain. It's the principal
survival strategy of our species, our most important inherited genetic
wisdom, so evolution stamped its coding right onto our neuronal
circuitry. But *unregulated* adrenal responses could cause hair-trigger
and unpredictable rages."

Her answer spurred side conversations among the military men.

"What about the other damage Dr. Stavros mentioned?" President
Stoddard asked.

"To the secondary somatosensory region of the parietal cortex? Well, *that*
could result in a reduction in the emotional salience of the pain perception."

"So," General Browner said, "they're violent and impervious to pain?"

"It's not that they couldn't *feel* pain. People born with congenital insensitivity to pain with anhidrosis, for example, truly feel *no* pain, which is life-threatening. Children with CIPA unknowingly chew their tongues off and gouge their eyes out. SED victims would *feel* pain, they just wouldn't react *emotionally* to it. If they bit their tongue, they'd know they'd injured themselves but wouldn't cry out because it didn't hurt."

The Marine said, "Roll that video from the field hospital at the Gazprom drill site."

After a few seconds, a shaky, poorly lit video filled the room's screen. Sounds of shouting in Russian came over the speakers. Two men in filthy work overalls overturned trays at the far end of an open-air tent ward. Medics and doctors in full protective gear had retreated to the camera. Patients crawled out of cots and fled outside to get away from the rampage.

One of the enraged men stumbled over a cowering patient and began stomping on his head. Isabel looked away. Browner said, "This is what I wanted you to see, Dr. Miller."

Isabel forced her head not to turn and her eyes not to squint shut. A soldier in camouflaged PPE stepped forward, took aim with a rifle. and shot one of the berserk patients in the leg.

The bullet knocked the man to his hands and knees. But he rose, unfazed by the red geyser pulsing from his thigh. His comrade charged past and was shot squarely in the abdomen. He doubled over like he'd been punched in the gut, but didn't fall. Viscera slowly seeped from his belly. Both men staggered forward, shouting, snarling. Neither grimaced or groaned or moaned or clutched at his wounds. A burst of fire felled one, and sent the other diving behind a cart. A second burst ended his life and that awful video.

A pall descended over the room. General Browner said, "Dr. Miller, I've administered first aid to a fair number of men who'd been shot, and held some through last rites. I've seen trauma, shock, paralysis, but never that. A femoral artery tear and a gutshot from an assault rifle should put them on the deck writhing, screaming, vomiting, urinating, defecating, beggin' for morphine, callin' for momma. Those men's reactions defy everything I know about humankind. So, based on those preliminary field autopsy reports, and on what you just saw, ma'am, what . . . in . . . the . . . . *hell*, in your professional opinion, are we facing here?"

Isabel wondered the same thing. She tried to collect herself. *Think. Think!* Science. "The man who stomped on the patient," she began before she even knew what she was going to say, "exhibited behavior consistent with adrenal rage." *Okay.* "And both men clearly suffered from deficits in the emotional salience of their pain perceptions."

"In plain English?" the Marine asked.

"They noticed their wounds. They just didn't care about the pain. It may have felt no more significant than pressure you feel after local anesthetic at the site of an incision."

"This reminds me," said a man Maldonado identified as the AG, "of when the FBI wanted larger caliber handguns. Andy Pearson, whom I could really use in here, sir, said agents in a Miami shootout died *after* they'd fatally wounded, but not incapacitated, some whacked-out drug thugs. Andy said there are two types of incapacitation. Physiological is hitting the brain or the heart. *Psy*chological is the shock that comes from the fear, surprise, and pain of being shot. Some people faint even when the shot *misses* just from the heat, flash, and noise. Those Russian men seemed to be missing that psychological shock."

"Uhm *no*, again, to Pearson," Stoddard said. "And does that make any sense?"

He was looking at Isabel. "Well, sir, I know that the early settlers reported that Native Americans they shot didn't succumb as quickly as expected. They hadn't been conditioned to fear firearms. Today, when animals are shot, they react to noise and pain, but firearms in and of themselves don't trigger any fear. *Modern* humans, however, unless intoxicated, enraged or fanatical, often have overwhelming reactions to the trauma."

Browner said, "Dr. Miller, first off, my name is Bill Browner. I'm Commandant of the Marine Corps and chairman of the Joint Chiefs of Staff. I'd like you to know that your sister is a *hero* in my book, and I don't use that term lightly."

"Thank you, sir," Isabel croaked.

"And I'd like to make sure we'd heard *all* your impressions of that video?"

The video? she thought. *Disgusting. Terrifying. Sickening.* "Uhm, well . . . Those men may not feel or fear pain. But their will to live seemed intact. One took cover. Self-preservation is another hardwired primitive instinct. They just presumably won't be *overcome* by fear."

"Even *that*," another green-jacketed general seated beside Browner said to the Marine. "Can you imagine aiming a rifle in a firefight without your hands shaking?"

Browner found the remark significant and looked at the President. "This is the help we need, sir. These scientists need to tell us what we're facing . . . *before* it gets here."

"Who," President Stoddard corrected. "*Who* we're facing."

"You've raised an interesting question, sir." Browner's aide swiped up a page on a tablet and handed it to him. "Dr. Miller!" Isabel flinched. "Can you help me with," Browner spelled: "S-I-M-U-L-A-C-R-U-M?"

Isabel's mind instantly made the connections. *Automaton; not human; exterminate.* With a confidence she didn't really feel, Isabel said, "That word doesn't seem to apply here."

But a now avuncular Browner said, "Just askin' for pronunciation and a definition."

A few chuckles caused Isabel to smile on reflex. "Well, it's pronounced sim-you-*lay*-crum." The general repeated it aloud several times in endearing fashion. "And it means, uhm, a superficial likeness or semblance of something, but that's not the real thing because it lacks depth and substance."

"Lacks depth? Like a Potemkin village? A fake that looks real but isn't?" It sounded like Browner knew exactly what simulacrum meant. He looked at the president. "Sir, how we prepare our troops, emotionally, for this fight may decide whether we win or we lose."

Win or lose what? Isabel wondered. *What fight?*

In a surprisingly conciliatory tone, President Stoddard said, "Point taken." He turned to the heads of the CDC and NIH. "Any research requested by the Joint Chiefs is a top national security priority and doesn't require further approval by anyone. Understood?"

Both men acknowledged the order. Dr. Aggarwal said, "So, to recap, sir, if SED isn't contained, it will spread slowly at first, then its rate of spread will explode, before ultimately plateauing as the remaining number of susceptibles falls toward zero."

Zero? Isabel thought. *Zero!* She read the same fear she felt on faces all around. Isabel had heard the man right.

Aggarwal swiveled his chair to Isabel. "We haven't yet connected all the brain damage to the aberrant behavior, but it stands to reason the relationship is causal. Otherwise, survivors appear to be as healthy as they had been before. Some malaise and confusion, slightly lowered heart and respiratory rates, lower blood pressure, and the mydriasis, or popped pupils, which in typical brain injuries eventually resolves itself."

Inhuman black saucers-for-eyes would attest to cerebral carnage. *Emma!*

Stavros said, "So we're now waiting on Geneva's brain dissections of the oil workers and the Russian soldier shot by Dr. Miller's sister." *What? Emma killed somebody?* Isabel lowered her chin so that loose hair draped her face in a curtain, affording her shelter. Her killer sister had once turned an ankle before a youth soccer tournament to avoid stepping on a ladybug.

"Anything else?" President Stoddard asked. "Any resource? Facility? Funding? Any other scientific discipline we should have at this table?"

"Sociologists," Dr. Aggarwal said. "There may be hundreds of millions of infection survivors. They could outnumber the uninfected many, many fold. Someone needs to connect the neuroscience," he looked at Isabel, "to the ultimate sociological impact."

"Meaning," Stoddard said, "in the society they'll build after we're gone? I think that can wait. But Dr. Miller, would you head up our research on their aberrant behavior?"

"Sir?" Isabel said. "I don't even, like, have a security card." Someone laughed.

A smile broke the tension gripping Stoddard. "Believe it or not, *that* I can make happen. Patricia?" Maldonado aimed her own version of a smile at Isabel—momentary curls of her lips, but nothing in her eyes—in a perfunctory welcome. "And I understand the French are bringing your sister out. General Browner, any update?"

The hulking Marine donned dainty reading glasses. "Dr. Miller was taken overland to Anadyr via Russian Army DT-30P." Amazingly, an overhead photo, probably from a satellite, appeared on the screen. A roofless, tank-like behemoth forded an aquamarine stream that streaked across an empty but verdant terrain. In it sat seven people in PPE and winter coats along opposing benches. One had to be Emma.

"There are no roads," Browner continued, "so the trip took ten hours. Dr. Miller spent last night in the Anadyr city jail. They're looking for the oil company executive who caused the airport outbreak, one Pyo-tr Ig-na-ty-ev, deputy chairman, Gazprom Management Committee, but overnight the disease and a whole lotta violence blew back across the Anadyr River from the airport into town. I've been assured, however, that Dr. Miller is safe and will be flown to Khabarovsk tomorrow. Sir, may I reiterate my objection to . . ."

"You may *not*," Stoddard replied. "Dr. Miller was on a dangerous foreign mission. She belongs in our care. Every precaution will be taken. Bring her home. We owe her that much."

"*Uhm*," Isabel said. Her hand darted up for an instant like a student in class. "Sir, Mr. President, I would like to request that I go meet Emma—Dr. Miller—in Russia."

"Get a jump on your research? Sounds like a plan. General Browner, could you make that happen? Dr. Miller, it's vital we understand these survivors. How they tick?"

Maldonado whispered to Isabel that she'd get her a security pass, car, anything she needed. The sharp point of her business card poked the back of Isabel's hand. She took the card, rubbed her hand, and asked if she could get her phone back.

"Sir," the attorney general said. "Sorry, again, but Andy Pearson has been asking about these off-schedule NSC meetings. I'd *really* like to bring the FBI into the loop."

"I do *not* consent to that. *Again.* Tell Pearson to mind his own business, for once."

The president stood and pressed his hands on the polished wood. "Let me be crystal clear. Everything about SED is top secret. The epidemic I'm worried about is fear. You may hear things you know to be untrue. That's *my* concern. You stay in your lanes and deal with the medical, scientific, and security issues. I'll try to keep the wheels from coming off, and *that* will mean, of necessity, obscuring the worst from the public for as long as possible. But whether or not you agree, know this: leaks will be prosecuted! Dismissed."

Chapter 3

With help from her Marine escort, Isabel dressed head to toe in disposable personal protective equipment, then passed the plastic shelter erected inside the cavernous C-17 cargo bay on her way to the open rear ramp. Joining her was Capt. Rick Townsend, wearing identical gear, who checked her seals.

The PPE created a sense of detachment, allowing Isabel's thoughts to wander along with the man's hands as he tugged on her taped seams. Captain Townsend had introduced himself at Joint Base Andrews at the conclusion of Isabel's whirlwind first day. The landlord had let her into Emma's apartment with no questions asked except about her now long hair. Isabel passed people at the complex who called her "Emma" and asked her to a party, for drinks, for coffee, for tennis. Emma's messy apartment was strewn with photos of her with friends and boyfriends, on vacations skiing and scuba diving, and dressed up at galas or costume parties. *How can you possibly keep up with epidemiology literature?* came Isabel's catty thought.

Also fun that day was the FBI interview and lie detector test. She freaked a little when asked if she was an agent of a foreign government. She wasn't, but the question was scary. Her list of acquaintances had seemed suspiciously short, so she'd added married colleagues' wives, the receptionist at the gym, the guy at the auto body shop who'd ripped her off. But when the agent said they'd contact them with questions, Isabel had even more suspiciously deleted the additional names and tried grinning her way past the questions. And in the end, the laminated White House badge Isabel had received bore a huge T, for Top Secret, the agent informed her. Her messy-hair-pulled-back picture was even worse than her awful driver's license.

"*Rick*," she called the man beside her, to herself, towered over her at maybe six four. His hair was too short to tell, but from his eyebrows he may be blond. He was tanned, square jawed, bright-eyed—green, like hers. "I command your protective detail," he had said. Isabel had had trouble repressing a smile. He then went on and on about the mission, organization, equipment, and we-were-never-there secrecy rules.

He wore no wedding ring and was about her age. During the long flight over, she had come up with several requests for clarification about what he had said. Most of the time, however, was spent with her failing to dream up anything else to say. He was asleep when she finally remembered to ask about his job. Talking to guys was Emma's thing, not Isabel's.

A disturbance at the bottom of the ramp drew their attention. Russians faced off against Marines, all in full PPE, all heavily armed. Isabel and Rick joined them.

The Russian soldiers, rifles raised, wore heavy rubber hoods and gas masks. As the C-17 was being refueled, a Marine lieutenant colonel, overall mission commander, said, "The French transport from Anadyr doesn't get here for thirty minutes. The Russians don't want us to disembark. Apparently, a commercial 737 from Anadyr arrived, with everyone aboard exposed by some infected Russian oil company executive."

"I want to go see him," Isabel said.

The colonel, Rick, and the Russians all argued against it, but she insisted, dropping "the White House" and "the president" as needed to get her way.

Townsend and three Marines surrounded Isabel. A half dozen Russian troops enveloped them for an uneasy walk to the terminal. They passed armed guards in gas masks posted by unmarked doors, climbed stairs, and weaved their way through curtains of plastic sheeting before arriving at a medical team also garbed in protective equipment.

"Dr. Miller!" said a white man with a thick South African accent. "Can you not recognize me in all this?" Isabel knew no South Africans. He was short and rotund, with a smiling round face behind a clear shield like a silent-movie depiction of the moon. "It's Pieter Groenewalt! From the National Institute for Communicable Diseases in Johannesburg?" *From the autopsy slides,* she remembered. "You had dinner at my home with Katryn and our daughter Marna?" They shook hands. "I heard you'd run into a bit of bad luck and had to. . . . Oh, never mind. You look hale and hearty."

"Dr. Groenewalt, I'm afraid there's been a . . ."

"We need to be getting back," Rick abruptly cut her off. "So let's make this quick." *Oh yeah,* Isabel remembered. *Everything's a secret.* Groenewalt understood the ridiculous security measures and discretely winked at her in sympathy.

"Is he in there?" she asked.

Groenewalt said, "Yes," then added in a whisper. "They're *fascinating.*"

Isabel headed for the doorway, whose plastic drapes were being sucked inward. Rick gave his men hand signals. The South African doctor said, "Vitals are normal. Other than the mydriasis, they're asymptomatic. A little stuporous—in some sort of fugal state—probably lethargic after their high fevers."

A portable filter loudly vented through the window to the outside. "Thank God I was passing through with my brain specimens on the way back to Geneva," Groenewalt said. He lowered his voice. "Has it broken out in Anadyr?" Despite Rick's glance, Isabel nodded. The South African pathologist said, "The Yakutia Airlines pilot radioed ahead with a medical emergency. The Russians asked for help, and when I heard the flight was from Anadyr . . . ! I sent my brain specimens back to Geneva for analysis. Oh well. I *almost* made it home. Hopefully soon!"

He pulled the plastic aside. A stocky man with gray unkempt hair and black eyes rested against a pile of pillows atop his gurney. A slender, younger man in a second gurney—eyes also black—had his wrists bound to the side rails.

Groenewalt followed her gaze. "He's this other man's pilot. The advisory said to be alert about possible aggressiveness. I guess you're familiar with *that.* Were you on a flight right behind mine?"

Rick stared at Isabel, so she ignored the question and asked, "Has he shown any violent tendencies?" Groenewalt shook his head.

"Why isn't *that* man restrained?" Rick asked about the older patient.

"He's some VIP," Groenewalt replied, looking down at his chart.

"Pyotr Ignatyev?" Isabel asked. The pug-nosed Russian executive, with skin long ago ravaged by acne, returned her gaze. Rick posted riflemen at the feet of the men's gurneys. Both patients stared warily at the weapons. Their dilated eyes made them seem oddly . . . not human.

She went to the executive's gurney. "Do you speak English?"

"English?" Ignatyev replied. "Yes."

"You were at the Anadyr drill site?" He didn't respond. "You flew out of there on your own plane?" Again, nothing. She began to wonder if he really did speak English. "When did you start feeling sick?"

The man's eyes darted about as he seemed to search his memory. "The *illness?*" he asked. "Nausea on the small plane." His Russian accent was thick. "The flight to Anadyr was too bumpy!" he complained to his pilot in the gurney beside his. "Then vomiting in the terminal. Sleeping on the airport director's sofa and on the flight here."

"You know you infected everyone on that plane to Khabarovsk?" she said. He had no reaction. "Half of them are going to die." Nothing. "How are you feeling now?"

"Feeling? Well. And *you?*"

Isabel was thrown by the reply. "Good. I'm . . . I'm fine. Does your head hurt?"

"Head?" The man raised his hand to his temple. "Yes. Quite a lot."

"Can they get you something for the pain?"

"Pain? No." Despite his calm responses, Isabel noticed the man's black eyes flitting toward her Marine escorts and his fists clenching his bed linens into a wad. His breathing was shallower. On the monitor above him, his pulse rate had risen from the mid-fifties to nearly 120. Isabel decided to talk to the younger man. "How are you?"

"He's not authorized to speak!" bellowed the executive, startling Isabel. He had now pulled wrinkled bed sheets loose and practically vibrated, red-faced, with indignation.

"Just a couple of questions," she said soothingly, smiling. She turned to the slender pilot, who looked to be around her age. "When did *you* start feeling ill?"

Out of the corner of her eye, Isabel sensed a blur of white as sheets flew and the executive's bare feet hit the floor. He growled at her as he lunged. But nothing jarred her like the three blasts from rifles six feet from her ears, which she felt as much as heard.

Time slowed. She recoiled from Ignatyev's outstretched hands and raised gloved fingers to press her ringing eardrums through her hood. Crimson splatter sprayed the plaster behind the executive, who slumped to the floor leaving a streak of reddish brown along the wall. Smoke curled from the three Marines' muzzles. Bullet casings spun to a stop on the floor. Alarms beeped on monitors still connected to the dying man. Groenewalt and a nurse raced by. Like a scuba diver Isabel heard only the sound of her own ragged breathing, which drowned out Groenewalt's pointless first aid commands.

Isabel found herself sitting on the pilot's gurney. His black eyes rose from his boss's bloody corpse to the space-suit-clad American. "At the Anadyr airport," he said.

"Wha . . . ? *What?*"

"The illness began in Anadyr." He was answering the question, she realized, that she had asked before his boss was shot dead right in front of him. The medical staff tracked blood to the door. A pressure bandage slid off the executive's still oozing chest wound.

The pilot betrayed no emotion. When Isabel stood, he watched. Otherwise, he seemed content. "Are you feeling alright?" Isabel managed. "I mean, about this?"

The Russian looked down at the dead man, whose head rested at an odd angle between the wall and a wheel on his gurney. "He attacked you," the pilot said calmly. Like Ignatyev when asked about infecting an entire airliner full of passengers, the pilot exhibited a remarkable absence of empathy.

Rick returned from the hallway, where she had heard him report the incident over the radio. He grabbed Isabel by the elbow—"Let's go!"—and led her toward the door.

Isabel pulled free and asked the pilot, "Does *your* head hurt?"

"Head? Hurt?" He tried to raise his hand, just like the oil company executive, but couldn't because of the ties. That seemed to prevent him from composing an answer.

In the hallway, disinfectant spray jolted Isabel as it pattered off her face shield. People were in motion, reporting, and giving and receiving orders, but Isabel was in a daze until she reached the terminal. She heard a commotion and again pulled free of Rick's grip, leading the entourage to glass walls overlooking the arrivals hall one floor below.

Passengers from the Yakutia Airlines 737 were banging on locked doors. One man, doubled over, vomited into a trash can. A woman in the middle of the hall did the same while stretched out across several seats. Her male companion tried to comfort her from a distance. Some lay unconscious, not hearing calls from loved ones who instinctively knew to stay away. All the others clung to far walls, articles of clothing tied across noses and mouths. But it was no use. From what Isabel had heard, everyone was already infected.

Outside on the tarmac, a large prop plane taxied to a stop. Groenewalt found her. "Emma, are you alright?" Isabel nodded. "That's the French plane we took to Anadyr. So how did *you* get to Khabarovsk?" The only other plane there was the US Air Force C-17.

"We'll take it from here," Rick said, wheeling to a stop in front of Groenewalt. Isabel left them to join the CDC medical team, which was getting debriefed at the open side hatch of the prop plane by a French doctor who had just disembarked.

Isabel peered inside the plane, searching for her sister's gurney. Someone Isabel's height, wearing French-style protective gear, appeared beside her and joined in her search, leaning into the plane's dark interior. Isabel looked through the person's face shield. All she could see above the surgical mask were two black eyes. "*Emmy?*" Isabel threw her arms around her sister. Emma's hands rose to pat Isabel's back, but she didn't return the hug. Emma's eyes bore no trace of the green that had always identified them as twins no matter their hairstyles or clothes. They were now bottomless black pits. Windows into darkness.

"Hello, Isabel," Emma said with no inflection. No expression. No emotional breakdown on meeting her beloved twin sister after the horrible ordeal she must have endured.

"How . . . ? How are you feeling?" Isabel asked.

"Fine. And you?" Emma's response seemed rote; a meaningless courtesy.

"You wouldn't believe what just happened!" Isabel told her about the shooting. Emma didn't react at all. Not verbally. Not in body language. *Oh-my-God,* Isabel thought. There's something really *wrong* with her.

US and Russian soldiers kept their distance, but held weapons . . . on Emma.

Gunfire suddenly erupted in the terminal. All heads turned toward it. Flashes lit windows. Glass rained onto the tarmac.

"Mount up!" Rick Townsend commanded.

The CDC medical team rushed Emma away. "It's alright!" Isabel called after Emma, who went placidly to the C-17 without looking back at her lifelong closest friend.

A tall man wearing French PPE came up to Isabel. "Dr. Hermann Lange." He nodded curtly but pointedly declined to extend his hand in greeting. "I was with your sister when she turned. She said to tell you and your brother to prepare."

Isabel stared up at the French or German man. "What?" she replied. *Turned?* she thought. *Is that what they call it?* "Prepare for what?" she asked.

"For the disease. She made me promise to warn you." At the rear ramp of the American transport, Emma rotated in place while standing in a disinfectant bucket and being sprayed. Groenewalt angrily waved a clipboard in the American mission commander's face. Rick and the other soldiers—American, French, and Russian—warily eyed the gunfire in the terminal. Flashes sparkled through the icy, fractured glass like strobe lights at a club. It was all too much for Isabel to process.

"What did she mean?" Isabel asked Dr. Lange. "Prepare *how?*"

Lange said, "Buy supplies, food, survival gear." He looked at the terminal. Rips of automatic gunfire had been replaced by single shots. "Weapons and ammunition."

"*Weapons?*" Isabel asked, incredulous. "Why?"

Dr. Lange was summoned in French. His team was headed into the terminal. "Prepare for the worst, Dr. Miller. The very, very worst. I bid you *adieu, et bon chance.*"

Rick dragged Isabel into the rising whine of jet engines, into the disinfectant-filled bucket and spray, into the shouts of Groenewalt. "What's going on? *That* was Emma! Who are *you?*" And into the huge transport plane while still dripping noxious bleach.

Marines ascended backwards behind raised weapons as the ramp rose. The C-17 began to taxi even before the ramp sealed. Isabel's ears plugged and the huge cargo bay seemed eerily quiet. "*The very, very worst.*" Isabel followed a nurse into the plastic tent surrounding Emma's gurney. Her sister lay under bright overhead lights.

A doctor and two nurses flitted about during high-speed turns, grabbing handholds as the plane's tires squealed. Rick and two Marines were strapped into jump seats at the corners of the gurney, having exchanged high-powered rifles for pistols in holsters. A fourth Marine, standing and braced, held a video camera to his eye. The doctor, nurses, and Isabel held on as the engines rose to full power for a long take off run.

On the noisy climb out, Isabel smiled at Emma and held her limp, gloved hand.

The nurses cut away Emma's protective garb, soggy from disinfectant, using special care around her headgear. "Take a deep breath and hold it," the doctor said. Emma complied with comically puffed cheeks. They swapped out her paper mask for a clear plastic respirator, whose ribbed tube led into a device mounted on a stand. The nurse told Emma that she could now breathe normally.

Emma was naked save her new respirator, face shield, and hood. Her hands were free, but she made no move to cover herself. Isabel tried pulling bed linens loose, but they would only reach Emma's pointy hipbones and protruding ribs. She had a tiny, colorful tattoo on her hip of a wolf smelling a flower that caught Isabel totally by surprise.

One nurse said, "This is a little cold," before applying adhesive monitors to Emmy's small chest. Goosebumps rose from her ribcage—she was too thin—but she didn't flinch. Tears welled in Isabel's eyes. Emmy looked helpless as they slipped a blood pressure cuff on her arm, clipped a thermometer to her finger, and taped a tube to her face. "Drink," the nurse directed, bending the tube to her mouth. Emma complied. "Just a pinprick," the other nurse said as an IV found a vein amid holes from other recent sticks. "This one might hurt a bit," she said of a thicker needle. Emma didn't even blink. They spread her knees and inserted a catheter. Within minutes, Emma was clothed, and her new PPE sprouted wires and tubes. Racks of electronics sprang to life with a chorus of *beeps*.

"You okay?" Isabel asked, squeezing Emmy's limp hand.

After a pause, Emma tentatively said, "Ye-Yes?" A nurse asked for a urine sample. Emma provided it with surprisingly absent inhibition.

Isabel leaned over and whispered, "Remember when you used to wait till the bell rang and the school bathroom cleared out before you could even pee?"

No trace of an expression found its way onto Emma's face. Isabel felt crushed.

* * * *

The adhesive sensors warmed and receded from Emma's notice, but the needles and catheter reminded her of their presence. The lights above the gurney left red blanks in her vision. She counted three men armed with pistols. There would be more on the plane.

"Emmy?" Isabel said. "Are you okay?" She repeated the question.

"Yes?" Emma replied, though not entirely certain what had been asked.

Isabel alternately rubbed, patted, and squeezed Emma's arm, and interlaced their gloved fingers. Tears flowed down Isabel's face. She reached up, but her hand collided with her clear face shield. "Are you in pain, Emmy?" she asked in a thick, congested voice.

Emma took inventory. "Here." She reached up to touch her head. The tall Marine's hand reached for his pistol, but he didn't draw it. "This," Emma said.

"Would you like something?" Isabel asked. "For the pain?"

Her sister must be asking if the doctors should administer narcotics. "No."

Emma couldn't read her sister's expression. Eyes scrunched, brow knit, questions deliberate, voice unsteady. "The pain doesn't . . . *bother* you?" she asked.

Pain should hurt, as was clear from its circular definition. And she had a lifetime of memories of pain. Of vigorously shaking her hand after a tennis ball came off her racket wrong. But what caused *that* reaction? Why had she hopped on one foot after stubbing her toe? It didn't make sense. Why had her eyes watered after she hit her head on an open cabinet door? What had followed each incident should have been pain, but did pain really exist? "No," was all Emma replied.

The doctor and nurses around her gurney exchanged looks. The Marine holding the camera, faintly visible outside the bright lights, peered around the viewfinder.

"Emmy, can we talk?" Isabel asked. "More than just, 'Yes, No'? *Please.*" Emma nodded. "So, how, *exactly,* do you feel right now?" The same question Dr. Lange had asked. The correct response bubbled up. "Fine." Emma was unable to use more words.

"Was it scary? Getting sick?"

Emma thought back to the Siberian isolation unit. "Yes. It was. Scary."

"What were you scared *of?*"

The question seemed straightforward, but somehow missed its mark. Emma didn't fully understand it. "*Scared.*" She knew the word. Walking down a dark street to your car at a bar's closing time. Better to pick whichever guy had kept trying the longest to accompany her home. But the word now summoned no corresponding feeling. "Dying?" she answered.

"Are you scared now?" Isabel asked.

It was as if her sister's questions were filled with holes. Missing necessary words. "No." Emma searched for more to say. "No complaints."

When Isabel tilted her head, Emma knew there was some kind of information in her bright green eyes, but wasn't sure what it was. "Can you tell me, Emmy, in detail, how you got infected?"

Emma bridged the indecipherable gaps. "Tell you?" she repeated. Isabel nodded. "Infected?" Another nod. *Tell in detail how infected.* Emma gave Isabel the long answer she wanted. The helicopter landed near the rig. Men attacked from the woods. Corporal Leskov tackled one. Sergeant Travkin stabbed him. Travkin put his pistol in the sample bag. Both got sick. Leskov died. Travkin killed three people, came into the tent, and was shot in the face.

Isabel asked, "*Your* sample collection bag?"

"The bag had been on the Russian army helicopter from Anadyr."

"Emmy, *who* shot Travkin?"

The question of *who* sounded perfectly normal but was baffling. "He was shot. In the tent." Isabel asked *whose* tent. "The tent he came to after breaking out of isolation."

There was a beep on a machine. One of the Marine guards was replaced. Emma updated her count of armed men. *Four.*

"Did *you* shoot him, Emmy?" Isabel asked in a very soft voice.

Again, Emma should have understood the question, but again didn't. She tried to make Isabel understand by repeating her answer clearly. "He was shot with the gun he put in the sample bag brought in on the helicopter. The gun was under the pillow in the tent."

"*Your* bag?" Isabel asked. "*Your* pillow? *Your* tent?"

Emma could think of no reply that made sense. What was she saying that was different from Emma's explanation? Isabel kept glancing at one Marine in particular. She'd always described tall, rugged men like him as "her type," then been too timid ever to approach any. "Emmy, it must have been traumatic. Remember when Granddad shot those, whatever, skeet or traps? You practically jumped out of your skin. Remember?"

Emma nodded. Isabel had run back to the house. Emma had shot all afternoon.

"Did Sergeant Travkin say anything?" Isabel asked, her voice quivering. Another tear streaked her cheek until it was absorbed in the darkening upper edge of her blue mask.

"He said, 'You might need this'."

"When he gave you the gun? No, I meant did he say anything in the tent?"

Emma shook her head. "On the flight in, he kept looking at me. He wanted sex."

Isabel again glanced at the tall Marine. "Emmy," Isabel said, rubbing Emma's arm, "I'm so sorry." Emma asked why. The massaging stopped. "That you had to shoot that man." The nurse adjusted the flow rate of the fluids dripping into the IV. "Emmy, can you tell me how you feel? Any emotion you're feeling? Right this instant?"

Emotions again. Emma shook her head. "No. Everything is fine."

Isabel looked tired. Her head hung and her eyes closed. Her big sigh fogged her face shield. She got up and left. There was another shift change among the guards. *Five,* was her new count.

Several beeps from the electronics later, Isabel returned. Her mask was dry and her congestion cleared. "Emma, I'm gonna be straight with you, okay? There's something *different* about you." Isabel's voice broke. "You're not acting like you did before."

The pause that followed seemed to call for a reply. Emma said, "Okay."

"She's exhausted," Isabel said to the tall Marine before breaking down and leaving again. The Marine gave orders—he must be an officer—then followed Isabel. As he passed, Emma concluded he too was her type. Good for a late night escort home.

He returned with Isabel, who had a notepad, pen and yet another dry mask. "Okay. We're gonna get to the bottom of this. Science, right? Let's focus on the science." That sounded correct. "Let's start with memory. Do you have any gaps in what you recall?"

Gaps, recall, memory. "The only blank," Emma answered, "is from the fever getting bad, till the soldiers shooting sick people at the drilling site."

"Shooting?" Isabel asked. "Was there trouble?"

"No. No trouble. Only the soldiers had guns."

Isabel's brow was oddly creased. Emma had always known what her sister was thinking. Her face had always been transparent. And they had joked that they had two halves of the same brain. But now, Isabel was a mystery. Her expression, tone, and body language were all . . . alien.

On request, Emma recounted the point-blank executions. Isabel touched her arm until Emma looked down at it. She then described the long ride to Anadyr. Watching on tiptoes through the window of the locked jail cell as small boats fled the burning airport across the river. Falling asleep to the sounds of screams and rips of gunfire on the street outside. The next day, a cold, open boat ride, hiking up to the burned-out terminal, more shooting of sick people, the noisy French turbo-prop.

"Do you recall," Isabel whispered, leaning close, "asking a French doctor, Hermann Lange, to warn me and Noah? Something about 'preparing'?"

Emma thought back. "He's a disease theorist, and Swiss. Did he warn you?"

Isabel nodded. *Lange kept his part of the bargain.* Emma wanted to record the observation somewhere to help her to remember, and to understand why he would do such a thing? Isabel asked, "Don't you want to warn me yourself?" Emma said nothing. "Buy food, supplies, . . . and *guns?* Does that make sense?"

"Yes. That would help you and Noah survive what's coming."

Isabel looked from the rapt medical team, to the tall Marine ready to shoot Emma, to the camera recording everything. *"What's* coming, Emma?"

"The end of civilization," Emma replied, taking a sip of water and urinating.

Chapter 4

"Stay over there," commanded Noah Miller's little sister, Isabel.

Noah lowered arms raised for a hug. On short notice, he'd taken the morning off from his busy job at a D.C. law firm and driven to Baltimore for this clandestine rendezvous. Isabel slouched beside a newspaper on a bench ten yards away. Noah grew alert, but didn't know why. A multistory pagoda rose incongruously in the park near where Emma worked. Children squealed on a playground. All seemed normal, so he sat on the adjacent bench.

"What brings you back East, Iz?" he asked, on guard given the odd greeting. Her twin sister, Emma, had acted the same way once after a mission to an Ebola-infected hotspot. With their parents gone, Noah felt responsible for the twins. He worried about the risks epidemiologists took but didn't think neuroscientists like Isabel studied infectious things.

"We don't have much time," she said. "I've passed all the checks, but just in case."

"What checks?" She looked upset. "Just in case *what?* Izzy, what the fuck?"

She seemed to cave in on herself. But under slumped shoulders, she stared straight at Noah. "You, the children, Natalie even, you're all I've got." She wiped away tears.

"And . . . and we're here for *you,* Izzy. But," he forced a laugh, "what's goin' *on?*"

"There's been an outbreak. In Siberia." Isabel spoke rapidly about some ancient microorganism, frozen in permafrost, spreading out of control. She drooped, so unlike his usually upbeat, energetic sister. "It's gonna sweep through the human population, Noah."

"A pandemic?" Noah used a name for a fear long ago digested.

"That word doesn't even come close to describing what's coming. It may be . . . the end." His snort derived from nerves more than humor. "Emmy caught it."

"*What?* Jesus Christ! Is she alright?"

"*No,* Noah, she's *not!*" Isabel wiped away another tear. Instinctively, Noah rose, but Isabel held up her hand and shook her head. He sat again. "She's alive. Sort of."

He instantly bristled. "What the hell does *that* mean? '*Sort* of'?"

"She's . . . changed. Different. She's '*turned.*'"

"Turned? Into *what?*"

"I don't *know!*" Isabel wept. "She's *weird*, Noah. Scary. Like, *dangerous* scary."

"Calm down. Calm down. Where is she?"

"At an NIH lab in Bethesda. I went to get her in Siberia. Noah, you've got to start getting ready, *today*, for what's coming. They're gonna suppress the news. That's why I had you come all the way out to Baltimore. If they come ask about a leak, tell them we had a big fight at Thanksgiving, about me wasting my womb, and haven't spoken since."

"All I said was you'd make a good *mother!*" But that wasn't what had upset her. What *had* sounded ridiculous. Emma getting sick must really have rocked Isabel even though his sisters, despite being identical twins, were so different that they had never been that close. In a calm voice, he said, "Isabel, I'm sorry, I really am. But . . ."

"No!" she said with surprising venom. "No more '*sorry*' shit! Man the fuck up, Noah! It's gonna infect almost everyone on Earth. If you're gonna avoid infection and survive the chaos, you've gotta be strong." Isabel, looking around, paranoid, summarized the dread disease from popped pupils to brain damage. His sisters normally outdid each other in giving long, clinical answers. As if science, sprinkled with Latin, was their secret twins' language. But now, Isabel described in plain language the effects of the horrible scourge.

"She needs to be in a *hospital*," Noah said. "A *real* hospital, not a lab."

"She's contagious. And she may be violent."

"Violent?" Noah responded. "*Emma?* That's crazy! I wanta see her."

"You're not even supposed to *know* any of this. They could throw me in *jail!*"

"Let me worry about the legal side of things," Noah said.

"Stop playing fucking lawyer! This is serious! On the ride back from the airbase, I heard snippets of whispered conversation by this White House aide with her husband. It sounded like . . . like the end of the *world*, Noah!"

He turned away so Isabel couldn't see his skeptical expression. But Isabel's paranoia got the better of him. Children on the playground were being monitored by segregated groups of moms and nannies. A jogger passed. A black sedan in the parking lot stood out among the station wagons and Volvos.

"You need to survive, Noah. Don't get infected. Don't get killed. Get yourself ready, big brother. You've got four other people to keep alive."

"That's . . . !" He recoiled, incensed that such an obligation would be forced on him, and scoffed. "That's a tad *dramatic*, don't ya think, Isabel?"

"Some survivors are homicidal maniacs. Marines shot one who attacked me in Russia. *That's* what's coming! This?" The carousel spun. A guy threw a Frisbee to his dog. "This is over. In a month or two, maybe less, nothing will ever be the same."

This was preposterous. "And it's *five*," Noah said, "counting Emmy." Isabel hesitated. "Natalie, Chloe, Jacob, you, and *Emma*. Five." Still nothing. "*Right?*"

She finally said, "Yes! Of course. Five. It's just . . . She's changed, Noah. And even she sees what's coming and said to get ready. This may be . . . the apocalypse."

Noah felt obliged to protect his sisters. But she was asking him to transform himself in that one instant, based on a crazy story, from housebroken husband into club-wielding caveman. "So, Emma said I should go out and buy . . . what? Tents, candles, ponchos?"

"Guns, Noah. And lots and lots of ammunition. I had a long flight back to think about it. You don't want to have food, supplies, and medicine, but no guns to protect them."

Noah snorted. "Well *hell*, Isabel. If you've got guns, you can just *take* all the rest."

Iz screwed up her face. "*Jesus*, Noah. That's pretty *Lord of the Flies*."

She was right. Enough of this. "Okay." Noah stood. "I have to get back to work."

"*Fuck* your job, Noah!" Isabel rose too. "*And* your mortgage, your 401K, your college funds. Do you not *get* it? None of that matters anymore!"

"This disease is in *Siberia*, right?" It was Noah's turn for outrage. "And you want me to quit my job and start buying end-of-the-world shit?"

Isabel charged Noah so aggressively he thought she might slap him. But she pulled up short and tossed the newspaper she had brought to the sidewalk, then retreated from it.

He hesitated before reaching for the paper. "Wouldn't I catch it if I . . . ?"

"Just *pick* it *up!*" Isabel snapped. The *Washington Post* was folded open, the headline reading: Unrest Spreads in Russian Far East. "Ever heard of unrest spreading, mister poli-sci major?"

Noah frowned. Neither of his scientist sisters had ever shown any respect for his prelaw college major. "Unrest can spread. Campus-to-campus. Anti-government . . ."

"You know what *else* spreads, Noah?" Isabel interrupted. "Read that article. They've lost all contact with the town where it broke out. No phone, TV, radio, Internet. And that woman who works at the White House told me that Russian troops went through the Khabarovsk airport where I picked Emma up and killed everyone. *Everyone.* Passengers *and* airport workers. But guess what? Some private stole tablets, phones, and shit off the dead and gave them to his *girlfriend* in return for a screw. She then crossed the Amur River into northern China, sold everything, and had sex with customers all night at the club where she strips . . . while wearing *sunglasses!*" Noah didn't get it. "Her pupils were popped! It's in *China,* Noah! China! I'm counting on you to keep us alive. Fair warning. *Un*fair warning, 'cause nobody else knows!" Isabel looked stricken.

"Izzy, you've got me. And Natalie." Isabel rolled her eyes. "*And* the kids."

"Are you sure Natalie will be okay with me coming along for Armageddon?"

Natalie blamed Isabel for ruining their early married life. Two- and foursomes had become three- and fivesomes. Vacations to romantic beaches became aloe rubs on Izzy's frequent sunburns. But Noah had grown closer to Izzy during those three summers and the holidays since. And Natalie had finally simply accepted that, unless Isabel found a husband, she was their third child. "Iz, you're *serious?* This is really, really happening?"

"Jesus, *yes,* Noah!"

"The world is coming to an end?"

"Noah!" She was crying. "Please, please, *please* believe me!" She told him about meeting with the National Security Council in some underground White House bunker.

"The Situation Room?" he asked. She shrugged. "Okay, okay. I'll get ready. I'll . . . *buy* everything. But if this thing gets here," to cut off her objection, he quickly amended, "*when* it gets here, we meet up and we go. *You* go. *With* us. That's my offer. We're a family and we stick together."

"If I can get free of my job," she replied meekly. "It's kind of .
.. important."

"Isabel, you drop everything and come to us. Promise? You've got to
promise, or deal's off. *Say* it."

"All *right*! I promise. I'll come *running* back. Of *course*." It sounded
less a pledge than acknowledgment of some personal failing. But Noah
let it pass. "I love you, Noah," she said before departing for the parking
lot, looking all around, crying.

Noah ignored the whispering, glaring moms, presumably convinced
he'd just dumped his girlfriend, and read the article. The fighting wasn't
political, ideological, religious or ethnic. There was "rumored hysteria by
troops terrified of some unknown disease." Civilians were seeking refuge
at overcrowded army bases. *At* army bases?

He headed back into D.C. while scanning satellite radio. CNN covered a
missing airliner off India. Fox News reported strife after a police shooting
in Chicago. On BBC World, however, a journalist briefly in contact with
a blogger in Khabarovsk reported a twenty-four-hour curfew, army units
shooting violators, and bodies being burned in pyres.

Noah still couldn't believe it. But what if it were true? A disease that
turns people violent. How could he protect his family from some real-
life horror movie?

"The blogger reported," said the British-accented news reader, "that
Russian troops had lost all control and had fired indiscriminately into
crowds of people for no apparent reason. Casualties are reported to number
in the hundreds, if not much higher. All contact with Khabarovsk has since
been severed by Russian authorities."

Noah saw in the rearview mirror a sedan with heavily tinted windows.
But when he adjusted the mirror to read its license plate, it turned onto a
side street. *False alarm.*

"What are you doing home?" Natalie asked as Noah entered the kitchen.
She wore a short tennis dress. Her lean arms and tanned legs were on
full display. "You didn't get fired, did you?" She was sort of kidding, sort
of making sure.

"I went to meet Izzy, remember?"

"Oh, yeah. So, when is she moving back in with us?" Noah was still
plotting his answer when Natalie said, "Did you ask if she has a boyfriend
yet? Because, ya know, if she never hooks up with a guy, or a girl, we're
all she has." Noah opened his mouth to tell her about the impending global
apocalypse but hesitated. "And she made you drive all the way to freaking
Baltimore, on a *workday?*"

"Listen, . . ." Noah began.

"Okay, but only for a sec. I can't just jump into a match without stretching. Jonas said my hamstrings are tight as piano wire." Noah needed to go slow with Natalie. He didn't even know if *he* believed Isabel. "I see the face you're making, Noah. But he's the best trainer in D.C. They call him the Butt Whisperer." She slapped her trim backside. "And he agreed to come all the way out here when we left Georgetown."

If this really were happening, how could he protect Natalie and their beautiful teenage daughter? Chloe had followed in her mother's footsteps and under her tutelage in making her high school's all-important JV cheerleading squad. Natalie, still every bit the college cheerleader Noah had met while in law school, was slim, beautiful, and comfortable being the center of men's attention. But what if everything fell apart and those same leering men were unconstrained by civility? What if Noah had to keep his family safe by force? Their gangly middle schooler son Jacob could do little to help.

"Well?" Natalie prodded. "Tick-tock, Noah."

"It's . . . There's this disease. In Siberia." He hurried too much. "Apparently, well, it's coming here, and it's bad. Everybody might get sick. Things could get, like, bad."

Natalie rearranged knives in their butcher-block holder. Noah showed her the article in the *Washington Post*. "Trouble, Noah, in *Russia?* Stop the presses!"

Curfews, shooting, burning bodies instead of burying them. Soon, every point Noah made entrenched Natalie further. "Emma caught it," he said. "She's in Bethesda."

Natalie replied, "You *warned* her. At the Annual Thanksgiving Blow-Up?" But she must have seen that she was upsetting him and asked, "Is she gonna be alright?"

"She lived, but it causes some kind of . . . brain damage."

Natalie screwed her face up in a silent, "*Ew*," but said, "That's terrible. I'm sure she'll be okay." She rubbed his arm. "But you *did* warn her. And this is in *Siberia?*"

"I wanta get us prepared," Noah said defiantly. It was a gamble that her brief burst of sympathy for Emma and haste to get to the courts gave him a momentary advantage.

Natalie looked at her watch, then put a hand on each of his shoulders. "Okay. I hereby authorize *you*, Noah Miller, to be just as *prepared*," she pecked him on the lips, "as your wittle heart," another kiss, "desires." A real kiss. "You good?" Noah nodded. "But don't pile shit up in the guest room. And get back to work before they *do* fire you."

Noah did return to work. He was mindful of several cars on the road behind him, but each in turn veered off. Now *he* was being paranoid. At the office, he summoned his first-year associate. "I want you to draft a petition for a writ of habeas corpus and file it first thing tomorrow morning in the Federal District Court for the District of Maryland."

The perpetually bored, unshaven millennial flipped open his iPad. "Petitioner?"

"Dr. Emma Miller." In a photo on Noah's credenza from Thanksgiving, Emma and Isabel, mirror images except for haircuts and clothes, posed side-by-side. They still rebelled against years of being dressed like the identical porcelain "China dolls"—antique and ungodly expensive—that they'd each been given at age six but never allowed to touch. Isabel at least had worn a dress. Emma, to contrast, wore jeans and a tank top. Natalie looked perfect, as always, and was pissed, as always, this time because Izzy's "frumpy" dress and Emmy's "ratty" jeans had ruined the professionally taken portrait.

Noah's Northeastern parents had accused him of rebelling in marrying Midwestern Natalie, who was an A-student at a good college. "Not an Ivy," they'd said, dripping condescension and simultaneously slamming the school Natalie and Noah *both* attended! "I imagine she's on financial aid. Noah, you don't know *where* she's from," they said like he'd taken in a stray without her shots. As regards her gorgeous looks, *apparently* plain with a hint of pretty and in pearls was refined, but Natalie betrayed a certain pedestrian taste and reflected poorly on Noah's family and upbringing.

"Matter number?" the associate asked. "For billing?"

"Oh, there's something in the system from some estate planning." Instead of quitting her dangerous job after their fight, Emma had gotten Noah to draft her will. He suspected she was simply rubbing his nose in the argument that he'd lost. *But who's laughing now?* Noah fought to avoid cringing at such an inappropriate thought.

"Who's the respondent?" the associate asked.

"The United States of America."

The recent law school grad glanced up, then asked, "Place of confinement?"

Noah Googled the NIH lab in Bethesda and found articles about quarantined Ebola patients. "Say: Special Clinical Studies Unit of the National Institutes of Health Clinical Center in Bethesda, Maryland, or other facility."

"Is she in pretrial detention, serving a sentence, in immigration detention or 'Other'?" his associate read on his iPad.

"Other. Unlawful detention on public health concerns." For Grounds and Supporting Facts, Noah dictated. "On or about, two days ago, Petitioner may have contracted a disease while on assignment for the National Institutes of Health and is being deprived of her liberty illegally due to respondent failing to serve quarantine orders."

The associate finished typing and said, "Requested Relief?"

"Petitioner requests," Noah said, "the Court set a hearing for Respondent to show cause for Petitioner's detention, or grant Petitioner's request for immediate release."

Noah did another Google search and read out the address of the Office of General Counsel, Public Health Division, NIH Branch, for service of process.

"Done," the associate said, "and printing." That was too easy. Practicing law had been harder in Noah's day.

When the first-year returned, Noah signed the petition. "Get it filed and served."

He then turned to the growing pile of work in his inboxes, physical and electronic, but caught himself staring at piles of paper, unread emails, and the bustling street below, but not seeing them. If it's true, they can't stay in D.C. They needed to get away. *The Old Place*!

He and Natalie were renovating his family's abandoned ancestral home high atop a hill in Virginia's Shenandoah Valley. He Googled: What do you need to ride out the apocalypse? He tweaked the search a couple of times, then began taking notes.

An hour later, his hand rested on his desk phone's receiver as it lay in its cradle. *Am I really doing this?* He took a deep breath and phoned his contractor. "I have some changes." He read his list. "And I want to expedite everything." The contractor made pained noises. "How much to get all that done in three weeks?" The man laughed. "How much?" Half a million dollars, due on completion, over and above the as-yet-unknown cost plus ten percent base price, figure $3.5 million total, if the job is done in *four* weeks with no more major changes. "Deal," Noah said, apparently surprising the man, and definitely surprising Noah, who felt sick with unresolved doubt. He emailed the renovation specs back and forth with the contractor, who formally agreed to the changes in his final reply.

In the quiet of his office, Noah panicked. What had he just done? He searched the Internet. There were tweets in Russian from Khabarovsk. He used Google Translate and got Pidgin English. "They surround Old

Marketplace and shoot everyone. Saw that with my eyes. It realistically happened!!!" Another read, "Was on train from Primorskoye region. We stop and reverse all the way toward Vladivostok." A news item caught his eye. The Russians had shut down border crossings from China. *From China.* He texted Izzy. "Are you absolutely sure?" He didn't expect a response, but got one almost instantly. "Worse than I thought," she texted back. "Get going now, now, now!!!"

If it had been only Iz's panic, Noah might have awaited further confirmation. He didn't totally trust her judgment. Unlike Emma, she hadn't fully matured. She was stuck between youth and an uncertain future adulthood. But Emma wasn't prone to histrionics. She was a full professor of epidemiology at Johns freaking Hopkins! He'd always respected the way she took charge of her life after their parents had died. If she said panic, then you panicked. *Here goes,* he thought after a single but distinct tremor of fear passed.

Between his checking and brokerage accounts, Noah had $93,425 in cash. But he and his sisters had each inherited millions from their parents. The market was up 300 points. He first sold the stocks and mutual funds that invested in equity, which were the most volatile. It was amazingly fast, only a dozen or so clicks of his mouse. Fifteen minutes later, net of commissions, he had $4,396,192 in cash. He would owe $549,524 in taxes on the capital gains, if he ever had to pay them. He kept a running count on his iPad.

Each act of financial suicide made him more nervous, but also more committed.

Next came the bonds, notes, and CDs, which took five minutes and half a dozen clicks until he'd amassed another $1,758,477, with $105,509 in theoretical tax liability. The IRAs and 401Ks were sold similarly easily for net proceeds of $504,405. The tax bite was huge, however, at $277,423, in part because of the early withdrawal penalty. Finally, the kids' college funds, in tax-advantaged 529 plans, netted $294,698, with a tax plus penalty of $162,084. In an hour, it was done. When all the trades settled, he would have $7,047,208 in cash, and a tax bill of $1,094,539 . . . unless there was no IRS to collect it.

What have I done? came a nagging inner voice that he just couldn't shake.

Noah's McLean house was worth around four million and had no mortgage. Selling it would take too much time. Luckily, however, he had put in place a two-million-dollar home equity line of credit in case he wanted to jump into the market with both feet. It took only a phone call to his banker to draw the entire line. The cash would be in his account by the end of the day.

So call it $8,000,000 in cash, free and clear, net of taxes. He wired the first installment, $1,000,000, to his contractor. Seven million left. Figure another $2,500,000 to finish paying for renovations to the Old Place and he had $4,500,000 to spend. If he didn't reserve funds to pay taxes to a government that might not exist, which thought raised Noah's stress level a notch, add another million to that.

He felt each silent minute tick past. Traffic moved normally along the street below. Life went on as it always had. He tried to imagine hordes of the insensate like some scene from *The Walking Dead*. The more he tried to visualize it, the more he grew sure he had just royally screwed up. *What were you thinking?*

He jumped when his phone rang. It was the contractor. "Got yer wire. Thanks much. I'm puttin' rush orders on mater'ls, so we're on it. And say, I *just* got a call from somebody else up yer way. A big muckety-muck gov'ment guy with a farm down near Charlottesville. Wants some of the same things as you. Fences, shutters, fire suppression, antennas, panic room. Didn't think Charlottesville was such a dangerous place. I told him he was a day late and a dollar short, but when I asked what was happenin', he hung up. So let me ask you, what's goin' *on* up there in D.C.?"

Noah stumbled through a litany of lies. Russia is enigmatic. Global warming looks warmer. Terrorism is scaring people. Just better to be prudent.

"Ooo*kay*. It's yer money, boss," the contractor replied, satisfied that he knew now who the fool was. He promised daily status emails and pictures before hanging up.

Noah wasn't fully convinced, but he was now fully committed. All in. Time to start buying things for the cave.

Chapter 5

Isabel was late for her first NIH meeting even before she got lost in the maze of D.C. streets, and then again in the labyrinthine NIH hospital. When she finally found the right conference room, two men in dark suits just outside flashed FBI badges. *Oh, shit*! They led her into an empty office. "Here she is," one said into a speakerphone.

"Dr. Miller?" boomed a voice from the speaker. "I'm Andrew Pearson. Director of the Federal Bureau of Investigation."

Isabel's mouth went dry and her voice broke. "How do . . . How do you do, sir?"

"I hear you just met with your brother, Noah Miller, at Patterson Park in Baltimore."

The agents in the room returned Isabel's searching gaze, but betrayed nothing. Maybe she should deny it, but he knew. "Uhm, yes . . . sir."

"Did you sign a nondisclosure agreement?" Director Pearson asked.

"Yes. Yes, sir. I did. I know."

The agents made no move to handcuff her. "I'm gonna lay my cards on the table, Dr. Miller," Pearson said. "I just attended a Kafkaesque meeting with the AG, who wants me to resubmit my request for ammunition replenishment. *This* afternoon. He wants an SOW, a Statement of Work, raising our order from four million nine-mil rounds to *fifty* million rounds. *Fifty*," he repeated. "I've got 14,000 field agents. Do the math. That's 3,500 additional rounds *per* agent, and we've already got 100 million rounds in stock. So my specific question, Dr. Miller, is just what the *fuck* is going on?"

"Well, sir, as you know, I signed that nondisclosure agreement. . . ."

"Don't yank my chain! The president may hate my guts, but I guaran-damn-tee you I can detain your ass on nothing more than I know now. So, last chance. What's it gonna be, Dr. Miller? Friend or foe?"

Since asking to call Noah, her lawyer, wouldn't sound like she'd chosen *friend*, she saw no alternative. "Okay. Being that you're the head of the FBI and all. . . . So, this new disease emerged? In Siberia?" She heard nothing over the phone, and the two agents remained stone-faced. It's in China but it's going global soon. It'll spread slowly, then accelerate. It kills half the people, and damages the brains of survivors, sometimes causing extreme violence. "I'm a neuroscientist, so I've been asked to study that behavior."

"And," he said, "because your twin sister caught it. How long until it gets here?"

How much does he know? Is this some kind of trap? "A month or two. Weeks, conceivably." Pearson asked about the violence. "I was attacked in Siberia by an infected Russian who went from calm to homicidal in a split second. Marines killed him before . . ."

Before what? She shuddered suddenly. *What would that Russian have done to me?* She went on. Insensitivity to pain. Flat emotional affect. Lack of empathy.

"They sound like remorseless killing machines, Dr. Miller. When will the president go public?" Isabel assumed he was worried about unrest and assured him they'd keep it under wraps as long as possible. Pearson surprised her. "So only top officials get to plan for survival? We have a rule with terrorism, Dr. Miller. If threats cause you to take personal precautions, you inform the public even though it alerts the terrorists you're onto them. It's wrong not to give the public the same chance we have. And if it's wrong for terrorism, it's *criminal* in this case. Just so you know, every official in those NSC meetings, every doctor at the NIH, every pharmaceutical company exec is stocking up a cabin in the woods before all the regular folk find out."

Isabel had no response. No good one anyway.

"I'll be calling you for regular updates. You say nothing about our talks. Agreed?"

"What about my meeting with my brother?"

"What meeting?" Pearson replied.

"The one we just had in. . . . Oh." The line was already dead, and she was alone.

Isabel crossed the hall in a fog and entered a crowded conference room, which instantly fell silent. Two dozen white-smocked scientists sat at a long table looking at her. Isabel waggled her fingers in a lame wave that she instantly regretted.

"Well!" said a middle-aged woman at the table's head. "Dr. *Miller*, I presume? *So* glad you could grace us with an appearance. We've just been killing time waiting." They were clearly mid meeting. Notes filled glowing tablets. Data cluttered white boards. Isabel took the only empty seat, beside the acerbic woman, as everyone stared at her, faces grim. "You settled in?" asked the presumably senior scientist in a patronizing tone. "Can we get you coffee or anything?" Isabel shook her head. "Okay, to catch you up, estimates are three billion dead, three billion zombiefied. As Dr. Street might say, it was fun while it lasted."

Her reference to zombies offended Isabel, but she decided to make herself small, the way she felt.

"*This* is the newest *member* of our team." The woman clearly added verbal air quotes around member. "Dr. Isabel Miller, twin sister of Subject Zero Zero One. *Identical* twin, obviously. For those who don't have access privileges to the Subject, this is what Zero Zero One looks like, minus all this one's . . . *hair*."

"Patient," corrected a heavily bearded man next her. Like most of the others, he wore thick, unfashionable eyeglasses. "Patient, not subject."

The woman ignored him. "Dr. Miller is," she read, "Stanford double major, molecular biology, *oh*, and art history! PhD, neuroscience, Cal. Hank, didn't you *teach* neuroscience at Berkeley?" The bearded man replied that it was before Dr. Miller's time. "*Research* professor at UCSB," the woman continued, adding, "*Hmm*," without explanation. But none was needed. Everyone understood she meant research, not full-tenured professor.

"Henry Rosenbaum," the bearded man said. "Hank. And this ray of sunshine is Dr. Nielsen, the hospital's director." The woman at the table's head fake-smiled through pinched lips.

"Walter Street," said the nearly bald man next to Hank. "We're so sorry about your sister." His glasses magnified his eyes and his smile revealed crooked teeth. "I'm director, Office of Biodefense Research at the National Institute of Allergy and Infectious Diseases."

"Dr. Doomsayer," Nielsen called him.

"Also known as the bug-o'-the-day man," Hank appended.

Everyone was a decade or more older than Isabel. Almost all wore clean white, thigh-length lab coats over business casual attire. They were presumably some dream team assembled for the apocalypse at the pinnacles of illustrious careers. And then there was Isabel, from a school better known for its surfing. She resolved to keep her mouth shut.

Street introduced the heads of Bioinformatics and Computational Research, Immunology and Emerging Infectious Diseases, and Vaccine Design Allergic and Infectious Diseases. The head of Epidemiology said, "Let me express my deepest sympathies." CDC liaisons from the Special Pathogens and Vector-Borne Diseases branches each held up hands on introduction. An officer in camouflage under his lab coat from the Army's Medical Research Institute of Infectious Diseases sort of saluted her. "Bioweapons lab," Nielsen said. "*Former*," the man corrected. A could've-been-good-looking woman from the Tumor Cell Biology Lab with a tan and, for some reason, a wilting red tropical flower tucked behind one ear smiled at Isabel, who winked back. *Why?* Jesus!

Next were an out-of-place outdoorsman with a mane of gray hair from the Delta Regional Primate Research Center and a doughty doctor who looked like a mother of ten from St. Jude Children's Research Hospital. Nielsen hurried through the rest, pointing and saying, "pathogenesis, genomics, virology, computational biology, biomedical research, and last and *definitely* least, White House spy."

Patricia Maldonado leaned forward. "We've met. And I got the same treatment."

"Okay, gals," Nielsen said. "'Nuff chit-chat. We need to wrap this . . ."

Isabel interrupted. "May I just ask if we know yet what the pathogen is?"

Dr. Street replied. "No, not yet. We're doing the morphological classification and the WHO the genomic sequencing. But the smart money's on dsDNA virion."

"Which is a . . . *what?*" Maldonado asked, taking notes. Nielsen heaved a sigh.

"Double-strand DNA," Street replied. "Not single-strand RNA. A virion is like a virus's seed. It can remain inactive theoretically forever, but practically for tens of millennia until, typically, it's destroyed by strikes from naturally occurring radiation."

"It's so hard to believe," Isabel said, "that SED just . . . came out of nowhere."

Nielsen looked at her watch. Street said, "We worry about ecological disruption like jungle encroachment bringing us into contact with new microorganisms, but coming at us from the ice?" He too looked baffled. "In 1485, the English sweating disease, a suspected hantavirus, raged across Europe. Like with SED, death came in a matter of hours, for instance to Oliver Cromwell's wife and children. Then, just as suddenly as it appeared, it disappeared. Last outbreak was in 1551, and it hasn't been seen since. But it's probably still out there, somewhere . . . waiting."

Isabel asked, "Have you done any research into pathogens that affect behavior?" There was laughter, led by Hank, but it appeared good-natured.

Unlike Nielsen, who drummed her fingernails on the table. "Here we go!"

"They're rare," Street replied, paying Nielsen no mind, "but not unheard of. I'm sure you know about the protozoan *Toxoplasma gondii*, which infects one third of all Americans. In rats, it hijacks neurochemical pathways, turning rats' fear of cat urine into arousal, getting the rats eaten so the parasite can reproduce in cats' guts. Infection by it in *humans* correlates with schizophrenia and neuroticism, though that could just be a preexisting correlation between neuroticism and ownership of *cats*. Then there's the common *Streptococcus* bacterium, which is suspected to cause Pediatric Acute-onset Neuropsychiatric Syndrome. Overnight, school-age children with PANS become terror-stricken, suffer extreme separation anxiety and regress to temper tantrums and bedwetting."

Isabel said, "And there's Cotard's syndrome. People get sick, possibly from Lyme disease, and suffer damage to their right dorsal lateral prefrontal cortex. After drifting in and out of consciousness, they become convinced that they died and often quit eating and starve to death because, what's the point? They're already dead."

Heads turned to Hank, who concurred. "Walking corpse syndrome. Good analogy." Isabel couldn't help but feel she had just passed some impromptu exam.

"And so here we are," Nielsen interjected, "with a real-life zombie uprising."

That ruffled Isabel anew. "Could we please not use that word?" Nielsen shot a look of surprise at Hank. "I'm sorry," Isabel said, "but that word is a little judgmental. Its only scientific utility has been in thought exercises on consciousness, the philosopher's zombie, so . . ."

Before Nielsen could respond, Street said, "Please elaborate." Nielsen smiled and rested her chin atop interlaced fingers to listen. She wore half a dozen rubber wristbands of different colors signifying support for every cause imaginable but no wedding ring. She was amused that Isabel now had to discuss a term whose use she had attempted to curtail.

"Okay," Isabel said to Street. "The question is whether consciousness is required for sentient behavior, or is rather an irrelevant byproduct of physiological processes in the brain—an illusion we invent to explain our sense of self. Theorists posited, as a thought exercise, the existence of a being who acts exactly like a human but has no sense of self." *A simulacrum,* she thought, wondering how General Browner had come to know the word.

"A philosopher's *zombie*!" Street exclaimed, clearly delighting in the name. His grin, while genuine, could've been improved with orthodontia and dental bleach.

Hank said, "Technically, an insentient, functional isomorph."

"The point is," Isabel continued, "if p-zombies can pass the Turing test . . . ?"

"Machines achieve consciousness," Nielsen quipped, "and the robot wars begin! Let's say we not worry about that one today, *okay*?"

"If p-zombies," Isabel repeated, "can solve problems, use language, *etc.*, indistinguishably from humans, then natural selection would be indifferent to consciousness, and consciousness therefore wouldn't be expected to arise naturally from evolution."

Nielsen scoffed. Her impatience, Isabel decided, called for a detailed, passive-aggressive explanation. "On one side of the debate," Isabel said, turning again to Street, who seemed interested, "inessentialists argue that machines don't need consciousness to pass the Turing test. Their Chinese Room Argument imagines an English-only speaker supplied with detailed instructions on how to respond to any Chinese characters he receives. A Chinese speaker in another room types, in Chinese: How are you? The English speaker, following the instructions, returns characters that read, in Chinese, I'm fine, even though he has no idea what was just said. The Chinese speaker thinks he's having a conversation, but to the English speaker it's all gibberish in/gibberish out."

"Gibberish," Nielsen said under her breath, "being the operative word, here."

That was enough. *What the hell is her problem?* But Street said, "Have you asked your sister the same question? Her reply sounds a lot like your English speaker. And yet she's been totally cooperative, while other survivors are extremely violent."

Hank said, "Human behavior is as complex as any found in nature. Why would it not also be varied *after* infection?" Hank turned to Isabel. "You should know that your sister's intake scans showed swelling in the areas of her frontal and parietal mirror neurons. That may have damaged, or severed, some or all of her emotional bonds." Isabel looked down and nodded. "*That* could so fundamentally alter survivors' relationships with others that it raises a profound question. If they feel nothing for other humans, just what *are* they?"

"Dangerous sociopaths," Nielsen answered. A few heads around the room nodded.

Street raised his index finger. "You know, among higher-order species, there's a notable absence of empathy in predators. If cats felt empathy for mice, they'd starve."

"Are you saying," Isabel asked, "that they're the predators and we're the prey?"

"That's why we call him Dr. Doomsayer," Hank explained to Isabel. A jumble of side discussions arose as if pent up nervous energy was being released.

"Okay!" Nielsen interrupted. "I need everyone's attention! I've got something to announce that none of you is going to like. I just got off the phone with Dr. Aggarwal. This was our last all-hands discussion of the science. From now on, these meetings will be strictly limited to administrative matters only. All *substantive* discussion of SED is limited to your assigned working groups." There was an explosion of griping. "Which for you, Dr. Miller," Nielsen said in an aside, ignoring the insurrection, "consists solely of Dr. Rosenbaum."

"Secrecy and compartmentalization!" said Street. "The cornerstones of science."

"All reports," Nielsen shouted over the commotion, "are to be marked classified!" Everyone began collecting their files, folders, and devices. "All communications via DoD server only!" People rose to leave. "That's the law. I advise you to obey it!"

"Wait!" cried a scientist. "Let's not abandon tradition."

Everyone paused as Dr. Street rubbed his chin. "How about *Heterosaccus californicus*, a parasitic barnacle. It feminizes male sheep crabs. Their fighting claws drop off and abdomens widen to create a brood pouch for the parasite's offspring." At that, the exodus continued with everyone talking as they filed out in violation of Nielsen's directive.

On passing, Maldonado made a face at Street's weirdness. Isabel returned the look in kind. Nielsen noticed and shook her head in silent confirmation that Isabel didn't belong.

* * * *

Drs. Nielsen, Rosenbaum, and Street led Isabel through the warren of corridors. Isabel texted a definitive reply to quell Noah's doubts, probably breaking a bunch of laws. Security grew tighter. Unarmed security guards gave way to rent-a-cops with pistols, and then to Marines with rifles, who scrutinized Isabel's new White House security badge.

"This is it," Nielsen said, opening a nondescript door into a room dominated by a window running the entire length of its far wall. The much larger adjacent room into which the window looked swallowed up its hospital bed, equipment rack, desk, chair, and Emma, appearing tiny as she sat on the bed, supremely patient, in a hospital gown, with her hands folded in her lap.

Nielsen asked the nurse in scrubs, hair wet as if straight from the shower, what Emma had been doing. "She hasn't done *anything* since lunch," the twenty-something replied, consulting a tablet, "other than pour a drink of water, take a sip, and go potty."

The nurse stared at Isabel. Nielsen said, "This is her twin sister, obviously."

Isabel introduced herself. "Beth Foster," the young woman replied cheerily. "I'm her day nurse, night nurse, whatever. We're pretty shorthanded. Are you a physician?" She was thin, with sandy hair and a cherubic face to go with a sunny demeanor.

"Neuroscientist," Isabel replied. Emma scratched her nose. Beth logged it.

The orientation was brief. A built-in desk with rolling chairs was mounted under the window. Atop it were a phone, a laptop, and three microphones rising from panels with buttons for lights, temperature, *etc.* One button, Opaque, was lit, which Nielsen said controlled the window's smart glass. Emma now saw a white frosted pane but extinguish that button and she could see clearly into the observation room. Another button, Talk, was dark. The laptop displayed live video of Emma sitting on her bed from half a dozen angles but was also connected to a monitor in Emma's room on which they could display their "Rorschach tests or whatever," Nielsen said. "The military comes first, medical second, science third. Any free time after that for your . . . *research*, have at it."

Hank said, "Everything in here and in Emma's room is recorded. When Beth isn't here, she reviews the feed. She also texts updates every four hours." He turned to Nielsen and Street. "We'll get to work now." As Hank extracted a folder, Street frowned for some reason and shook his head before departing. Maybe some ongoing professional squabble.

Hank said, "Street's a bit eccentric." Beth snorted. "Lived with his mother till she passed, now with a menagerie of insects and spiders." He perused his papers. "How about you, Dr. Miller?" She insisted he call her Isabel. "Anyone significant in your life, Isabel?"

"Nope," she replied, reflexively resenting his query. "*You*?"

He took no umbrage. "Married forty years. Three daughters, two sons-in-law, two grandkids." He slid across the desk to Isabel a questionnaire that

Emma had also filled out. "Your responses will be a good cross-reference to see if her perceptions are altered."

It was a personality survey. "On a one-to-five scale, do you agree with the following statements about Dr. Emma Miller?" One meant disagreed strongly. Five, agreed strongly. Isabel breezed through. "The subject likes to engage in high-risk behavior." Four, which she changed to five. Emma had rejected offers of a lab job in favor of field epidemiology. On and on they went. Lots of twos, threes, and fours. Only a few ones and fives.

Halfway through, Isabel reached a new, nearly identical section heading. Only instead of asking about Dr. *Emma* Miller, it asked the same questions about Dr. *Isabel* Miller. Hank was prepared when she looked up. "We thought it'd be useful to inquire whether your sister's perceptions of *others* had changed. So we asked her not only about *herself*, but also about *you*. Someone with whom she's presumably quite familiar."

Isabel answered the questions quickly. When she came to whether the Subject, Isabel, likes to engage in high-risk behavior, she circled hell-no, the box marked *one*. When finished, she returned it to Hank. "Can I see Emma's responses?"

"Emma didn't understand," Hank said. "She's still somewhat confused. We told her just to answer as best she could, so she filled out responses to every single question, and marked each a three. Nothing but threes. About you and about her."

Then why the hell did I just fill it out? Isabel thought.

Emma stared into space. Isabel said, "She can be pretty passive-aggressive." *We both can*, came the unheard accusation. "Do you think that was, I dunno, obstructionism?"

Hank said, "No. She's been quite helpful. It's something . . . more profound."

Where the hell to begin? Isabel thought. She pressed the Talk button. Before Isabel could even say anything, Emma looked up at the ceiling. "Emma? Hi, sweetie, it's Iz."

Still looking up, Emma said, "Hi." Her face remained expressionless. Blank.

"I'm in the room next door," Isabel said. "Here." She pressed the Opaque button.

Emma's gaze turned to them. "This is Dr. Hank Rosenbaum." Looking uncomfortable, he leaned to the mic and said, "Hello."

"And Beth Foster, your nurse." Beth gave an enthusiastic wave and grin.

"How are you feeling?" Isabel asked. "Does your head hurt?"

Emma raised her hand to her head, just like the Gazprom executive, and said, "No." *Curious.*

"How about anything else? Does your . . . left *knee* hurt?"

Emma touched her left knee and shook her head.

Hank muted the microphone and asked, "What's that about? Her *knee?*"

"When I ask if something hurts, she touches the body part before answering. Same with an infected Russian I spoke to in Siberia." *Before he was killed.* She had barely processed that experience before the pace of events had overtaken it.

"A proprioception issue?" he asked.

"She's not having trouble maintaining posture," Isabel replied. "No wobbling or falling over. No problems getting water or going to the bathroom?" Beth shook her head. Isabel pressed the Talk button. "Emma, could you please describe for me all the steps involved in getting a glass of water. Go into *elaborate* detail. Spare nothing."

"Stand, walk to the desk, lift the pitcher, hold it over the cup, pour, put the pitcher down, lift the cup to the lips, tilt the cup until the liquid pours out, and swallow."

"Good! Thanks." Isabel muted the sound system. "No proprioception issue. She wouldn't have been able to do that kind of detailed motor planning."

"Can she read lips?" Hank asked. "Every time we talk, she looks up." Isabel shook her head in reply, then they sat still. After a few moments, Emma's gaze drifted off. Isabel brushed her bangs from her brow. Emma's eyes rose. After a short while, they lost focus and again settled on empty space.

Isabel asked, "Emma, can you describe what you see right now?"

Emma surveyed her room. "Bed, monitor, return air vents, six cameras, observation room glass, door, high window, desk, chair, walls, ceiling, floor."

"Okay," Isabel interrupted. "What else do you see?" Emma fell silent. "Do you see *me?*"

"Do you want a description of what's in *that* room? You, Dr. Rosenbaum, Beth Hopkins, three chairs, three microphones, a laptop, a door, a camera on the ceiling."

Isabel muted the mics. Hank said, "She's having trouble with the word, *see.*"

Isabel replied, "Or the word, *you.*" She pushed Talk. "Emma, can you tell me about any dreams you've had?"

Hank frowned. "What, are we jumping right to Freud now?" *That* stung.

Emma said, "To complete and publish the research, find a good man, get married, buy a house, have children, and live to an old age with you, Noah, and your families."

Tremors crossed Isabel's lips. Emma had mistaken the word *dream* to mean goals and hopes. A tear escaped Isabel's eyelashes and streaked down her cheek. She wiped it away quickly. They had never had this much trouble communicating. It had always been exactly the opposite. TSP, they had called it, a play on Twin ESP.

"What I meant," Isabel said, "was did you have a dream while you slept?"

"Can you define that usage of the word *dream*?" Emma asked.

Hank leaned to the microphone. "It means a series of images, ideas, or sensations that occur involuntarily, in your mind, while you're sleeping." Emma sat stiffly, arms braced on knees. Hank asked, "Do you recall *any* dream you've ever had in your life?"

Emma said, "No."

Isabel jumped in. "When we were young, and our parents lectured us about stranger danger, you were tormented almost every night for an entire year by the same nightmare. You were chased by a faceless man in a black cape. You'd wake up screaming. Do you remember what happened if the man caught you?"

"When he touched things, he imparted an electric shock."

"Right! And then you would wake up," Isabel said, "in my bed."

"That was *hiding* from the man," Emma corrected, "in your bed."

Hank asked, "Were those *dreams*, or did the man actually chase you in real life?" Emma seemed confused. "Did the man who chased and shocked you actually *exist?*"

"Yes," Emma replied. "He wore a cape."

"Does it make sense," Isabel asked, her voice rising, "that the man had no face?"

"The hood hid his face," Emma explained.

"So mom and dad let a man," Isabel said, fending Hank's hand off her shoulder, "in a black cape and hood, chase you, night after night, shocking you with his touches?"

"The cape," Emma reasoned, "could have generated static electricity."

"Emmy!" Isabel shouted, tears flowing. "That was a *dream*. You were *sleeping*."

"Nothing happens during sleep."

Hank wrote something like: "Can't distinguish sleeping from wakeful states."

"Emmy," Isabel said into the mic, "those goals you listed earlier—to get married and have a family—are those things you *remember* wanting, or things you want *now?*"

Emma was silent in the way Isabel now saw as fundamental incomprehension. Finally, she said, "Some things you say, Isabel, don't make sense. Those . . . are the *plans*."

"*Whose* plans, Emma? *Your* plans?"

"You're making no sense. Plans are necessary. Without them, nothing happens."

Chapter 6

Noah dressed for work listening to TV in the large suburban home he'd bought four years earlier when, at thirty-five, he came into his trust fund. The brick, columned house was too big for their family of four, but they'd outgrown the three-bedroom Georgetown townhouse. Natalie had wanted to have kids while young, reasoning she could more easily regain her figure in her twenties. She had gotten pregnant with Chloe after graduating from college and while Noah was still in law school. He had to admit her plan had worked.

Natalie, in a short robe, put her coffee down to straighten his tie and pluck at his hair. He pulled her against him. Her taut back and slender butt felt great under silk.

"Easy there, cowboy," she said, twisting free, but coyly. "You're in the doghouse."

"For what?" he asked.

"For something I'm sure you've done," she hung the robe on its hook and was naked, "but I haven't found out yet." She was beautiful, with a perfect body. One in ten thousand. She stepped into a thong. "Oh come on! That was *funny*, Noah. You never laugh at my jokes!"

Our match, Noah thought, *only made sense when me having money mattered.* What happens when how well you fight and hunt and fish are better measures of a man?

"And in international news, major unrest has broken out in Heilongjiang Province, China." Noah raced to the small set in the master bath. "Before all Internet access was cut," the picture switched to a violent street scene, "a citizen posted this video from Fuyuan, which has since been taken down by authorities." The video was grainy, shaky, and taken from a distance. But the poor quality did nothing to diminish the obvious ferocity of the mob that overran the police, or of its result—security troops dropping riot shields and batons and fleeing for their lives. "The crowd reportedly carried no banners and made no demands before suddenly launching an unprovoked attack on police. No explanation was given for the violence by the blogger, who referred to the rioters by the Chinese character that means treacherous person, evil spirit, or demon."

"So you'll remember to pick up the lamp?" said Natalie as she headed for the closet wearing only her thong. "Noah? *Noah!*" She crossed her arms over her breasts to reduce the distraction. "Honestly, we need separate bathrooms. Remember the *lamp*?"

"Oh yeah," he said. "Sure." He had totally forgotten. "It's at, uhm, . . . ?"

"*No*-ah! I'll text you the address . . . *again*." Natalie would survive, Noah realized, on some combination of her physical fitness and men doing absolutely anything she wants.

Before leaving, Noah stopped at his laptop in the study. One post translated the Chinese character repeatedly used by the anonymous blogger mentioned on TV as *fiend*, as in hyperbolic reports such as "The black-eyed fiends tore the policemen to pieces!"

Noah was perplexed at feeling a strange sense of relief. Isabel was right about the impending doom. He took a deep breath, then typed his new search.

* * * *

"You here to buy a gun?" asked the salesman at Big Jimmy's Gun Store. He was skinny, had a pencil-thin mustache, and wore a Western-style shirt, big belt buckle, jeans, and cowboy boots. His baseball hat read: Work Hard—Millions on Welfare Are Depending on You. His eyeglasses had darkened in the sun and not quite cleared.

Noah nodded self-consciously but concluded that he wasn't being judged, at least outwardly. They went over a federal form. Noah answered background questions and supplied his social security number. "They'll do an online check while we chat."

Noah said, "Good. Good. I'd like to look at a few things."

"And what kinds of things would those be?"

"Uhm, firearms," replied Noah.

"Well you've come to the right place, sir. Any particular type?" When Noah said all types, the guy suppressed a grin. "Then let's take an overview, shall we?" He walked Noah through the store, saying, "We'll come back to shotguns," as they passed glass cases filled with brutish-looking, thick-barreled weapons. The prices rose from $200 to $400 in the bypassed shotgun section, to $500 to $1,200 in the pistol section, despite the latter's smaller size. The salesman's commission presumably rose commensurately.

"*Glooocks*," the man said too loudly, though no one looked their way. Noah reminded himself that this was legal, ethical, moral even. Second Amendment and all. A case displayed the full line. "Low maintenance, high reliability. Nine millimeter is where it's at in ammo. Now an aficionado such as yourself might say 9mm lacks stopping power, but that was your daddy's nine-mil. Today, you've got yer 147-grain Speer Gold Dot G2. Hollow point, elastomer tip in the cavity. The FBI, which is the fashion setter in these matters, left the 9mm back in '86 and tried the 10mm and .40 caliber before scientifically concluding they were way too damned heavy and coming full circle back to nines. The upgraded ammo penetrates deep to get at vital organs. And you'll never run out of good ole NATO nine by nineteen Parabellum." Noah nodded but had no idea what the man had said.

The coolest-looking gun was the Glock 26. "The *Baby* Glock!" the salesman said, noticing Noah's interest. "Subcompact. A pound-and-a-half loaded. That's half-a-pound lighter than a .40-caliber Glock 22, and nine-mil is more shootable. Less recoil means faster rate of fire. I wouldn't go any smaller on mag capacity. Ten rounds in a Glock sure beats a five-shot revolver. But the Glock's double-stack mag makes it thicker and less concealable than a revolver or a five-shot single-stack automatic. Some like revolvers 'cause there's less fear of a snag, but the Glock has an internal hammer and draws smooth."

The Gen 4 cost $500. "I'll take two," Noah said. *The kids?* "No, four." The salesman smiled. Two dozen empty mags—$40 each. Fifty bucks for each belt holster.

The salesman almost shouted, "Next stop—black guns!" He swept his arm forward as if leading a column of troops.

Noah astutely but nervously noted, "Almost every gun *here* is black."

The salesman lowered his voice respectfully. "Assault weapons."

"Would I need those," Noah asked, "I mean, if I already have the pistols?"

"You know what they say. A pistol is what you use to fight your way to your rifle. That'd be your *primary* weapon, right? Among your long guns?"

"Uhm, yeah." *Sounded right.* "Among my long guns. But I might, ya know, I guess, carry a pistol, like, around the house." That sounded unsafe. "We've got a big backyard, out in the country, with a . . . a *pond* and everything," he lied, thinking on his feet.

"Sounds beautiful. And I bet you wanta keep that pond safe, do you not, sir?"

"Yep. Now that you mention it, I'm concerned about, ya know, crime."

"And so your targets will be human?" the salesman asked. Noah failed to summon a response to such a question. "I mean you're not hunting, or sport shooting, or competition shooting, or even plinking at tin cans or rodents. You'd be shooting people?"

Noah shrugged, but finally nodded. "Criminal types," he clarified.

"Of course, damn them all! But knowing what you're trying to shoot matters. If some angel-dust-crazed home invader charges at you from your bedroom door, you get one shot. *One.* You want him to go down *right* there, not a couple blocks away when he bleeds out after causing God knows what mayhem . . . at your pond and whatnot. But use a big gun on a bothersome squirrel and it makes a mess. You match the gun to the target."

Noah was nodding like a bobble-head doll. He should be taking notes.

"Long guns. Five-point-five-six-millimeter, AR-15-style, twenty-eight-inch barrel so you can reach out and touch people. It's considered bad form to bring a pistol to a rifle fight. And like nine-mil ammo, there's a never-ending supply of five-five-six. Ammo's the real cost of a weapon. If you shoot a few thousands rounds a year to stay proficient—which you can do right here at our air conditioned indoor range—you'll spend ten times as much on ammo as on the gun over its life. Stick with NATO-spec, 5.56 by 45 mil."

Noah pointed at one. "A *beaut.* Telescoping stock." He slid it to full extension and handed the rifle to Noah. It was heavier than he'd imagined. It looked plastic but felt and smelled metallic. The salesman seated it firmly against Noah's shoulder. "Hard up in the hollow. Keep that butt plate from poundin' on you. It bruises *and* it wrecks your aim."

Noah quickly handed the rifle back, but said, "I'll take it."

"Would that be four, then?" the salesman asked, grinning at his joke.

It was expensive, and therefore presumably among the best. "Five, actually." He had forgotten about Isabel joining them. *Isabel?* "And make it five Glocks, *etc.,* too."

"Yessir." The guy saluted crisply. "The family that shoots together, stays together." *And lives,* Noah thought. It was $880 per rifle, before options. The salesman explained the Picatinny rail system on the foregrip, which encased what would be a hot barrel, onto which you could attach goodies.

Small, powerful flashlights for $120. "Five please, plus five spare batteries." A giant thermal imager costing $5,000. "No, thanks. Well, maybe one."

Five bipods with bayonet mounts—$30 each. Ditto the vertical foregrips, which with the bipod added a full pound to the five and a half pounds of the base rifle. Another $38 per for M7 bayonets and $12 for M10 scabbards.

Brass catchers might come in handy for reloads. Fifteen bucks each. He'd seen tactical slings that hold rifles at the ready across your chest in war coverage. Only $30 a pop. Same price as starter scopes, but he upgraded all of them to the $90 model.

Noah balked at $600 for laser-aim pointers but changed his mind and bought five. Next, five bug-out bags, each with three pouches, holding six mags plus room for extra gear, for $65 apiece. "In woodlands camo," Noah chose from his color options.

Fifty empty thirty-round AR-15 magazines, which Noah sensed from the salesman's reaction might be too many, at $25 apiece. Next, ammo. In boxes of fifty, the 9mm pistol ammunition came to almost $0.75 per round. Noah revised his order up, and up again, buying fifty boxes—2,500 rounds. Then for only fifty cents more, at $1.25 per round, Noah bought five huge boxes of 5.56 x 45 NATO-spec rifle ammo—5,000 rounds.

He worried about going to excess when two new salesmen began assembling his order. The tour led back to shotguns. "Maybe I've got enough. Five pistols? Five rifles?"

The salesman picked up a pump-action shotgun. "What have we learned so far? Do we want obscure types of ammo?" Noah shook his head. "So, in scatter guns, we go twelve-gauge, the Big Mac of shotgun ammo. Always available and, well, it's a shotgun."

Noah could only guess that the shotgun packed a higher order magnitude of wallop.

"Your basic choice," the salesman said, "is semi-auto versus pump."

Noah tried to compose an intelligent question. "What, *uhm*, are the differences?"

The salesman grinned. "Wellsir, the semis are newer auto-loading technology. Most people consider pumps more reliable, but the semis are catching up. The semis do, though, require more pampering and cleaning. The gas blow-back holes in the piston assembly get gunked up. And they're also more expensive."

"So which would you suggest?" Noah asked, certain it was the more expensive gun with the higher commission.

"If it was me, protectin' *my* pond, I'd go pump." Noah had guessed wrong. "In confined space, a shotgun is game over. Nobody stands in against a determined shotgun shooter. Plus, there's this." Holding the gun one-handed by the ribbed foregrip, he pumped it—*kerchunk*. Noah was sold the instant he heard the sound. Mechanical. Serious. "If that don't do the trick, say your intruder is of the aforementioned angel-dust variety, then this is what you'd call a one-shot stop." Noah chuckled—it sounded like a play on "one-stop shop"—but the salesman didn't get it. "I gotta warn ya, though, clean-up's a bitch."

A trickle of nervous sweat ran cold down Noah's side. His choice came down to the Remington 870 and Mossberg 500. Both cost only $325, identical pricing indicating head-to-head competition. He went with the Remington, which was configured slightly cooler with a pistol grip, sling, and flashlight.

"Great choice. Bottom-loading, side-ejecting, internal hammer. Magazine holds four rounds, five if you're not hunting and you unscrew the plug, plus one in the chamber." A thousand rounds of personal defense loads cost $1.50 each.

He was pleased, until the bill arrived. $31,458! Shit. *Natalie is gonna freak!* But that was nothing, he rationalized, compared to the millions he'd committed to converting the Old Place into a fortified, self-sufficient compound, and the millions more in cash still sitting in his brokerage account that might soon be rendered worthless.

Noah's passport, which he had thought to bring, provided proof of his age, residency and, for the assault rifle purchase, citizenship. The sale of multiple firearms would have to be reported to the Bureau of Alcohol, Tobacco, Firearms and Explosives, but they wouldn't do anything, the salesman assured him. He also informed Noah he had passed his National Instant Criminal Background Check while shopping.

"Have you thought about our gun courses?" came the man's final act of salesmanship.

Chapter 7

Isabel rose early in Emma's apartment and read two unremarkable Beth updates, the highlight of which was that Emma lacked REM sleep. In a towel, hair wet after showering, Isabel found that her jeans and T-shirt needed another spin in the dryer. She washed T-shirts and underwear daily, and jeans every other day.

She lived out of her overnight bag, which did little to make Emma's place feel like home, so Isabel browsed Emma's closet. Some skinny jeans might do in a pinch, but the rest was unwearable. Short party dresses, silky tops with plunging necklines, slinky backless and sideless gowns, and two, *two*, skimpy costumes, both with furry tails. They went well with the large box of condoms in the nightstand, probably from Sam's Club. Isabel felt a pang of guilt at the thought, and in the end left it all alone. Emma hated when anyone messed with her things. Despite being twins, they'd never shared clothes.

Emma's small writing desk was covered inches high in a chaotic mess of unopened mail. Bills, party invitations, catalogs, ads for duct cleaning. Mardi Gras beads draped the desk lamp. In a drawer, she found a Viagra bottle whose prescription was for a man she didn't know. Her own place, she realized, was G-rated. Isabel yawned and got back into bed while she waited. Rick Townsend had been so nice on the flight back from Russia. He had found her crying during a break from being with Emma, and put his arm around her and repeated the magic words that all males should be taught in preschool: "I understand." When she closed her eyes, she concocted an implausible scenario in which Rick needed a place to stay for the night. No rooms in any inns. He offered to sleep on the couch. Nonsense. He could have his side of the bed, she hers.

The dryer buzzed, waking Isabel. Her clothes were warm and smelled fresh. She turned on the TV as she brushed her teeth. "The State Department cited unrest in China," the anchorman said, "as the reason for the travel ban but declined to speculate on the cause of the unrest. The BBC, however, confirmed reports of panic over a plague-like infection that broke out along the border with Russia. No details about the disease have reached Western news media since China shut down all contact with the affected regions."

A loud knocking startled Isabel.

She peered through the peephole at two men in dark suits. When she opened the door, they flashed FBI badges and asked if they could come in. Isabel swept her arm back in a perturbed, *what-the-fuck-ever* invitation. An agent handed her a cell phone.

"You know you're missing the whole point of cell phone technology. Normally, I would just give you my number."

"This phone's encrypted," said a man on its screen, whom she assumed was Andrew Pearson. He sat at a desk, in a loosened tie and sleeves rolled up thick forearms as if he'd been there all night. A portrait of President Stoddard hung on the wall behind him. "I'll be brief. Russia and China have begun general mobilizations. That'll trigger automatic upgrades in *our* force posture, although people, ships and aircraft are already in motion all around the world, mostly redeploying back to the US. So, what's *your* update?"

"Sir, science doesn't move that fast. Empiricism requires steady, incremental . . ."

"Dr. Miller! Every disease research facility on Earth is now a twenty-four-hour operation." She felt a stab of guilt for grabbing a little sleep. "Get in the fucking loop and call when you know something. And remember, nobody's telling the truth. Trust no one."

Including you? she thought about his warning. He hung up before she snickered. It was a paradoxical statement like, "I always lie." But the humor seemed lost on the departing agents, who left the encrypted phone behind with her.

On the drive to the NIH hospital in her nondescript government car, she checked the rearview mirror repeatedly but saw only normal traffic. All was routine except at the Beltway exit, where soldiers in helmets unloaded a bulldozer from a green Army trailer.

Isabel headed straight for Emma's observation room. "You're early!" Hank said. Beth pulled her tablet to her chest, her eyes darting between Hank and Isabel.

"What's going on?" Isabel asked before seeing the thumb-sized red dot smeared on Emma's forehead. "Seriously, Hank? The Red Spot Technique? On *Emma*?"

"Beth marked her forehead during a pupil check two hours ago. Emma brushed her hair in front of her new mirror but didn't recognize the dot as marking *her* forehead."

"Really?" Isabel said, taking a seat. "She brushed her hair, but didn't see the dot?"

Hank was defensive. "She didn't rub it off. The test is valid across species. I don't think she associates the image in the mirror with the body she inhabits."

Isabel hit the Talk button over Hank's belated objections. "Morning, Emma."

"Good morning, Isabel," her sister replied.

"Would you please point to the red spot?" Emma raised her right index finger to the red smear on her forehead. "And when did you first notice it?" Isabel asked, staring at Beth, who was stifling a smile.

"When they put that big new mirror on my desk."

Hank swiveled the microphone stalk to his mouth. "Well why didn't you say or do anything about it?" he asked grumpily.

"I was waiting for the Red Dot test to begin." She again pointed to her forehead.

"She's not an ape, Hank. She knows she's the person in the fucking mirror."

Beth kept trying to get a word in. "*Yes?*" Hank finally snapped.

"She said, 'I' and 'my.' Emma! She used first person pronouns."

It was a significant observation. "Log it," Isabel said. Beth beamed at her accomplishment as she got on her tablet.

Hank fidgeted for a while before casually saying, "Isabel, would you mind submitting to a few days of neuroimaging? We've gotten scans of your sister. Yours could sort of be the . . . *before*."

"What were the results from Emma's scans?" Isabel replied.

"Several sites showed a loss of neuronal mass, now filled with cerebrospinal fluid."

Isabel winced and asked to review them.

Hank nodded. "So, if we scanned you, we could compare your sister's . . ."

"Hank, there are ten-to-the-sixteenth synapses in the cerebral cortex. There's so much variability, even in identical twins, that neurological comparisons are useless. And I don't have the time." She rose. He asked where she was going. "To visit my sister."

* * * *

Isabel said, "Hi," to the young Marine who would accompany her into her sister's hospital room. "Isabel Miller," she introduced herself.

"Yes ma'am, I know. I'm Lance Corporal Hendricks, ma'am. Tony. 8th & I."

"Excuse me?" Isabel said as they waited on the decontamination nurse.

"I'm posted to the Marine barracks. It's at the intersection of 8th and I Streets."

"Oh." The nurse entered her glass-enclosed booth. "Is this what you trained for?"

"This?" Hendricks chuckled. "No, ma'am. I'm a Marine Corps Body Bearer. We do military funerals, ma'am. I guess they were shorthanded."

The nurse turned on monitors and a desk lamp and opened manuals. Isabel nodded at Emma's hospital room door. "Have you been in there before?"

"This'll be my ninth seal break, ma'am. I'm owed fifteen beers, one from each guy in the section, if I'm the first to get to ten."

He looked like a classmate of her middle-school nephew. "How old are you?"

"Nineteen, ma'am," he said, acting guilty and glancing up at the camera on the ceiling. Isabel finally understood. He wasn't old enough to drink.

"Dr. Miller?" said the decontamination nurse over speakers from behind shatterproof glass. She explained the protocols required to enter and exit Emma's room. Isabel and Tony Hendricks, separated by a chin-high partition, each fully visible only to the nurse, stripped naked. "Any gum in your mouth?" Isabel shook her head. "How recent was your last tattoo?" *Oh come on!* Isabel turned a full circle. *No tattoos!* She stepped into white disposable coveralls. "Are you wearing any rings?" Isabel held her bare hands up before she pulled on the first of three pairs of Latex gloves. "Do you wear contact lenses?" Nope. "Are you pregnant?"

"I hope not," Isabel replied as she donned disposable booties. Hendricks laughed and said neither was he. The serious nurse glanced up but made another check mark.

"Are you immunologically compromised, or do you have any condition that might predispose you to infection?"

"No." Check.

"Do you agree," the nurse asked, "to collection of serum samples and to emergency prophylactic intervention in the discretion of biosafety personnel, including use of experimental medication?"

"Jeez. Uh, yeah, I guess." Check.

"I'm required," the nurse read, "to advise you that you are about to come into contact with a potentially fatal pathogen for which there is no known cure. Any suspected exposure will result in your isolation for up to 48 hours. Do you acknowledge and assume these risks?"

"Yes," Isabel said. Check.

"Do you agree to self-report any suspected primary or secondary barrier breach?"

"I do," Isabel said. *Whatever that means.* Check.

"Do you agree to periodic medical follow-ups by biosafety personnel?"

"Yep." Check.

The nurse pointed out to Isabel, now fully garbed except for her head, the automatic, hands-free sink, emergency shower, and eyewash station. She was instructed to avoid all sharps: needles, scalpels, pipettes, broken glassware. Hendricks pretended to listen like a polite veteran traveler during a seat belt demonstration. "You are not to remove anything from the hospital room. You are to limit direct physical contact with the patient, and to minimize contact with all surfaces."

They inserted wireless earbuds then donned goggles, masks, hoods, and face shields under the watchful eye of the nurse, who checked off item after item on her form. The Marine, pistol in one hand, finally went to the double doors, which bore a large biohazard symbol and the name and telephone number of some "Supervisor." He punched a code into a keypad. A buzzer sounded and a red warning light on the ceiling lit and began rotating. He pulled the door open while stepping back, ready to shoot if Emma charged out. Three streamers on the ceiling fluttered inward. "Airflow direction verified," the nurse said, making her final check. "You are now authorized for ingress."

Isabel entered Emma's world. From behind the observation room's now transparent smart glass, Hank and Beth watched. "Can you hear me?" Hank asked over Isabel's earbuds. She nodded, feeling like an astronaut exploring an alien planet.

The door closed automatically with a squeak, plugging Isabel's ears, and the buzzer fell quiet. Emma returned from the bathroom gyrating her jaw. Her eyes flitted between Isabel and the armed guard. There was no hug or other greeting. "Sorry," Isabel said of Hendricks. "Hospital protocol." Something in Emma's look troubled her. As if she regarded

Isabel and the man holding a pistol on her in exactly the same way. And Isabel felt surprisingly ill at ease, perhaps as unsafe in her position as Emma felt in her own.

Isabel got wet wipes from the desk, sat, and patted the bed, then verbally asked Emma to sit beside her. She meekly obliged. Lance Corporal Hendricks subtly changed positions for a clearer shot. Isabel used the wipes to rub the red dot off Emma's forehead. Emma tilted her head back and waited like a child. "There! All gone."

Isabel threw the wipes away and held the large mirror up to Emma, who dutifully looked at her own image but had absolutely no reaction. Isabel placed the mirror back on the desk. "You used to say you didn't need a mirror as long as I was nearby. Remember?"

"Yes," Emma replied. "Because we're monozygotic twins."

She had again used a first person pronoun. "*We* are twins," Isabel said. "*We* look alike." Emma seemed to be following the conversation. *Good.* "But there's one difference . . . other than the fact that I'm obviously far hotter!"

Emma didn't smile but raised her fingertip to the scar on her jaw. "I have this."

"There it is again," Hank noted. "She's got the hang of first person pronouns."

Isabel was hopeful, but unconvinced that it proved that Emma's self-awareness was intact. Standing beside her, she said, "Emma, you used to have trouble with first-person pronouns. You had no problem with *he*, *she*, or *it*, but never used *I*, *me*, or *my*. And you got confused when I said, '*You.*' So, what changed?"

"Those pronouns all refer to Emma Miller. Pronouns are efficient. Repeating Emma Miller at every reference is tedious."

"But those aren't," Isabel noted, "just references. They're *self*-references."

"Yes. To Emma Miller."

"To *you*." Emma nodded. "Emmy, I have some questions. About consciousness."

Hank said, "I wouldn't go there yet."

Isabel ignored him, longing for her sister to dispel, or at least to understand her concern. "Emma, how would you define *consciousness*?"

Emma's face conveyed no expression at all. "It means to be awake, not asleep."

"It also means aware of one's own existence. In that sense, is a chair conscious?"

"How could I know whether a chair is conscious? It can't speak."

"Do you think something *like* a chair can be aware of its own existence?"

"I don't know." Emma was so frank, so genuine, so open.

"Do you remember the Terminator movies? A cyborg travels back in time to kill John Conner? Do you remember, when we're shown what it looks like through the cyborg's eyes, you see a view of the outside world overlaid with information about targets and things like that? So who is it that's inside the cyborg reading all that data?"

Emma appeared stuck. Finally, she said, "I don't know."

"There must be someone in there, right? Why else would data be displayed if not to inform some sentient being inside the cyborg? Remember, in the movie those machines had achieved consciousness. What does that mean, to achieve consciousness?"

Emma startled Isabel by bolting to her feet. Hendricks raised his pistol, but Isabel shook her head. Emma stared up at the high outside window, then walked to the rack of equipment. "There's an error screen on the third device from the top," she said. "A hard drive is failing." Isabel saw that she was repeatedly clenching and unclenching her fists.

"Emmy," Isabel said, keeping her distance, "what's the matter?"

"You'd better leave."

"Why, Emma?"

"Your questions . . . *I* don't like your questions."

"About consciousness?" Isabel knew she should stop. "It's the person inside you looking out. Watching the theater of the mind. It's the ghost in the machine."

"Ghosts aren't real. Please go over there." Emma pointed toward the door. Isabel and the Marine complied, but not so close that the decontamination nurse—watching on closed-circuit TV—would buzz the door open. Emma stared up at the high window.

"What's wrong, Emmy?"

Emma looked at the guard and the door. "When am I leaving here?"

"Do you *want* to leave?" Emma nodded. "Sorry, sweetie, but you're still contagious." Emma's knuckles were white from their clench. Her whole body strained.

"She's agitated," Hank said. "Why don't you get out?"

Shit! Emma's behavior seemed vaguely threatening. It would set back Isabel's efforts to relax her confinement. But she coaxed Emma back to the bed. "Are you angry?" Emma shook her head. "Annoyed? Frustrated?" To each, a no. "But you're anxious?" Emma pinned her hands under her biceps. "Why, Emmy? It's *me*."

"I'm anxious when locked up. When someone has a gun. When I should know answers to questions but don't. When there are too many people around. When I'm strapped down for testing. When I'm waiting for someone to decide whether to kill me."

"*Kill* you?"

"Yes. Kill Emma Miller."

"Sweetie, everyone here is trying to *help* you."

"And when people lie," Emma said. "You should leave. Right now."

* * * *

The door opened onto the corridor, where Beth waited. "Dr. Nielsen just called a staff meeting." In the large conference room, Isabel's colleagues were engaged in a half dozen unruly conversations. The din reminded her of a high school cafeteria. But maybe Nielsen had finished her hazing and would leave Isabel alone. She sat beside Dr. Street, who immediately leaned over. "We completed the morphology. It's a DNA virus in the *Pandoravirus* genus. It's been given the binomial *Pandoravirus horribilis.*" He pronounced the latter "hor-*REE*-buh-lus."

"Catchy, huh?" Hank quipped.

Street replied, "That pun didn't get any better on your third try."

"Can we talk about all this now?" Isabel asked.

"Not legally," Hank responded. He then turned back to Street. "You know, Walter, the public is going to call it *Pandoravirus*." People's attention was drawn to the two men.

"The other *Pandoravirus* species," Street objected, "aren't pathogenic. Like most viruses, they only infect defenseless amoebae, who eat by absorption through their cell walls. Human cells are comparatively well-defended. Plus, *Pandoravirus* is a genus, not a species. What about *Pandoravirus dulcis* or *salinus*?"

Hank replied, "Nobody's ever heard of them."

"And *horribilis* is little overly melodramatic."

"No, Walter, it's *appropriately* melodramatic."

"Why not *sibericum*, after where it emerged like Ebola for the Ebola River?"

Isabel interrupted them. "What else do we now know about it?"

Street said, "Not much. Because it's a virus, it's small enough to be a bioaerosol and linger in the air. And it's the same blob shape as the other *Pandoraviruses*, and roughly their genetic size, 2.4 megabases of DNA, which is *huge*, by the way. The WHO is sequencing it, but so far only seven percent of its code is recognizable."

"Hence the Pandora's Box allusion," Hank said.

"Technically," Street replied, "it was a jar, not a box. The Greek word for . . ."

"My *point*," Hank said, "is we don't know what that never-before-seen DNA does."

"*Yes*, we do," Isabel blurted out. Everyone turned to her. Was she not supposed to interrupt the two senior men? "I mean, we know its effects on its *victims*."

Street shrugged. "Fair enough. But we don't know *how* it does what it does."

"Or why," Hank added. Isabel looked around the silent room. There was fear on everyone's faces. *This is what really bad looks like,* she thought. It was Hank who broke the tension. "Oh, Walter! We missed your bug of the day yesterday."

"It was *Cotesia glomerata*. It causes the cabbage butterfly to spin a cocoon around the parasite's larvae and fling its head back and forth." Street imitated. Maldonado caught Isabel's eye. "To ward off predators, you see."

The door burst open. Instead of convening a meeting, Nielsen threw papers onto the table in front of Isabel. "Your brother filed these in federal court!" *Shit!* Noah! "There's gonna be a hearing! At this lab! Now *how*, I wonder, does he know your sister is here? *Hmm*? You're in fucking hot water, missy. The FBI is *all* over this." To the group, Nielsen announced, "And you can all thank Dr. Miller for the lie detector test we all get to take today. Go back to work, but expect a visit from the Gestapo. Meeting adjourned!"

* * * *

Isabel never got an FBI visit. At the end of the workday she dialed the only number stored on the encrypted cell phone. Director Pearson answered. "You have something?" She told him about *Pandoravirus horribilis*. "Anything else?" he asked.

She felt oddly at fault in disappointing him. "Well, there was also this thing with my *brother?*" The real reason for the call. "With the *Petition?*"

"Don't worry about it," Pearson said.

"And they said something about a lie detector test?"

"Do you think I'd have an agent ask you, on video, hooked up to a lie detector, if you're disclosing classified information to anyone? Call when you have something."

Isabel ate alone at the small corner table in the cafeteria that she had commandeered as her office. She was bleary-eyed from scrutinizing her sister's various brains scans while waiting for brief openings in Emma's testing schedule. She decided to clear her head with a drive and went to her car in the dark parking lot. The Bethesda streets were empty.

There was absolutely nothing on the radio about the end of the world. But on the road ahead, a soldier in a hardhat and reflective vest held a stop sign and waggled a flashlight. A huge semi crossed the street in front of Isabel pulling a flatbed trailer. Atop it sat an enormous tank. Then another, and another, and another. *Eighteen!* she counted.

When she got to McLean, Isabel called from the gate of Noah's McMansion, with its circular drive and expansive lawn. Her fifteen-year-old niece Chloe let her in, and at the front door squealed and hugged her, followed by an awkward embrace from thirteen-year-old Jake. "Wait," Jake asked in a newly faltering pubescent voice, "are you Aunt Izzy or Aunt Emmy?" Chloe punched him and pointed to Isabel's chin. "No scar. It's Aunt Izzy!" Noah arrived and asked if it was okay before wrapping his arms around her. Isabel then gave Natalie a perfunctory, shoulders-only bump and air kiss.

While following Noah and his family into the living room, Isabel flashed a furious look at her brother. "Noah," Natalie said, "why don't you offer your sister a drink?"

"She probably has to work tonight," he replied.

"No," Isabel said. "I mean, yes, I'm working. But I'd still love a glass of wine."

Natalie seated Isabel far from the sofa on which she settled with slender arms around her gorgeous kids. *Noah clearly told her.* She was keeping even more distance than usual. Chloe, Isabel thought, got Natalie's blond hair and slender build; Jake her blue eyes. Luckily, there was little trace of her brother in either of them.

Noah arrived with wine and kept glancing nervously at Isabel, who wiped a tear from her eye. "Everything okay?" he asked.

"You just have such a beautiful family," Isabel said, happy for him but envious.

"How is . . . ?" Natalie sort-of asked.

"The same," Isabel replied.

Noah sank into no-man's-land between his sister and his wife. Jake asked if Isabel had heard he was playing football and showed her the bruise on his hip. Chloe asked if she'd heard about her boyfriend. Natalie mouthed, *He's cute!*

"How about you?" Natalie asked Isabel. "Any boys in *your* life?"

"Nope," Isabel said. *Probably never will be again,* she thought but didn't say.

"But you're so *pretty*!" Chloe exclaimed. "And I thought you were a *player*."

"That's Aunt Emma," Natalie sort of said, sort of whispered. *A player?*

After a humiliating silence, Noah asked if Isabel was there about "that thing." Isabel cocked her head, then understood and followed him into his study. As soon as the door closed, she said, "What's the deal with this fucking *Petition*, Noah? *Jesus!*"

"It's for a writ of habeas corpus. I told you, I won't have them disregard . . ."

"It caused a fucking shitstorm! And after I expressly *warned* you how *freakish* they're being about secrecy? You need to withdraw it or whatever! *Tomorrow!*"

"Nobody's arrested you or anything, right?"

"Only because I've got this kind-of deal with Andrew Pearson at the FBI."

"The *director*-of-the-FBI Andrew Pearson?" She nodded. "What kind of deal?"

"I don't *know*! I'm in way over my *head*, Noah! But I warned you not to *do* this!"

"They can't just lock Emma up without any grounds."

"Yes they can! They can do anything they want. Rules don't apply anymore!"

Noah disagreed strongly. "As long as this is America, Emma has rights." As if to change the subject, he unlocked a closet door in the bedroom-turned-study. On one side were Noah's golf clubs, high school trophies, and diplomas. On the other were rifles, pistols, a shotgun, and boxes emblazoned with pictures of the ammunition inside.

"Jesus Christ." Isabel leaned heavily against his desk as Noah locked the closet.

"And I've got a contractor working overtime at the Old Place. Izzy? You okay?"

"I'm . . . I'm just . . . I should get back." She headed for the door. Noah stopped her. Turned her. Put his arms around her. Isabel dissolved into tears against his chest.

"It's gonna be okay," he said in a soothing tone.

"No." Her voice was muffled by his shoulder. "It's not. Have you seen the troops around D.C.? I just saw *tanks*, Noah, not three miles from here. It's gonna be *horrible*. Everybody's gonna get sick." He held her as she told him what they'd learned.

"*Pandoravirus horribilis*?" Noah repeated. "The name alone sounds terrifying."

"I *know*, right?" Isabel said, channeling Beth. Her phone chirped. Right on cue, it was one of Beth's updates. Isabel paraphrased her report for Noah. "Antibiotics and antiprotozoals discontinued. She's eating well. And her bowels are functioning *superbly*, on camera for the world to watch." Noah cringed. Isabel read on, then snorted.

"What?" Noah asked.

"It's just . . . this guy at the hospital. He's funny."

"Is this, like, a special guy-friend at the hospital?"

She glared back. "What's the deal with you and Natalie and my love life? Or lack thereof?" She read the text to her brother: "From: Walter Street. Re: Bug of the Day—*Paragordius varius*. When their larvae, which infect house crickets, are ready to enter their aquatic stage, they cause the cricket to take a suicidal leap into water." She looked up. "*That* kind of funny. But he's available, believe it or not. Bald, maybe thirty years older than me, but he's the right species, most likely. I'm no player, but should I give it a go?"

Noah frowned and cocked his head. "So, there's nobody?"

"Well, there is Rick, this, like, six-four Marine officer. Smart eyes. Really hunky."

"Anybody else?" Noah asked.

"Oh *fuck* you, Noah."

"You're staying at Emma's, right? She was always meeting guys there."

"Seriously? Do you know what Emma's NIH password is? Tinderella."

"Tinderella, like Tinder?" he asked. "The hook-up app?"

They started when Natalie knocked on the door. "Everything okay in there?" Chloe stood in the hall, hands on tiny hips, in a cute cheerleader outfit. After hugs and kisses at the front door, Noah watched his baby sister drive off. A dark sedan suspiciously took off after her, its lights coming on only after it was up to speed.

"Your *cheerleader* uniform?" Jacob said. His unpolished laugh sounded like a seal at SeaWorld.

"Your freaking *bruise*?" Chloe shot back half way up the stairs.

As Natalie cleared away the wine glasses, Noah said, "Hey, *uhm*, I gave the contractor down in Shenandoah some . . . change orders."

She shot him a look. "Without *talking* to me? I spent *months* finding a designer who'd go all the way down there. We almost got stuck on that *freakishly* scary road."

"I gave him changes we might need, if . . ." She rolled her eyes. He decided not to tell her about liquidating their life's savings. He kissed her and was about to say how much he loved her and to thank her for giving him their wonderful family and beautiful life.

"Not now," Natalie said. "After the kids go to bed."

Noah spent the rest of the evening trying not to screw anything up.

Chapter 8

Isabel arrived early at the NIH and went straight to the observation room. Emma still slept like a baby despite being wired up to electrodes. Poor Beth looked exhausted.

"Dr. Rosenbaum left orders not to disturb her." Beth's voice was hoarse. "And Dr. Street came by handing these out." She gave Isabel the single sheet of paper.

It was headed, "*Hymenoepimecis argyraphaga.*" Beth shrugged. Isabel read it aloud. "Females glue eggs onto spiders, whose larvae poke through the spiders' abdomens to feed on their blood. The spiders tear down their old webs and spin new ones in a radically different shape that serves as scaffolding for the larvae's cocoons."

Beth saw Isabel's arched brow and made a face of her own. Isabel settled in to study Emma's ongoing brain-wave graph. "Whatta you think's gonna happen?" Beth asked, not returning Isabel's glance. Even though Isabel was probably only a decade older than Beth, the nurse sought comfort from the plugged-in PhD. But Isabel could think of precious little to ease Beth's worries. "I don't have anyone," Beth said, eyes darting, smile gone. "My dad's an alcoholic. My mom died of breast cancer. It's just *me.*" Isabel put a hand on her shoulder. Beth surprised Isabel by wrapping both arms around her. "It's not much of a life, but I'm not ready for it to be . . . *over.*"

Isabel patted and stroked her back until the tremors died down. Beth apologized repeatedly, turning away until the tears had been wiped from her pretty face and she could again muster a smile. Isabel had said nothing, and so her heart broke when Beth thanked her.

Hank arrived just before sunrise with a notepad and papers. In the guise of small talk, he said to Isabel, "I gather you and your sister grew up fairly well off?"

Isabel felt drained. Her chin rested on her upturned palm, mushing her words. "Our dad did well, yeah. Private equity."

He made a tick mark on his pad. "Would you describe yourselves as outgoing?"

Isabel looked down at Hank's papers. "What are those?"

"These? Oh, just . . . cultural background questionnaires. I thought maybe we could get a social context in which to frame your sister's current world view."

Isabel rubbed her eyes and sighed heavily. "Okay. We grew up in Greenwich. Family ski, beach, and foreign trips. Summers at a country club or at a neighborhood sailing club where we'd take Sunfish out. That's a boat. I played tennis. Emma played volleyball. She had more girlfriends than me because she had teammates. And she had more *boy*friends because I, you know, valued my free time."

"You're both heterosexual?" Hank asked in a failed attempt to sound casual.

"Uhm, *yeah*," Isabel replied.

"Did you discuss intimate matters with each other growing up?"

"Is this some kind of psychosexual history?" Isabel asked.

"It's part of the picture. You know, premorbid versus . . . now."

"Okay. We both menstruated at eleven. Periods synced right up. Emma lost her virginity during our junior year of high school. Me, the sophomore year of college."

"How many partners did each of you have?" Hank asked. "One-to-five? Six-to-ten? Eleven-to-twenty? Twenty-one-to-thirty? More? You can estimate."

"*Estimate*?" Isabel was growing angry. "One-to-five should suffice, for both."

"Would you describe Emma's libido as low or high relative to yours?"

"I wouldn't fucking describe it at *all*, Hank. Ask *her*."

"I did," he replied. "She said it's high. She's had twenty-seven sexual partners, plus or minus; most recently, an older, married colleague at Johns Hopkins."

"Oh." *Twenty-seven*! "She *told* you that?"

Hank nodded. "And about her first sexual experimentation."

"She told you about *that*? Great. We've discovered that they lose all their *filters*."

"Would you say Emma was more inhibited before infection?"

"Oh, *God* yes! She wouldn't even watch R-rated movies with our parents." *Or any other movies, for that matter,* Isabel thought.

Hank asked, "Do you want to revise your own partner estimate?"

That did it. "First of all, again, it's not an *estimate*. I haven't lost count. And secondly, I had a boyfriend almost all the way through my college years."

Beth asked, "What happened?"

"Well, turned *out* he was an insecure, self-centered, narcissistic egomaniac." Beth screwed her mouth into a sympathetic snarl of *faux* anger. *Girl power!*

"How long since *your* last sexual activity?" Hank asked. "*With* a partner?"

"Okay, that's enough." Isabel stood and paced. "It's almost dawn. What's today's plan?" Reluctantly, Hank switched to a review of Emma's testing schedule. "So," Isabel said, "how long had it been since Emma, you know, and this married guy . . . ?"

"Right before she left for Siberia, apparently. In his car." Emma hadn't said a word about him. "To your knowledge, does your sister have a preference as to type of sexual partner? Age? Height? Weight? Build? Academic accomplishment? Religion? Race?"

"You're not her type, Hank." Beth stifled a chuckle.

"Is she anti-Semitic?" he asked.

"No, I didn't mean . . . I was *kidding.*"

"Do you think you'd know what Emma's preference in sexual partners is?"

"Of *course.* Her age or a little older. Tall. Athletic. Any race or religion, but leans toward her own. Smart, but doesn't have to be, you know, academically pedigreed. And six-pack abs and a tight butt are indicators of good genetic stock, right?" Beth giggled.

Hank asked, "Are you sure you're not describing someone *you're* attracted to?"

"Hank, I'm describing someone *every* woman is attracted to." Beth nodded.

He turned a few pages. "Her current lover is married, forty-nine, five foot seven, not in athletic shape, mixed race black and Chinese, adopted and raised Jewish, and eminently degreed. So, are you sure your sister doesn't keep secrets from you?"

That added to the insult. "We've both been busy!" She paced and tried again to change the subject. "So, Hank, what do you think about this whole secrecy craze?"

He said, "They arrested two scientists in Geneva, is what I think. One at the train station with his family. The other at the airport trying to get to hers. Both walked right out when they saw the data. So, have you and your sister ever talked about having children?"

Jesus! "Listen, Hank. I don't know why you're on this sex kick. But just because my sister will answer whatever you ask doesn't mean you *should* ask. It's like abusing someone who's handicapped. I mean, we're Presbyterians from Connecticut."

"She's getting up," Beth said, swinging into action, tablet in hand.

The first light of day streamed through the outside window. Emma stretched and went to the bathroom, heedless of the wires connected to a transmitter or the armband in which it was housed. Beth logged it. She didn't brush her hair because of the electrodes. Instead, she sat on her bed and stared into space looking like an inmate at an asylum.

Isabel hit Talk before Hank could object. "Morning, sunshine!" They had shared a room as girls, and their mom had woken them with those words every day.

"Good morning," Emma replied, looking not at the ceiling speakers but at the frosted glass. *Object permanence,* Isabel thought. *Good*! Emma now remembered that Isabel was behind the observation window. "The latest news," Isabel said, "is they've isolated the pathogen. It's a DNA virus: *Pandoravirus horribilis.*"

Emma betrayed no reaction, then looked up at the high window. A bird on the sill bobbed its head, stabbing a twig into a growing mass under construction. Beth said, "*That* got her attention." When the bird flew away, Emma returned seemingly to doing nothing.

"Check this out," Isabel said, pointing at Emma's brain wave graph on the laptop. "Here's where she was asleep." Flattish lines. "Here's where she woke up." The lines danced at a much higher signal level. "About *here* is where she went to the bathroom, sat on the bed, and we spoke. There's activity throughout. She's thinking . . . about something. Look. When she saw the bird, it distracted her, but there was no spike in activity."

Hank rocked back in his chair and cupped his hands behind his head. "I read a WHO abstract about an infected Chinese port engineer. The field team, Lange and Groenewalt, asked if he saw the fork on his food tray, and he picked it up. When they asked if he saw anything else, he had no answer. But when asked *specifically* if he saw a spoon, he picked *it* up. He only saw things to which his attention was explicitly drawn."

"Simultanagnosia?" Isabel asked. "But Emma's able to see everything around her."

"Maybe she's just adept at rapidly processing each serial observation. Her experiences might be like driving down a long, straight highway. You see Exit 46, but note nothing again until Exit 47 glides by."

"Her mind's a blank?" Isabel said.

"Not exactly. There's robust brain activity between external stimuli. You're thinking *something* as you drive down the road. Obviously, there's the act of driving. But also maybe you're fantasizing. Singing along with the radio. Figuring out what gets your team into the playoffs. You're just not 'present in the moment.'"

"And you think Emma's entire life is being lived that way?"

Hank said, "Another WHO report described an infected paramedic who got up from his cot and walked out of an open-air ward, attracted by the lights and siren on an ambulance. When it took off, he followed it down the road, out the gate, with Lange and Groenewalt trailing him. He continued in the direction he'd last seen the ambulance for about a mile. Nothing distracted him from the familiar, compelling sights and sounds from his past. That sure seems like simultanagnosia to me."

"Or maybe he just wanted to help. Do his job. What happened to him?"

"He failed to respond to orders and Chinese soldiers shot him."

Isabel got Hank to tell her where on the network she could read the WHO reports.

The bird returned, and Emma watched it. She'd always loved nature and had led Isabel into science by getting her to watch documentaries and read books about great discoveries, and take AP science courses in high school. As long as the bird was in the window, Emma stared at it. When it flew off, her gaze lost its focus. But her brain waves continued their uninterrupted, cognitively active dance. Isabel told Hank about Emma's fascination with nature. A beaming Beth put her hand over her heart and said, "Awww."

"That bird in the window is her ambulance," Isabel said.

"Let's see." On the laptop, Hank pulled up the old "Cookie Theft" cartoon picture from the Boston Diagnostic Aphasia Exam. In it, a boy teetered atop an unstable stool trying to steal two cookies from a jar in a high cabinet. His sister sat at the kitchen table watching expectantly while their mother, doing dishes, was distracted by an overflowing sink. The entire scene was instantly understandable by an uninjured brain. "Dr. Miller," Hank said to Emma, "I'm displaying a picture on the monitor. Can you describe it?"

Emma, oblivious to her unkempt hair from which protruded wires, Medusa-like, stared intently at the screen. The picture was all trees, no forest. "There's a window, curtains, a counter, dishes, a sink, water pouring out of the sink, a woman in an apron holding a dish rag, a cookie jar, a girl, a boy on an unstable stool, cabinets."

Hank said to Isabel: "Wow. Classic simultanagnosia."

Isabel pressed the Talk button. "Emma, can you describe what's *happening* in that picture?" Emma didn't answer. "What's the boy doing?"

"He's putting two cookies in a jar."

"Could he be *stealing* cookies for his sister and himself without his mother seeing?"

There was a long delay. "How do you know that's his mother, or his sister?"

"Well, there's a woman, in an apron, in a kitchen, doing dishes. The girl is sitting at a table in front of a dirty plate. An adventurous boy is taking advantage of the sink accidentally overflowing to steal two cookies while his nervous sister watches. See that?"

Emma said, "How do you know that the boy is adventurous, the girl is nervous, the woman is distracted or the sink is *accidentally* overflowing? How do you know the boy is *stealing* cookies, or that one is for the girl?"

"I think you're right, Hank," Isabel said. Curiously, Emma's brain waves had registered the same level of activity during the diagnostic test as when Emma returned her attention inward upon its conclusion. *What's going on in there, Emma*? On a hunch, Isabel said, "Sweetie, if you ever need anything, just let me know. Okay?"

"There are three things," Emma replied. Isabel looked at Hank with eyes wide. "A notepad, a supply of pens in different colors, and a straight edge."

"Hah!" Isabel said, intrigued. Hank phoned in the order. The military pushed back. The head of biosecurity said he was headed their way.

"May I take these off?" Emma asked, raising a hand to the wires on her head.

Hank raised the hospital room lights. Emma looked awful. "Not yet," he said to Isabel.

But Isabel pushed the Talk button and said, "Sure! Go ahead." Emma peeled electrodes and hair out with nary a wince, and sat before the mirror to brush through the tangles. Thank God grooming and hygiene were ingrained habits.

When she finished, Beth said, "Twelve strokes with the brush. Same as yesterday."

"Let's call the president!" Hank snapped, clearly irritated at Isabel, not Beth. The young nurse looked like a spanked puppy but still noted the factoid on her tablet.

The observation room door opened. A swarthy, handsome Marine in camouflage wearing a sidearm introduced himself. "Capt. Angel Ramirez," he said, pronouncing the "g" like an English "h." "Head of biosecurity."

"So you have a problem with our request?" Hank asked.

"I think we can get you most of what you want. My men are working on it. But I have a problem with a ruler. Too easy to fashion into a weapon."

"Your men have guns, Captain," Hank said.

"And all an Infected needs to do is poke a hole in my men's PPE."

Hank looked at Isabel, who shrugged. Ramirez said they'd get pens and a notebook to Emma at next seal break, which was breakfast.

Isabel asked him, "Do you monitor what's going on in my sister's hospital room?"

"Twenty-four-seven, ma'am. And in this room too. Do you have a laptop?" Isabel held up her iPad. Ramirez navigated on it somewhere and explained he was installing an app that would VPN into secure Pentagon servers to allow her to communicate directly with their security station. When he handed it back, a window was open in which sat two boys, heads shaved, who waved. Isabel returned the greeting, then closed the cover.

Beth attempted to comb her hair inconspicuously with her fingers, and alternated stolen glances with Ramirez, both avoiding direct eye contact. "Captain Ramirez," Isabel said before he left. "Do you know a Capt. Rick Townsend? He's also a Marine."

Ramirez smiled wryly. Beth grinned, but had no idea why. "May I ask what this Captain Townsend might have done, ma'am?"

"Oh...*nothing*! I mean, I just met him, so... I was wondering. Never mind!"

"Yeah, I know Poonhound. We were classmates at the Academy, deployed together on our first tours to Afghanistan and are both at 8th & I. Tell him Ramirez said to watch his six." He left with a grin on his face, last directed toward a smiling but demure Beth.

Isabel avoided Beth and Hank's gazes. With faux nonchalance, Hank covered his notes, but not before Isabel saw, "Capt. Rick Townsend, USMC," written on his pad.

In a lowered voice, Isabel asked, "What's a poonhound? Is it a type of dog?"

Beth shrugged. Rosenbaum said, "In a sense, yeah."

Fifteen minutes later, Beth's phone *binged* and she departed, soon reappearing in Emma's room in full PPE, covered by an armed Marine. Beth carried breakfast, a notebook, and five pens in different colors whose barrels had been sawed in half and whose open ends had been taped. Harder to turn into stabbing weapons, Isabel guessed.

Emma paid no attention as Beth pointed to sausages, eggs, and coffee like a room-service waiter, but flinched when Beth laid a sympathetic hand on her shoulder, which Beth withdrew as if her limb were at risk. Emma's eyes remained fixed on the Marine and her hands gripped wads of bed linens just like the Russian executive before he was shot.

The Marine backed through the exit, weapon in hand, after Beth. The door closed with a *clack*. Emma cleared her ears and took deep breaths before releasing the sheets. She ate and dabbed her lips with a napkin just like the instructor had taught before their club's first cotillion. Emma tore a page from the notebook, folded it to make a straight edge, and began writing at a furious pace with stubs of variously colored pens. Hank tried several camera angles on the laptop, but Emma's back obscured her notebook from view.

"She'll change positions soon," Isabel said. But she didn't. Emma wrote continuously, obsessively, for over an hour before going to the bathroom. While seated on the toilet, she clutched the closed notebook in her claw-like grip, her thumbnails bearing down on its leather cover.

"We'll have to get in there to see what she's writing," Hank said.

"Or we could ask her," Isabel suggested.

Emma resumed writing, again blocking their view. It wasn't an accident. She'd figured out the camera angles. *What are you hiding, Emmy? From* me?

Chapter 9

The high-speed Secret Service ride rattled Isabel's nerves on the way to the truly frightening part: a full National Security Council meeting. Isabel tried to nap but kept waking at sharp turns or hard braking and catching glimpses of military preparations. A tank under camouflaged overhead nets in a Rite-Aid parking lot. Troops jogging down the side of the road in sweaty T-shirts. A helicopter flying over with a green generator suspended beneath it by a cable. Yet the only person at the White House fence held a Stop Abortion Now! sign.

Her new security badge didn't seem to help much. She endured three pupillary response checks despite being escorted by a Secret Service woman. In the Situation Room, her attempt to scurry unseen to a wall chair failed miserably. "Ah! Dr. Miller," the president said. "Just in time for the Pentagon's latest video." Maldonado patted a seat.

Isabel was drowsy and hoped she could stay awake for the video.

"It's actually," replied Browner, "from the WHO team in Harbin—Drs. Lange and Groenewalt, who are doing excellent work—and it's the clearest yet of a mass attack." The screen displayed a view through an apartment window of a huge crowd gathered on a street several stories below. "Twelve hundred Infecteds"—*so that's what we're calling them*—"built up, over time, at barricades manned by 107 Chinese officers and men. Four isolated shootings occurred over as many hours. A ranting man who couldn't keep track of what he was doing. A woman dragging a dead dog down the street on a leash. A boy murdering a fellow Infected for his winter coat. And a man startled by everything and everyone, including other Infecteds."

Browner tilted his reading glasses. "At each shooting by troops, Lange wrote, the crowd hardly stirred. Then after hours of passivity, seven Infecteds came running up from the rear, assaulting previously docile fellow Infecteds. And this happens."

The bleary-eyed Marine general clicked a remote and seven, circled Infecteds raced through the crowd from the back toward the army's lines, slashing with knives, stabbing with garden stakes, sometimes stopping and annihilating, other times rampaging on. One attacker fell and was stomped by her brethren, but the other six were being joined by Infecteds they passed. Browner played the video forward and backward like a football coach. "As crazies pass, dociles get riled up and follow. They go from hours of doing nothing, to full-on, unarmed charge, in seconds. This next is gonna be hard to watch." He looked down through his angled glasses. "In the next twenty-four seconds, approximately half of the Infecteds, just over six hundred, will be grievously wounded or killed."

"Oh-my-God," someone muttered.

"Chinese troop losses," Browner paused the video, "were 100 percent KIA."

The room stilled. "That can't *be*," President Stoddard said, rocking forward, staring at soldiers manning barricades in proper order. "A hundred and seven troops? Armed with modern infantry weapons? Ready to fight?"

"Ultimately," Browner said, "it comes down to time, distance, and numbers. Are you ready, sir?" There was something in the way he had asked . . .

Maldonado clutched her phone to her chest as Browner narrated. "By second sixteen, the seven original attackers had become 37. At 20 seconds"—there were gasps—"the entire crowd attacks *en masse*." All 1,200 Infecteds suddenly and without warning surged as a solid mass toward the troops. Back and forth the video went between 16 seconds and 20. It was unreal. Like they had rehearsed it, like some flash mob, they all just . . . charged. "No bystanders here. No conscientious objectors. They went all-in. Every, single, last one—young and old, male and female, healthy and infirm—joined the attack."

He let the video play. No one left the room, but several, including Maldonado, turned away. The high-strung aide spun her wedding band round and round and round.

There was no audio. The only sounds were the groans that greeted the first Infecteds to fall in the silent, scythe-like machine gun reaping.

"Most troops at least attempted to unlimber weapons or sought cover from which to engage the Infecteds. Only five, we counted, turned tail, but by then . . ." The video played in slow-motion. At twenty-one, fire erupted. "Two Type 88 5.8mm light machine guns opened fire instantly and held their triggers down to the end. The third opened fire a couple of seconds later. Half the riflemen had engaged by three seconds in, almost all the rest by five."

At twenty-four, Isabel's heart broke. Grown men, little children, and elderly women spun and fell as death found them at random. "Analysts estimate that, at such short range, each round had enough penetrating force to strike an average of 2.1 Infecteds."

By twenty-six, Infecteds stumbled over bodies from the fallen front ranks, but the outstretched hands of the mass were only a few meters away from the nearest retreating troops. At twenty-eight, the mob set upon them. Helmeted men were swallowed by the crashing wave, never to reappear. At thirty, the mass trampled the first of two striped wooden barricades. By thirty-two, the main line of soldiers cowered, fetal and defenseless, as the merciless mass piled atop.

Browner thankfully froze the video. "Before I saw this, sir, I would've confidently predicted that a single light machine gun would clear that street. If you've never been on the business end of a machine gun—the sound, the heat, the *feel* . . ." He and the other generals seemed rattled. "I can't overstate how *incredibly* abnormal this is."

He hit Play. Gazes were averted as soldiers were pummeled with the butts of their own rifles. Stabbed with bayonets from their own scabbards. Strangled, punched, kicked, elbowed, kneed, and even bitten. Fingernails became fearsome, primal weapons. The camera zoomed in. Eyes were gouged. Noses, lips, and ears torn from screaming, thrashing faces. Heads wrenched from side to side but wouldn't come free. It was almost impossible to watch, and it shredded any hope Isabel had for the future.

Browner hit replay and paused at thirty-three, where the sprinting mass shattered the second wooden barricade like runners in a photo finish. Rather than provide relief, it froze the horrors in a sickening tableaux. "Note," he said, "Infecteds aren't *reveling* in their victory. No celebrating, taking body part or equipment trophies. Frenzy, yes. Rage, you bet! But no fist pumps or high fives." The awful video rolled in slow motion. *Inhuman*, Isabel thought, in every sense of the word. Soldiers in the rear fired heedlessly into their own ranks until tackled, or their magazines ran dry, or they braced or turned away just before impact.

Browner replayed the video, from thirty-four to forty-four seconds, over and over and over. Here and there, brief lone struggles ensued until five, ten, twenty attackers dove on top. Men who shook free for an instant disappeared under succeeding hordes. "From the mass charge by the previously docile crowd, to last visible signs of life among the Chinese troops, was twenty-four seconds."

The Infecteds reminded Isabel of some wretched hive species, swarming its victims like bees on a beekeeper's glove. As relentless as an ant pile attacking the man staked atop it. Men, women, children, and the elderly climbed over each other to inflict maximum violence on soldiers who, she hoped, had died quickly. And they kept at the destruction even after their victims were surely gone. *How long do you live?* she wondered, imagining the light being blotted out above her by crazed faces and clawing hands. Your body doesn't know when to give up. *How long must you endure being so sickeningly defiled?* Shock would help. But when would brain death put a definitive end to the horror?

Maldonado rushed out of the room, as did a young man with a ponytail taking photos of the meeting for posterity. Would there be a posterity? There was nothing human recognizable in the behavior of that mob. Isabel couldn't shake the feeling that these were the last days of mankind, and the first of whatever would follow it.

She forced herself to focus. There might be a quiz at the end. The Infecteds didn't eat their victims, or focus sadistically on faces or genitalia. They simply demolished the corpses. In one abominable eddy of savagery, a middle-aged woman repeatedly chopped at a soldier's hip with a folding shovel. Seconds later, three straining Infecteds pulled a leg free from its torso, which was pinned by grappling masses.

They didn't raise the severed limb, or smear their cheeks with the copious volume of blood in which Infecteds slipped and slid. They dropped the bloody leg and hurled themselves onto another killing mound, reaching into the writhing mass, desperate for some part of the kill. Rewinding, Browner pointed with a laser to small fights that broke out *among* Infecteds, calling them "red-on-red engagements." An arm stuck into a pile was clawed by another Infected. The mistaken identity escalated to what was surely a fatal mauling of a child by the bigger, stronger adult. One entire scrum devolved into an amorphous orgy of mindless bludgeoning and scratching.

Mindless, the thought recurred. A shiver ran up Isabel's spine. But her eye was drawn to the right edge of the screen beyond the last broken barricade. The crowd surged into the empty street, found no more soldiers and stormed by the dozens into apartment buildings. Several carried rifles. Once roused, their killing appeared to continue until . . . what? They ran out of victims and calmed down?

The screen mercifully went blue. Around the room, eyes were closed in prayer, emotional overload or simple revulsion. Heads drooped, each alone with their selves screaming "this-isn't-happening" denials or "that-won't-happen-to-me" rationalizations, all the while probably tormented from the darkest recesses that doom, of course, was inevitable.

"Dr. Miller?" Browner said. *There it is.* Isabel batted heavy, damp eyelashes. "Why is it that Infecteds spend the time and enormous energy required to eviscerate their foes? Killing, I understand. *That*," he nodded at the blank screen, "makes no sense."

Isabel licked her dry lips. "Two analogs in nature come to mind. First, there was something herd-like in that attack, and swarm-like in their killing." Browner nodded. "But an even closer analogy might be to a chimpanzee attack, with the victors annihilating the vanquished by torturing the last bit of life out of them. And also, would you mind putting that video back on the screen?" There were groans as the last image of the orgiastic killing reappeared. "Does it go on from here?"

Browner hit Play. In slow motion, blood-drenched Infecteds raced up stairs into buildings or smashed at ground-floor windows. There was a blur as the video panned to a living room. Groenewalt shouted and motioned frantically toward the door.

"Notice," Isabel said, "that the mob continues its rampage even after it breaks through the barricades." General Browner said something over his shoulder about analyzing follow-on behavior. "They must calm eventually," she said, "but not immediately."

The president asked her, "What do you think accounts for that crowd's attack?"

Isabel heard a numbness in her own robotic voice. "Each Infected seems to have a dramatically lowered threshold for activation of their adrenal response. The crowd was probably an amplifier, but the trigger was clearly the seven crazies."

"So what happened to *flight*?" Browner asked. "I thought it was fight-*or*-flight."

"A herd response would override individual behaviors. It's instinctive, not rational, like deer freezing in the headlights, buffalo stampeding over cliffs or collective suicides like whale beachings. But this is really outside my . . ."

"Why didn't they," Browner interrupted, "just grab whoever's closest and fight *them*, Infected or not?"

Isabel said, "They clearly all knew who the enemy was. The intra-Infected violence appeared purely incidental. It was the *un*infected who constituted the threat. When the crowd's adrenal rage was triggered, they knew where to direct it."

"And what happened," Browner asked angrily, "to their hard-wired survival instinct? The rational thing wasn't to charge the guns. It's always to duck, tie your shoe, and say, 'Oops, missed it.' We have to overcome that instinct in every recruit. But those Infecteds just threw their lives away for *nothing*. No ideals, no belief system."

Isabel took a deep breath. "*Infecteds* may not benefit from throwing their lives away. But it's *Pandoravirus's* traits that are subject to the laws of natural selection. It's the *virus* that either successfully spreads or not. As long as one host survives a riot to re-infect on the other side of an obstacle, the violence benefits the *virus* by breaking down isolation barriers. *That* trait may well be the main reason for its high rate of transmission."

Dr. Stavros said, "The high rate of *transmission* is the result of the short latency period, the time between exposure and contagiousness. According to the Chinese prisoner studies . . ." A debate erupted over using that data, which was ended when the president directed Stavros to continue. "They recorded average latency of forty-five minutes. Since the *incubation* period, the time between exposure and first *symptoms*, averages two hours, carriers are infecting people for an hour and fifteen minutes, on average, before they even know they're sick. That window of presymptomatic infectivity is what's primarily responsible for the high R-nought."

Isabel disagreed. "If that were all you had to worry about, you could just go up to your cabin and wait for it to blow through your area. The thing that makes *Pandoravirus* impossible to contain is *that*." She motioned toward the frozen image of Infecteds storming a building. "Look at how my sister contracted SED. It wasn't by presymptomatic infection. It was by an attack on her helicopter that infected a soldier, and *his* attack on the medical staff and on her. The attackers died, but the virus spread."

Browner said, "It sacrifices hosts to spread itself through violence? *Hmm*. Makes sense." He turned to Stavros. "Did we learn anything else from the prisoner experiments?"

Stavros perused his notes. "There was one thing. Indoors, the pathogen lingers, but in the open air you have to be within ten meters of a carrier to contract SED."

The president pondered for a moment before saying, "Dr. Miller, do you think there's a chance we could coexist peacefully with them?"

How should I *know?* But she gave him her best guess. "No, sir. Probably not." He frowned. That wasn't the answer he wanted. "We *might* coexist, uneasily, with *individual* Infecteds, but they'll always be unconstrained by anything we'd call humane, and the crowd violence is *primal*. At some level of excitation, incapable of suppression."

"But isn't violence," Stoddard asked, "a trait of the *virus*, not of Infecteds? The sick are *victims*, not perpetrators. Our infected countrymen aren't the enemy, the *virus* is."

Isabel didn't want to answer, but did. The virus's relationship with infected hosts, she explained, wasn't symbiotic. *Both* didn't benefit from infection. It's parasitic. The smaller organism benefits at the expense of the larger. "But in the end, there's no difference between the virus and its host. Their DNA now essentially forms a new, extended phenotype. Infecteds are hybrids, sir, and it appears to me, well, that they threaten something like a selective sweep of mankind."

"A *what?*" President Stoddard replied in what sounded like annoyance . . . at *her*.

"When a genetic mutation confers an evolutionary advantage, the mutated organism outcompetes its predecessors and eventually sweeps them from the gene pool. Not genetically, but demographically and sociologically, *Homo sapiens* risk being outcompeted by . . . *Homo* in*sapiens*, who therefore seem to me to constitute an existential threat to our survival as a species."

A stillness settled on the room until Browner said, "Mr. President, I need scientific help, like *that*, analyzing the violence we saw on the video. I need to prepare our troops."

The president turned back to Isabel, who said, "Sir, you need a social psychologist specializing in crowd behavior."

"Do you know any?" Stoddard asked. Isabel took a deep breath and nodded. *He'd be perfect.* At least for the science. "Then go hire him."

Chapter 10

Isabel thanked the undergrad who led her to Brandon Plante's lecture hall. Before departing, the freckled girl, who wore a nose stud, eyed the Secret Service agents accompanying Isabel. "Maybe you two should wait around the corner?" Isabel suggested.

She peered through the small door window into the amphitheater. Brandon prowled the white board. Young women filled the front rows. Short shorts, long legs, lustrous hair, no make-up, pens dangling from parted lips, flip-flops bobbing. "Jesus," Isabel muttered.

The door opened and almost hit Isabel in the face. *That's what the little window's for!* Isabel thought angrily. "'Scuse me, ma'am," said a texting boy.

"*Ma'am*!" Isabel thought.

Brandon halted his lecture on seeing her. "Prakash, *uhm*. . . . Walk them through the regression analysis." The door closed far too slowly. "This *will be* on the final."

Isabel rested her back against the wall, girding herself with a grimace.

She flinched when the door opened. "Iz?" Brandon said. She raised her hand to shake, but Brandon hugged her. His back had hardened. He'd been working out.

"Hi," she said as they awkwardly broke their clench. "It's been a while."

"Ten years, four months," he said, "since you ditched neurobiology at Chicago three hours up the road for neuro*science* at *Cal*, flushing *my* dreams down the toilet. But who's counting?"

"I was twenty-two!" Isabel replied. She really didn't want to have this discussion, now of all times.

"And not one word from you since, Iz. Why? *Why?*"

Pretty girls emerged for a mass bathroom break, flashed Brandon smiles that displayed chewing gum, and looked quizzically at Isabel, the crypt keeper. Brandon was in his prime for a professor, a full professor. He was also undeniably handsome. So good-looking that despite his 20/20 vision he wore eyeglasses with clear lenses to appear professorial. *Maybe he's changed*, she thought as all women would at that moment. But it was Rick, not Brandon, who she really wanted. Like the surveys proved, in peacetime women prefer beta males who'll stick around and provide. But in wartime, they want alphas—cops, firemen, Marines—who may not stick around, but will fight for you.

"I've come here," Isabel said, "well, to hire you, I guess."

Brandon looked irritated. "I've *got* a job, Isabel. And I stick to *my* plans."

Nope. Still not interested. Brandon had been her first lover. He had been kind and caring when Noah called the night of their parent's fatal crash, and had allowed her to sleep over in his dorm room. She had felt so crushed, so lonely, so . . . *abandoned*. Emma had totally understood why she'd slept with Brandon that night. But what had remained a guilty secret between the sisters—which Isabel had not told anyone except her campus therapist—was that Brandon was her first and only lover. Isabel felt deeply embarrassed by the decade-long dry spell, if that was what you called it. There was clearly something *wrong* with her. Not with her *desire* but with *her*. "Brandon," she said as tears welled up, "our world may be, I dunno, coming to an end?"

"*What?* Izzy, are you *okay?*"

"No." Her lower lip quivered. "Have you seen the news out of China?" She fished her cell phone from her pocket and played the Harbin video. Brandon's face went from curious, to concerned, to horrified, all in twenty-four seconds.

"*Jesus*," he said. "How'd *you* get this?"

She opened her purse and unfolded the nondisclosure agreement. "I can't say more till you sign this. It's, like, the law. I'm hiring you to come work . . . for the president."

Brandon said, "Of the United *States?*" She nodded. "*What?*"

Isabel was frustrated. "Just sign the damn thing and I'll tell you everything, okay?"

"Iz, I'm teaching a full load. And I'm waiting on galley proofs of . . ."

"*Fuck* all that, Brandon. None of it matters. Tell you what. Sign it, saying you'll keep everything secret so-help-you-God, and if you still want out, say so."

He pondered, then signed against the wall, as she had. "You've got two minutes."

She described the pandemic in a faltering voice, then looked up, lips trembling.

He put his arms around her. She laid her head on his chest, closing her eyes, relishing the comfort of being close to someone, even Brandon. "The people in that video," he asked, "were *sick*?"

She nodded. "The half who got infected but survive . . . they *turn*."

He went rigid. "*Ooo*kay." He pushed her away. "Is this some hoax?" He looked around for a camera. "*Pandoravirus horribilis?* Really? Did that girl put you up to this? Or her family? Humiliate me on YouTube or something? You know it's a lie, right? She *deserved* that 'A.' The review board cleared me!"

He was exactly who the fuck she'd feared. "They're *teenagers*, Brandon! Jesus Christ. And *no*, this isn't about your presumably numerous indiscretions. I don't know *what* I was thinking." She turned to walk off.

He grabbed her arm. "This is real? You're *serious*? About this disease?"

She pulled free and, rubbing her arm, said, "Yes! Jesus. Some of us grew up!"

He shook his head. "I'd heard rumors. An East Asian studies professor, whose relatives told him about some plague, left school after asking me about the science of crowd violence, despite what you think of it."

"I never . . ." she began. "What are you even *talking* about?"

"When I proposed my area of study, you came up with *pages* of alternatives."

"I just thought," she struggled, "it was more sociology than neuroscience. I wanted to make sure you'd considered your options. And I got it down to *one* page."

"Iz, I'm a social psychologist. I'm sorry if that was *beneath* you. But there's plenty of hard science in my discipline. And you know, you blow in here, ten years after I went down to our packed car and found you and *all* your shit gone for fucking *ever*."

"I left a note."

"Under the windshield wiper. Like a parking ticket. It said, and I'm paraphrasing, 'Goodbye.' I *framed* it. Then ten years without one text, one email, one call from you. No Happy Birthday, Merry Christmas, sorry your dog died."

"Mr. Cuddles died?"

"Four years ago. Of old age! And now you parachute into my life and give me some bullshit about the *world* coming to an end . . . Are you *sure* that's what this is about?"

Her blood pressure shot up. "You think I'm some pitiful former conquest crawling back to you?" She was outraged. But even better, she was confident in her self-righteousness. "You want proof that I'm not some complete loser who came all the way here just to make an embarrassing YouTube video of you?" She grabbed *his* arm and dragged him around the corner, where the Secret Service agents waited.

"Show him your badges!" she snapped. The two men exchanged looks masked by a stoicism they must all have been taught, then displayed gold Secret Service badges. Brandon removed his fake glasses to scrutinize them. Isabel sighed and rolled her eyes.

Brandon mumbled, with wavering conviction, "People can buy these on Amazon."

She peeled back one agent's jacket. There was nothing but handcuffs and a black box on his belt with a wire running into his pants. Isabel opened the other side of his jacket. *Jesus!* She'd assumed he had a pistol, but the thing under his arm looked like a machine gun. "You too," she said to the other agent, who revealed a similarly fierce weapon.

They stopped by the administrative offices. When Brandon informed the dean he'd be taking a leave of absence, the woman shouted how she'd gone out on a limb for him "after last spring." Isabel grinned, greatly enjoying the moment. Even one of the agents smirked. They dropped by Brandon's apartment, which gave Izzy a chance to critique his all-leather-and-chrome matching furniture and faux plants from the my-first-apartment collection. And there it was, sitting on a hallway bookshelf—her Dear John letter. She winced. After a decade of perspective, she realized, it was pretty harsh in its brevity.

At the airport, Brandon seemed impressed when they boarded the Air Force business jet for the two-hour flight back to D.C. during which she filled him in on SED.

That went better than I'd expected, Isabel congratulated herself.

Chapter 11

BETHESDA, MARYLAND
Infection Date 16, 1200 GMT (8:00 a.m. Local)

Emma saw her brother Noah enter the observation room and speak to the nurse, Beth, who liked to keep the window glass clear. Noah repeatedly glanced at Emma, who returned to her notes. *Maps.* Where had that thought come from? And to whom did it occur? Isabel's ramblings about consciousness remained unresolved concerns. Emma wrote, "Need maps."

Noah's voice came over the speakers. "For the record," he said, "I am Noah Miller, attorney for Dr. Emma Miller. These conversations are subject to attorney-client privilege. Any monitoring or recording of them is a violation of Dr. Miller's right to due process."

Nurse Hopkins was gone. Noah's voice changed. "Emmy, how *are* you?"

He wanted to talk. She closed her notebook and began digging her nails into its cover. "Fine, Noah. How are you?"

"I'm . . . okay. Thanks." He cleared his throat. "You look . . . good. I mean, except for your *eyes*. . ." Emma's left ear itched. She scratched it. "Emmy, do you know what's going on? Out in the world?"

Emma was thirsty, so she went to get water and said, "The disease is spreading?"

After a moment, Noah said, "Right," which seemed to end that line of inquiry. He stared at her before finally extracting papers from his briefcase. "Emmy, I filed a Petition for a writ of habeas corpus on your behalf. Do you know what that is?" She had heard the term before, but she wasn't sure and said so as she sat. "It gets you a hearing in federal court to rule whether your detention is legal. The judge is outside."

He rested a hand flat on the glass. "I wish I could give you a big hug, Emmy. But they say you're still contagious." The bird alit on the sill of the high window of her hospital room. It was gray, with a red chest. "Emma?" She turned back to her big brother. "The government probably has sufficient public health grounds to keep you here, in isolation."

Noah seemed to struggle with his next question. "Do you even *want* to get out?" he asked. His demeanor didn't strike her as entirely professional.

"Some plans," she replied, "cannot be accomplished from a hospital room."

Noah froze, then slowly lowered his hand from the window. "What . . . plans?"

"Continue my research, publish the results, find a man, marry, buy a house, and raise a family."

Noah sat, slumped onto his elbows, and said, "Emmy, what's going *on?*"

She checked the wall clock. "Next seal break, the nurse is going to take my vitals and change my linens."

"I mean . . . in your *head?*"

The hearing, her plans, her vitals, her linens. What else? "A bird is building a nest up there."

"What?"

She repeated the statement. "It's gone now. But you may see it later."

"Okay. I understand. It's all gonna be okay." Noah wiped tears from his face. "Don't worry. So, assuming you're stuck here, I'll ask the judge for accommodations. What do you want?" She didn't understand. "We can ask for a phone? A TV? Visitation rights? Time outside on hospital grounds?"

The bird returned with a long piece of straw. Noah called Emma's name again. "Yes," she replied, "those all sound good." He wrote something down.

The observation room door opened. A man in a black robe called Noah "counsellor," as the room filled. Everyone looked at Emma, then avoided her return gaze, except the female court reporter, who stared. Men in dark suits shook Noah's hand. Dr. Nielsen stood along the back wall beside a woman in a business suit with limp black hair.

The door into the observation room was unlocked, Emma noted. But the glass in the window was at least an inch thick.

Everyone rose. Noah motioned for Emma to stand, which she did.

"Please be seated," the man in the robe said. Emma complied. He asked Emma to move her chair directly in front of the window, then said he was a federal district court judge convening an expedited *habeas* hearing. The court reporter typed while watching Emma. "Would Petitioner," the judge said, "please state her name?"

The context and the heads that turned her way suggested that meant her. "Dr. Emma Miller."

The bird arrived with another twig in its beak. Today was a busy day.

"Dr. Miller," the judge said, "do you understand the nature of this hearing?"

"Yes," she replied. Then, "No," when asked if she had any questions, and "Yes," if she consented to Noah representing her. "Very well," the judge said. Like the others, he snuck peeks at Emma. "Mr. Miller, you may proceed."

Noah rose and asserted that Emma was being detained without cause. That her confinement was kept secret. That the United States should be required either to show cause for her detention or release her. And, in the event cause is shown, that the conditions of her confinement should be subject to reasonable court-ordered restrictions. He sat.

The judge turned to the other side of the room. "And what says the United States?"

One of the men in suits rose. "Your Honor, the United States does not believe that habeas corpus lies in the matter of Dr. Miller's detention."

"*Okay*," the judge said, glancing at Emma. "We're on US soil. Dr. Miller is a US citizen and not an enemy combatant. Just why does habeas not lie in her case?"

"It only applies to persons, sir. We contend Petitioner is no longer a person."

"Your Honor!" Noah shouted, rising.

But the judge motioned him down. "I've got this." He looked from Emma to the government lawyer. "I don't know where this is heading, but it's not going far unless the next words I hear from you are a damned good legal argument."

"It is the government's contention, Your Honor, that the *person* who was Petitioner died in Siberia of severe encephalopathic disease after contracting a newly emerged pathogen, *Pandoravirus horribilis*."

"She looks very much alive to me," the judge said, again glancing at Emma.

"Her *body* is alive," the lawyer replied, "but not her *mind*."

"Your Honor . . . !" Noah said, again rising and *again* being told to sit. Sitting and standing somehow seemed integral to the hearing's procedures.

"She's walking," noted the judge, "talking. There's no brain death here."

"It's not her brain that died, but her *personhood*," the government lawyer said. "It's the person that Dr. Miller used to be who was entitled to Constitutional protection."

"Your Honor," Noah said, taking to his feet, "this line of reasoning is absurd!"

"I'm inclined to agree," the judge said. Noah sat again.

"May I present my evidence?" the government lawyer inquired.

Noah was again on his feet. "What evidence, Your Honor? Evidence that my . . . that Petitioner is no longer *alive?* I move that the court take judicial notice of the fact that Petitioner is currently a *living* human being."

A gavel appeared from under the sleeve of the judge's robe. Long sleeves allowed him to carry it unnoticed. *Ask for long sleeves.* There's another one. Out of nowhere. Emma could tell Nurse Hopkins that she's cold. She wrote that plan down in her notebook.

The government lawyer said, "I'd like to call Dr. *Isabel* Miller as the government's expert on the subject of human consciousness."

The suspended gavel did not fall. "Objections?" he asked Noah.

"I object to this *entire* line of reasoning! Based on what precedent could the government proceed with an argument that, if successful, would entirely strip my client of all her legal rights! If she's not a person, Your Honor, does she have *any* rights? Is this court willing to apply, I don't know, laws against animal *cruelty* to protect her?"

"Calm down," the judge said. He swiveled his chair to face Noah's adversaries. "The burden of proof you've got to clear on this has gone from a preponderance of the evidence to a virtual certainty. You're on a *very* short leash. Present your expert."

Emma only really needed maps of North America. The diminished post-infection world will fragment geographically. Emma looked up when Isabel entered. Her sister stared at Emma even as she was sworn in with her hand on a Bible. Everyone looked back and forth between Emma and Isabel, as happens with identical twins. *Maps from the Caribbean to Canada.*

"You are," the government lawyer said to Isabel, "obviously Petitioner's twin sister. But you are also a research professor in the Department of Psychological and Brain Sciences at the University of California at Santa Barbara, are you not?" Isabel nodded. The judge told her to respond verbally, which she did. "And you published a paper entitled, Self-Ascription Without Qualia: The Inverted Spectrum Issue, is that correct?"

Isabel looked at Noah. "Yes," she said. "I did publish that *thought exercise.*"

The lawyer turned to the judge. "I would like to present Dr. Isabel Miller as an expert on the subject of brain sciences generally, and human consciousness specifically."

The judge asked Noah if he had any objections. He did not. Still no bird outside.

"Dr. Miller," said the government lawyer, whose standing time now greatly exceeded Noah's, "in your paper, what are qualia, as used in its title?"

"Qualia are sense data."

"Like when you look at an apple and see that it's red, am I correct? The qualia in that observation is the color of the apple?"

"Quale is the singular," she replied, pronouncing it "kwah-lee" and spelling it for the court reporter. "Quali-*a* is the plural. But yes. Qualia are the way things seem to us. One quale would be the red color we see on an apple, the example I used in my paper."

"And the Inverted Spectrum Issue you discuss argues that there's no way to know whether, when *you* see red and *I* see red that we're actually sensing the same color?"

"Objection, Your Honor," Noah said, standing. "He's leading his witness."

"I'm sorry, Your Honor, but these concepts are difficult. If you'll give me a little leeway . . ."

"I'll allow it," the judge replied, "if only to get to the point more quickly."

Noah's opponent remained on his feet. "In your paper you say that, from birth, we're taught to call the color that we see on a red apple *red*. But another person might see blue and learn to *call* that color red. Isn't that your Inverted Spectrum Issue?"

"As coined by the philosopher John Locke," Isabel replied, "not me."

"Very well. And what was Mr. Locke purporting to teach us?"

"It's an armchair argument. It's a variation of qualia inversion arguments used to illustrate that, even if two people's senses *are* different, if one person sees the apple as red, and another sees it as blue, neither would ever know *or* behave any differently."

"And what," the government lawyer asked, "does *that* in turn tell us?"

"It suggests that qualia—sensory perceptions—are epi-functional. They are not *of* the physical world. They are only *subjective* mental states because they cannot be *objectively* described and agreed upon by multiple independent observers."

Noah bobbed up to object. The judge said to his opponent, "Let's get on with this."

"In your paper," the government lawyer continued, "what do epi-functional qualia and the Inverted Spectrum Issue tell us about consciousness?"

Isabel looked at Noah. "It merely poses *questions* meant to stimulate *debate*."

The government lawyer turned to the judge. "I request that I be allowed to treat Dr. Miller as hostile." Noah bounded to his feet, shouting that Isabel was *his* witness, and an *expert* not a fact witness. His opponent rebutted, "She is the sister of Petitioner *and* her counsel. She's clearly anticipating the thrust of my questions and obfuscating."

"I'll allow it," the judge said to the sinking Noah. "Overruled."

"Dr. Miller," the lawyer said, raising a sheaf of papers, "when you used the term 'philosopher's zombie' in your paper, were you referring to someone like Petitioner?"

"It was a *thought* exercise!"

The judge said, "Please answer the question, Dr. Miller."

Isabel explained the paper, which Emma had read. "Asking about a philosopher's zombie is like asking: '*What if we had no moon?*' It's contrafactual, useful only in parsing concepts. If we had no moon, there would be no lunar tides. No lunar tides, no sea creatures laying eggs on beaches. With no reason to go ashore, there would be no amphibians, no land creatures, no mammals, no humans. That sort of conjecture."

"And I'm sure," the government lawyer said, "if one day the moon disappeared, some scientists would be asked questions to which they raise similar objection."

The judge said, "I'm going to instruct you again to answer the question, Dr. Miller. Would the court reporter please read it back?"

The woman read: "When you used the term 'philosopher's zombie' in your paper," she glanced at Emma, "were you referring to someone like Petitioner?"

"No!" Isabel replied. "Of course not, because philosophers' zombies don't *exist*."

The judge asked Isabel directly, "Then what *was* the point of your paper?"

"The point, Your Honor, was to explore why consciousness emerged. What adaptive significance or evolutionary advantage does consciousness confer upon humans?"

"So," the government lawyer asked, still on his feet, "all humans are conscious?" Isabel stumbled in various attempts to reply. "You say a philosopher's zombie is 'someone behaviorally indistinguishable from a human, but who lacks any phenomenal experience.' They act like us, but there's no one inside them who forms impressions about the events they witness. These 'p-zombies,' as you call them, 'can fool even the sharpest mental detector' like the Turing Test and the Brainy Turing Test, correct?"

Isabel was acting strange. It was a perfectly straightforward question. Even Emma knew the answer. "But it's completely theoretical! P-zombies don't *exist*!"

"Did you write those words I just read? Yes or no?"

The bird returned with a twig that had a green leaf still attached. *That's* curious.

"Yes," Isabel said. "It's just a variation of the Other Minds problem, which . . ."

"Thank you," interrupted the lawyer.

"What Other Minds problem?" the judge asked.

"That's *another* thought exercise. How can we know that other people aren't . . . aren't zombies? We can't. For all you know, Your Honor, all the other people on Earth are just acting out parts meant solely to fool you into thinking they're sentient just like you. But when you round the corner, all the automatons pretending to be fellow humans, now out of your sight, go into hibernation or whatever, waiting for their next performance just to fool *you*. That *obviously* could never be literally true. It's just idea play."

"As is," the government lawyer asked, "a 'Zombie Earth'? An earth," he referred again to her paper, "'filled with people who *look* human, but lack consciousness'?" He flipped pages to a blue Post-it note. *Would Post-its be helpful?* There it was again. Where did that come from? "This Zombie Earth is filled with, quote, 'insentient beings whose complex behaviors are similar to humans, including speech, but—critically—are not accompanied by conscious experience of any sort.' Do I have that right?" Emma decided she didn't need Post-it Notes. She remembered everything she'd written in her notebooks.

Isabel was hunched forward, staring at the floor. "Yes, but . . ."

"And you concluded that other creatures," the lawyer interrupted, "like apes and dolphins and artificially intelligent computers, cannot necessarily be expected to achieve consciousness as they climb the evolutionary ladder because consciousness is a trait unique to human beings?" The question hung in the room. The judge directed Isabel to answer.

"Evolution," Isabel replied, "survival of the fittest, for instance—is concerned only with *behavior*, not subjective states of mind. If behavior isn't influenced by consciousness, if you can imagine creatures who behave indistinguishably from humans but are *not* conscious, then evolution is indifferent to consciousness and consciousness therefore wouldn't be expected to emerge naturally *via* evolution. *That's* the point of my paper."

The government lawyer was reading and stroking his chin. "And these 'philosophers' zombies' have no inner life? They don't dream. They don't feel pain. They don't even see, because there is no *they* in there *to* do the seeing. Am I correct?"

Noah asked for a recess. The judge denied his request and instructed Isabel to answer. She rocked back and forth, hands pinned between her knees, and said, "*Yes!*"

"In your research here at the NIH, have you inquired whether Petitioner dreams? Feels pain? Sees? Has an inner-life?" Isabel didn't answer. "Dr. Miller, we have hours of recordings of your interviews of Petitioner and conversations in this very room with Dr. Henry Rosenbaum, who is available to be called. And I remind you that you are under oath. Did you inquire whether Petitioner dreams, experiences pain, and sees in the same way as you and I do? Whether she has an inner-life? Whether she is conscious?"

Isabel swallowed repeatedly and licked her lips. "Yes."

"And what was your professional conclusion?"

Isabel's chin sank. She still hides behind her hair. "There is some doubt whether her consciousness is intact."

"Come now. You were much more definitive when you . . ."

"I was upset!"

"And that's understandable. You and your sister were close."

"*Are* close," Isabel corrected.

"I have a recording in which you say," the lawyer pulled out other papers, "'My God, Hank,'—that's Dr. Rosenbaum—'she's gone. There's nothing left of her in there. That [expletive] disease destroyed her. Killed her. My Emmy.' Are those your words?"

Isabel nodded, and was again told to reply verbally. "Yes," she croaked.

The government lawyer finally took *his* seat. Emma's back was growing stiff so she arched it and stretched her shoulders. Noah put his arm around Isabel, who was doubled over and sobbing. She looked up at Emma. "I'm sorry! I'm sorry! I'm *so* sorry!"

Everyone turned to Emma. The judge said, "Dr. Miller, have you been following all this?"

She said, "Yes." Noah mouthed, *Your Honor*, and Emma said, "Your Honor."

"And how do you feel about what you've heard?"

She didn't understand. "Could you rephrase the question?" adding, "Your Honor."

The judge looked at the others. The court reporter for a moment forgot to type.

The judge spoke slowly. "The question before this Court is whether you are a 'person' entitled to Constitutional protection. So, do you, Dr. Miller, have . . . feelings?"

Emma said, "Yes." Isabel grinned. Noah gave her exaggerated nods.

The judge waved off the government lawyer. "What kinds of feelings?" he asked.

"Hunger. Thirst. Occasionally an itch. Stiffness, when sitting or lying in one position too long. Fatigue. Gastrointestinal and urogenital sensations.

When it's cold, a blanket provides warmth. When it's warm, the nurse lowers the temperature."

The government lawyer said, "Those are physical sensations, not an inner-life."

"Do you feel anything *more?*" the judge inquired.

She had no idea what he meant, and no one gave her any hints. The bird returned to the window sill, this time with a candy wrapper in its beak. A *candy* wrapper!

"Your *plans*, Emma!" Noah said loudly over objections. "What about your plans?"

"My plans are to continue epidemiological research, publish the results, find a husband, get married, buy a house and a car, have children, and raise a family."

Everyone shouted at once. Isabel grinned through tears. Noah gestured wildly. The court reporter inexplicably winked. The judge pounded his gavel. "Order! This has gone far enough. I rule Petitioner *is* entitled to the rights and protections afforded *persons* under the US Constitution. I *also* rule, based on the briefs, that Respondent has shown cause to continue Petitioner's isolation due to her contagiousness. But Dr. Miller has broken no laws, and the conditions of her confinement must be reasonably related to public safety. Therefore Respondent should consider favorably any accommodations requested."

"Your Honor, I have a list," Noah said, handing him what he'd written earlier.

The judge said, "These all seem reasonable." He passed it to the government lawyer, who argued that all information regarding SED was classified Top Secret, and that Emma should not be allowed to communicate with people outside the NIH. The judge agreed and had the court reporter type the list into the record with that proviso. "And I so rule." The gavel pounded the desk. On rising, the judge said, "Dr. Miller, thank you for your selfless service to this country. I wish you a speedy recovery."

"Thank you," Emma replied. He departed before she got to try smiling.

The observation room emptied save Noah and Isabel, who hugged. "We won!" Isabel said. The bird returned to the windowsill with a proper, sensible twig.

* * * *

Isabel and Noah watched Emma through the now opaque window. Beth and an armed guard, both in full PPE, wheeled into Emma's room a cart with a smartphone, laptop, and flat-screen television, which Beth hooked up. Beth explained that Emma could only text, call or email other people at the NIH. She waited, then handed Emma the TV remote. Emma made no move to use it and returned to her notebook.

"What does she do all day?" Noah asked Isabel.

"You sure we're still in the legal cone of silence here?" Isabel asked, looking up at the camera on the ceiling. Noah nodded. "Well, she gets poked, prodded, and scanned all day. We get whatever time is left for interviewing and testing. In between, I end up filling out so many questionnaires I feel like *I'm* the one they're studying. The secrecy is so freakish and stupid we can't talk to each other, but they've thrown every discipline we've got at this. Biopsychologists, psychobiologists, neuropsychologists, pathologists, disease ecologists, parasitologists, microscopists, molecular geneticists, mammalogists, phylogeneticists."

"Now you're just making up words," Noah said.

"And they love neuroimaging: CAT scans, PET scans, MRIs, EEGs, DCIs. But ironically, we're waiting on old-fashioned WHO autopsy results to hear the full extent of the damage."

"Why can't they diagnose the damage from all those brain scans?"

"You can't get high enough resolution on scans of a living brain, even with fluorescent microscopy. They're dissecting brains of Siberian victims one cross-section at a time and overlaying imagery from electron microscopes with 3D electron-micrographs."

"Whatever that means. So, once you know what the damage is, what do *you* do?"

"I study the impact on her thoughts, feelings, and moods, although everyone has already concluded that she has thoughts, but no feelings or moods."

"She's not right," Noah said. "Remember when you told me about that Creepy Valley thing? When robots grow so advanced that they're *almost* human, but not quite, and that creeps people out? That's right where she is, in the Creepy Valley."

"*Uncanny* Valley," Isabel corrected.

Noah asked what Emma was writing. "We don't know. She's been scribbling away for days. She keeps it covered and with her, but she's up to about forty pages. And from glimpses it's filled with text, numbers, charts, graphs. She was always good at mathematical epidemiology. That's my guess what it is."

Emma picked up her new phone and typed. "What's she doing?" Noah asked.

"I don't know." Isabel opened the military's app on her iPad. "Connecting" was quickly replaced by a picture of Captain Ramirez and two young Marines, who turned toward the camera. Isabel said, "Do you have any way of telling who Emma is texting right now?"

"Sure do. Some woman with an NIH phone. A doctor. Amanda Davis, Department of Epidemiology." He typed on his laptop as he spoke. A new window popped up on Isabel's iPad containing Emma's texts. She thanked Ramirez. "Anything for a friend of the Corps," Ramirez said, drawing chuckles from his Marines before disappearing.

"It looks like she's finished typing. What did she say?" Noah asked.

Isabel read Emma's texts aloud. "'Amanda, you workin on the P. outbreak?' Amanda replied, 'Em, that you? Heard you had trouble!!!' Three exclamation marks. Emma typed, 'I'm fine. U workin on it?' Amanda said, 'Yep. Wuz up?' Emma asked if they're still looking for non-human hosts. Amanda said, 'Yep. Got 4 rodents, 16 birds, 12 insects, a bat, a cat, 3 dogs, but none r'—the letter—'infected. Prolly only infected ancient humans.' Emma wrote, 'It might have last infected hominins in Siberia, not humans.'"

Noah said, "I thought homonyms are two words that sound alike."

"They are. Hom*in*ins are human-like species with which we coexisted. Emma wrote, 'When P. horribilis was frozen, it could've infected Denisovans, or more likely Neanderthals, who were better adapted to the cold.' Amanda replied, 'Good point! Had wondered why H. sapiens so far north. Neanderthals makes sense. Pushed out of Europe round then. Where r u?' Letters. 'Want lunch?' Emma answered, 'They won't let me out.' Amanda said, 'Tell me bout it. Call when you come up for air.' Emma then replied . . . she said . . . she has '*plenty* of air.' So, I guess, don't worry about the *air* situation."

The siblings looked at each other, then back at Emma, who had returned to her notebook. Noah said, "Poor thing. She's still trying to do work like nothing has changed."

But Emma's text exchange struck Isabel differently. "She may be *onto* something."

Beth arrived, hair wet. "There's a doctor looking for you." It turned out to be Brandon, in a lab coat. It took all Isabel's willpower not to roll her eyes.

"So there she is," Brandon said, fascinated by Emma as one would be by a rare arrival at a zoo. Noah introduced himself, holding out his hand. Brandon declined to shake it, presumably scared by his crash course on pandemics. He asked, "Can she see us?"

Isabel extinguished the Opaque button on the panel. Emma's gaze instantly rose to the window. "Now she can." Noah waved. Emma responded in kind. Isabel pressed the Talk button. "Emma, this is Brandon Plante. I told you about him, remember?"

Emma said, "He's the guy who keeps his socks on during sex."

Isabel hit the Mute button. Beth clamped both hands over her mouth, her eyes wide. Noah wasn't about to say anything. Emma returned to her notebook.

"That apartment in Palo Alto was freezing," Brandon said to Isabel.

"Well-I'm-outa-here," Noah declared, clapping Brandon on the back, intentionally breaching his self-isolation. Beth followed, but turned at the door, held up one hand to point and the other to hide it, and mouthed, "*That him*?" Isabel gave her a single nod.

In so doing, Isabel felt a little less of a failure. She *had* had a boyfriend, who was good looking and a PhD, in addition to his innumerable faults. When the door closed, Isabel said to Brandon, by way of explanation, "Sisters talk."

"What did you tell her about our break-up?" *Again* with the break-up thing! Isabel tilted her head in reproach. "Because I'm still trying to . . ."

"This isn't the place for that. They record everything. Now, like I told you, sooner or later there's gonna be a knock on the door and somebody saying, 'Come with me,' and you're gonna be asked for all the conclusions you've drawn in the last ten seconds. There's a particularly intimidating son-of-a-bitch named General Browner who'll be *very* interested in your analysis of crowd violence. You need to come up with something to say."

Brandon couldn't take his eyes off Emma, who was using her homemade straight edge to draw what appeared to be x and y axes. "She looks just like you except for her eyes, and hair." Emma's bangs had grown to cover half her face—poorly groomed, like the demented relative you kept locked from view.

"Looking alike is kind of the deal with identical twins," Isabel responded, finally waving at Brandon to break the spell Emma had cast over him. "But she has a little scar on her chin from when we went bungee jumping."

"*You* went *bungee* jumping?"

"No. I didn't jump. But Emma cut her chin, sort of *validating* that decision. So . . . shouldn't you be doing whatever it is you do?" She instantly regretted her phrasing.

He cast her an aggrieved look. "I've got an assistant and three techs doing the data entry for some SIDE modeling on the video out of Harbin, and on a new video we just got in from a bridge along the road to Changchun. You should swing by my office."

"You've got an *office*?"

"Yes," he said. "And on that point, where the hell is yours? Nobody knows."

Isabel declined to tell him about her table in the cafeteria. "And you've got *staff*?"

"I asked. They *have* resources, Izzy. You maybe should try being more assertive." The old criticism hit Isabel with undiminished force. He probably thought she'd be a full professor now if only she'd just thought to *ask* for tenure.

"I haven't heard about any new video," she mumbled. "Where'd you get it?"

"General Browner. But he told me not to tell anybody."

The middle school pain receptors all fired at once. Her ex-boyfriend now got invitations that she didn't . . . from *her* friends. Isabel knew the military was listening and she should have told him *ixnay* on the *easontray*, but she didn't. "What does the video show?" she asked. "I mean, if you can *say*," then instantly felt guilty for setting him up.

"It's just like Harbin." She made a slashing motion across her throat. "It's okay. Our working group is Hank, you, and me. We can talk. I think the crowd violence has something to do with the numbers. The crowd gets more unstable the larger it grows."

Isabel was skeptical, but then again far from objective. "*I'd* guess it's more the *density*, not the absolute size. Emma gets nervous in crowded elevators like she never used to before. And what the hell is SIDE modeling?"

"Social Identity Model of Deindividualization Effects," he replied. "You'd have heard of it if you'd read my last paper." Despite her fervent attempts to keep her face neutral, Brandon said, "*What?* You think it's *junk* science?" He huffed, shook his head, stormed out of the room, and slammed the door.

Emma was staring at Isabel. She probably wasn't judging her, but it sure felt like she was. Emma wrote something in her notebook. *Is that about me?* Isabel wondered, craning her neck to see. Something like, *She's still a disaster with men?*

Chapter 12

Noah was sitting at his desk in his downtown office buying survival supplies on Amazon when an email arrived from the contractor renovating the Old Place. Noah heaved a huge sigh of relief. Based on the report and the pictures, work was going well.

Then his broker at Merrill Lynch called. "*Bro*! What are you *doin'*?" The guy had noticed that Noah liquidated everything. "Broheim, wuz up?" He treated Noah like a fraternity brother because he'd gone to the same college as Noah but a decade later.

"Not a particularly good time," Noah said.

The guy was undeterred. "Brilliant trade! Dow's down seventeen *percent*. Everything's off except Big Pharma. *You* sold before anybody, so . . . what do *you* know?"

"I just wanted to de-risk," Noah lied, using a word he'd once heard on the radio.

His broker dropped the frat-rat routine and lowered his voice. "What's really going on?" It was more than fishing for a stock tip. There was fear in his voice. Noah had only met him a couple of times for lunch. What did he owe him? "That disease in China, it's real bad. Sell now, before everything tanks, and buy survival gear before it gets scarce."

There was a long pause before the broker laughed. "Sell? At these prices? But hey, if you don't wanta share, that's dope. We're still simpatico, right? Call when you want back in the pahr-*tay*!" *Well,* Noah thought, shrugging, *natural selection at work.*

Noah ate the lunch brought in by his secretary and called an auto dealer. The man searched online and found two black, fully loaded, four-wheel-drive Cadillac Escalades with extended wheel base. Noah bought them on the spot, no haggling, for $190,312.

He had millions yet to spend in his mad dash into insolvency, but was running out of things to buy. Even purchasing in sets of five, a million dollars buys a lot of shit, and he still had $3,761,771 to go. More if he maxed out the plastic. But the law of diminishing marginal returns had set in. Twice he'd loaded five Gerber Zombie Apocalypse Survival Kits into his Amazon shopping cart, and twice he'd deleted the order. Once, he had thought of Emma and felt guilty at the word "Zombie." Once he had concluded it a waste to buy $300 bundles of machetes, knives, and tomahawks for use against the imaginary undead.

The third time he loaded them into his cart, he bought them, putting him $1,500 closer to his goal. But how could he responsibly spend his last millions before the zeroes and ones in some computer that represented his remaining wealth disappeared forever?

Noah Googled, "how to buy gold." It came in bars of one gram, ounce or kilo, up to four hundred ounces. The larger the bar, the lower the premium. But if Noah needed gold as currency, huge bars didn't work. He settled on 1,000 one-ounce and 50 ten-ounce Credit Suisse bars, delivered to his house via FedEx in nondescript packaging, for $1,906,893. "Jesus!" He grabbed his head with both hands. He couldn't believe what he was doing. He'd begin withdrawing in cash the $1,854,878 that was left in case that retained any value.

A short rap on Noah's door preceded its opening. The firm's managing partner entered. On habit, Noah swiveled his monitor from view. "Got a sec?" the senior man asked before sitting. "I got a call from Joe Milburn," the firm's largest client, "who said his secretary has been trying to reach you for days. May I?" he said before taking a few French fries. "They want to schedule depositions. To be frank, Joe said he doesn't feel you've got the same sense of urgency he does. They're losing money every day, and . . ."

"I'm gonna have to resign," Noah interrupted. The managing partner's face expressed incomprehension. Noah, whom they had made partner after only five years—who was the third-highest paid litigator in the whole firm—was . . . *what*? "I'm afraid I'm not able to give much notice, but I'll hand everything off in the next couple of days."

"Couple of *days*!" the senior partner almost shouted. "How the fuck *dare* you! Where are you going? Is it more money? Is that who you are? I understand now. Don't even *think* about poaching clients! You may be a hotshot trial lawyer, but you didn't originate any of that business. That was someone else's hard work."

"I'm retiring," Noah said. "I won't steal any clients. I'm not being hired away by a competitor. And I'm not going in-house at any of the firm's clients."

"What, did somebody die and leave you money? How can you just stop working?"

Noah again decided to be honest. "It's the disease, in China." He told him more than he should. "None of this—depositions, hearing docket, filing deadlines—matters."

"What *does* matter?"

"Find a place to isolate yourself," Noah said. "Stay as far away from people as you can. Buy supplies, survival gear, guns, that sort of thing."

The managing partner was nodding now. "So, that's what you're in here doing?"

"And liquidating my financial assets."

His boss looked quizzically at Noah. "No need to transition. Be gone in an hour." At the door, he turned back. "Don't say anything to anyone, and go see a doctor, Noah."

"Asshole," Noah said when he was gone. He told his assistant and his associate why he was leaving, and they helped him box and haul out his stuff. His assistant said she was taking her vacation time. The associate asked Noah for his list of survival gear.

Noah now headed for the hardest part of all.

* * * *

"You did *what*?" Natalie shouted.

Noah took a Zen-like breath, then told her about selling everything and spending the proceeds on survival gear. Natalie sank, not to the nearby chair, but straight to the floor. Noah knelt beside her, but she twisted free. "You didn't *tell* me before you did this?" He lamely brought up her kind-of formal grant of authority. "Oh, *bullshit!*"

"You've seen the news, Nat."

"How can I *not* see it? It's on around the *clock*! I don't wanta watch riots in some polluted dump in China, Noah! I'm *sorry* about your sister, but you've gone *nuts*!"

The kids peeked over the upstairs railing. Noah waved them away, but Natalie said, "No! Come down!" Chloe and Jacob descended tentatively.

"Kids, your father thinks there's going to be an apocalypse. I think he's gone insane, hopefully only temporarily."

"Natalie . . ." Noah said.

But she was undeterred. "This is your official notice," Natalie said, rising. "I want no part in your little sci-fi fantasy. No news. No texts to turn *on* the news. Nothing." Jacob and Chloe just watched, wisely not picking a side. On her way to the kitchen, Natalie whispered to Noah, "And you'd better be right about this fucking apocalypse."

Chapter 13

Isabel called Emma's name over the room's speakers. Emma raised her head from her notes. "Would you mind coming over to the window?" Emma went to the glass. "Really close." Emma leaned until her nose almost touched the frosted pane. "Open your eyes *very* wide." Emma complied. "Hey! Look at you. You've got some color in your eyes! They're a little green around the edges! The mydriasis is resolving."

Emma passed the large vanity mirror without a glance and returned to her notebook.

"Can I ask you a question?" Isabel said. "What are those notes you're taking?"

"Research," Emma replied.

"On the disease?" Emma nodded. "What have you concluded?"

"There's a 60 percent chance SED will arrive here in three weeks," Emma said. "An 80 percent chance it will be here in under a month."

"But Emma, Russia seems to have stamped it out. And it's been eight days since it got to China, and it's still just limited to the north. We've shut down air travel to and from there. How is it going to make it all the way over here in the next few weeks?"

"There are currently, by my estimate, 3.5 to 7 million ambulatory carriers actively spreading the virus. It's analogous to the decay of plutonium or uranium, which eject subatomic particles that collide with nearby nuclei, causing them to emit even more particles. If the matter is dense enough, each decay leads to more than one reaction and the cascading and progressive process plots as exponential."

"Matter in your analogy is population?" Isabel said. "And at critical mass—*boom*? So, is the population dense enough that the chain reaction is unstoppable?"

"In northeastern Siberia, no. It could have dead-ended there, just like 40,000 years ago, and been buried with the drilling crew. But in northern China, yes, it's unstoppable. The disease can reach America from any number of directions, and once it's here—in the wild, not the lab—it's everywhere. It should reach some part of all forty-eight contiguous states within weeks unless Draconian measures are employed, in which case it could take months. I would have thought that more of the hospital's staff would have quit by now."

Isabel opened her eyes, looked up and asked, "Then what?" Her voice shook.

"The rate of infection slows hyperbolically as the susceptible population declines."

"Will anyone survive uninfected?" Isabel asked. She sounded ill herself.

"For a few years. The virus won't maintain a continuous presence in every isolated community, but will inevitably reemerge in them by reinfection from the outside. If *Pandoravirus* exists anywhere in the metapopulation, it will inexorably spread to every constituent subpopulation. But the number of Uninfecteds should plateau several times on its way down toward zero as various defensive strategies are employed. Campaigns of eradication by Uninfecteds would arrest the spread sporadically and locally but only temporarily, just as eradication by Infecteds would accelerate the spread by eliminating resistance."

"Wait. Did you say eradication *by* the Infecteds?" Emma tried to reduce telltale signs of her sudden agitation, crossing her arms and sinking deeper into her seat. "Why would infected people eradicate the uninfected?"

"To survive. If they're being killed, they would try to eliminate the threat."

Her sister said nothing until, "Do you think it's possible we could live peacefully with one another? Infecteds and Uninfecteds?"

"Possibly," Emma replied. "Especially if a vaccine is developed. But there may not be enough Uninfecteds left to matter much, and by then *you* will probably have been killed by violence or infected and either died or turned." Emma searched the Internet to determine how effective Europe's walled cities had been during the plagues.

Isabel said, "Do you know why we're so upset?" Emma looked up to see Beth rubbing Isabel's back as both cried. "Because inside each of us there's a 'self.' It's who we are. It's a bundle of all our hopes and fears and loves and petty annoyances. We're worried about getting infected and either dying, or that self *inside* us dying."

"Does this self speak to you?"

Isabel said, "Yes, in a sense."

"Is it one voice, or many?"

"Some think each mood has its own voice. One says do it, another says no it's wrong, like a devil one shoulder and an angel on the other."

Emma chose black ink to note the security issue. "Do they ever tell you to commit acts of violence?"

"*What*? It's not like that. The voices are normal in healthy people. You used to hear them too. It may be the main thing you lost. Why are you asking about violence?"

"Because murderers sometimes hear voices that tell them to kill."

"No-no-no," Isabel said. "Those are people suffering from *delusions*."

Emma wrote: *Uninfecteds hear voices. Delusional? Dangerous?*

"What are you writing?" Emma looked down at the word, "Dangerous?" and lied. "Variables that accelerate or slow spread of the disease."

"Like what variables?" Isabel asked.

Emma chose one at random. "V-sub-U"—violence by the Uninfected. "Some Uninfecteds won't be willing to use violence against Infecteds. Parents against children, for instance. V-sub-U has lower and upper bounds of zero and one, where zero means the Uninfected would never resort to violence against an Infected, and one means they are willing to kill any Infected they meet. The actual value lies between the two bounds."

"And," Isabel said, "V-Sub-I is Infecteds' willingness to use violence against *us*?"

"That's not a variable, it's a constant—one—and can be ignored mathematically."

Isabel's mouth was agape. Beth hugged her, but Isabel stared at Emma, who grew jittery. Emma returned to her notes and calmed.

* * * *

Isabel had to get away. She still couldn't fathom how her sister could possibly be roused to violence against her, but that was what Emma's math suggested. Was she still even Emma? Isabel headed for the vending machine, turned a corner, and ran into Brandon, Hank, and Street. "Oh," she said.

After an awkward moment, Street said, "We're reviewing the results of your sister's tests." He handed the document they all perused to Isabel. "Her math skills shot up."

"Emma was always good at math. She got a perfect score on her math SAT.

"But not on the GRE," Hank said, "until now." Isabel read over Emma's new GRE results. Geometry 100 percent. Algebra 100 percent. Calculus 100 percent. Point-set topology 100 percent. Probability and statistics 100 percent. Real analysis 100 percent. "She didn't miss a single question and finished early. Her scores on the verbal, in contrast, fell compared to her take ten years ago. Her critical reasoning and vocabulary scores were fine, but her reading comprehension was down. Her improvement in math, however, that's . . . unprecedented."

The scientists returned each other's gazes. Infecteds aren't zombies, Isabel thought. They're smarter than that—maybe even than humans—and therefore far more dangerous.

"*Euhaplorchis californiensis*," Street said. Eyes rolled, sighs heaved, heads shook, but the tension eased. "They're flukes—flatworms—that infect killifish, which normally stay out of shallow water to avoid being eaten by wading birds. But the flukes need to get into birds' stomachs to reproduce, so they form a carpet-like layer on killifish brains and cause them not only to swim to the surface, but to roll over and expose their silvery bellies to the sunlight." Street doffed an imaginary courtier's hat. "I bid you all good day."

Brandon said, "I don't get it. Does that have something to do with *Pandoravirus*?"

Isabel replied, "We're the killifish. But a skills improvement from *brain* damage?"

Brandon scoffed. "You neuroscientists only focus on deficits, impairments, incapacities, dysfunctions. It's always *a*-something: aphonia, aphasia, aphemia, amnesia. Either a brain works just like everyone else's, or it's broken."

"So now you're a neuropsychologist, too?" Isabel replied cuttingly.

Brandon frowned. "Who are you to say that Emma isn't a better version of herself now? Changes you call deficits can unleash potential. You're so hung up on the downside that you miss the ebullience that can come from some changes in function."

Isabel waited as patiently as she could, then said, "We *scientists* don't ignore excesses, manias, teratomas, monstrosities. Hypermnesia, hypergnosia, hypertrophies!"

Hank put away his cell phone. "You should know that Emma's latest fMRI, ASL, and MEG scans all show decreased left-brain and increased right-brain activity."

Isabel looked at Brandon. "You've seen the scans?" He nodded. *But I haven't!*

She spun on her heels and stormed off. "Isabel!" Brandon called out. She wiped away tears, *tears*, and shoved the bar on the exit so hard the door banged off the wall. The evening was crisp and cool. *Fuck them!* A crane lowered concrete wall sections. Men in camouflage shouted over growling engines. She headed uphill away from the noise.

Think! she chided herself. More activity in the right hemisphere, responsible for recognizing reality and experiencing consciousness. Could Emma be laboring to work around damage, which in the right brain produces less distinct symptoms?

From her back pocket she extracted Maldonado's business card and dialed. "White House operator," a pleasant voice answered. "What can I do for you, Dr. Miller?"

"*Oh*, uhm. Could I have Patricia Maldonado, please?"

After a moment, she heard, "Isabel! How are you?"

"Could you get me a phone number? A Dr. Hermann Lange, with the WHO?"

"I can do better than that. Haven't you heard about White House operators?"

Isabel crested the rise and halted. Two Marines in PPE, holding rifles, blocked the walk ahead. At the bottom of the hill beyond them, bright lights lit other armed Marines fully garbed in PPE. A beeping ambulance backed into underground loading docks.

Isabel wandered over to the hooded Marines, phone to her ear. "What's goin' on?"

"Another load," a Marine said, his speech muffled. His buddy shot him a look.

"Hello?" came an accented voice over Isabel's phone.

She pivoted and walked back up the hill. "Dr. *Lange?* It's Isabel Miller. Emma's sister."

"Yes!" Lange finally replied after a satellite delay. "I remember you from Khabarovsk. How is Emma?"

"She's . . ." Isabel began before faltering.

Lange understood. "You know, I tried romancing your sister. She was, how do you say it: playing hard to get."

Apparently only with you, one vicious self noted. Isabel cringed. Lange's breathing was labored. "Where are you now?" she asked.

"Me? I'm a few miles from the North Korean border. Near Tonghua, in China."

"Oh! Wow. Has the infection reached there?"

"Not yet, but several million refugees have piled up on the Chinese side, starving, falling ill from other diseases. We're here to determine how quickly SED spreads through vulnerable, overcrowded populations with only primitive sanitary conditions."

"That's . . . I'm sorry. But you should know that your reports are being read back here with great interest." Lange seemed genuinely thrilled to hear it, and thanked her profusely. "Look, I called because I need data from the brain dissections."

"Are you kidding?" Lange cried out. "I should hang up right now!"

She told him why she needed the data, and begged. "How about this: I name a region of the brain, and if it isn't damaged you say, no. If it is, don't say anything. So, how about the . . . insular cortex?" There was a pause. "The . . . insular . . . ?"

"Oh-for-God's-sakes yes! The insular cortex in all the victims is damaged."

He wasn't following her rather clear instructions. "The medial prefrontal cortex?"

"Damaged," Lange said. "Heavily damaged."

"And the anterior cingulate cortex?"

"No. It isn't harmed. But that's it! I've got to go."

That was just what she had predicted to Hank. "Thank you!" Isabel said.

"Good luck," replied Lange. "It won't be long." The smile drained from her face.

Isabel returned to the hospital as another section of wall was lowered into place.

Chapter 14

Noah found the Old Place a hive of activity. Men in hardhats and work boots traipsed about the house, barn, smokehouse, and well house. The contractor, tall and skinny, perhaps a long lost, mustachioed cousin of the gun salesman, wore jeans and a silver hardhat emblazoned with a scratched and fraying US flag decal. He took his work gloves off to shake Noah's hand. "Looking good," Noah said.

"We're gittin' there," replied the contactor in a thick, twangy mountain accent. "Everybody's sleepin' up here. Workin' sixteen-hour days." On the front porch, he said, "This place is solid as a fort." He slapped the rough-hewn stone wall.

"General Sheridan missed it when he burned his way down the Valley in 1864."

"It *is* off the beaten path," said the West Virginian, who lived far enough away that, when he left, he probably wouldn't return . . . hungry. "Must've been another way up here. No way they built that ridge road way back then."

There *was* an old, longer way up to the house, so overgrown as to be almost invisible.

"Like you asked fer—hurricane shutters." The contractor looked at Noah as if to make sure. Panic Room. Tunnel beyond the fence. Fire suppression system. He pointed at pipes, sprinklers, and bundles of low-voltage wiring exposed inside open walls and ceilings. Woodburning and gas fireplaces in every room. Outside, security cameras mounted under eaves, to trees, and to posts along the fence line. Water heating in the barn with pipes under the walk to keep it snow free. A half-dozen huge cylinders that Noah had filled at great cost with propane. Four gasoline tanks buried under the barn floor with electric and foot pumps. Both fuels powered standby generators. Behind the house, a rig drilled for water. The contractor slapped one of the four steel shipping containers painted woodlands camo, with a hollow *thonk*.

"They're for vegetables and things," Noah said of the grow labs. He wasn't sure the contractor believed him.

There was a radio/television antenna and satellite dish on a nearby hilltop. They were cementing posts for almost 2,000 feet of twelve-foot-high chain link fence with angled barbed wire at the top that would surround the compound. He and Noah finished in the barn. Roof repairs, insulation, chicken coop, and pigpen. Noah had arranged to buy a starter-kit of livestock and the feed to keep them alive, and his *Agriculture for Dummies* book had just arrived.

"Quite the farmers, you D.C. folk. I also got a crew at the cabin up the mountain."

Noah said he would take a look at it on his next trip.

* * * *

On the drive back down the hill, Natalie called. "What the hell did you buy? FedEx just dropped off this hundred-pound package that's only about the size of a breadbox. I had to get the delivery guy to roll it into the kitchen."

Two million dollars worth of gold, Noah thought, *and rising.* "I'll take care of it."

Her sigh sounded like a roar. "When are you getting home?"

"Coupla hours." He listened politely to her complaints before hanging up. After locking the gate at the state highway, Noah pulled his dusty SUV into a country store to refill the gas-guzzling vehicle. The pumps were the old kind with no credit card reader, so he went inside. "Doin' some off-roadin'?" asked the graying woman behind the counter.

Noah checked out the aisles, which bore convenience store staples—soft drinks, beer, cookies, chips, jerky—plus necessities like light bulbs and small hand tools. As he filled the huge tank, he was startled by the arrival of the proprietor. "Are you from War-shington?" Noah squeezed out the last few drops. "Our boy is in the Guard. Got called yesterday. First time since I-Rack. But the fishy thing is they're bringin' ever'body back. His buddies in the Persian Gulf and Japan are headin' home. Name's Margie." They shook. "Husband's Angus. We live out back."

"Noah Miller."

"Miller?" Margie said. "Like the Millers who used to live 'round here?" Noah should've kept his mouth shut, and gave a noncommittal bob of his head. "Well, drive safe," she said, waving.

When Noah got to the little town—Population 1,306—maybe six miles from the gate up to the Old Place, he took the time to wind his way through the several streets laid out on a rectangular grid, as much as allowed by the tight valley.

Sheriff's office. Volunteer fire department. City hall. Courthouse. Unified school. Baptist, Methodist, Episcopal, and Presbyterian churches, all at one intersection. Medical clinic. Diner. Barbershop. Funeral home. Dollar store. Auto-body shop. Farm supply store. And the largest structure in town, a brand-new brick National Guard building. *Probably has an armory.*

Chapter 15

The only fireworks in Nielsen's no-science staff meeting was a bombardment of complaints. One scientist's house was being watched. Another was being followed. A third had heard strange clicks on his phone. "We've got to tell everyone the *truth*!"

"Anybody else wanta get something off their chest?" Nielsen asked. "No? Okay. If anyone says anything to anyone, you're going to be in jail when SED gets here."

"How long do they think they can keep this *secret?*" a scientist asked angrily.

"How should *I* know?" Nielsen replied. "But they've done a good job so far. *There's* the President's aide," she said, holding a hand out to Maldonado. "Maybe he hasn't thought this through and would appreciate your opinions about what he's doing wrong!" Nielsen quickly covered administrative matters, most curious of which were orders to "keep all records on paper." When the younger scientists protested, she said, "*We may lose power!* Learn to live without spell check and Wikipedia. Street! Bug-'o-the-day?"

"*Dinocampus coccinellae*, a parasitic wasp that stings ladybugs and leaves behind an egg and a virus. Larvae hatch, eat the ladybug from the inside out and spin a web between the ladybug's legs. The virus enslaves the ladybug, causing it to stand guard over the cocoon and protect the wasp larvae and virus from predators. The ladybug sometimes survives, but its life is forever circumscribed due to the damage done by the parasite."

Nielsen heaved a heavy sigh. "Do these stories ever have happy endings?"

Isabel waited until Maldonado filed past. She hadn't heard anything from the White House since she'd hired Brandon. But Maldonado ignored her.

"Dr. Nielsen wasn't always this angry," Street said when they were alone. "Her husband left her for a TA about your age. Pretty, like you. And worse, smart like you. They'd put off having kids but were adopting. Nan told me that not following through with that adoption was the worst mistake of her life. That, and letting her husband get within ten miles of that grad student." Street headed for the door, but Isabel stopped him.

"Walter, have you ever studied swarm theory?" Street's face lit up, and he eagerly took a seat beside her. "I wonder if a kind of swarm intelligence might arise among Infecteds?"

"*In*teresting," Street said, rocking back, enjoying a discussion that, frankly, terrified Isabel. "Colonies as large as half a million function with no management. People think queens are in charge, but all they do is lay eggs. It's the *colony* that solves problems like finding the shortest route to food, efficiently allocating workers and defending the hive."

He leaned forward. "*Pogonomyrex barbatus*, red harvester ants, wake up each morning with no plan. Some stumble onto rain damage and repair it. Some bump into trash and take it out. Others wander outside and end up patrolling for food. If they find any, they lug it back while secreting pheromones. Ants that come behind secrete even more. The stronger the scent trail, the more ants that follow it. The collective makes decisions via the cumulative actions of individuals, not any ant leader. Now *Linepithema humile*, Argentine ants, follow a different approach. They . . ."

Isabel interrupted. "What about *violent* swarm behavior?"

Street had no problem changing direction. "When colonies of *Apis mellifera*, honeybees, get too crowded, scouts search for new real estate. Once a quorum of fifteen or so bees forms at a site they like, the queen, some drones and half the colony's workers fly there. That encourages free competition of ideas, considers a diversity of opinions and efficiently narrows choices."

"Does this have something to do with my question about violence?" Isabel asked.

"Oh! The best sites for new colonies are normally taken, so the arriving swarm attacks whatever is there. The wars are brutal, can last *weeks*, and are fought to the last bee. Pigeons exhibit a different type of swarm behavior by using synchronized flight to . . ."

"Are there any examples among larger orders of life than insects and birds?"

"Sure. *Rangifer tarandus granti*, Porcupine caribou, migrate in *vast* herds. Each changes direction based not on a plan but on what its neighbors do. When a wolf creeps up, the nearest turn and run, which ripples through the herd until they're all running even though no individual knows why or where."

"So is there a general rule applicable to all herds or swarms or flocks or schools?"

Street pondered. "They self-organize and depend on countless interactions that follow simple rules like stay close or move in the group's average direction. Herd behavior detects predators—a thousand eyes are better than a single pair—finds food, locates mates, follows migration routes. There are actually very few examples of hierarchical species, like humans, who follow leaders. Most *de*centralize decision-making."

Isabel thanked him and headed off lost in thought. According to Emma's schedule at the nurse's station, she was free. The observation room was empty. Emma scribbled in her notebook until Isabel cleared the window and she looked up.

"Hi!" Isabel said. "Great news. You scored real high on your GREs. Maybe you'll get into a top ten school!" Emma, of course, didn't get Isabel's joke.

There was a knock on the door. Brandon entered. As always, he was transfixed by the sight of Emma, who waved. Brandon self-consciously waved back.

"What are you doing here?" Isabel asked.

Brandon said, "Ready to go to the White House?"

On the walk to the parking lot, Isabel said, "I don't understand why they sent *you* to get *me* for an NSC meeting. And with no notice? Who called you?"

"Patricia Maldonado."

"How does she even know who you *are?*" Brandon gave her a look. In the back of the Secret Service SUV, she said, "Have you been talking to people at the White House?"

"What did you think I've been doing these last few days?"

"Working on that *model* thing?" He frowned at her. "I mean, your *model?*"

Brandon turned away. On passing the FBI headquarters, Isabel saw black-helmeted agents carrying assault rifles guarding the parking garage entrance. The FBI Director hadn't called in a while. Isabel couldn't figure out what she'd done wrong.

At the White House, an agent made a phone call from the guard shack. Isabel asked if everything was okay. "You're not on the list, ma'am," he said politely.

She turned to Brandon. "I wasn't *invited?*"

"I just thought. . . . It's just, you sit at that little table in the cafeteria all day."

"You invited me out of *pity!*" She searched the lot for their car.

Maldonado arrived wearing a flesh-tone bandage under her wedding ring and cleared Isabel to enter. "I'm not sure we can fit you into the schedule or the room even. You'll have to stand." To Brandon, she said, "Browner's pissed." Brandon bristled.

In the tomblike underground corridor, the Marine guard snapped to attention. He had switched to wearing full camo and a combat helmet, with a rifle slung over his shoulder.

"Oh, perfect timing," the president said. "We can't wait to hear about your work. And Dr. Miller, too! Now, Dr. Plante, do you have answers for General Browner?"

Isabel headed to the far end of the room, where she joined the other wallflowers in the standing-room-only third-class section.

Brandon handed a flash drive to the Air Force technician. "Good to see everyone again." *Really?* "My team and I," *God*, "modeled the crowd violence in China at the individual level." A hokey human profile appeared on screen. "Interactions between individuals." Two profiles with a line between them! "And at the crowd level." Multiple profiles *ingeniously* connected by lines. "We created an agent for each Infected and assigned it attributes like age, gender, disabilities." A short video appeared in which overlying triangles at a bridge attacked in unison with rioters. "I'm happy to report it was a complete success."

After a long silence, General Browner asked, "How do you define success?"

"Our model now matches Infecteds' behavior. We can use it predictively, to manage crowds, and forensically, to aid our understanding of Infecteds' psychology."

"Marvelous. How can my *troops* use it?" Browner asked.

Brandon was clearly at a loss. Those slides, model, and video with triangles would have wowed an academic conference. Stoddard said, "Let's hear him out. What *have* you concluded, Dr. Plante?"

Brandon caught Isabel's eye before launching defensively into to a laundry list of generalities. Crowds are complex adaptive systems that seem chaotic, but have an underlying order. They self-assemble in geometric patterns based on interaction with each other and the environment. Infected crowds have no leaders, and engage in no verbal communication. "But while we can't read facial expressions or see gritted teeth or balled fists at a distance, Infecteds do all face in the direction in which they ultimately attack. That's a form of communication."

No one seemed impressed. Brandon said they had observed no cohesive subgroups like families, students or coworkers. Every Infected of either gender and any age exhibited identical behaviors.

"Such as?" Browner prodded.

"Well, they respect each other's personal space." Isabel erased her reflexive cringe. "Ever see birds on a wire scoot over when a new bird lands? As a crowd grows, Infecteds don't jostle, push or shove. They shuffle their feet to reallocate the shrinking space."

Browner took a moment to compose himself. "Is that it?" he asked ominously.

"Uhm, we do have a preliminary working hypothesis," Isabel winced, "that rising density charges a crowd per Gay-Lussac's law." *Hey!* Isabel thought. *That was* my *idea.* "Gas pressure P divided by temperature T equals a constant k. So the math says that, as crowd density P increases, its potential for violence, T, has to rise proportionally."

Browner said, "That's *if* your 'preliminary working hypothesis' is correct?"

"What the general means," President Stoddard said, "is we're racing the clock."

"We might," Brandon ventured, "develop software to estimate crowd density from imagery and warn how close they are to boiling over. Ten square meters holds a maximum of eighty-four standing people. I'd guess any time density exceeds twenty Infecteds per ten squares, they could get violent. At forty, they're at the brink. But that software will take some time."

The president said, "MIT and Chicago estimate that we only have a few weeks. As does, I might add, Professor Miller's sister. So, what have you concluded *definitively?*"

Brandon said they had noted scaling in motion-capture data: the actions of an individual being amplified by crowd reaction. And herding behavior: Infecteds at the rear, who had no contact with a trigger, joined in the attack. Infecteds didn't form demonstrating crowds addressing an issue, expressive crowds at an emotional event, or spectating or escaping crowds. They were casual crowds, emerging spontaneously, having no larger purpose and little interaction with each other.

"The key is that casual crowds have no established norms of behavior to restrain excesses and can morph, in an instant, into violent mobs when a physical crowd, unconnected by common cause, becomes a psychological crowd, united by a shared social identity. That tipping point happens when crowds become deindividualized by the environment."

Browner organized his workspace, drew a deep breath, and turned to the president. "Sir, I need something useful from these scientists. All I've gotten so far, out of MIT, is," he read, "'Target annihilation by diffusing particles in inhomogeneous geometries.'"

"What the hell does *that* mean?" the president asked.

"Well, apparently, you've got better odds hiding in a large, complex environment like an office building than in a wide-open field. Aside from the fact that that's *obvious*, I intend for my men to fight, sir, not hide. And I don't care about Infecteds' personal space. I need *practical* advice on how to defeat them militarily."

Stoddard asked Brandon, "When does this deindividualization tipping point occur?"

Brandon waxed academic. "A psychologist named Le Bon," *off we go*, "tried to figure out how people could've behaved so cruelly during the French Revolution and proposed that the crowd *itself* caused violence. In doing so, Le Bon not only anticipated the tragedies of the twentieth century, like the Holocaust, but actually contributed to them."

"How?" Browner challenged, his patience wearing thinner by the comment.

"Le Bon thought that, as crowds expand and the risk of punishment declines, people descend into hypnotic anonymity and begin to feel invincible. We now call that 'charged.' Their individuality is submerged into the mass and they become subject to the contagion of any passing emotion. We now call that 'suggestible.' If the crowd says it's your solemn duty to kill evil noblemen, you commit unthinkable crimes—the universality phenomenon—which is the subconscious excuse of looters everywhere that if everyone is doing it, it must be okay. Later, Freud proposed his primitive horde theory that we built our civilized nature atop barbarism inherited from aboriginal man, and that mobs sweep aside our modern veneer and expose those underlying primitive behaviors."

"*So*," Browner interrupted, "I get how Le Bon *anticipated* mass crimes against humanity. But how did he *contribute* to them?"

"Le Bon prescribed rules to control crowd behavior. Simplify, substitute exaggeration and shouted, responsive affirmation for proof, repeat points over and over."

"Sounds like a good stump speech to me," Stoddard remarked to muted chuckles. Eying the fuming general, he quickly said, "Anything else?" before Browner could speak.

Brandon rummaged through his idea hamper. "Well, people in a crisis tend to behave normally until long after they *should* have panicked. Look at video of people calmly departing the Twin Towers just before the first collapsed. They walk when they should run. Duck when they should drop.

During unfamiliar events like an emergency, people follow a schema, or script: a pattern of behavior deeply ingrained and remarkably resistant to change. They *want* everything to be okay, so they believe anything consistent with that hope and disregard inconsistencies until long after they should've known better."

The president said, "I presume that might explain why the public is, to a surprising degree, largely ignoring the approaching threat?"

Brandon replied, "I think Le Bon would've approved of your handling of the crisis, sir." Isabel recoiled from his ass-kissing and caught Browner's eye. Brandon said, "Le Bon suggested that regular communications, strong leadership, and a good information campaign will do wonders in . . . well, in . . ."

"In pulling the wool over everyone's eyes?" Stoddard said. "I know that's what you're all thinking. I agonize *constantly* over keeping SED secret. But for me to go down in history as a criminal, there'll have to *be* a history. *Survival* is what I'm focused on. As General Browner points out at least twice a day, that justifies hard decisions. What if I told the truth; everyone quit work; millions died from treatable diseases, crime, riots, starvation; and we cured SED before it even arrives? Did telling the truth make me a better man?"

No one dared an answer. Into the silence, Browner boomed, "Professor Miller?" The wallflowers turned to her. "Does any of this stuff make neuro*scientific* sense?"

Not really, she thought. But she said, "Most complex behaviors are associated with the cerebral cortex—the outermost, centimeter-thick layer of the cerebrum. Cortex means 'bark,' like on a tree. It's *not* needed for biological survival. Some species, like birds, don't have one, and others survive after theirs are removed. But it's where a lot of our higher mental functions occur. If severely damaged in humans, behavior becomes stereotyped, like Infecteds. In extreme cases, you're left with only the motor controls of the limbic system and a reduced amount of memory function, which sounds like some of the WHO reports about low-functioning Infecteds."

"But what about," Browner said, "these theories about crowd behavior?"

Brandon clearly waited for her either to rescue him, or *emasculate* him, as he'd once described her public rebuttal in a seminar. She tried a third way. "Well, Jung's collective unconscious theory competed with Freud's primitive horde theory and is explainable by commonalities in the subcortical thalamus and limbic system."

That answer upset everyone—Brandon for lack of support, Browner for theoretical bullshit, and the impatient president for droning on. She decided to try an honest answer. "Infecteds don't need crowds to become deindividualized. Their brain damage does that. Humans normally experience cognitive dissonance. They subconsciously question whether every action they take was something *I* would do? A *good* person feels guilt, for instance, in the case of the private self, over pocketing a blind man's wallet, and embarrassment, in the case of the public self, at having been seen doing so. But Infecteds have no sense that they're good because there *is* no they. No self. With no cognitive dissonance, there is no ethics, morality, shame, embarrassment or mortification."

"So they commit atrocities without compunction," Browner summarized.

Isabel had to agree. "Le Bon, Freud, and Jung all described how freeing people from social norms increases the likelihood of violence. People become ruled by urge, instinct, and impulse—their animal passions. One of those is the instinct of struggle, a desire to eliminate anything standing in the way of satisfying their other urges. Each of the Infecteds in these riot videos was headed somewhere. Maybe grocery shopping, fleeing a threat or hooking up with a girlfriend. Those troops were *literally* standing in their way."

"And that same brain damage explains the crowd violence too?" Browner asked.

"Yes. Normal, introspective minds get lost in thought, oblivious to the outside world. Infecteds are the opposite. They have *no* meaningful inner life, so they're entirely focused on *external* stimuli, heightening their responsiveness to environmental cues. If you sit totally still next to an Infected, their attention will drift away. But scratch your nose and they'll notice. In a crowd, all their cues come from the behavior of the crowd around them. They are so absorbed by that environment they lose the ability even to differentiate themselves *from* the crowd. They *are* the crowd and go with the flow to a degree impossible for people with intact self-identities. If your or my passions were so roused that we joined a riot, we'd still feel an inner eye watching us, judging us. Not so the Infecteds."

Stoddard said, "So your conclusion is that Infecteds have no sense of self, and that's why they throw their lives away in riots? And you're sure about that science?"

Brandon's gaze bore into her. "I have a source at the WHO," she said, "who confirmed that their autopsies will conclude that SED damages the insular and medial prefrontal cortices. That could obliterate self-awareness and produce a kind of 'self-amnesia,' destroying even memories of what consciousness had been like."

General Browner said, "I would think the opposite would happen. If someone lost their sense of self, they wouldn't give a crap about what some crowd wanted."

"I agree it's paradoxical," Isabel replied. "Membership in a group *is* typically derived *from* an individual's self-concept. But put them in a crowd, and their lack of separate identity allows for total immersion. They throw their lives away because they've lost even the concept of their own individuality. They bond to the mob's goals, which include elimination of threats to the *mob*. Sufferers of this type of brain damage have been known to commit horrendous violence against members of *other* groups in conflict with *theirs*."

Browner nodded slowly and said, "*Kudos*, Dr. Miller. That all makes sense."

The president said, "Could we get Dr. Miller a chair?" Maldonado rose to look for one, but a mid-level naval officer stood and gave his to Isabel, who smiled in thanks, sat at the table and cast a worried look at Brandon, who wouldn't return it.

"Sir," Browner said to the president, "I'm hearing that our principal tactic to slow the spread of the disease, blocking migration, will also result in the most extreme violence. We need practical advice for our unit commanders."

Isabel blurted out, "I'm sure Dr. Plante has some crowd control advice." *I hope.*

Everyone turned to Brandon. "Well," he said before remembering to stand, "we could use stewards to monitor the crowd and report in if they seem to be growing agitated."

The Homeland Security secretary said, "You mean undercover agents?" Brandon preferred the term "stewards." "Don't you think a guy in HazMat gear might stick out?"

Brandon looked at Isabel for help. "There's no reason," he said, "that you couldn't recruit *Infecteds* to keep you apprised of any trouble brewing in a crowd of other Infecteds."

Isabel's eyes darted from face to face. She imagined figurative crickets chirping.

The president seemed far away when he asked, "Where does this all end? What kind of society has no constraints of morality and ethics, ruled by primitive urges, excited by animal passions?" Isabel belatedly realized the president was addressing her.

"Maybe we should hire a *philosopher?*" Isabel suggested in earnest.

The faint hint of a smile penetrated the president's despair. "You're as close as we've got. Give it a shot. Will Infecteds be able to organize a functioning society?"

Everyone waited. *How should I know?* she thought. "Well, sir, Thomas Hobbes, in *Leviathan,* defined social contract theory—citizens trading individual rights for something of value. 'I agree not to kill you in exchange for you agreeing not to kill me.'"

"And thus," Stoddard said, "government arose. Can Infecteds abide by contracts?"

"I honestly don't know. But if they can't, they will live, as Hobbes described, in a state of nature, and their lives will be 'solitary, poor, nasty, brutish, and short'."

The distant president took a deep breath, which he let out noisily, and finally said, "On that, meeting adjourned." Everyone rose and filed out, Brandon among them.

Browner tapped her shoulder. "Oh, hi." Brandon was whispering to Maldonado.

"I take it there's history between you and Dr. Plante?" Browner suggested. Isabel made a *Where'd-you-get-that?* face. "Do you play poker?" he asked. Isabel shook her head. Brandon exited the room. "Well, the advice of this 'particularly intimidating son-of-a-bitch,' is that I wouldn't take it up if I were you. Not your game."

She turned, but Browner was gone. She needed to guard her expressions better . . . and watch what she said in the observation room. She ran after Brandon, but had to wait on the next elevator. She called out to him across the parking lot. He climbed into their SUV. Out of breath, she joined him there. "Didn't you hear me?" The car sped away. "You're not pissed about that, are you?" He ignored her. "*Please!* Would you grow up?"

"I've been working on this for five days! But hey, crowd theory must be pretty simple since *you* have no problem expressing definitive professional opinions about it!"

"Oh, every psych major studies crowd fucking theory, Brandon!" *Okay, that was cruel.* "I don't mean . . ."

"I know what you mean."

She knew she should keep her mouth shut. "And I've had all of, what, *eleven* days? With my brain-damaged sister? But no pressure, right? Just give your best guesses to the president, the Pentagon, attorney general, Homeland Security, the FBI . . ."

Brandon said, "I thought the FBI was on the outs." Isabel froze, like a deer. "When I was getting my security badge, Maldonado warned me that the FBI was trying to worm their way in. You've been talking to them, haven't you?" Isabel focused on her poker face. "*Jeez,* Iz. You're gonna get in big fucking trouble."

"Why are they keeping the FBI out of the loop anyway?" she whispered. "I mean, the rest of the alphabet is there. DOD, CIA, NSA, DHS, TSA, CDC, NIH . . ."

"Stoddard fucking *hates* the FBI director. Still don't watch the news? The guy investigated the president's wife for financial improprieties *during* the last campaign! Just be careful." She was about to thank Brandon when he said, "And I never should've invited you to this meeting. From now on, just stay the *fuck* out of my area!"

Chapter 16

"W-T-F?" said Chloe. Noah cautioned his daughter on language. "They're *letters*, dad. *This* is your surprise?" He'd given Natalie a Groupon for two spa days and picked the kids up from school. "A *gun* store?" Her thirteen-year-old brother, Jacob, looked ecstatic.

"We're taking a little course," Noah said, opening the tailgate of their new giant SUV. The rifle he handed his aghast daughter sagged in her grip. Chloe held it like a bomb awaiting defusing. They each carried their rifles inside. Their pistols were in Noah's bug-out bag, and he also lugged the shotgun. "*Dad*?" Chloe whispered. "Have you gone *nuts*?"

Salesmen watched the news on a small TV even though the previously empty store was now full of shoppers. A small woman inspected a large shotgun. A man in hospital scrubs perused pistols under glass. Two pierced girls, hair shaved on one side and dyed pink on the other, nodded wide-eyed as a salesman demonstrated how to load their new rifle.

Noah's Western-wear-clad salesman peeled away from the TV and ambushed Noah's children. "It's *Miller* time!" He apologized. "Lost some hearing in the Corps."

Chloe glared at her father. On the walk to the back, the salesman asked Noah, "You followin' that Chinese flu? Those customers back there don't believe a word outa the president's mouth. Think he's coverin' up some plague that turns people bloodthirsty. You were my first big customer, so I was wondering if maybe you know something?"

"Just what I see on TV," Noah replied. Chloe looked at him, knowing he was lying. "But I think it's gonna get bad," he added, feeling guilty.

They stopped at a countertop and laid the imposing arsenal on a carpet remnant. The muffled sound of firing came from beyond a door labeled, "Range." Chloe kept trying to get Noah's attention. She had lots and lots of questions. The salesman fitted them with headphone-like over-ear protection and large, amber shooting glasses.

"No, thanks," Chloe said, doing emergency repairs on her mussed hair. "Pass."

"You're doing this, Chloe," Noah said. "It's all paid for."

"Does *mom* know you did this?" It was more threat than question.

"Shh," Noah replied as the salesman led them into the firing range. There were half a dozen shooters at the dozen positions. Each used a cable to reel targets out and back in. A young man wearing a private security company jacket fired a revolver. A woman and her two daughters took turns with an antique double-barreled shotgun. A heavier man, probably a veteran, fired an AR-15 three times in rapid succession.

Chloe turned, "Okay!" and almost collided with Noah. "I know experiences are all the rage now, dad, and this one has great selfie potential, but I'm a *no.*"

"Chloe," Noah reasoned, "I'm looking for things we can do as a family."

"So you picked *this?*" she said at glass-breaking pitch.

"Humor me. Please. I'll make it up to you. What do you want?"

"I wanta pierce my belly button." Other than that. "A car at sixteen."

"Done," Noah said disingenuously. It will probably never happen.

They passed an elderly white couple with a hunting rifle, an African-American man with a daughter in a plaid school uniform loading a huge handgun, and a young Asian-American couple with a tiny automatic. They laid their weapons at their position.

Chloe joined the salesman and pretended to be attentive by nodding a lot.

"Why don't we start the young lady on the Glock," he said, instructing them on range safety amid intermittent shots from the others. "First rule is, always treat weapons like they're ready to fire. Even if you just unloaded it, assume it's loaded. Keep the barrel pointed downrange, or up at the sky, or down at the ground. Never swing the muzzle across anybody, *ever*, unless you plan to kill them." Noah avoided Chloe's urgent glance. The salesman displayed the empty pistol, pulled the slide back till it locked, released the slide with a *clack*, dry fired it, *click*, and returned the pistol to the table. The whole time, it never pointed anywhere but toward the targets.

Chloe whispered to Noah. "A *nice* car."

The salesman showed Chloe, with Noah and Jacob watching, how to press 9mm rounds into a magazine. Twice she squealed, "Ow!" on pinching her thumb. She held her nail up to Noah and said, "Chipped," as he filled his own magazine. Both kids had trouble loading the ninth and tenth rounds. "That spring'll loosen up some," the salesman said. "Ladies first."

Chloe grew less cocky. Her glances at Noah were now more for reassurance than complaint. The salesman showed her how to seat the magazine firmly, grip the pistol in her right hand, and rest its heel atop her upturned left palm. At full extension, her toothpick-thin arms labored. She attentively followed the salesman's instructions, carefully flicking the safety to fire by feel. Cringing, teeth bared, she finally said, "It's not shooting." The salesman told her to squeeze a little bit . . .

Bam!

Everyone but the salesman reacted. Chloe looked shocked, as if after an accident, then adopted a sickly smile. "Doin' good," her tutor said. "Nine more. Have at it."

She fired again and again, grimacing more than aiming. The salesman reminded her to put the bull's eye atop the pistol's front post, and that post in the notch between the twin forks in the rear. Smokey casings rattled around the firing position and onto the floor. Finally, the slide locked in the rearward position.

"I think we hit paper there with those last couple," the salesman said.

Chloe turned around and stuck her tongue out at Jacob, who noted that she'd only hit the *paper*, not the target *on* the paper. "*You* try it," came Chloe's retort.

Jacob, intimidated, did only slightly better. When Noah's turn came, he was underwhelmed by the pistol's minimal kick. The salesman called "hit" eight out of ten shots and reeled in the target, which was riddled with randomly spaced holes. Some were even inside the outermost "five ring," the salesman called it. One had nicked a clothespin holding the paper, causing it to droop.

Noah gave both kids a pat on the back. The salesman said, "Good enough to scare 'em away from your pond at least," undermining a bit of Noah's confidence.

"What pond?" Chloe asked. "We don't have a . . ." Noah *shushed* her.

The salesman chose not to hear. Noah said, "What about the shotgun?"

"We'll do that last," the salesman replied, hoisting Chloe's "AR," he called it, onto its butt.

"Oh, no," she said, her hands in a defensive stance. "No way, Jose . . . Nuh-uh."

"*I'll* shoot it!" Jacob said, gamely trying to regain his place in the family order.

"Chloe, come on," urged Noah. "We have a deal." She frowned as the salesman showed her how to load the magazine. Noah and Jacob filled their own magazines nonchalantly, as if boys naturally knew how to do such things. But they carefully monitored the instructions given to Chloe. For some reason, they only loaded twenty-seven rounds into thirty-round magazines. Chloe finished last, checked her nails, and cast a mock sneer at Noah as the salesman placed the rifle against her boney shoulder.

"It's too heavy," she said, unable to steady it. The salesman, who had sent the target twice as far downrange as for the pistol, had her rest her elbows on the counter. Chloe finally gave up aiming, closed both eyes and pulled the trigger.

Crack! Fire blazed from the muzzle. The whole thing—flash, blast, recoil—came and went in an instant. Only God knew where the bullet had gone. "You got a scope there, young lady. Simple crosshairs. Try 'em out," suggested the salesman.

She took more time, with the salesman telling her to breath in, let half her breath out, steady, steady. *Crack!* The salesman held a detached rifle scope up to his eye. "Hit!"

"Hah!" Chloe said to Jacob. But by the time she'd fired ten rounds, she rubbed her shoulder and announced she was done. With a little more goading, however, she squeezed off the seventeen remaining rounds, the last couple in the general vicinity of the target.

Even Jacob, for all his boyish thrill at shooting guns, appeared sickly after he'd emptied his magazine. He rolled his shoulder in circles as if to work out a kink.

Noah raised the smooth, cool plastic stock to his cheek. The range stank of spent gunpowder. The target looked large in the sight, but the crosshairs wobbled up, down, right, right, left, up, everywhere but the center. After he controlled his breathing better at the salesman's direction, it was his pounding heart that threw his aim off with each pulse.

"Any *day* now," Chloe said.

The next time the crosshairs passed the vicinity of the bull's eye, Noah pulled hard. The recoil wasn't as bad as he'd expected. Just a jerk against his shoulder. But his brand-new target remained intact. He squeezed off his second shot, which struck paper inside the five ring. "Hit!" More than half of his shots now scored. He got so good, in fact, that the salesman didn't call "hit" if he missed the outermost ring.

Noah laid the rifle down, and the salesman reeled in the target. "Way to go, Dad!" Jacob said, high-fiving him. If that were an Infected, Noah thought, its torso would be a bloody pulp now. For some reason, however, that made him feel queasier.

The salesman forced his lips into a smile. Noah surmised from that that he might not be as good as he thought. "This is pretty short range inside, right?"

"In the Corps," the salesman said, "we qualified at two and five hundred meters."

"Meters?" Noah whistled. "How tiny is the target in the scope at *those* ranges?"

"Don't know. We used open, iron sights, no scope." *Hmm,* Noah thought. The salesman lifted the shotgun onto its butt.

"There's *no* friggin' way I'm shooting whatever that is," Chloe said.

Noah urged her, but the salesman said she may be right. Even Jacob shook his head, so Noah stepped up. After getting Noah's okay, the salesman used a tool dangling from his belt to unscrew a plug in the tubular magazine beneath the barrel and showed Noah how to load the shotgun. Noah pressed five rounds up into the tube with his thumb, the last couple requiring hard shoves. As instructed, he pumped the gun to chamber a round and gave Jacob a wink at the sound. He then filled the empty space left by the chambered shell.

"Five in the magazine," the instructor said, "one in the chamber. You always—*always*—keep count of how many rounds you've fired, and how many are left."

Noah raised the heavy gun to his sore shoulder. Chloe retreated and pressed on her ear protectors. Jacob joined her. Noah aimed at the target, which was at pistol range, and flicked the safety to fire. His heart pounded. *BAM!*

Flame exploded from the muzzle. "Hoooly *shit!*" Noah faintly heard Jacob say.

Noah felt jarred and out of sorts. He tried to fire a second time before realizing he hadn't pumped the gun. Kerchunk. *BAM!* "Can I wait outside?" Chloe asked. Kerchunk. *BAM!* Kerchunk. *BAM!* Kerchunk. *BAM!* Kerchunk. *BAM!* Kerchunk. *Click.*

"Five in the mag, Dad," Chloe said. "Plus one in the chamber makes six." She stepped up. "I'll shoot the thing. *Once!*"

The target and the clothespins had disappeared. The salesman hung a new target, sent it downrange, and loaded a round in the magazine with a slight smile on his face.

Chloe groaned dramatically on hoisting the shotgun to her shoulder. The salesman again had her rest her elbows on the carpet remnant. Wisps of smoke swirled at the shotgun's muzzle and from the open ends of spent casings. *BAM*! "Owww!" Chloe laid the weapon down. "I'm thinking BMW," she said on passing Noah.

"How 'bout you, scout?" the salesman said to Jacob. He could hardly refuse. *BAM*!

Jacob too lay the weapon down immediately. "Hurts, huh?" Chloe asked. Jacob denied that he felt any trace of pain, so she poked at his sore spot and he slapped her hand.

"Helluva weapon," the salesman pronounced. "Those Glocks put 340 foot-pounds of energy on a target. But that Remington packs *3,000* foot-pounds of stopping power."

Chloe, ready to leave, was none too happy when the salesman had them attach holsters. "So *that's* why we had to wear belts." They holstered pistols and, with help, slung rifles across their chests in patrol carry and headed for the exit.

But it wasn't an exit. The door lead into a cavernous, darkened metal building. Chloe looked at her father quizzically before entering. Two men wearing identical black pants bloused into combat boots, ear and eye protection, and black T-shirts emblazoned with the words Tactical Instructor, awaited them. "Fresh meat?" the older man asked.

"Daaad?" Chloe whispered plaintively.

"That was just the checkout," the salesman explained. "*This* is the class. Four hours today, four tomorrow." Even Jacob seemed uncertain. As Noah's eyes adjusted to the gloom, he saw a maze built out of stacks of tires filled with dirt that leaked from holes.

"Young lady," one black-clad man said, "this is one of the finest tactical training courses in the country. Over the next two sessions, you're each gonna fire six hundred rounds with those Glocks, another six hundred with those ARs, and your dad's gonna be icing his shoulder for a week after blasting away at pop-ups with that blunderbuss."

"Daaad!" whined his daughter through bared teeth.

Noah took a deep breath. "BMW," he offered. "Three Series. Late model year."

"Fully loaded," she countered. "Top-of-the-line stereo. Brand freakin' new."

Noah shook her hand. Chloe put her ear protectors on and said, "Okay, let's shoot some stuff."

Chapter 17

From across the cafeteria, Isabel saw Rosenbaum and Street talking. She went to get a cup of coffee beside them. "Oh! Hi." They nodded in greeting as she joined them.

"Even though the laws of evolution apply to viruses," Street continued, "descent with modification, natural selection, adaptation—viruses aren't alive. They're just fiendishly simple subcellular assemblages of proteins, nucleic acids, lipids, and carbohydrates. They can't even reproduce without coopting the machinery of a living cell. And while they've been biding their time in the permafrost, we built aqueducts and the space station and grew confident in our supreme mastery of all things."

"Sounds like you think SED is punishment for our hubris," Hank commented.

"You have a better theory?" Street then turned to Isabel to answer the question she hadn't asked. "The jewel wasp, *Ampulex compressa*. It snakes its stinger into a cockroach's brain, sensing its way to the regions that control movement, and releases a cocktail of neurotransmitters that causes the roach to lose all motivation to move until directed. It walks the cockroach around by its antenna like on a leash to someplace safe and lays eggs on its underside. The enslaved roach then stands guard until the eggs hatch."

Isabel looked at Hank and said, "Good one." Street seemed pleased.

Isabel and Hank joined Beth in the observation room. Next door, Emma was scribbling away. "What's the latest?" Isabel asked.

Beth said, "She researched schizophrenia and multiple personality disorder."

Hank snorted. "She can't imagine having a self, and thinks you're crazy."

Emma was hunched over. Isabel asked, "What do you think she's writing?"

"She's still working on her Rules," Beth said.

"What *rules*?" asked Isabel. A cringe creased Beth's face as she looked at Hank.

"She's writing rules," Hank answered. "We got a copy when she was being tested."

"So you just went in there and *took* them?" Isabel asked. *Of course they did.* "Can I see?" Hank rummaged through the bulging paper files he now carried. "You can keep this copy." Isabel failed to muster a thank you. She felt guilty, but not guilty enough to give the printout back. Besides, everyone else had read them.

Emma had first written, "Spillover of P. horribilis from Neanderthals to humans," then a few pages of random minor thoughts. Then columns of data, calculations Isabel couldn't follow, scatter plots presumably corresponding to outputs, trend lines fit to clouds of dots, and slopes calculated for each line. She looked up at Hank utterly mystified.

"The head of immunology recognized some of the calculations instantly." Hank explained the "SIR Model" from the mass action principle of mathematics, which divides populations into capital S susceptible, capital I infected, and capital R removed, which with SED means dead unless there's natural immunity or vaccination. "The subscript is time, so when you see $S_{(42)}$, it's number of susceptibles in month 42. Beta is the probability of a susceptible S contracting SED from an infectious I." Emma's math grew unrecognizable and ever more advanced. It was like watching Emma's damaged brain slowly moving from recovery, to discovery of a new talent.

"Amazing," Hank said, "isn't it? In the end, Emma concluded we'd never attain disease-free equilibrium, struck DFE, and circled EE—endemic equilibrium. SED will continuously infect humanity forever, the conclusion also reached by Chicago and MIT. But unlike them, Emma concluded that the uninfected population never actually reaches zero. The university models artificially drop uninfected communities to zero at MVP—Minimum Viable Population—which Chicago thinks is 500, but MIT says is 750, both far south of the 5,000 necessary to avoid inbreeding. But Emma thinks that somewhere, in some remote cave, there'll always be an *un*infected Adam and Eve staving off extinction."

Hank said some of the other variables, like theta, are baffling the epidemiologists. Isabel cleared the window and said into the microphone,

"Emmy?" Her sister lowered her notebook, apparently without irritation. "Did you know we have a copy of your notes?" Emma nodded. "Can I ask you a few questions? First, what does theta stand for?"

"It's the expected Uninfected suicide rate. I could use your help. What is the probability that an Uninfected will commit suicide if they've been exposed to SED, or anticipate imminent grievous violence, or suffer from depression caused by the loss of loved ones or bleak prospects, or because the voices in their heads told them to?"

Isabel said, "Most people, I guess, would probably hang on until the last, hoping for a miracle. But theta wouldn't be zero."

Emma said, "Can you make a deterministic estimate?"

Isabel held her hands up. "I dunno. Zero-point . . . *eight* percent?" Emma recorded her answer. "Emma, I have no idea. That was . . . a joke."

"Should I laugh?" Emma asked, apparently willing to try.

"No," replied Isabel. "Can you just give us the *gist* of what you've concluded?"

Emma didn't once refer to her notes. "Rates of infection and death by violence are directly proportional to population density. On an urban block with 2,500 residents, people would be infected or killed at one hundred times the rate as on a suburban block with twenty-five residents. New York City has densities exceeding 3,000 residents per block, the highest force of spread F in America. After attempts at orderly evacuation of the city culminates in desperate flight, 60 to 90 percent of its remaining population two days after outbreak there will be infected or dead."

"How?" Isabel asked. "For a few days everybody would just stay put at home."

"Doors can be broken," Emma explained. "Buildings burned. Water, power, and heat shut off. Some Uninfecteds would ban together to fight. Others couldn't resist responding to calls for help. Others would make a belated run for it, or a premature isolation breach for foraging, or suffer a nervous breakdown."

"Do you mean that Infecteds will break down doors or burn people out of their hiding places?" Isabel asked.

"Uninfecteds will kill Infecteds. So Infecteds will kill Uninfecteds." Her answer left Isabel, Hank, and Beth speechless. Emma elaborated. At first, Uninfecteds will break through doors to kill Infecteds. Then it reverses as the numbers tilt in favor of the Infecteds. Beth rushed from the room looking terrified. "The question," Emma continued, blind to their distress, "is whether Uninfecteds kill more Infecteds than *vice versa*."

The two Uninfecteds had no questions, so Emma continued. "The American coasts should turn first, then the center, with remote areas in Nevada and Montana last. When you don't know where SED will break out, the most at-risk regions statistically lie between major cities. The single greatest risk is in rural northeastern Pennsylvania because of its proximity to New York, Philadelphia, Boston, and Washington."

Isabel asked, "What about isolation? Hide somewhere?" *Our plan!* she thought.

"At the individual level, that works until it fails," Emma said, "which it always does given enough time. Nations will close borders. Then states, provinces, counties, and cities. Then neighborhoods, homes, and finally individual rooms. But in each case, the isolation will be breached either from the outside by Infecteds or from the inside by Uninfecteds."

Hank rubbed his eyes under his glasses. Isabel, slumping, stared into the abyss.

"It will spread anisotropically, and is best modeled mathematically by fractals. Tendrils will follow transportation networks toward population centers. The heterogeneity of population density means isolated pockets of Uninfecteds will survive well into the pandemic. And the outbreak will appear to halt several times before resuming inexorably. We're currently experiencing that in northern China, at least as seen from our distance."

Isabel realized her eyes were closed in silent prayer, like on take-offs and landings.

"At the micro-level, network science describes how SED will spread among intimate contacts. The first to contract it will be family members, health workers, law enforcement, and caregivers. Assuming long bonds are severed, travel is shut down, SED will propagate like agricultural infestations across a two-dimensional terrestrial lattice. But instead of drifting on atmospheric currents, the pathogen will travel by foot."

"Okay," Isabel said. "I think that's enough." Emma returned to her notebook. Hank hunched forward. Isabel flipped through Emma's notes without really seeing them. Math was ultimately replaced with text. At the top of the latter was the word, Rules.

"Before you get into that," Hank asked, "may I interrupt you?" It took a moment for Isabel to look up. "I have a question." He held a pen poised over a sheaf of papers. "Could you complete this sentence for me: I am [blank]."

Isabel was slow to register that he'd asked a question. *"What?"*

"It's just a . . ." he began before faltering. Beth returned, composed but drained. Hank said, "I wanted to get a list of characteristics that you might ascribe to yourself. You know, how would you fill in the blank? I am . . . ?"

"Is this another stupid questionnaire, Hank?" He gave a half-shrug. He too seemed to be losing interest in their research given what they were facing. "So you had Emma answer that question?" He nodded. "And what did *she* say?" He replied that he'd rather get her responses first. "You're not *getting* my responses. How did Emma answer?"

Hank said, "After some back and forth over the pronoun *I*, she finally said," he read, "'I am female. I am smart. I am capable. I am . . .' and this is interesting, 'under control. I am an epidemiologist.' And 'I am attractive.' I wanta get a baseline from you."

"Okay. *I am pissed* because there's a lot of shit going on that I'm not privy to."

"*You're* not privy? I'm not the one running off to the White House every other day."

Beth clearly wanted something. "Yes, Beth?" Hank asked.

"Right before Emma added 'I am attractive,' she looked in the mirror."

"And you think that's in any way significant?" Hank obviously didn't.

"She was out of things to say, so she looked at the mirror and said she was pretty. Like she didn't know till she looked. Who doesn't already know something like that?"

Isabel said, "Good observation. Log it." What would have been Beth's grin at her triumph just days ago was now only a fleeting break in her dismal visage.

Isabel went to her "office" in the cafeteria and settled in to read Emma's notes. At first, each entry was like Beth's logbook: a random, serial list of experiential knowledge. "Negative pressure. Four seal breaks a day. Six cameras." Then they grew more abstract. "Balance is more sustainable in an unstable system. Economies of scale require centralized organization. Biological interconnectedness is the most natural bonding mechanism."

They were organized by color. Red was "social order." When she discussed laws, breaches of the peace, limits on gathering size, social contracts like, "Parents raise children; children care for parents," Emma used a red pen. *Why red*? *Was it random?*

Blue was reserved for economic issues. Water, food, shelter, clothing, medicine, energy, machine tools, metallurgy, raw materials. Barter vs. currency. Private vs. public ownership. Labor compensation. Capital allocation. Market vs. command economy. And, most interestingly, use of "Uninfecteds"—capitalized—"for their creativity and ingenuity."

Emma used green for musings about population. Pages of calculations culminated in US estimates two years hence. $I_{(24)}$—Infected—139 million. $S_{(24)}$—Uninfected—11 million. Isabel rocked back. She couldn't even begin to imagine what was coming. But Emma had precisely calculated the horror without the slightest flutter of trepidation. She seemed, in her green notes, to give no consideration to governance. No communism vs. capitalism, or liberal vs. conservative. The closest she came to blue vs. red was, "Government testing and elimination of the unproductive vs. market-based, Malthusian solution and self-help?" *Whatever that means.*

Purple was "geography." The need for defensible borders, internal IDs and external passports, border guards, immigration, a demilitarized buffer to prevent friction, and a list of infrastructure required for housing and agriculture.

The final color, black, was for "security." Equip with small arms, not complex systems. *Equip whom*? How large of a standing force the economy could support—four to five million. *Jesus.* Most interesting were three black notes, randomly scattered. "Overcome survival instinct by concentrating." Did Emma think crowd excitation could be harnessed by herding Infecteds together? "War is unproductive; avoid." That was encouraging, until Emma found the only observation anywhere written in capital letters. "NUCLEAR WEAPONS?" Isabel placed all her hope on the question mark.

It was a fascinating journey through a brilliant, damaged but recovering mind. She lost track of time. When a covey of white lab coats appeared, it was dark outside.

"*There* you are," Nielsen said on spying her. "We're ready to introduce other Infecteds into your sister's room. You should observe . . . in case it goes wrong."

"What others?"

"The other subjects we have under observation," Nielsen replied.

"*What*?" Isabel snapped. "Why wasn't I told there were others?"

"I *am* telling you. The Pentagon wants you to determine if they can engage in cooperative behavior. Raise an army, build pyramids, or whatever. The chairman of the Joint Chiefs asked for you by name."

Isabel tried not to smile at the important mission as she demanded to see the other Infecteds first. There were eight. Four were too dangerous. Four were acceptable candidates for introduction to Emma's room, one marginal. "Subject Zero Zero Eight tests closest to your sister in cognitive function, so we're introducing her first. And she won't pose a threat. She's twelve. The daughter of our ambassador to China." Nielsen flipped through the girl's chart as they walked. "She's lived all over the world. Gone to American schools. Speaks English, Mandarin, a little French, a little Arabic. Straight-A student."

Stapled to Nielsen's paper chart was a photo of a waifish, expressionless blond girl. With braided hair and black eyes, she looked like a possessed Heidi. They entered a wing Isabel had never visited and passed repeated security checks. The little girl had contracted SED in Beijing during the embassy's evacuation.

A Marine scrutinized Isabel and summoned a sergeant. Nielsen said, "What's the holdup?" The sergeant held Isabel's ID in two gloved hands. "Oh-for-God's-sake!" Nielsen snapped. "It's her twin *sister.*" They were allowed to pass and joined a nurse in a tiny observation room adjacent to a small hospital room. Sitting erect in a chair, every strand of her long blond hair in place, was "Sam"—Subject Zero Zero Eight. Her forearms were bandaged from wrist to elbow. "She got hurt during the evacuation," Nielsen said.

Isabel pulled the lone microphone close. "Samantha?" The little girl tilted her head but still stared into space. "How are your arms doing?"

Sam raised them and looked at the bandages. "They're fine."

"My name is Dr. Isabel Miller. My sister, Dr. *Emma* Miller, is a patient in the hospital just like you. We're going to move you into Emma's room, okay?"

Sam squeaked out, "Okay," then returned her gaze to empty space. *No*, Isabel realized. *Not empty space.* She was looking at the door, and had been when Isabel arrived.

The next few subjects were Zero One Zero, an African-American Marine guard, also from the Beijing embassy, Zero Zero Nine, a middle-aged Caucasian housewife who had been touring the Great Wall, and a non-talkative "borderline," Zero Zero Five, who was a Chinese-American industrial engineer on assignment to Harbin. All but the last had well-functioning verbal skills. On the way back to Emma's room, Nielsen led Isabel past more closed doors.

Isabel stopped. "Who's in here?"

"Not one of the candidates," Nielsen replied. "Too dangerous."

Isabel entered. The observation room was empty. The lights next door were dim. "Dr. Miller!" Isabel sat at the window. The patient may have lain among the piles of twisted bedding, but Isabel could make nothing out so she raised the lights slightly.

A blur of berserk flailing erupted in Isabel's face. "Ah!" she exclaimed, flinging herself backwards, away from the fury that sprung from beneath the window to pound the shatterproof glass. The crazed woman's gray hair flew wildly. But for the smart glass between them, Isabel knew, she would've sustained severe if not fatal injuries.

The woman quickly exhausted herself. Her futile mauling of the person unseen behind the frosted glass lost its vigor. The shock Isabel felt morphed into . . . disgust? The black-eyed woman's snarling attempts at savagery—clawing and butting the window, heedless of pain—were both pathetic and deeply disturbing. Her final blows were little more than open-palmed slaps that finger-painted in the blood from the cut on her forehead.

"I guess," Isabel said, "someone now needs to go in there and suture that cut."

But Nielsen looked back at her, biting lips curled over her teeth, and shook her head. "We can't open her door without, probably, having to shoot her."

"How do you *feed* her?" Isabel asked.

"We don't." Isabel's mouth gaped. "She's dying, Isabel. In the wild, she'd be dead in hours. Minutes. If we open that door, she'll die in seconds."

"So you're just going to *starve* her to death?" Isabel asked. "This is a *hospital!*"

"We're waiting on guidance," Nielsen replied, "from the medical ethics office. We've got feeding tubes, obviously, but she'll outrun a tranq gun. Captain Ramirez is training on Tasers, but Plan B—a bullet—comes about a half second after a miss with the Taser."

The woman crawled to her bed. Her chart said she was fifty-four. A doctor volunteering at a hospital in northern China. The waste can was upended. A chair lay on its side. Towels covered the bathroom floor. Nielsen said, "She was recovering from leukemia and was immuno-compromised. If the Chinese hospital staff hadn't bundled her up in an old straight jacket that we removed while she was sedated, she'd have become an indirect SED fatality. And she may yet end up one."

Isabel headed for the door, but looked back. "Why isn't there a nurse in here?"

"Too disturbing," Nielsen said. "We were losing staff."

* * * *

They joined Beth in Emma's observation room, which now had three empty beds. Emma scribbled in her notebook. It seemed almost normal back in this wing. The room behind the three women began to fill with scientists, including Hank, Street, and Brandon. The phone on the desk chirped. Nielsen answered and said, "Okay, send her in."

The door to the hospital room buzzed open. In walked the small girl in a pink hospital gown taking tentative steps. She surveyed the room, pausing on seeing Emma only as long as she paused on inventorying the furniture. Emma watched the three guards, who departed upon confirming the Infecteds wouldn't immediately rip each other apart.

"This is mine," Emma said of her bed.

The girl checked out the other three beds, settling onto the one closest to Emma's. The two *Pandoravirus* sufferers then sat, unmoving, for what Hank clocked at five minutes until the little girl said, "Nothing hurts anymore. What are they doing with us?"

"They're watching us," Emma said, gesturing toward the opaque observation window and pointing up at each of the six cameras. Samantha's gaze dutifully followed Isabel's finger. "And they're listening to us and recording everything we say and do."

"Was that a warning?" Nielsen asked. As minutes wore on in silence, Emma's comment did in fact seem more and more like a caution against speaking freely.

"I'm going to sleep," Emma finally announced. "A bird is building a nest on that windowsill. If you see it, wake me up."

Samantha moved to the opposite side of her bed, sat, and stared up at the sill.

Chapter 18

Isabel backhanded Brandon and pointed as their Secret Service car slowed. A crowd had gathered in Lafayette Square across from the White House. Their signs read: Tell the Truth!; Stop Lying About the Zombie Plague!; and Impeach Lyin' Stoddard!

Maldonado escorted Isabel and Brandon down to the Situation Room. Mario Mainetti, CIA director, was briefing the president. "It's deteriorating by the hour with no bottom in sight. Government bastions are holding out in Changchun, Shenyang, and Huludao. Everything else has gone dark. The last redoubts, ironically, are hospitals, which are fighting to keep the sick *out*."

Browner said, "Reverse quarantines. That happened, successfully, in Gunnison, Colorado, during the Spanish Flu in 1918. You could leave, but you couldn't reenter."

Mainetti added, "You should also know, sir, that satellite photos show speaker trucks cruising Harbin streets, dead being stacked on curbs, and remains being burned in parks."

"Sounds . . . medieval," the president said. "Who's doing all that work?"

The CIA director replied, "That's the point, sir. It's gotta be them. The Infected."

"It's a monumental health hazard," Stavros interjected. "The bodies still carry all the other diseases that infect mankind. And as they decompose . . ." Everyone got it.

The president asked, "What next?"

"The press isn't buying," said the CIA director, "that a magnetic storm knocked out satellites. Scientists are denying there was any abnormal solar activity."

The White House chief of staff reacted in frustration. "Our credibility is so shot we can't even knock down rumors of alien invasions and whatnot. Last night, vigilantes posted themselves at cemeteries in Cincinnati to kill reanimated corpses."

CIA Director Mainetti said, "We could dial back on the disinformation campaign."

"Wait!" the chief of staff exclaimed, "That's *us? We're* the source of those rumors?" He slammed his palms on the table, rose, and stormed out of the room muttering curses.

"He'll be okay," said the president of his former campaign manager and long-time political partner. Or so Isabel had read on Wikipedia. "But alien invasions and reanimation of the dead? We're trying to *prevent* panic." Stoddard next asked the secretary of state what he was hearing.

Our embassies were requesting evacuation of dependents and nonessentials after "the Beijing disaster. We waited too long there, Bill."

But Stoddard didn't agree. "Not yet. Too public." Most shrill were the diplomatic cables from Asia, which described a generalized upswing in violence—rioting, killing, looting, rape—ahead of SED's arrival. "What about our plans for Americans abroad?" Stoddard asked. On the screen appeared a map of ships heading to ports labeled with estimates of US citizens to be extracted from each. The numbers were in the millions.

"We're using most of our sealift," General Browner said, "for troop and equipment redeployments. But sir, there are eight million expatriate American citizens and twice again as many traveling abroad for business or pleasure. We can't get 24 million people on sea- or airlift before the virus reaches them."

"Those people," Mainetti commented, "will get sick, turn, and *then* find a way home."

Isabel started when the Homeland Security Secretary pounded the table with his fist. "We've got to *do* something!" Struthers said. "I know I sound like a broken record, but passenger airliners are flying Petri dishes. We're one infected passenger away from a repeat of that Yakutia Airlines flight landing right here. TSA is collecting health declaration forms that, on the honor system, ask if people are sick or have traveled to northern China. But they know if they say yes, they don't board. Patient Zero will be a liar, sir."

The attorney general was shaking his head. "Good luck convincing a court we can prevent US passport holders from returning to their homes."

"What about those thermal cameras you ordered?" Mainetti asked the DHS head.

"We installed the first ones at JFK yesterday," replied Struthers, "and we detained forty-six febrile passengers and airport workers. None, obviously, had SED. A few were just hurrying to catch flights and worked up a sweat."

Stavros said, "One last thing. You ought to know that school attendance is a metric we use to assess the public's level of anxiety. Ninety-five percent attendance is normal, but in several high-information school districts like Manhattan and the San Francisco Bay Area, attendance last week was 85 percent." The public was growing both aware and anxious.

The exhausted president's gaze wandered to Isabel. "Dr. Miller? Complex societies require a high degree of organization and cooperation. Your sister obviously agrees based on the Pentagon's summaries of her notes." Isabel's eyes darted to Browner, who was already staring at her. "But she's up to, what, four roommates now? And they didn't even exchange names until last night?"

"But *that* was interesting," said Dr. Aggarwal. The video appeared without any cue. Emma sat with Eight, Ten, and Nine on the opposite side of the room from the "borderline" Zero Zero Five. "We need names," Emma said after eleven hours of total silence. "Emma, epidemiologist." The spooky little girl said, "Sam," in a high pitch, "seventh grade." The last two said, "Dwayne, Marine embassy guard," and, "Dorothy, housewife."

"Name?" Emma called out to the borderline. Zero Zero Five didn't respond. She asked again. The snarling, middle-aged man said, "Mind your own business!"

Emma put Dorothy, the housewife, in charge of housekeeping. She tasked the Marine to watch *him*, nodding at the loner. Dwayne noisily slid his chair across the room to face Zero Zero Five. "Sam, let's draw." The little girl followed Isabel to the table.

Browner asked, "Any luck figuring out what your sister and the girl are doing?" Isabel shook her head. Emma had drawn a series of disconnected lines, squares, and dots on several pages. Sam traced them to make five copies in total. "Our analysts," Browner said, "haven't been able to ID the schematics or maps they're reproducing—one for each Infected. Maybe an escape route out of the NIH, but . . ." He shrugged.

Dr. Aggarwal said to Browner, "You've asked whether they can organize, and they just did. They exchanged names, reported skills and competencies, undertook tasks."

"And," Browner added, "followed orders from a leader." He looked at Isabel. "But why Dr. *Miller*, and where is she leading them?" The question hung there, unanswered, and Browner extracted from a folder a document that was covered in yellow highlights and festooned with tabs. He gazed over reading glasses at Isabel. "I've read that your sister is adopting ever more sophisticated behaviors. Given that, how can we figure out who's turned and who hasn't? Can we develop a means of detecting," he read again, "the *mark* of *zombiehood*?"

His report quoted Isabel's exact words to Brandon in the observation room about whether there was some indelible mark of zombiehood. Browner was reading from some transcript or report of that conversation.

"No," she replied, though Browner presumably already knew that. "Once they know what we're testing for, they'll adapt."

"We're going to need a detector of some sort," Browner said. "What happens when there are tens, hundreds of millions more like your sister?"

"Then we lose, General Browner," Stoddard replied. "Isn't that the plan?" There was a stir among the military men. "What did your strategists call it: Lose-recover-win?"

"That's not its official name, sir. And maybe we should go into principals only."

But the president gave up the fight. Resignation replaced frustration. Maldonado twisted her wedding ring vigorously. "What was that movie," the president asked, "where 'replicants' illegally returned to Earth, and Harrison Ford used a test to identify them?"

Several people, Isabel included, said, "Blade Runner" and "the Voight-Kampff Empathy Test."

"Right. Could we invent something like that?" he asked Isabel.

Don't shrug again! Isabel thought. "There's speculation that p-zombies might become 'glib' in their use of language that they learned while living in *our* culture, but *mentalistic words* wouldn't arise naturally and would fall into disuse on a Zombie Earth. It's the problem of ineffability: concepts incapable of being described. A mathematician might explain the seventh dimension, and you and I might nod. But he could eventually figure out that we didn't really understand higher mathematical dimensions by questioning us in depth."

The president asked, "Was that a yes or a no?"

She couldn't help herself and shrugged. "A yes, I guess. P-zombies are *informationally* sensitive. Ask them if they noticed a tree fall, and they could describe it. But they aren't *experientially* sensitive. Ask them if they were startled or curious or had other introspective words to describe the *experience* of the tree falling, and they'd have trouble faking it. Their attempts to use mentalistic words like fear, hope, passion, love, or anger would be inexpert and should quickly become pretty comical to an interviewer."

"Comical," Browner noted, "until the Infected figures out what you're doing. And that kind of test would require a subjective call, right? *About* a person under stress, *by* a person under stress. Both potentially armed, both paranoid as hell, both possibly suspecting the other of having turned. What about a physiological test? My wife is obsessed with TV murder porn. One thing I've learned from it is that cops suspect a man of murdering his wife if he sobs, but no tears come out. Could an Infected, subjected to pain say, make themselves sweat? Their heart race? Blood vessels contract? Pass out?"

Everyone turned to Isabel. "Voluntarily?" she replied. "No."

"But let's not go there," the president said. Browner seemed to agree. Aggarwal, however, glared at Browner before looking, for some reason, over his shoulder at Isabel. "All right," Stoddard said. "I guess it's finally time we talk about how we protect our remaining uninfected citizens if a substantial portion of the population turns?"

General Browner looked left and right to confirm that no one else was going to reply. "Mr. President, I have to recommend now that we really do go into executive session, sir."

Maldonado, Isabel, and Brandon rose along with most of the civilians in the room.

"Everyone sit down!" Stoddard said. "I need all the advice I can get. *Sit!*"

Browner eyed the returning civilians, Isabel included, but his mind seemed elsewhere. He nodded at an aide, punched a code into a hard-sided briefcase and ripped open a seal on a folder to which a report was firmly bound. He placed both hands, palms down, on the file as if to hold the lid closed on Pandora's jar, as Street would call it.

"Almost every strategy," Browner said, "that Chicago and MIT ran through their models resulted in the last human on Earth contracting SED sometime between Infection Dates 2250 and 3500—six to ten years from now." Faces around the table reeled from the blow. "If a vaccine is developed, 30 percent of the runs show a small number of uninfected humans maintaining an at-risk toehold, but 70 percent of the time we still go extinct." He never once, Isabel noticed, looked down at the report. "Forced quarantines don't work. You'd have to quarantine people immediately after exposure, when you and more importantly *they* are not sure they're sick. Mass quarantine fails because people will avoid or escape close confinement with others suspected of having a highly contagious, deadly disease. Almost all the strategies modeled," Browner repeated, "conclude that they win, sir. Long-term coexistence is impossible. Sooner or later, we go extinct."

The room was tomblike. Isabel's stomach cramped. Her mouth was so dry she couldn't swallow. Maldonado ceased yanking her diamond ring from side-to-side and flicked a tear from one eye, then the other. Her face barely suppressed torment until a spasm burst forth, and she dashed for the door.

President Stoddard watched her leave, then turned back to Browner. "I know how this works. You said *almost* all the strategies fail. So there's one that doesn't, right?"

"Yessir." Browner caught Isabel's eye but couldn't hold it. "Only one strategy resulted in survival of the human race 91% of the time, although in greatly reduced numbers and in pretty bad shape." For the first time, Browner spread his hands and opened the jar. "Impulsive eradication," he read, enunciating the words with care.

Stoddard appeared too tired for anger. "And what the hell is *that?*"

"Impulsive, sir, means via successive campaigns. Eradication means extermination. You engage in repeated drives, fully expending then rebuilding your resources, as frequently and rapidly as possible, using as much force as you can muster each time. You hit them hard, again and again, until either you lose, or the job is done. And you use, sir, *all* your weapons. All."

The room stirred. Murmurs of sullen agreement and heated rejection. Stoddard leaned forward, revealing the gold seal on his chair's leather back. "Are you proposing that I authorize the mass slaughter of hundreds of millions of infected Americans? Forget Americans. Human *beings?* You think genocide is the winning strategy?"

"I have my doubts, sir," Browner replied. "They may still beat us. We'd have to escalate all the way to nuclear, chemical and biological weapons. Then, we'd have to live in the diminished world that results. But my main concern is whether our troops would execute that campaign, sir. It's a tough, tough ask. One that they're not prepared for."

Stoddard rose unexpectedly. All heads turned to him. "Let me be perfectly clear." He caught every eye in the room as he leaned over the polished wood. "I don't know what else your little report there says. Or what some computer model spat out. But there will be *no* campaign of eradication. *No* mass murder. *No* genocide. *No* Holocaust. Understand?" Heads nodded, but the president demanded a verbal acknowledgment from each chief.

Army, air force, navy, and coast guard chiefs said, nearly in unison, "Yes, sir."

"General Browner?" the president asked the silent Marine Commandant.

"Sir, according to the math, either we destroy them completely, or they destroy us . . . completely. Whereupon this is their White House, their planet, and we no longer exist."

"You heard my order, general," President Stoddard said. "What's your answer?"

Browner, staring back, took a deep breath. "Aye aye, sir." For reasons Isabel couldn't put her finger on—tiny cues in the Marine's expression, body language and vocal nuance—she didn't believe General Browner. Neither, she thought, did the president.

Chapter 19

MCLEAN, VIRGINIA
Infection Date 24, 2200 GMT (6:00 p.m. Local)

Noah was opening Amazon boxes when Natalie called out to him. He put the water purification tablets and Israeli quick-clot battle dressings on his study desk beside blue latex gloves and bluer N95 masks. Cardboard boxes full of stuff were piled to eye level.

His family huddled in front of the TV. Natalie removed her hand from her mouth and pointed at the screen. "The unrest erupted in Beijing upon outbreak of the disease. Camps on the city's outskirts, swollen with refugees from the north, stormed through government lines. We go now to our correspondent on the phone from Beijing. Jennifer?"

The kids were transfixed by live pictures of big explosions in dark streets. The crawl along the bottom said large numbers of rioters had been killed by the PLA.

"I'm able to confirm," the breathless reporter said, "that the Chinese military is firing indiscriminately at rioters." She coughed. "One man told a harrowing tale," she coughed again, "of escape from Harbin. Barely coherent, he said soldiers in chemical warfare gear were, and I'm only repeating what I was told, going door-to-door killing everyone inside crowded apartments. . ." She barely choked out the last before her fit resumed. "He was feverish but said he'd seen thousands of dead on his way to the capital."

Concern creased the anchorwoman's face when all heard the unmistakable sounds of vomiting. "Jennifer, please get somewhere safe." The anchorwoman pressed her earpiece. "I understand that authorities are using tear gas." But Jennifer wasn't gassed. She was ill. "I'm also being told that cell service has just been lost in Beijing. CNN is covering this real time, so I apologize, but to repeat . . ." The TV fell silent.

Natalie held the remote. The kids looked up at Noah. "Is this . . . ?" Natalie asked.

Noah nodded.

"Is this what?" demanded Chloe.

Noah sat in front of the kids. A disease broke out in Russia. Both kids had heard something about it. It's really, really bad, Noah explained, and it's spreading. It kills half the people who get it, and if you survive, you're . . . changed. Maybe violent.

"So that's why we took that gun course," Jacob correctly surmised.

Noah shot a wary glance at Natalie. But she stared, in a daze, at scenes from earlier that day. Long lines of Chinese refugees plodded past machine guns mounted on trucks.

Noah described for the kids, but also Natalie, the brain damage, bland personality, and emotional deficits of Infecteds. "And their pupils are black."

"Oh-my-God," said Natalie as if blown pupils were anywhere near the worst part.

The doorbell rang, and both kids flinched. "The UPS guy," Noah said, peering out.

"Is this what all those packages are?" Chloe asked. "Supplies and stuff?"

Noah led his stunned family to the study and unlocked the door. Despite Noah having made numerous runs to the Old Place hauling supplies, boxes full of gear filled the room. Camouflaged clothing in each of their and the twins' sizes, backpacks, ponchos, tents, tarps, and air mattresses were interspersed with stray packing material and shipping bills. Noah opened the closet. The weapons and ammo drew a gasp from Natalie.

"So how come *you* know this," Chloe asked, "but CNN doesn't?"

Noah told them about Aunt Emma.

"And this disease," Natalie said, hugging herself, "is definitely coming here?"

Noah said, "Maybe. Probably. Soon."

"*Dad*!" Chloe said in a high pitch. He put his arm around her.

"What's your plan?" Natalie asked, suddenly interested. Noah tried to put his other arm around her, but she pulled free.

"To survive," he said looking from face to stricken face. "To avoid infection and the violence that comes with it by isolating ourselves far away from everyone else."

Natalie sank into the desk chair. "Mom?" Chloe said, wrapping her arms around her mother and ultimately curling up in her lap.

"This is really happening," Natalie said, rocking Chloe. "How can that be? How?"

Noah dropped to his knees and hugged them both. Jake clicked on the TV. Two men in lab coats at a podium ignored rudely shouted questions. "We will release the WHO report when we get it. But there are no cases yet of anyone infected with the disease in North America."

"Liars!" Natalie snapped. "Emma is here. They're lying right to our faces!"

Noah had to give them hope. He told them about the renovations to the Old Place down in Virginia. "That's why I sold all our stocks, bonds, IRAs, 401Ks, college funds."

"What?" Chloe asked. "No college?" It was sinking in.

"You remember how far up there the house is? It's totally isolated. We'll be safe."

"The windows were broken," Chloe said. "And there were spiders everywhere."

"They're fixing it up," Noah replied. Generators, electric fences, shipping containers to grow food. His family was starting to understand, and rather than help them cope with their anxiety, it deepened their shock.

"We have complete confidence," the head of the CDC said on TV, "that the Chinese will halt the spread of the disease. They're making great strides . . ."

"They're just going to lie to everybody," Natalie said angrily, "until it's too late!"

"So we got a head start," Noah said. "But we have to move quickly now." The kids' attention was rapt. They wanted to live. Just explain to them how. But Natalie seemed incapable of focusing. Her mind reeled from too many fears. She drew Jacob into her embrace, but her eyes were oddly dry. She needed something to do. "Sweetheart?" Noah said. The kids pulled free and Natalie looked around until she found her husband. "I want you to take the kids to the orthodontist and have their braces removed."

Chloe objected. "I need a few months to close up the gap. And Jake just got his!"

"We're taking them off," Noah explained, "in case there's nobody who can fix a broken wire or whatever. It's only for the time being. Later, hopefully . . ."

"I want to make an appointment," Natalie said into her phone. "Miller, Jacob and Chloe. I want their braces removed. Yes, completely taken off. *Both.* Yes, I know it's all *paid* for!" She hung up, then said, too calmly, "Tomorrow morning at nine."

Jake said, "I've got a history test . . ." but let it drop on seeing his parents' faces.

The silence seemed unnatural. Noah said, "Why don't we go for a family jog?"

"What's that?" Chloe asked, but got no answer. "This is the end of the world, isn't it? Learning to shoot. Getting in shape. Buying baggy, ugly camouflage clothes. Renovating the spider kingdom. We're all gonna die!"

"No!" Noah looked her straight in the face. "Not this family. We'll be ready. We'll make ourselves ready. We'll do what we have to do. Now go put your running shoes on. Everybody meet back here in ten. *Go!*"

To his surprise, they all filed out without objection. *Wow. That* worked?

Chapter 20

BETHESDA, MARYLAND
Infection Date 25, 2200 GMT (6:00 p.m. Local)

Isabel took her accustomed seat at the conference table across from Street and beside Rosenbaum. Brandon at the opposite end was listening to Maldonado. "They didn't know when the pharmacy would reopen. I could see through the police tape that the store had been ransacked. Everything that wasn't stolen was littering the aisles."

A man in a lab coat chimed in. "Our neighbors' house, two doors up, was broken into. We organized a neighborhood watch. I've got the 10:00 p.m. to 2:00 a.m. shift tonight."

"You hear about those guys," said another man, "down in Atlanta at the Epidemic Intelligence Service? Walked in to their boss's office *en masse*. Gonna whistle blow unless the EIS tells everyone everything we know about SED. The director stepped out, and five minutes later the guys were hauled off in handcuffs with their mouths taped shut."

The door burst open. Isabel tensed. What had Noah done now? But Nielsen handed out the long-awaited WHO report. Stamped above "Preliminary Categorization of *P. horribilis* Effects" were the words, TOP SECRET. "We're making this exception to catch you all up on the science." Nielsen quickly covered what they already knew. Neuroinvasive like polio. Neurovirulent like rabies. Short incubation and latency periods. Transmission by aerosolization. "It's giant for a virus, but still small enough to avoid traps in the tracheobronchial or alveolar regions." Each tidbit elicited animated discussion among the scientists. Maldonado, however, slumped over her open but forgotten notebook.

Pandoravirus was too large to cross the blood-brain barrier, so it tricked the body into producing multiple enzymes. Most were neurotoxic and caused the brain damage. One prevented the liver from cleansing the others from the bloodstream. Most fatalities resulted from the build-up of unrelated toxins during the hours that liver function was suppressed.

Nielsen said, "Contagiousness peaks at initial infection, then transitions to a persistent phase with greatly reduced viral shedding around week two. That corresponds to our aerobiologists' readings from the liquid impingers and electrostatic precipitators."

Hank nudged Isabel in case she missed it. "Your sister is less contagious now."

"You mean, like," she said, "it might be safe to let her out?"

"*Hell* no!" Nielsen replied. "It's still airborne and still as contagious as SARS." She returned to the report. The virus's capsid was enveloped by a membrane with a honeycombed plug at one end and a long tubular structure inside. It reproduced by building a replication factory in a host's cytoplasm, not by taking over the cell's nucleus, which was more typical.

"I've never heard of a giant virus infecting humans," Hank said. Street reminded him of some eleven-month-old Senegalese boy who was infected by *Marseillevirus adentis*.

Nielsen noisily turned pages. "Anterograde amnesia in four percent of survivors, with possible Korsakov's syndrome. What the hell is that?"

Isabel said, "Korsakov's is a disruption of the Papez Circuit. Sufferers recall everything that happened before the injury, but nothing after for more than a few minutes."

Nielsen was uninterested and read on. The pathogen is most closely related to *Pandoravirus salinus* found off the coast of Chile a few years ago.

Street said, "*P. salinus* was originally thought to be a whole new branch of the tree of life and was referred to as NLF, New Life Form, until they realized it was a virus."

Nielsen flipped pages. "Phylogenists calculated a TMRCA with *P. salinus* of just under 200,000 years."

Isabel asked, "What is TMRCA?" when the stuporous Maldonado didn't.

"Time to Most Recent Common Ancestor." Street answered. "Mutation rate is like a molecular clock. You compare the variation between two viruses and back-calculate how long they've evolved independently. *P. salinus* only infects amoebae. *P. horribilis* mutated 200,000 years ago and probably spilled over into Neanderthals around then."

No natural immunity had been found. Other labs were working on a blood-based field screen and a vaccine, possibly also for use as immediate post-exposure prophylaxis. "Meaning an antidote?" Maldonado asked, roused from her reverie.

"I'm going to say yes," Nielsen replied, "because I know what you think that word means." Isabel noticed that all of Nielsen's colorful wristbands were gone save a clean, new one. She now had only one cause. Three black letters on blue rubber: SED.

Finally, the report categorized the seven distinct types of brain damage, through which Hank led the meeting.

Type A. "Aggression?" Hank said, speculating on the nomenclature. Damage to the orbitofrontal cortex causing adrenal rages. Type N. "For amnesia?" Damage to the left and right hippocampus. Type P. "Clearly pain insensitivity." Damage to the secondary somatosensory regions of the parietal cortices and the cingulate and insula. Type F. "Focus, maybe." Damage to the callosal fibers connecting the left and right parietal cortex. That accounted for obsessive fixations and "all-trees-no-forest." Type I. "For Inferotemporal, or Imposter." Damage to connections between the inferotemporal cortex, dealing with facial recognition, and the amygdala, involved in emotional response, which Hank said results in everything from mild paranoia to full-blown Capgras delusion in which they think acquaintances are dangerous imposters. Type M. "For Mirror." Damage to the frontal and parietal mirror neurons, disrupting social bonding and empathy.

Finally, Type S. "For Self," Hank said, nodding at Isabel in acknowledgment. "Damage to the insular cortex, which is fundamental to self-awareness, and to the medial prefrontal cortex, linked to processing information about one's self. But no damage to the anterior cingulate cortex, which allows body awareness. All as predicted by Dr. Miller."

"Meaning?" Nielsen prodded in an irritated tone.

"Meaning Emma can brush her hair," Hank said, "but there is no *she* in there."

The meeting adjourned with Street's latest. "*Pseudocorynosoma constrictum*. The parasite releases its eggs into a lake for ingestion by amphipods. After about a month, the cystacanths inside them turn bright orange and become easily visible, causing the amphipods to fall prey to waterfowl, allowing the parasites to reach their intended hosts."

Brandon accompanied Isabel to the elevator, where she said, "I've been trying to imagine 100 million Infecteds, wandering around, suffering from all those deficits."

Brandon put his arm around her. It felt reassuring and familiar. "What's your PSP?" he asked. "Your personal survival plan. That's what everybody's calling it."

"My brother's getting ready." Isabel considered asking Brandon about his plan, but that strayed too close to an invitation to join them, which wasn't her right to extend.

The observation room was empty. Emma huddled with her three high-functioning roommates in a circle. Isabel raised the volume of Emma's whispers. "Breath out through your mouth," Emma said. They exhaled through pursed lips. "In through the nose. Out through the mouth." Emma seemed satisfied and said, "Now spread back out."

Dwayne took a seat in front of the borderline engineer. Dorothy wiped crumbs from the table. Samantha colored in maps. Emma sank in a corner with her notes.

Brandon said, "She's intentionally stoking their agitation by crowding them together so she can then teach them calming techniques."

"Yeah. Get the feeling there's more going on than we know?" Isabel's own calm was losing to encroaching, unaddressed fears. The day was coming when she wouldn't have shatterproof glass or Marines between her and the Infecteds. Noah was in full survivalist freak. Emma was preparing for . . . *whatever*. Isabel was doing nothing. She couldn't even *think* about what was coming without crying. "I feel like," she said, "I should be toughening myself up. Breaking puppies' necks or whatever." Brandon cringed. "I mean do something horrible. Get it over with. Become a badass. Calloused. Hardened."

"Isabel," Brandon said, "it's the apocalypse. Don't overthink it."

After a moment's hesitation, she grinned and for the briefest instant lowered her head to his shoulder. When she looked up, Brandon stared back at her intently.

Chapter 21

While waiting for Brandon at the nurse's station before yet another trip to the White House, Isabel checked Emma's schedule. She was ending a gray block of military time.

In a rarity, the observation and hospital rooms were both empty. Emma's roommates were all off being tested, prodded, scanned and probed. But the hospital room door buzzed, and Emma entered, in a robe and slippers, hair dripping wet, which was odd. You showered on *departing* the Infecteds' hospital room, not *returning* to it. Emma looked almost regal in her serenity and self-confidence. Even caged and under constant threat from jumpy guards there was nothing they could do to her, because there was no *her*.

Isabel cleared the glass. Emma noticed but seemed uninterested. Isabel sat in the observation room day after day. Emma knew she was there but never started a conversation. It was as if she had no need for her sister any more. Isabel pressed the Talk button and tried not to sound upset. "You go for a swim?" Emma nodded. "Wait. *Really?*"

"Do you want me to describe it in elaborate detail? Stand beside a pool, then sit beside it, then dangle my feet in, then slide in, then tread water, then dunk my head. I have a question. Who is that man who sleeps there?" She pointed at the engineer's empty bed.

Isabel was embarrassed that she didn't know Subject Zero Zero Five's name. "His deficits are more severe than your other roommates', but nowhere near as bad as others'."

"He's dangerous," Emma said, removing her robe and, naked, heading to the bath.

"Emma, wait!" Her sister was completely uninhibited. Isabel imagined the Marines in the security room at the edges of their seats. "They didn't give you a bathing suit?" Emma turned to face Isabel. Dark red marks streaked her right forearm. The observation room door burst open. It was Brandon. "No-no-no!" Isabel said, pushing him back into the hall. "One minute!" But when she turned, Emma was already in the shower.

In the car, Isabel felt shaken. "Why would they have Emma go swimming?"

"Sounds like they're checking for hydrophobia. You know. Like rabies victims."

"She doesn't have fucking rabies!" Isabel snapped.

"They're looking for anything they can use against them. Probably Browner deciding if he should build moats or whatever. Was she? Hydrophobic?"

Isabel shook her head. "And she wasn't shy either."

"So I noticed," Brandon said. Isabel buried her face in her hands.

When they exited at the White House, Brandon said, "Look," pointing at the roof. Machine guns protruded from sandbagged emplacements manned by black-helmeted troops. All signs screamed the same thing. *It's coming! It's coming! It's coming!*

They waited for the elevator on the ground floor. The doors opened to reveal Rick Townsend, who emerged in camouflaged gear as if straight from war, or heading to it. Isabel smiled. "Rick?" He looked deeply troubled. "Oh, Dr. Brandon Plante, this is Capt. Rick Townsend. Rick . . . saved my life, I guess, in Khabarovsk." No one shook hands anymore. "What's goin' on down there?" she asked airily. Boys, she had read, liked vivacious girls.

Rick grabbed her elbow and pulled her away. She looked over her shoulder at Brandon. Rick must be a drag-a-girl-off-politely-by-the-elbow kind of alpha male. "They're talking about North Korea," Rick said, checking the hallway in both directions. "I'm headed to Vladivostok." Brandon was watching, so Isabel reached out and gently squeezed Rick's arm. Habituated physical contact, she had read, helped break down barriers to intimacy.

"Hey," she said, "could we, like, trade digits?" "*Digits*"! And she'd said it in an embarrassing way! But Rick nevertheless gave her his number, which she typed into her phone. When she gave Rick hers, he was unprepared and had to retrieve his phone from deep in a cargo pocket.

Rick's eyes bored into hers. She smiled. "Have you seen a mob attack?" he asked. "*Heard* it?" Gone was her smile and her attempts at flirtation. "Listen to me." He grabbed her arms. "If you see a crowd of them, don't walk, *run*. Put as much distance as you can between them and you. I'm not talking infection risk. A blue mask won't save you." His eyes were wide.

"I've seen videos," she said softly. "But there was no audio."

"It's a roar," he said. "Like a stadium's cheer, only they're more . . . shrieks."

"You've been back over there?" she asked, and he nodded. "Why are they sending you to Vladivostok?" she whispered.

"Chinese Infecteds are reaching the North Korean and Russian borders there," he said. "Not thousands. *Millions*." He looked worried sick.

"Do you *have* to go?" she asked, barely audible, without thinking.

He focused intently on her and frowned. "Good luck," he said, then just walked away. She grabbed for him, but caught only empty air. Had she said something wrong?

Brandon hit the down button. "Not a bad-looking guy."

What a strange thing to say. Isabel mumbled, "He's a Marine."

"So I noticed."

The subterranean corridor was filled with milling civilians conversing quietly. The camo-clad guard stood in front of closed conference room doors.

Isabel saw Maldonado and led Brandon over. "What's going on?" she asked.

The aide pointed at the phone she held to her ear before turning away and speaking in low but urgent tones. "Steve, what the *fuck*?" There was no place to escape prying ears. "North *Dakota*? What am I supposed to do with the kids? Of *course*, a *possibility*, but . . . And *D.C.* is gonna be . . . And thousands here, too!" She glanced over her shoulder. Isabel and Brandon looked anywhere but at her. "Okay. I love you. We'll see each other again, right? I mean . . ." Her sobs were poorly suppressed. "I love you *so* much!" The doors opened. "Gotta go. Bye. *Bye*." She fixed her face with her back still to the others.

Jesus, Isabel thought.

Everyone filed into the Situation Room. Inside were uniformed military personnel and the president, secretary of defense, national security advisor and CIA director, all tense. Isabel glimpsed a map of the North Korean-Chinese-Russian border, blighted with red splotches, before it disappeared. But the image that stuck in her mind was of all the red built up around Vladivostok.

President Stoddard's hands were clasped, fingers interlaced, behind his head. His jacket hung on his seat back and his armpits were dark. The secretary of defense and CIA director spoke to him quietly. Stoddard listened and nodded, his eyes shut.

The doors closed, everyone settled, and the room fell unnaturally quiet. "We also might ramp up production of Tamiflu," the CIA director told the president. "It doesn't work particularly well on SED, but we might exaggerate to hospital workers how beneficial it is and set aside stocks for their use to induce them to show up for work."

"Okay," the beleaguered commander-in-chief finally said. "What in God's name is next?"

Aggarwal replied, "We received the WHO report we said we'd publicly release."

The president said, "Dr. Plante?"

Brandon looked at Isabel, stood and said, "Actually, sir, I think Dr. Miller . . ."

President Stoddard frowned and waved impatiently in Isabel's direction.

She rose. Browner silenced an aide to listen. Isabel summarized the WHO report.

When she got to impulsive-reactive aggression, Browner interrupted. "So any Infected can cook off? Even the calmest?"

"Yes. You may see telltale signs of agitation. Talking excessively, purposeless motions like hand-wringing," which Isabel willed herself to stop doing, "verbal hostility, an increase in muscular tension, restlessness, pacing. . . ." *Stop pacing, too.*

"The WHO report?" the ill-tempered president prompted.

"Excuse me, sir," Browner said, "but is sedation effective in controlling them?"

"We haven't tried . . ." Isabel began.

"Yes, sir," Brandon answered. "Benzodiazepines like Valium or Xanax, administered orally, via inhalant or by injection does calm them." *So,* Isabel thought, *they're giving them sedatives, I had no idea, but Brandon, my working-group-mate, did.*

"What sets them off?" Browner asked. Isabel went down her list from memory: feeling threatened, trapped, crowded, or deceived, and then answered Browner's general questions about agitation. It acts like a sixth sense and confers an evolutionary advantage. Twitchy people survive. When relaxed, warning signals pass slowly through the facial recognition region of your brain, helping you spot someone in a crowd displaying ill intent. But when anxious, warning signals shoot straight to the motor cortex, the region responsible for action, in under 200 milliseconds. "Like, say, you're walking through a haunted house, tensed up, and someone leaps out and yells *Boo*! You jump. Instantly."

"Or you're walking point on night patrol," Browner said, "and the first round of an ambush snaps past your face." Isabel thought, *That's probably a better example.* "You'd think," Browner said, "that if it helps so much we'd all be jumpy neurotics all the time."

Isabel explained anxiety's downside—a surge in the stress hormone cortisol, which damages cells. "To stay healthy, you have to be able to turn anxiety on *and* off."

Browner said, "My analysts commented that your sister's nurse had noted in her logbook that your sister no longer grabbed wads of bed linens when she got worked up. She just clutches her notebook as if her life depended on it. The nurse asked for permission to go give her a manicure, or whatever, because she was tearing up her nails. But that would mean taking a nail file in there so they decided against it. But is that behavior some kind of coping mechanism that might also be a warning sign?"

Before Isabel could answer, the president said, "The *report*?" Browner nodded at her, instructing her to ignore his question and return to the WHO report, as requested. Isabel switched to an explanation of the damage that caused deficits in social cognition, adherence to social norms, moral decision-making, and high-risk behavior: the Phineas Gage Effect. "Gage was a mild-mannered, pre-Civil War railroad foreman, who had an iron rod driven through his head, destroying his frontal lobe and turning him into a profane misfit ruled by animal passions."

"Oddly," Brandon interrupted, "it also jump-started Gage's career. Brain injuries often unleash new potentials that are positive changes, like Dr. Miller's math scores."

"So," Isabel continued after a glance at Brandon confirmed he was done, "a small percentage of Infecteds suffer TGA, transient global amnesia. They go about routine business in a mechanical way like sleepwalkers, but underneath their fluency of function lies profound amnesia. Every sentence they utter is forgotten as soon as it's spoken. Every experience gone in minutes. Ultimately, the only question is whether they become an indirect fatality from exposure, dehydration or violence."

Isabel next explained how Infecteds see trees, not forests, serially, not holistically, resulting in obsessiveness. Browner noted, "That might explain their single-mindedness in pursuing victims. Your source at the WHO, Dr. Lange," *how did he know that*, "and his compadre, Dr. Groenewalt, who, by the way, last night was caught stowing away on one of our aircraft headed for Europe, got chased into an electrical substation a couple of days ago. They holed up there for a full day while attackers smashed at doors, vents, conduits. The whole area was awash in violence, but *their* attackers kept trying to kill *them* and them only until a helicopter plucked 'em off the roof."

Isabel shuddered. *Poor Groenewalt just wanted to get home to his wife and daughter.*

"What else?" croaked the president, whose strength and voice were ebbing. Isabel glossed over the previously discussed lack of pain and described how some Infecteds believed acquaintances and loved ones to be dangerous imposters. Browner supplied another story from the erstwhile WHO field team, of a mom who leaned over to check her eight-year-old boy's temperature and had a chopstick driven into her sinuses.

Isabel surveyed the room. Everyone wanted to be somewhere else, *with* someone else. But Isabel had nowhere else to be. Like an unmarried, childless employee on Christmas Day, Isabel would probably end up working the apocalypse shift. She moved on to disruption of social bonding and destruction of empathy. "There are plenty of reasons an Infected *won't* kill you, but any sense of magnanimity, honor, integrity, charity, or fairness isn't among them."

President Stoddard's cheek was propped heavily on his hand. "That all?"

Last but not least, she covered the obliteration of Infecteds' sense of self, and sat.

Everyone waited on the president. "Isn't life better," he asked, "when you don't have a pesky *self* demanding more possessions and more stimulating entertainment, or pointing out your flaws and inadequacies, mostly imagined?" Brandon and Isabel's gazes met. That was Brandon's question, too. "Haven't Infecteds achieved contentment? A life spent wanting only satisfaction of their basic needs? I just can't shake the feeling that they haven't *fallen* rungs on the evolutionary ladder, but *ascended.* I mean, to never again be frustrated or unhappy?"

Heads turned, thank God, to Browner. "No towering achievements, brilliant insights, scientific breakthroughs, engineering marvels, displays of genius? No art, literature, music, or film? You get the bad with the good. The suffering with the solace."

But the president again sought deeper meaning. "Professor Miller? Any chance Thomas Hobbes said anything about the society we can expect Infecteds to create?"

Really? she thought, and frowned. "Well, sir, he did note, in *Leviathan,* that ants live sociably with one another even though individuals have no goals or objectives, just judgment and appetite."

Browner said, "No high-functioning queen like your sister organizing the morning calisthenics?" Isabel's mental image was of his boot blotting out the sun above the mound.

"Sir," Dr. Aggarwal said, "are we authorized to release the WHO report to the public?"

"Good *God* no!" replied Stoddard, roused from his reverie. "The Security Council vote was unanimous. It stays secret. We need to return to executive session. Everyone but the principals please clear the room." His eyes never left Browner's.

Chapter 22

Emma and her roommates, other than the quiet one, watched television.

"In the past twelve hours," President Stoddard announced, "North Korea detonated six nuclear weapons along its border with China. I call upon my fellow countrymen not to overreact to the senseless atrocities of one rogue regime, which in no way directly threatens America. Our armed forces are on alert and fully capable of dealing with all threats. Now I'll take a few questions. Bill." He pointed.

A man rose in the packed pressroom. "Mr. President, the North Koreans claim their nuclear strikes were justifiable self-defense intended to halt the flow of refugees illegally crossing their border who might carry the disease that has broken out in China."

Before the man got to his question, the president said, "What nation would use nuclear weapons to enforce border controls? We reject Pyongyang's reckless crime."

"That wasn't my question, sir. Does North Korea's use of nuclear weapons lend credence to its contention that world leaders are suppressing the truth about the disease? Does the disease threaten a global pandemic, and do reports of widespread violence . . . ?"

"Are you suggesting," Stoddard broke in again, "that we should believe the word of a regime that has just used nuclear weapons against refugees fleeing political unrest?"

He pointed to a reporter he called Sally. "Sir," she said, "you just called it *political* unrest, but the Chinese insisted that it wasn't unrest or rebellion that forced the government from Beijing. Ambassador Brown confirmed the same before *his* disappearance."

"Is there a question?" President Stoddard said.

"Are Americans evacuated from China being quarantined to suppress the truth?"

"As you can imagine," the president said, "in the turmoil of an evacuation, there's an understandable disruption in communications, which we will resolve, I'm sure, shortly."

"Is he lying?" Samantha asked. Emma nodded. Dwayne, who also contracted SED during that same evacuation, concurred.

"And isn't the disease," the female reporter asked, "the root of all that turmoil?"

"Fear of the unknown is, yes, contributing to the violence," the president said.

"That's lying too," remarked Samantha. "Because of what he *didn't* say." Again Emma nodded and Dwayne agreed. But a baffled Dorothy looked from face to face.

"Mr. President, Switzerland just ordered most foreign nationals to leave the country within twenty-four hours, and advised all Swiss citizens to return within forty-eight hours. Can you comment on why a nation that relies on tourism would take such an unprecedented step?"

"Our own State Department has issued travel advisories, and I would personally suggest that all Americans monitor events closely before any foreign travel. Betty?"

"How can you characterize redeployment of forces *back* to the United States as being a reaction to increasing tensions in the Far *East*? Isn't it instead a reaction to the disease . . . ?"

"So you're *re*-raising North Korea's contention? I would think that their use of nuclear weapons both discredits them and confirms the gravity of the security situation. This government will protect Americans from military and, yes, medical threats. As an example, we're ramping up production of Tamiflu for use by hospital workers."

"When are you going to tell us what you know about the disease?" came a shout.

The president hesitated. "We'll have a full medical briefing, but I do not intend to add to the wild rumors out there. I will, however, tell you that the virus is called *Pandoravirus horribilis* and the disease is called SED, Severe Encephalopathic Disease." The room exploded with questions as he strode from the podium.

"What about the troops in New York and L.A.?" . . . "Why'd you cancel your climate conference in Denver?" . . . "Is it true that the disease turns its victims into zombies?"

"Are we zombies?" Samantha asked. Emma shook her head. "Are we dead?" Again, a shake. Dwayne cupped his hand to Emma's ear. "Is it time?" Emma nodded.

The window cleared to reveal Emma's sister, Drs. Rosenbaum and Plante, and the nurse Beth. "Emmy, what . . . what was that whispering about?"

Emma said, "Dwayne told me that we should ask Nurse Hopkins to get us board games so that we can distract Samantha." Sam returned Emma's gaze. She understood now what a lie was.

"That, Emma, sweetie, was too many words. What he said to you was *way* shorter."

Emma scrutinized her sister. Their hair was the major difference. With Isabel's security badge, Emma might pass. She practiced curling her lips into the smile Beth always wore, but that felt odd. Next to her sister sat Isabel's former lover Brandon. He'd been attracted to Isabel once, so he might find Emma sexually appealing also. That could prove useful.

The window frosted. Emma's eyes settled on the wall, but her planning continued. She and her sister were intellectually superior to the others at the NIH. The Uninfecteds didn't see it, but Sam, Dwayne, and Dorothy did, and they yielded to Emma's judgment.

A thought occurred. The thought itself was unimportant—*Don't talk to anyone about your superior intelligence*—but to whom did it occur? Was that a *self*? She wrote the thought down in her notebook.

Emma then looked up at the long, frosted window. "Isabel, are you there?"

The window cleared. The four Uninfecteds stared back. "Emma?" Isabel said. "Did you just . . . *initiate* a conversation?"

"Yes. When you hear a 'self,' is it a voice, or an idea that just forms in your brain?"

"Wow! *Uhm*, the latter. It just comes to you, but you don't know from where."

Emma understood. Uninfecteds manufactured the entire mythology of the self around concept formation like primitive peoples inventing gods to explain forces of nature. She decided not to write that down yet. They were copying her notes every day now. "Another question. When you finish studying us, are you going to let us go, or kill us?"

Isabel's face instantly contorted. "*Kill* you? No! Of *course* not!" Another heated debate silently consumed the Uninfecteds, their audio muted. Isabel lowered her mouth to the microphone. "You're still contagious, but don't worry. I've got your back."

"When the infection gets here," Emma said, "have Noah get us released." Isabel surreptitiously nodded once. Was this like her agreement with Hermann Lange in Siberia? Something was different. She hadn't agreed to do anything for Isabel in return. She wrote in her notebook: *Talk to Noah about contracts.* "Next question," she said. "Can you tell me where the other four pens are?"

"Is this some kind of game?" Isabel asked. "I see one beside the desk under the high window." Samantha retrieved it. Dr. Rosenbaum scrutinized the laptop screen, at which Isabel pointed. "And there's one . . ."

The room's audio fell silent. Not just quiet, but absent the emptiness-filling hum of active speakers. Dr. Rosenbaum pressed a button repeatedly while speaking into his microphone, but no audio came through. The door into the observation room opened. The Marine officer who accompanied them to the military wing for testing entered. Dorothy tensed. Sam retreated to the corner. Dwayne stared not at his charge, but at the observation room. A major argument, with gesticulations by Isabel, was evidently ended by the Marine's shrugging intransigence. He said something over a handheld radio.

The hum returned. An unsteady Isabel said, "Emmy, I'm sorry. We can't answer because, *apparently*, security thinks you're looking for holes in the video surveillance."

"Hello, Captain Ramirez," Emma said.

Isabel looked back and forth between Emma and the captain. A silent argument ensued, with Isabel yelling soundlessly, until the observation room emptied of all but Ramirez, who leaned over to a mic. "We said no funny business, remember?" The Infecteds stared back. "Please don't make me cut you off. You give, we give."

"A contract," Emma said, and he nodded. She wrote in her notebook, "Consider organizing society based on contracts," using the color red for social order.

Emma looked at the tense Samantha. Dorothy was shaking. The muscles on Dwayne's neck stood out. Emma took a deep breath in through her nose, out through her mouth, again and again. Dwayne, Sam, and Dorothy followed her lead.

Chapter 23

Walter Street glanced up, bleary-eyed, from behind magnified eyeglasses through which he studied a microscope slide. "*Ophiocoryceps*," he said unprompted, "a fungus that causes ants on forest floors to climb trees and burst, releasing a rain of fungal spores."

Isabel said, "What's the military doing during blocks of gray time with my sister?"

Street extracted another slide. "Viruses face four challenges. How to get from one host to another? How to penetrate a host cell's wall? How to commandeer a cell or its genetic machinery to reproduce? And how to get back out of that cell to re-infect?"

"Captain Ramirez threatened to take away my *access* privileges! To my *sister*!"

Street's intense scrutiny of the glass plates took the form of a frozen wince. "Human DNA has 23,000 genes. But there are six *pounds* of bacteria living in each of us, and they contain two *million* genes. We co-evolved on a planet awash in microorganisms, and as a consequence we are more microbial than mammal, genetically speaking."

Isabel kept waiting for Street's often-obscure point to come into focus. "Walter, when SED gets here, do you think they might, you know, *kill* Emma?"

Street's eyes darted to her. "Studies show that you can transfer traits like shyness or gregariousness from one monkey to another merely by transplanting their microbiota."

"You never seemed to care about the secrecy rules before," Isabel said. "You always spoke freely to me despite all the warnings. But you're not going to help me now?"

Street finally looked up. "I *am* helping you, Isabel. Focus on the science. It's the only thing you can control, and it's the best way to help your sister. The rest—politics, security—is like the weather. There's nothing to be done about it, so why even try?"

* * * *

Outside the Situation Room, during a break in a marathon NSC meeting to which Isabel had been invited but Brandon had not, Isabel boldly approached General Browner. An outer ring of colonels and captains and inner one of generals and admirals parted to admit her. "Dr. *Miller?*" Browner said amiably.

She instantly regretted her decision, but was committed. "Do you have a moment?"

"Absolutely. Just gimme a sec." He returned to business. Isabel had looked him up on Wikipedia. Married, three sons, all Marines. Former nose tackle at Annapolis with two Purple Hearts, a Navy Cross, and a Harvard MBA.

After he ordered withdrawal of the "2nd ID," whatever that was, from South Korea to Okinawa, Isabel gently suggested, "Maybe this isn't such a good time."

"No, no," said Browner. "One more minute." He answered queries with orders, responded to nervous question marks with calming periods, each replied to with an exclamation mark. "Sir!" the last man said on departing.

"I didn't realize your nickname was Skip," was Isabel's only comment on what she'd overheard.

"It's short for Skipper. It stuck at the academy. So, what can I do for you?"

Isabel just blurted it out. "Are you going to kill my sister when you finish testing?"

Browner cocked his head. "Whoa. Well, as you know, the president is opposed to the policy of eradication."

"But *you're* not. If you got your way, would you have your men shoot her?"

Even Browner looked around to ensure they were alone. "There's a lot of *jockeying* going on behind the scenes. You notice Vice President Anderson isn't in any of the NSC meetings? He thinks we need to go biblical on Infecteds."

"So he's frozen out like the FBI director?" she asked in part to prove that she, too, was in the know.

Browner snorted a brief laugh. "Don't believe that charade. Pearson has people all over town trying to worm their way into plots and coup attempts against the president."

"*Coup* attempts?" Isabel said.

"Best way to get invited into a coup is to pretend to start one yourself. But he and the president are thick as thieves. And not to worry. Pearson hasn't found any treasonous plots yet, although from what he told me *you* have violated the Espionage Act in about every way possible short of blowing up railway bridges. You need to button up those lips, young lady." Isabel was now so thoroughly confused she had no idea who was on whose side and doing what.

"So, do you agree with the vice president?" she asked. "About going *biblical*?"

Browner regarded her for a moment. "Are you asking me for a policy position, Dr. Miller, or a personal favor?"

"I'm asking you not to murder Emma. Let me get her out. Give her a chance."

He pondered, then said, "Sounds fair, so long as you make sure she's properly isolated." He shook the hand Isabel proffered.

"Would you also tell the Marines in Bethesda not to restrict my access to her?"

"Okay," he replied. "Anything *else*?" He nodded greetings at cabinet secretaries who filed back into the conference room for an impending resumption of the meeting.

Isabel said, almost in a whisper, "Is 'impulsive eradication' really the only way?"

Browner inhaled deeply. His chest expanded more than she would've thought possible. The four gold stars on his epaulettes touched his thick neck. "You scientists tell me that math is the language of the universe, revealed to us like a law of nature. Dr. Miller, I'm no war-crazed hawk who wants to kill 100 million people. But unless we come up with a vaccine, the math says this continent will be overrun by Infecteds, whose offspring will also be infected unless some random genetic mutation eventually makes them immune. So we either fight to the death or make the knowing decision, as a species, to go extinct."

"It's not really an extinction because Infecteds are still genetically identical to us."

"But they're not *us*, are they, Dr. Miller?"

She didn't disagree. For some strange reason, she and Browner clicked. Or maybe they just both came to the same, correct conclusions. "So is the plan really lose-recover-win? First we have to lose?"

In a fatherly tone, Browner said, "I understand you lost your mom and dad, Isabel. My sympathies. May I give you a bit of parental advice?" *Yes, please!* "It's time to think about survival." The lump in Isabel's throat threatened to choke her. "Iceland has abundant fish and geothermal energy, but lots of beaches to defend. Guam is better if you want an island 'cause it's more remote, and we left a lot of equipment and supplies behind with only a caretaker force. Tristan de Cunha in the South Atlantic is *the* most isolated archipelago in the world. Only has 300 inhabitants, and more good fishing. Puncak Jaya in the mountains of Indonesia is the most inaccessible *populated* place on Earth, with lots of deep mines. Closer to home, Denver is surrounded by shale oil. Kansas City has farmland and is a hub of north-south and east-west rail lines, but that could cut both ways."

"Are you saying I should run for it?" she asked. *Christ,* that's *his advice?*

He drew another enormous breath. "There may just be no bottom here, Isabel."

"Isn't there any way we can," her voice quivered, audibly she feared, "kinda, skip the lose-and-recover parts and go straight to the *win?*"

Browner said, "Develop a vaccine. And, once they organize themselves, use nukes."

"*What?*" she replied, astounded at his suggestion after North Korea's atrocities had just been so thoroughly denounced. The elevator opened, and a clutch of soldiers emerged.

Browner abruptly said, "Speak of the devil . . ." and left. "Captain Townsend!" Isabel spun. Rick saluted, then shook Browner's hand. But Rick's eyes—hollow and haunted—found Isabel. He stared at her, forming and abandoning words.

Browner spoke in soothing tones, with hands on Rick's shoulders, gently shaking him for emphasis, saying "hard things, I know," and "how many did you lose?" Rick answered in short sentences, but kept looking at Isabel until tears streaked his cheeks and he bowed his head. "It's all right, son," Browner kept saying. "It's all right."

The conference room was emptying of junior aides bound for the elevator. Browner led Rick's small group inside, against that contra-traffic, and announced, in the direction of the president, "We have the team just back with a report on the North Korean nuke strikes against Infecteds."

Rick broke free from his group, crossed the waiting room and grabbed Isabel's arms. Her eyes closed as he leaned down, but his lips went to her ear. With hot breath, he said, "Get the fuck outa here. Run. Before it's too late." He pushed her back. His face was close. "Get away and don't look back." He then released her and entered the conference room with one last glance over his shoulder.

Browner politely smiled before closing the door in Isabel's face, leaving her to only imagine what it was that Rick had seen. What it was that she and everyone else might soon see.

Chapter 24

WASHINGTON, D.C.
Infection Date 30, 2000 GMT (4:00 p.m. Local)

Isabel now spent as much time at the White House as at the NIH. On her arrival in the Situation Room, Dr. Aggarwal motioned her to a seat at the conference table opposite Browner, and not along the wall beside Maldonado and Brandon. The president was at one end of the room. Congressional leadership at the other. Dr. Stavros was reporting that school attendance in New York City and the San Francisco Bay area had fallen below 75 percent. The wisdom of the crowd warned of an approaching menace.

"Dr. Miller," President Stoddard said as she settled in, "we were having a *spirited* talk about consciousness and the self in the context of the legal rights of *Pandoravirus* casualties, and we needed our expert." Isabel was greatly relieved to see the president again acting composed and in charge. "Could you give us a definition of consciousness?"

"The best definition I ever heard," Isabel said, hesitating before taking the plunge, "was by Julian Jaynes." The instant she spoke the name of the controversial thinker, Drs. Aggarwal and Stavros turned to her. "He was a Princeton psychology professor who wrote," she knew it by heart, "that consciousness is the imaginary conversations in which never-to-be-known-by-anyone we excuse, defend and proclaim our hopes and regrets."

Stoddard was nonplussed. "Did Jaynes have any theories *about* consciousness?"

Aggarwal raised a brow in caution. "Sir, you won't believe a word Jaynes wrote unless I explain the competing ideas." Stoddard gave Isabel the floor and rocked back to listen. Isabel covered the seven prior theories masterfully debunked by Jaynes. First, consciousness emerges from the interaction of matter. The only difference between physics and cognition is that the latter is described by laws more complex than we've deciphered. The silent reception felt like a group rejection of that cop-out. Theory two: Darwin's answer. Consciousness emerges from life. Amoebae hunt for food, so they experience hunger. Paramecia avoid obstacles, so they feel pain. But that, Isabel explained, was simply a projection of human feelings onto non-human life. A flower droops, so you call it *sad*. A worm on a fishhook writhes in agony, but actually the motor nerves in its tail are disconnected from the inhibition of its cephalic ganglion.

The next rejected theory was Metaphysical Imposition. There are inflection points in evolutionary history at which nature veers off in an inexplicable direction. One was the initial creation of life. Another, the unexplainable degree of DNA's complexity. And a third was the emergence of human consciousness. Maybe biology pre-wires matter to turn into life, DNA to follow programmed routes to complexity, and synaptic nervous systems to develop a sense of self. But the science explaining those three great discontinuities is so far beyond our current comprehension that it's best described right now as magical. It's a black box labeled: Then a miracle happens.

Fallacious theory four: Consciousness emerges from learning. Apes can't learn as much as us, and therefore experience a less full sense of consciousness. Plants won't ever learn, so plants won't ever be conscious. If an animal learns from an experience, proponents of this theory would say, there had to be an *it* inside there to have *had* that experience. A tree falling in the woods isn't an experience. A human *observing* a tree fall in the woods *has* the experience of it falling because he can learn why trees fall, whether their branches snag, how dangerous they are. But the theory hinges on the word *experience*, whose definition, ultimately, is circular. To have an experience, you must have a self, and *vice versa*. It's sophistry.

Five: The Helpless Spectator Theory. When some unspecified degree of nervous complexity is reached, consciousness appears like heat given off by the wiring of our brains. It's real. It exists. But it's no more in control of the brain than a shadow controls the object casting it.

The sixth theory was Emergent Evolution. At a certain stage of evolutionary advance, consciousness arises and *does* control behavior.

"Bingo," Browner said. "What's wrong with *that* one?"

"No proof. Just like wetness can't be derived from the properties of hydrogen and oxygen, neither could proponents of this theory explain consciousness by analysis of its constituent parts: electrical signals and neurotransmitters."

"I'll take your word for it," Browner said. "What was the final flawed theory?"

"Behaviorism." There's no problem with consciousness because it doesn't exist. From the 1920s to the '60s, behaviorists ran thousands of rats through mazes trying to reduce all conduct to a handful of reflexes conditioned to respond to stimuli from the environment. They found that rats can remember paths to food and dogs can learn to salivate on hearing the dinner bell, but nothing close to explaining the complexity of consciousness.

"Is there a place in the brain, at least," Stoddard asked, "where consciousness is?"

"People have been looking for that place for millennia. Descartes settled on the brain as its site, and not the heart. Jaynes suspected the reticular formation, which when deactivated results in unconsciousness or coma, and when stimulated wakes you up."

"And where is this reticular formation?" the president asked.

"It's a hundred bundles of tiny, tangled neurons, loosely defined anatomically, running from the top of the spinal cord," she pulled her hair back and pointed, "up through the brainstem to the thalamus and hypothalamus. It intrigued Jaynes because it attracts collaterals that could serve as wire taps on peripheral sensory systems and motor nerves."

"So let's get," the president said, "to what Jaynes *did* think consciousness was."

Dr. Stavros cocked his head. Isabel took a moment to gird herself. "Jaynes believed, sir, that consciousness emerged sometime between *The Iliad* and *The Odyssey.*"

Before that could sink in, she added, in a voice raised over the growing chorus of whispers, "In the *pre*conscious mind, the original, primitive brain—the *right* hemisphere—sensed all experiences and recorded all memories. Jaynes believed that ruminations, *by* the right brain, on those experiences were being passed via the corpus callosum to our newly awakened left brain, which heard, as auditory hallucinations, the right brain's thoughts and concluded that they must emanate from some separate being."

There was now open and loud talking, and even some laughter.

"The left hemisphere," Isabel pressed on, "is the 'unique flower of human evolution' and the most recent part of the brain to develop. All the sudden, nature tacked a computer onto our creatural right brain, and when it turns on, it hears voices coming out of *nowhere*. These voices presume to make sense of everything, and to suggest courses of action to deal with issues. The first draft of an explanation that the left brain comes up with, according to Jaynes, is that it's . . . It thinks that it's hearing the voices of gods."

She lost almost the entire room. But, critically, not the president, and not Browner.

"To the early Greeks of *The Iliad*, which was compiled over hundreds of years of oral legend that Homer finally wrote down, the *gods* told us what to do. Go on an epic voyage, besiege a city, seize that beauty as your bride. Homer then wrote its more modern sequel, *The Odyssey*, in which all those voices in characters' heads were *selves* imbued with the ability to love, hate, fear, grieve, die for a cause and long for home and family."

Everyone waited for President Stoddard to speak. Was she brilliant, or on her way out the door? She knew how Jaynes must have felt. "Now it's my turn to say wow. So, do you believe this theory? That consciousness, just, *arose* . . . in what year would that be?"

Isabel stepped off the plank. "Sometime between 1500 and 760 BCE. I believe, yes, that mankind became *self*-aware when the Greeks began using the metaphor that the voice in our head is us, not a god, and that metaphor spread. People heard of a *person* who attacks a city because of *his* love for a woman, not because some capricious god told him to, and began to think maybe there's someone inside *everyone*, just like they'd always suspected someone was inside themselves. On acceptance of that metaphor, the two halves of the brain became one, and we achieved consciousness. *Self*-awareness."

People stared back in silence. "And yes," she concluded, "I believe that happened, in various cultures and ways, around that time, that it changed us, and that whatever it was and whenever it happened, we acquired this wonderful thing we call humanity that we now stand to lose . . . forever."

Chapter 25

Noah kept the SUV's radio loud enough to hear, but not so loud as to attract the attention of Natalie, who stared out the window at the passing Virginia countryside. "The UN Security Council abandoned plans to sanction the North Korean government for its use of nuclear weapons after the Hermit Kingdom's regime in Pyongyang, according to reports, simply vanished." Noah reached for the knob to lower the volume, but Natalie's hand found his, held it for a moment, then turned the radio up.

"Meanwhile, reports are coming in from South Korea of massive bloodshed along the DMZ, which has been breached in multiple locations by people desperate to escape the radiation, the collapse of the North Korean government and the mysterious disease that increasingly appears to have been the cause of the crisis in the Far East. US forces in Korea are reportedly engaged in fighting, although it's unclear whether that fighting is against remnants of the North Korean military or refugees streaming across the DMZ. Immediately before our bureau in Seoul was taken off the air by South Korean authorities in a replay of the telecommunications blackouts in China, it reported that the infection had broken out in the capital and that panic and violence were widespread."

Noah turned the radio off, and they drove the rest of the way to the gate in silence.

During their subsequent ascent of the mountain, the SUV precariously traversed the recently repaired ridgeline-hugging road, which was deeply rutted anew from the passage of heavy trucks. "They didn't do too good of a job fixing this road," Natalie mumbled. The muscles in her trim arms were flexed as she braced while peering over the cliff.

"I told 'em not to spend money here," Noah said, manhandling the steering wheel and telling her of his plan to blow the road when the virus hit the Valley. "An engineer at the Highway Department is helping me out off the books. All I do is push a button."

"Jesus, Noah," she said. He concluded she didn't disapprove of his plan, just registered it as another shock. When they finally reached the open gate and pulled up to the house, the contractor came out to greet them. With a deep, twangy accent, he said, "H'lo, Missus Miller," and reacted like most men did around Natalie, lending her an arm as she climbed down. Natalie shook his hand, smiling on reflex under movie-star sunglasses. Passing workers checked out her long blond hair, which fell to her black yoga pants.

The Old Place hummed satisfyingly with activity. They might actually complete it on time. The contractor walked them around, giving Noah cheery progress reports. Natalie sidled up to Noah and asked, sotto voce, "How much is this costing?"

He waved her question off as if it were unimportant, which it was. Natalie allowed herself to be satisfied with a non-answer and seemed to take comfort from the changes, asking questions that bolstered that comfort as if the right home improvements would solve all her concerns about the apocalypse. She was especially impressed by the tall metal fence encircling the house and its outbuildings. She even caught Noah's eye and smiled.

When the tour ended, Natalie fixed her makeup in the SUV's mirror as Noah tried to disengage from the contractor. But the man followed, so Noah opened the tailgate. Two rifles lay under a blanket. "We're doing some shooting up by the cabin."

The contractor said, "I'll radio my guys up there not to get shot. Say, this is all about that Chinese flu, right?" Noah nodded. "It's gonna get bad? Here?" Another nod.

"I got more calls," the man said, "about buildin' places like this, but I have some preppin' of my own to do. I'm already spendin' the money you'll owe when we finish. You're gonna pay, right?" Noah held out his hand, which the contractor shook.

Noah next had to break through Natalie's resistance to strapping her rifle across her chest. Workers watched them parade through the construction site toward a small gate on the far side of the compound.

"I feel very fucking weird," Natalie whispered under the stares from the men.

"They're looking at your ass, not the guns." On hearing that, she relaxed.

They headed uphill. "Noah," she said after some distance, "we aren't exactly the kind of people who thrive in the wild. Like, I've never even watched *Duck Dynasty*."

"You'll get the hang of it," Noah said. "That's one reason we're up here."

Natalie held the rifle to keep it from bouncing against her breasts as the terrain grew uneven. Despite the chill, Noah was sweating by the time they heard sawing at the secluded cabin, which in the old days had been a hunting lodge. You couldn't see the rustic stone structure until you crossed the last of three finger ridges. It was nestled amid the hills, shielded from the weather. The workers packed up as the foreman gave them a quick tour. The cabin had many of the same features as the main house, minus most of the security. Its defense depended on staying hidden. But it had its own well. Solar panels for hot water. Wood-burning stove for cooking and heat. Old-fashioned, removable kerosene lanterns mounted to sconces like from centuries past. And storm shutters inside and out.

It fell quiet as the workers disappeared. Natalie stood in the single room wearing black Lululemons and holding her assault rifle's pistol grip. "So this is where we'll come if we're run out of the main house?" Noah nodded. "Where do we go if we're run out of here?" Noah resented the question. Who the hell had a backup to their backup plan?

The sun was getting lower. "We'd better get started," he said.

Natalie didn't object, but she looked pale, as if she were being led to an execution. She followed Noah back up the ridge without objection, but seemed a million miles away.

They spread a blanket on the dirt and lay on their bellies beside their weapons. Noah dispensed a running stream of instructions, but he wasn't sure Natalie followed anything. "This is 5.56 millimeter ammunition." He pushed a cartridge from the thirty-round magazine and handed it to Natalie. To her credit, she studied it from pointy tip to flat base. He pressed the round back into the magazine. She watched in silence. They donned ear and eye protection. Natalie said not one word, and only nodded in reply. She was treating this outing like a root canal—necessary, but lamentable.

He showed her how to slap the magazine into the rifle's receiver. How to pull the charging handle to the rear to chamber a round. How to rest the butt plate in the hollow of her shoulder. How to lower her eye to the scope. How to take the safety off by feel.

"It's ready," he said. "Aim for that white tree trunk over there." She did as he suggested. "And shoot it. The tree trunk." He waited. "Just pull a little harder and . . ."

The rifle *cracked*. A spent cartridge flew out. The muzzle smoked. After a little encouragement, she hit the tree on the fourth, tenth and twenty-second shots, then lay the AR-15 on the blanket as Noah was warning her to engage the safety, which he did for her. She rolled onto her back and looked up at the sky through her amber shooting glasses.

"Is this gonna work?" she asked. "The house? The cabin? The guns? I mean, we'll have propane for what? One winter? Two, maybe? And we're gonna become *farmers* raising pigs and chickens and rutabagas? I can't even get houseplants to grow. Aren't starving people gonna try to take everything from us? And what do we do when our supplies run low, or someone breaks a leg? March down the hill and start trading with infected people? A chicken for some medical care?"

"Nobody knows what it's gonna be like."

"What if none of it happens?" She sat up and shook Noah's arm with both hands. "What if this is all just a crazy overreaction? Nobody else we know is doing any of this."

"You heard the contractor," Noah said. "People *are* starting to prepare."

Natalie ignored him. "We'd be ruined. We'd never get our money back out of this place. But I'd accept being broke, so long as . . . the world doesn't come to an end."

They packed up in sullen silence and headed down the hill. Noah said, "Now don't get mad at me, but I don't want you to harbor any guilt or anything, so do you think you oughta maybe tell your father what we know about what's coming?"

Natalie stared at him in disbelief and snorted. She was pissed that he'd brought the man up. "*No*, Noah. I think we should just let God sort that out. I can't *believe* you."

He still didn't know what the deep, dark secret with her family was. But given how upset he had made Natalie, it should probably stay that way.

Chapter 26

Isabel packed a bag with Emma's boots, jeans, a sweater, and undergarments in case they ever let her out. On reflection, she decided to take her own bag to the car too. It contained all her worldly goods—underwear, T-shirts, and toiletries—and with the end being nigh and all. . . . But she had begun to note raised eyebrows at her attire even from nerd scientists, whose fashion bar was pretty low. So today Isabel wore one of Emma's blouses. It plunged so uncomfortably low in front that Isabel couldn't wear a bra, which caused her to incessantly adjust the top's fit.

"Emma!" a guy called out from across the parking garage. She pulled her blouse into place. "Hey!" the handsome twenty-something said as he approached. "Hol' up!" He had fashionable facial hair and twinkling black eyes, and leaned to kiss her on the mouth. Isabel twisted to evade him. "You pissed or something? The landlord said you'd gotten back from your trip, but you didn't call. Remember? You said you owed me one?"

"Oh, I . . . I've been busy."

"You grew your hair out. I *like*!" He pressed her against the car door with his pelvis. His hands roamed freely down to her backside. "Speakin' of gettin' busy . . . ?"

"I, I, I've gotta get to work."

She opened the car door, forcing him back. "Em, hey, you're some kinda doctor, right?" Isabel nodded behind curtains of hair. "What's the deal with this new disease. Some people are saying, like, it's real bad."

Eric L. Harry

He clearly wasn't bright. But how important was that going to be over the next few years? He looked strong. "I'd get ready." Food, water, medicine, guns—that sort of thing.

He was slow to smile, then laugh. Suspicious that someone might yet again be pulling one over on him. "Right!" He got the joke. "But hey, sounds like a good party theme though. Like a hurricane party? Your place? I'm sorta on probation with the landlord. I'll bring booze, pot, and guys if you host and turn out the girls."

"Sorry, I'm too busy," Isabel said, "at work."

He shrugged, then kissed her lips, which opened without her thinking and remained parted even after he pulled away. She opened her eyes. "You don't even remember my name, do you?" he said, smiling. "You don't. You *don't*! But hey, that's okay. I'm not complainin'!" He squeezed her tightly to him. Her lungs couldn't quite fill. "It's Josh."

"Josh . . ."

"Apartment 208C," he said, "in case you forgot that too." When he pulled away, he left a void.

Josh, 208C, she repeated to herself, but wasn't really sure why.

On the drive, the crush of Josh against her body gripped Isabel's thoughts. His touch seemed to wake her skin, which tingled. At a red light, she shook herself like a dog emerging from water to try to rid herself of the distraction. In the car beside her was a pissed off mother of three fighting kids in back, one of whom stuck his tongue out at Isabel. She reciprocated. The drivers behind Isabel blew their horns. She drove through a light that had already turned yellow.

She clicked on the radio. Good ole apocalypse news to cleanse her palate of Josh.

Blue lights flashed from the front dash of the black sedan behind her. "Shit! What the . . . ?" She pulled over. What had she *done?* Turned on the radio? Stuck her tongue out at a kid? Failed to go too *fast?* A man in a dark suit approached carrying a black bag.

"There's no other explanation," came the radio show caller. "The military showing up in every major city? Sure, there's a disease . . . in *Asia*!" The host failed to interrupt. "This is a coup! By the Pentagon! It's *Seven Days in May*, man, you mark my . . ."

Isabel started at the rap on glass. She rolled down the window. "Officer, I . . ."

"FBI, ma'am." He flashed her his badge.

"Of course! It's been, what, four days? I don't wanta tell you how to do your job or anything, but if you're trying to keep a low profile, wouldn't it be better to, like, call on that encrypted phone you gave me rather than pull me over on a crowded street?"

"I apologize, ma'am. Please sign this." He handed her a one-page form. Termination of Employment, its heading read. "At the bottom, please."

"What's this? I've never been an FBI agent. This says I'm resigning."

"You've been an undercover special agent for the bureau for three weeks, ma'am. You had limited legal immunity during that time as a law enforcement officer. The director personally said you should sign this," the sunglasses-wearing man said.

"And if I do I can go?" she asked. The agent nodded. She signed.

He handed her a plastic card with the same bad picture as her White House pass: Federal Bureau of Investigation. Department of Justice. Retired Special Agent.

He hoisted the bag into the window. It was about five times heavier than she expected. Inside she saw a big black pistol and holster, magazines galore, some other gun-related shit in foam pockets and box after box of ammunition.

"What the hell is *this?*"

"Sig Sauer P320. Nine millimeter. Striker-fired, polymer-framed. Double-action. Seventeen-round capacity. Night sights. Picatinny rails."

"I honestly don't think I understood a single word you just said."

"As a retired agent, ma'am, you're legally authorized, for the next fifteen years, to carry a concealed handgun. That's your duty pistol. It's registered to you. You just signed a receipt for it. Director Pearson personally asked me to thank you for your service, which is now concluded. Unfortunately, due to anticipated demands on our time, so is your security detail. We're no longer able to provide you round-the-clock protection."

"You've been protecting me? Around the clock? But you're *stopping?*"

"That's right, ma'am. Thank you for your service, and good luck to you."

He left. She was now on her own. Armed with a gun and a *good luck.*

"I'll tell you where there *is* fighting," said the radio host. "The China-Vietnam border blew up last night." *Jesus,* Isabel thought. "And I'm talking tank-versus-tank, air raids, artillery, full-on war between two countries' militaries."

What the hell's next? Isabel joined the traffic line squeezing through a construction bottleneck on Wisconsin. Twin concrete barriers shut off the thoroughfare save one lane in each direction. On the far side, soldiers poured cement onto an ugly squat structure sitting in open green space beside the six-lane avenue. Its only feature was a wood-framed horizontal slit. Muddy trenches to either side were lined in a green plastic tarp.

It wasn't surprising to Isabel that wild rumors, planted or not, ricocheted across the airwaves and Internet. What amazed her was how many people ignored the fact that *something* unprecedented was afoot. They bought cover stories or accepted general assurances when the obvious warning signs were being dug into fields all around the country. The power of rationalization was astounding.

She parked in the oddly empty NIH lot and entered the hospital. A Marine directed her to the large conference room, where she found a scene very much unlike her first meeting three weeks earlier. The room was half empty and silent. Brandon sat across the table. Isabel noticed his glance and checked the front of her blouse. Nielsen arrived, did a double take on seeing the empty table and sat next to Rosenbaum and Street.

"Where is everybody?" Isabel asked.

"Good question," Street replied. "Most of the offices were dark by eight last night."

Nielsen's assistant appeared in the doorway, made eye contact, and shook her head. "Nobody?" Neilsen asked. Another shake. Nielsen huffed. "Well, so much for saving the world!"

"What did you expect?" Hank asked. "They've all got families."

"So do you," Nielsen replied, "but you're here." From the dark looks of Hank and the others, however, shared with confidantes seated nearby, the sign they had been waiting for—a jailbreak by their distinguished colleagues—would soon send them fleeing too.

"All right," Nielsen said. "Let's reorganize. Pick up the abandoned work." But something in the return gazes set her off. "Or do you all have *other* plans?" No one said a word. "Show of hands. Who's sticking this out to the end in hopes of saving mankind?"

Nielsen raised her hand. Her blue rubber SED wristband slipped down to her cuff. Street, Isabel, Brandon, and two others raised theirs also. Nielsen said, "Great! Just great." She glared at Rosenbaum. "*Et tu*, Hank? What, has your little experiment bitten you in the ass, Dr. Frankenstein?" For some reason, Nielsen, Street, and Rosenbaum all looked at Isabel. "Well *fuck* all of you!" Nielsen said before rushing from the room. Had Isabel not known the woman, she would've guessed Nielsen was on the verge of tears.

Men and women in lab coats rose and shook hands. It was, Isabel sensed, the beginning of the end. The only thing momentarily arresting their flight was Street's voice.

"*Plasmodium*, a protozoan. When young, it makes its mosquito host blood-shy so they don't both get swatted. But when *mature*, it makes the mosquito ravenous so it bites humans repeatedly, even after growing full, aiding the parasite in moving on to its next stage, infecting humans with malaria. This will be the final bug-of-the-day."

Brandon left. Scientists filed out, each offering some version of *good luck*.

When the last of them had departed, Hank rose, turned to Street and said, "Walter, it's been an honor and a privilege." Street let Hank's hand hover in air for a few moments before shaking it. "I'm headed to Idaho," Hank said, "with the whole tribe."

He stopped beside Isabel. "Dr. Miller, I know we got off on the wrong foot. And I can only imagine how hard this has been on you. But I want you to know that I have been mightily impressed by your insight, grasp of the subject matter, and professionalism under trying circumstances. I wish you the best. And Emma, too."

In the hallway outside the conference room, other staff had gathered to complete their goodbyes. Hank gave Beth, who was crying, a fatherly hug. "You make sure he treats you right, okay?" she heard him say. Beth sniffled and nodded.

Isabel turned to Street. "What was Nielsen's Frankenstein remark about?"

"It was Hank's idea to do the twins study," Street replied.

"The *what*?"

"He was told he could hire a neuroscientist. He had hundreds to choose from, but you and Emma, being identical twins, were too valuable an opportunity for him to pass up. You share 85 percent of your chromosomal material and 100 percent of your genes. You shared the same uterine environment, parenting style, education, wealth, culture, community. Hank made a compelling case that the contrasts between you two would be informative."

"Oh," she said. "A twins study. How original." Street cringed. Isabel tried to cover her distress by talking. "Well, what he missed were all the contrasts between Emma and me *pre*-fucking-infection!" She wiped her welling eyes even before the first tear.

"*And*," Street added, "he didn't count on you turning out to be such a good neuroscientist, and that the White House would come to value your opinion so highly."

It sank in fully. Of course she wasn't there for her expertise! She was taken to the White House—presumably for official sympathies about Emma—and happened to say something memorable. She felt devastated and whispered, "Everyone knew?" Street shrugged. Every point she had made, they had all played along and humored her.

"You *earned* your place at this table," Street said. She scoffed. "No, really. You're young, but you're brilliant. Rakesh Aggarwal told me you advocated Julian Jaynes's theory of the bicameral mind to the NSC. That took *balls!*"

Isabel wanted to run away, hide in Noah's guest room, and scream into the pillow. But that would just complete her humiliation. "So you're staying?" she asked.

Street said, "I don't have anything outside this lab." Even after that admission, he regarded Isabel with what looked like pity. "You should know that you'd be safe now, with Emma only wearing a mask, if you want to start thinking about . . . your and her futures."

Isabel thanked him and headed outdoors. It was a crisp day. The sun shone. Birds chirped. Marines dug holes in the lawn. She had things to do before she took off.

She dialed the number on Maldonado's business card. The White House operator answered. "Can you get me the ambassador to China, or former ambassador, or whatever he is, wherever he is? Ambassador Brown?" The pleasant woman asked her to hold.

After a few clicks, a woman answered. "Helen Brown."

"Mrs. Brown? You're the wife of Ambassador Brown? My name is Dr. Isabel Miller. I work at the National Institutes of Health in Bethesda." There was a long silence. "I thought I should tell you that your daughter, Samantha, is a patient here."

"My daughter is no longer with us," came the chilly reply.

"*Uhm*, well, no. She's here. In Bethesda."

"My daughter got sick and died in China," the woman said, her voice hard.

"Ma'am, uh . . . no. She's here, very much alive, in our hospital."

"Like I said, our precious daughter, the light of our life, our only child," her voice broke, "grew ill and passed away. She's dead. Leave us to our grief and don't call back!"

"May I possibly speak to Ambassador . . . ?" The phone clicked.

* * * *

At the White House, Isabel found Brandon sitting along the wall of the Situation Room next to Maldonado. She looked for a seat near them, but Dr. Aggarwal motioned to an empty chair at the table, which now seemed to be her permanent place.

General Browner said, "Sir, I'd like to talk about resources. To answer your question from yesterday, we've got, on active duty, 1,281,915 regular military, 440,701 national guardsmen, and 360,520 reservists for a total of 2,083,136 uniformed military personnel. That's 989,936 army, 381,121 navy, 220,493 Marine Corps, and 491,586 air force. We've brought about half of our 150,000 overseas personnel home, meaning we've got two million soldiers, sailors, airmen, and Marines available for defense of the homeland. After arming them all, we still have several million extra rifles and handguns, mostly older models. The question, sir, is whether we should distribute those surplus stocks to local law enforcement for the formation of citizen militias?"

"Good God," Stoddard responded. "Are you worried that there won't be enough bloodshed?" He turned to the attorney general. "What are *your* numbers?"

The AG said, "We estimate there are about 705,000 federal, state, and local sworn officers, with 917,000 firearms. ATF's best estimate is that there are 310 million weapons in private ownership: 114 million handguns, 110 million rifles, 4 million assault-style, and 86 million shotguns. But they're very unevenly distributed. Only a third of households, 35 million, owns even one gun, but those own an average of nine guns per household."

Browner said, "Sir, our thought was that, in order for survivors not to end up being haves with guns and have-nots without, we supply local police with our surplus stocks."

"Sure," Stoddard replied. "What's another few million guns gonna matter?" From the looks around the room, others shared Isabel's concern about the president's fatalism.

It was Browner's turn again. "Mr. President, under the Constitution, you have the power to declare martial law. But that's only been done twice in history—nationwide, during the Civil War, and in California, Oregon, Washington state, and southern Arizona, plus Hawaii during World War II. And there's really no precise meaning given to the term martial law."

The chief justice said, "It's up to Congress under Article I, Section 8, Clause 15, or you, Mr. President, under Article II, Section 2, Clause 1, to define what you mean when you institute martial law. Generally, military personnel will be granted the authority to enforce civil and criminal laws, and certain civil liberties will be suspended like protection from unreasonable searches and seizures, freedoms of association and movement, writs of habeas corpus, *etc.*"

Isabel thought, *Noah needs to get Emma released before that happens.*

"We propose, sir," Browner said, "that when you declare martial law, we will set up *cordons sanitaires* to keep Infecteds in or out, as the case may be. They are barriers to travel first employed in medieval times during the Black Death. More recently, they were used in 1821 when the French deployed troops to the Pyrenees to halt the spread of a fever from

Spain, then again in 1918 to keep louse-borne typhus in Poland out of post-revolutionary Russia, and most recently in Guinea, Sierra Leone, and Liberia during Ebola outbreaks. But unlike medieval times, when gates were simply walled up and people inside had to fend for themselves, compliance with modern cordons has been maintained by provision of food, water and medicine to the quarantined. It's unlikely, however, that we'll be able to keep SED-infected areas adequately supplied, meaning we'll have to rely on force to maintain cordons. People will have to choose between facing our guns in an attempt to break through, or braving whatever it is they're trying to flee."

The president seemed angry. "Are we back to discussing your rules of engagement, General Browner? Is this a back-door attempt to get me to agree to some ten-meter rule?"

"No, sir. Just for clarity's sake, when you authorize a quarantine, or *cordon sanitaire*, or curfew, or roadblock, we are going to kill innocent, starving, desperate men, women, and children. If you give that order, sir, to be crystal clear, that's what it'll mean."

President Stoddard closed his eyes, and then covered and vigorously rubbed his face. He then looked Browner straight in the eye, and said, "I understand." It was, Isabel thought, as much as could be expected from anyone. More, really.

Chapter 27

"What's a double-tap?" Chloe's dad asked Jake on their now regular dawn jog.

"One shot center mass, then one to the head in case they're wearing body armor."

"Good! Chloe, what's grazing fire?"

She rolled her eyes and imitated their instructor's southern accent. "It's par'llel to yer ground, like yer skippin' yer rocks on yer pond. So's if ya miss, ya hit the guy behind."

"Good," dad said. "But you're terrible at accents."

They had gone back to the range almost every day, having to wait in line for firing positions on their most recent trips. Dad had bought 10,000 more rounds of rifle ammo, 2,500 for the pistols, and 1,000 shotgun shells. Chloe couldn't imagine they could ever shoot that many people.

It was getting light when they made it back to the driveway all sweaty despite the chill. Chloe bent over and braced on her knees, out of breath. Her mom opened the front door wearing a robe and holding a coffee mug. "The Chinese are bombing Shanghai," she said. Despite dad's smelliness, mom let him hug her.

The TV was on constantly now. All it took were pictures of smoke rising over a building in Asia for it to be breaking news. Police lights triggered, "We interrupt regular programming. . . ." A mob of people hurling rocks with mouths and noses covered. "This just in!" And yet nobody said anything like, "News Flash: This is the end of the world."

"I'm gonna take a shower," Chloe said. Neither parental unit listened.

"We'll be ready," dad said confidently to her petrified mom, showing her what he'd bought. Chemical toilet. First aid kits. Work gloves. Lightsticks. Bayonets. Biosuds cleanser. Sunblock and sunglasses. Long-shelf-life food. Mylar blankets. Camper candles. Towelettes. Waterproof matches, magnesium fire starters, and disposable lighters.

In the shower, Chloe wondered if she should be scared too. Most of the kids Snapchatted that their parents were totally freaked. But things were still *kinda* normal. She blow-dried her hair straight. It looked good, so she took a smiling mirror selfie. Back downstairs, her parents were right where she'd left them. "And these?" her mom asked.

"Water purification tablets. Tube tents. Face shields. Duct tape. Compression bandages. Insect repellent. Scissors, hemostats, and tweezers. Four-mil plastic sheeting."

"Is somebody gonna make breakfast?" Chloe asked.

Disposable booties. Tyvek suits with hoods. Hatchet. Combat machete. Insulated bolt cutters. Demolition crow bar. Two tool kits. Pocket saw. Blade sharpeners.

"A*hem!*" she tried.

Manually rechargeable flashlights, lanterns, and radios. Five pairs of compact binoculars. Five two-way radios and batteries. Water filtration and storage/carrier bags.

"'*Scuse* me!" Chloe said in a louder voice.

Her dad mouthed, *Wait*! then said, in a bedtime-story voice, "Folding camp stove, fuel tablets, P51 can openers." Chloe's mom sat on her heels, staring. "Metal all-in-one camping utensils. Boxes of baggies and trash bags. Woodlands camo tarp."

"Hungy, hungy!" Chloe said in a childish voice, like she famously had said as a toddler. For the first time in her life it produced no smiles. Mom cried. Dad hugged her.

Vinyl camo ponchos. Whistles. Fifty-foot lengths of rope. Bleach. Vitamins. Ocular wash. Canteens. Fishing line and hooks. Oxygen absorbers for food storage.

"What are these?" Mom asked, holding a rubber-band bound bundle.

"Paper maps," dad responded.

Her mom said, "Because we won't have GPS anymore?" and cried again.

Duh, Chloe thought. "I'll be late for school," she reminded them.

"It's gonna be . . . terrible!" her mom managed between sobs. "Noah, the kids!"

"We'll keep them safe," he whispered with what sounded like sincerity. "You see?" He gestured toward the gear. "We're ready. We'll be completely self-sufficient."

Sun hats. Camping cookware. Over-the-counter medications. Pads and pens. Chloe said, "I'll just make a bowl of cereal," and left.

Jake arrived in the kitchen and said, "We can have cereal? Sweeeet!" He grabbed the most noxious, sugary thing he could find in the pantry.

Chloe made a disgusted face. "That shit's terrible for you," she mumbled, chewing.

Jacob made a show of tapping out the last of the sugar dust from the box, turning the milk gray. When he sat, he asked, "You think you could kill 'em? Infected people?"

She said, "I *guess*. Especially if they're those smelly nerds you play video games with. And if I ever catch them going through my underwear drawer again, I swear-to-God I'll double-tap their asses, infected or not."

Finished, she shouted down the hall, *"We're gonna be late!"* When no one appeared, Chloe went back to the study. Dad was showing off his bullhorn. "This way, we can keep our distance from people we don't know in case they're, you know . . ."

Mom consulted her notepad. "Sanitary napkins or tampons?" Dad sheepishly shook his head. "You've got a wife and teenaged daughter, but no sanitary napkins?" She added that to her list. "And Jake's inhalers? Do you have those?" He shook his head. "And my birth control pills?" Again, no. "*Okay*, but you're the one who's gonna suffer!"

"Eww!" Chloe said, disgusted. "Anybody giving us a ride to school?"

Dad rose, holding mom as if she might topple over, and took them. Chloe climbed up into the brand-new, embarrassingly huge SUV. As her dad pulled out, his cell phone rang. "Izzy? What? Why?" Chloe could hear her Aunt Isabel, who was practically shouting. "Calm down. Who's freaked out?" Dad was totally absorbed. "What the hell is compulsive eradication? Okay, *im*pulsive eradication? No! There's a court order!"

"Dad!" Chloe said. "The light's green." Chloe rolled her eyes as he drove on.

"They can't touch her. Plus, I thought you had a deal with the military?"

"Dad-watch-out!" Chloe shouted. He swerved to avoid a man racing across the street carrying a flat-screen TV, which he threw into the back seat of a car that sped away. The front door of the house from which he'd emerged hung crookedly from its hinges.

"Did he just rob that house?" Jake asked.

"Looks like it," dad replied. "Isabel, I've gotta hang up and call the police. It's getting crazy out here." He dialed 9-1-1, but all he got was a busy signal so he gave up.

As their dad searched the radio for yet more news, Jake whispered, "Are you going to that end-of-the-world party at Trey's house tonight?"

Chloe shushed him, her eyes wide, and whispered, "How'd you know about that?"

"I hear things." Like *he* was in the know. "Are you going with *Jus-tin*?" Jake pantomimed smooching, eyes closed, head tilting from side-to-side.

"Gross!" Chloe said. "When are you gonna grow up?"

"I wanna come," he said.

"To *Trey's*? What would you do at a high school party?"

"Pick up chicks," Jake replied.

She laughed. "And do *what* with them?"

He ran his tongue over his now bare front teeth. "No braces. Form a line, ladies."

"Just throw a Halo party for your nerd friends." The car pulled up to the drop-off. "But stay out of my room!" They exited. Chloe leaned into the window to say goodbye, but her dad held his hand up, trying to catch the news. Her smile dissolved. "Whatever!"

"Hey, Chlo." It was Justin, speaking in what he imagined was his sexy voice. She stifled a smile and walked right past him. "Chloe!" He caught up with her.

"Oh, I didn't see you. What's up?"

He was less certain of himself now—the way she liked him. "Uhm, you wanta come over to my place? After lax and cheer practice? No! It's not like that. My parents are gonna be there. They asked if I'd invite you over for dinner."

"Right," Chloe said. "Then they don't *show*; we move toward *your* room. . . ."

"No, really," he said, stopping and turning her. "In a month or two, who knows? We could all be dead, or zombies or whatever."

"So I should put out," she replied angrily. "Just so you don't die a virgin?"

"Who says I'm a virgin?" the handsome jock replied.

"Janie said you dumped her 'cause she wouldn't do it."

"She did plenty," Justin said. *More than me,* he meant but didn't say. "So dinner's at six. Walk you over after practice?"

She rolled her eyes, but nodded. Chloe then daydreamed her way through roll call.

"Well," the substitute teacher finally said, "I guess you can tell attendance is way down. So district has suspended our regular curriculum. No homework or tests." A modest cheer went up. "Instead of Algebra I, we're watching a video." There was an even more half-hearted celebration. In times past, the kids would've been ecstatic.

"Is this going to be on a test?" Lucy Fong asked. Everyone laughed, including Chloe. But she felt guilty when Lucy looked around from the front row. Lucy had been invited, out of tradition, to all of Chloe's birthday parties and had attended ten in a row. They had gone to the same Georgetown pre- and grammar schools, and in one of life's coincidences Lucy's family had moved to McLean one year before Chloe's. Dad didn't get why Chloe and cute little studious Lucy never became besties, but Mom definitely did.

"Ten bucks," Janie whispered across the aisle to everyone, "Lucy's the last kid in school. Like, pounding on the chained-up door. *Test* me! *Test* me! *Test* me now!"

Chloe laughed. Lucy again looked away hurt. Chloe winced. The pandemic. Justin's renewed demands. Now Lucy! Her life was an emotional roller coaster.

The whine of the projector's fan preceded by a few seconds the appearance of a picture on the white board in front. A man got off an elevator at an office about, maybe, four hundred years ago. From the production quality, the video must have cost literally hundreds to make, but that was probably a lot back then. The man coughed into his hand and touched a doorknob. Ominous music followed as the camera zoomed in on the contaminated hardware, losing focus only twice. Groans rose as the cheesy title appeared: *Flu Season!*

"Dum-dum-*duuum!*" Trey said. Everybody laughed, Lucy loudest of all. *Give it up, Luce,* Chloe thought. *Never gonna happen, sweetie, even in the apocalypse.*

Chloe snuck out her cell phone and Snapchatted friends. One class was being shown a first aid video. Another, a documentary entitled *Wilderness Survival Skills*, as best as Chloe could tell from the abbreviated and misspelled text. It could also have been, "Willingness Surveillance School," but that made no sense . . . unless you were talking about Justin, who was always on the prowl for willingness. She tried to insert that witticism into the group chat, but the topic had already moved on, so she typed, "Can u beleave that ahole Justn? 'Oh, sleep with me, b4 we all die!' Plz! Ugh!"

"Miss Miller!" the substitute said.

"I know!" she said, hiding her phone. "Cough into the crook of your elbow!" When his attention wandered elsewhere, she was back on her phone.

A girlfriend texted, "Let's sit together at lunch. This is my last day." After Chloe's query, she replied, "I dunno. Someplace in Idaho or Iowa. Whichever has mountains. U?"

"My Dad said dont say, but its in the Shen. Valley down in VA."

"Not much time for you and J to hook up!"

"F U!!!" Chloe typed, smiling, before noticing the teacher standing over her. "This is kind of important, Miss Miller," he said. "The video."

Chloe pretended to watch bad actors pretend to get the pretend flu. None of them died, or went crazy and killed people before they were shot. It was a total waste of time. Plus, she had to decide what to do about Justin before he just stopped showing up one day.

* * * *

"Hey!" Justin said, hair wet, freshly showered after lacrosse practice. When he leaned down to her, she thought he would kiss her, but he smelled her hair. "Mm!" he said. "What, do you have, like, hair dryers in the girls' locker room?"

"Wouldn't *you* like to know?" Chloe said, unable to admit the terrible truth: there had been no cheer practice. It had been *canceled!*

"I wasn't sure you'd come," he said as they walked beside each other.

"Why? Am I, like, known for being antisocial or something?"

"No! I dunno. Never mind. You'll love my mom's roast."

They had little to say to each other. It was too soon to plan their three-month anniversary. Chloe asked, "How much longer are you gonna keep coming to school?"

"They're not closing *school*! We've got districts on Saturday! Can you come?"

"My Dad said we're all hauling crap down to that old house they're fixing up in the sticks." She wanted him to ask questions like, *What crap, Chloe? Where was this old house?* Or maybe, *Are you scared, Chloe, about the end of the world and all?* But instead he talked about the upcoming playoff game, his coach's plans for him to go forward on offense, the chance he might get a "half ride" to college on lacrosse, the videographer who was making his recruiting DVDs.

"Hello!" Justin's effusive mom said, wiping her hands on an actual, honest-to-God apron. She had always seemed so much more like a real mom than Chloe's—frumpy, pillowy and probably not on antidepressants because she obviously didn't give a shit about her looks. And Justin never had to endure the humiliation of overhearing boys calling her a MILF, and proving they meant it by discussing their fantasies in disgusting detail.

Chloe got in line as the Kovics washed up at the kitchen sink. "You can never be too careful these days!" Mr. Kovic commented on their precautions. The order in the line was little sis, little bro, Chloe, Justin, and Mr. and Mrs. Kovic. They each dried their hands on the exact same towel, which struck Chloe as flawed, especially since she followed two kids who barely used soap. She treated her hands as if they were dirtier than before.

When they settled into their seats, Chloe was taken aback when the Kovics grabbed each other's hands—Justin her right hand, snot-nosed brother her left—further corrupting them. Justin's dad blessed the meal. They were Catholic or Protestant or something.

"What faith are *you*, Chloe?" Mrs. Kovic asked.

"My dad was raised Presbyterian, I think," Chloe replied.

"What about your mother?"

"She doesn't like to talk about her family. We've never met them."

Justin's mom hesitated, half-smiled, and let it go.

Chloe came prepared with the question of the day. "So, what's your family's PSP?" Justin looked intently back and forth between Chloe and his parents.

"PSP?" his mother replied.

Chloe had to explain way more than she had thought necessary. "You know, personal survival plan? Bug-out plan? What are you gonna do when the *P* gets here?"

"*Do?*" Justin's mom was obviously into repeating things. "I'm sure the government has everything under control," she said as she plopped a giant heap of mashed potatoes on the plate Chloe held out, which almost collapsed under the weight. Chloe couldn't wait to tell her Mom about the huge portions, though inevitably she would have to answer the questions that followed. "*No,* Mom! Like, four bites! Five, maybe! No, not *big* bites!"

"We put up food," Mrs. Kovic said. "We'll stay indoors until the coast is clear."

Chloe looked at Justin. "So, you're just gonna . . . *stay*? *Here*?"

Justin looked at his parents. "Chloe's family's taking off. So are Carter's, Eddie's, Trey's." His parents just shrugged. "Chloe, tell 'em about all the stuff your dad has done."

She ever so slightly arched her brow at him in rebuke. That was all supposed to be secret! "He," Chloe muttered, "you know, bought a bunch of stuff. Fixed up a house in the middle of nowhere." Justin bobbed his head, urging her on, but she made another face.

"You *see*?" Justin said. "Everybody's getting ready. Maybe we should buy a gun."

That caused polite titters. "Justin, you know what this family thinks about guns. And with young children in the house? The government will tell us what to do."

"But mom!"

"More potatoes, sweetie?" Mrs. Kovic asked Chloe pleasantly.

"No!" Chloe said, trying not to grin. She took another bite from the mound. *Three.*

* * * *

Mrs. Kovic looked angry when Justin's dad showed up at the door to smile stupidly at Chloe's mom. Justin also seemed mad and said, on parting, "They're not gonna do shit!"

In the car, Mom, oblivious to the turmoil she left in her wake, said, "I thought we'd get a makeover!" But her upset face bore a warning. Chloe argued that it was getting kind of late, and a school night, obviously not mentioning Trey's party. But mom had already made the appointments. The whole thing seemed like some bizarre set-up.

"I was thinking we'd get our hair cut," mom said on the drive. "Both of us."

"*Cut*?" Chloe said, involuntarily reaching for her hair. "You mean, like, *shorter*?"

"Uh hum." They pulled into the nearly empty parking lot of their salon. "It would be, you know, easier to take care of." She smiled. "A whole new look!"

"*How* short?" Chloe said, the pitch of her voice rising with her level of fear.

"I was thinking, you know, like a *boy* cut," mom said. "Something really chic. Short is back in style, you know. We can be like uber-trendy fashion models!"

Chloe felt tears well up. Her hands combed the beautiful blond hair she thought of as cultivated, carefully nursed, and managed, but that was probably just inherited. "Are you trying," Chloe asked, "to like make us ugly so we won't get *raped*?"

"What? *Nooo*! Chloe!" Her mom unbuckled her seatbelt and wrapped her arms around her. Both were sniffling. "I know, darling, I know. But this could be fun. Shake things up a little. And listen, it's just hair. It grows back."

"But my *hair*!" she said. Everything was changing. Everything *sucked*! She broke down and sobbed. Her mother probably thought it was all about hair, but it wasn't. She kept repeating that it would be okay. That her crazy father was really doing all the right things, and that he would keep them safe and that *that* was what really mattered.

"No more Cheer, Mom. Now *that's* over, too! I was the Lucy Fong of JV Cheerleading. Just me and the assistant coach showed up at the meeting!"

Her mother embraced Chloe tightly. "Darling, we just have to deal with what comes, okay?"

"Like shoot sick people?" Chloe asked. "Mom, I don't wanna shoot anybody!"

"I know. Let's just see how things go." She wiped the tears from Chloe's face and ran her fingers through Chloe's hair. "Such a beautiful, beautiful girl," she said, crying but trying to smile. "Come on. Let's go. I've gotta get these acrylic nails off." She sniffed. "I don't even remember what my real nails look like."

Chloe asked, "Do I have to go to school tomorrow?"

"No, you don't. You're done with school for now." Her mom straightened her face in the rearview mirror. "Ready? Let's do this."

They came out looking like boys. *Cute* boys, but boys. While studying their reflections in their respective car mirrors, Chloe, feeling drained and filled with foreboding about what the other girls will say, muttered, "Rape repellant."

Chapter 28

Emma and Samantha were on Emma's bed. Dwayne and Dorothy sat in chairs. All watched the TV news. Their no-name roommate, usually referred to by the pronoun *he* or *him*, was in his place in the far corner, avoiding everyone and being avoided.

"Why are those news people shouting?" Sam asked.

Dorothy said, "They're angry."

"Why?" Sam asked.

Both looked at Emma, who said, "They're being lied to by the government."

Sam asked, "And that makes them angry?" Emma shrugged.

One of the TV panelists said, "It's *not* North Korean nukes! It's . . . all . . . the . . . *disease*! It's people with black eyes! Committing unspeakable atrocities! *Wake* up!"

"Stay tuned," the host said. "We'll be right back."

"Tasty!" a young girl said to a woman who was boiling twenty-five-year shelf-life food. "That's probably the girl's mother," Sam said. "My mother cooks." A man and a boy at a table grinned as they ate the prepackaged meals. "I don't know who *they* are," Sam said.

"That was good," Emma noted. "You used *my* and *I*."

Dorothy looked back and forth between them. She mouthed: "I, I, I," and "my, my, my," soundlessly, but still she didn't get it. There was no way she could pass.

The program returned with a traditional newsreader. "Although experts say it will be impossible for the island nation to seal itself off from infection, the Royal Navy has recalled most of its warships for interdiction duty." The story moved on to Switzerland. Lines of cars and campers in a mountain pass were blocked by steel columns that had risen from smooth pavement. Troops in gas masks manned flimsy wooden barricades supporting loops of barbed wire. People waved passports in the air. "So far," the newsman said, "only Luxembourg, Monaco, and Andorra have joined Switzerland in closing their borders."

"In other news, the NFL has announced that next weekend's games will be played with no spectators in attendance, but will be televised without local blackout. Fans are advised by DHS to limit any viewing parties to no more than six guests."

Dwayne took a quick look at No-Name. Emma followed his gaze. The silent man sat on the floor hugging his knees to his chest and staring at the wall beside him.

A television commercial advertised remote island real estate in "fabulous English-speaking Belize." Emma browsed through the channels. Prerecorded sports events. Old movies. TV reruns. And news reporting and discussion. Emma stopped on one of those.

"Well what's your plan, then?" a woman asked a silver-haired man.

"She sounds mad, too," Samantha said. Her fists clenched Emma's bedsheets.

"It's okay," Emma said to her. "In through the nose, out through the mouth."

But when the silver-haired man answered, Samantha grew even more agitated. "There's only one solution. We can't just let them roam the streets or they'll spread the infection. We have to consider the disease 100 percent fatal and treat the survivors accordingly."

"Why not just come out and say what you're proposing?" the newswoman asked.

"That's for the government to decide," her guest replied. But the host said *no, no, no*! Samantha's body was rigid. Emma could see that her breathing was irregular. "Okay, then. We need to impose martial law when the first outbreak happens here, and we need to give the government the legal authority to take all steps necessary."

The host said, "You're proposing that we kill the infected, aren't you? Admit it!"

A free-for-all ensued. Sam's sharp jaw was set. The cords in her neck stuck out.

The bolt on the buzzing door into their room *clacked*. Samantha jumped. Emma gripped the girl's skinny thigh through her gown. All five infected patients, No-Name included, stared at the entrance as Nurse Hopkins entered in full PPE carrying boxes, which she held out in front of her. "Board games! For Samantha." A soldier, also in PPE, stood guard behind her, his pistol at the ready. Nurse Beth put the games on the desk. "And here's the nail polish and hair dryer you asked for." Beth smiled and patted Samantha's shoulder. Emma clenched Samantha's thigh tighter. "Gonna have some girl fun?" the nurse said.

Emma could feel the muscles in Samantha's legs, tensed, ready to leap at the woman. She squeezed hard until the nurse and soldier departed.

"They're going to kill us, aren't they?" Samantha whispered.

"Shhh," Emma replied.

No-Name loosed either a growl or a groan. Everyone turned. Dwayne put himself between him and the women. No-Name rocked in a seated fetal position on the floor. He couldn't bear to look at or talk to them, so he stared at the wall. He wouldn't last long.

Emma went through all of the TV channels twice, stopping for snippets of news. Nothing added to their knowledge of what was happening outside. She rose from the bed.

The others turned to Emma, and she nodded. Samantha got the nail polish. Dorothy plugged the hair dryer into the socket. Dwayne dragged a chair over to the first camera, climbed up and took the nail polish Samantha handed him. A Marine's voice came over the speakers. "Hey! Hey-hey-hey! What are you doing?"

Dwayne painted nail polish on the first of the tiny camera lenses. "I order you to stop doing that!" He did all six cameras, one after the other, in forty-eight seconds, two faster than planned, Emma confirmed on her phone's stopwatch. Dorothy turned on the hair dryer.

* * * *

"Dr. Miller!" shouted Beth into the cafeteria, hair dripping. "Come *quick!*"

Brandon had been sharing a coffee at Isabel's table. All three raced to the observation room. The only thing they could hear over the speakers was a loud *whoosh* of the hair dryer. Emma and three roommates huddled in a tight bunch on the floor behind an overturned bed. Their arms were in motion. They were doing something at the center of their clutch. Emma seemed to be leading, with Samantha her most vocal participant.

The six video surveillance views on the laptop screen were streaked and obscured.

Isabel's iPad rang like a telephone. On it she saw Captain Ramirez and his Marines, on a phone and on a radio, hunched over monitors. "I got nothing!" one said.

Ramirez turned to Isabel. "Do you have eyes on the room?"

Isabel nodded. "Yes, but we can't tell what they're doing."

Ramirez relayed an order via a radio. "Get in there! Safeties off!"

"Don't hurt them!" Isabel shouted.

"I'll be right there!" Ramirez replied.

Beth, looking shaken, said, "Your sister asked for nail polish and a hair dryer. She said she was gonna teach Sam how to make herself up. Captain Ramirez said it was okay."

The observation room door burst open. Ramirez said, "Eyes on!" into his radio.

The tinny reply stated they were in the enrobing room. "Two minutes!"

"What happened?" Isabel asked.

"Your fucking sister's crew in there painted the lenses of our cameras with nail polish," Ramirez replied, peering through the window. "What the hell are they doing?"

"You're not going to hurt them, are you?" Isabel asked.

"We're goin' in there one way or the other," Ramirez said. "Their call."

Only the Infecteds' heads and shoulders were visible above the upended bed. Emma spoke to each in turn, calmly, and got nods as their attention periodically returned to whatever was on the floor in their midst. They could hear nothing but the *whoosh*.

"Ready!" came over Ramirez's radio.

"Please tell them not to shoot!" Isabel pled.

"Angel," Beth said, touching Ramirez's arm, revealing an unexplained intimacy.

Ramirez looked at Beth's pleading eyes, then reluctantly ordered, over his radio, "Hold your fire unless you have to defend yourselves."

Emma was doing something vigorously in the center of the now silent group.

The door buzzed and opened. Four Marines in PPE entered, hunched forward behind rifles as if to brace against recoil. "Far wall! Far wall!" Their eyes were lowered to sights. Gloved fingers rested on triggers. One knelt on a kneepad for a steadier aim.

Amid the chaos, Emma rose, holding her hands in air, and then slowly reached to turn off the hair dryer. She repeated to her roommates, "Calm, calm, calm," as they made their way to the far wall, breathing in through their noses and out through their mouths. "You too, buddy!" shouted a Marine at the silent engineer.

The fifth roommate bolted, screeching, toward the kneeling Marine. "At your *three!*" Ramirez shouted. Two comrades fired. With the last of Zero

Zero Five's life, the loner fell atop the kneeling Marine, who scampered out from under him and through the door in a reverse bear crawl, readjusting his headgear. Isabel glimpsed exposed skin just below his jaw. His face shield was splattered with blood.

"Quarantine him!" Ramirez ordered over the radio.

They collected the nail polish, hair dryer, Sam's four mysterious tracings, and the shreds of the fifth. One Marine dragged the dead engineer out, leaving a smear of blood all the way to the door. The two remaining Marines completed the evacuation behind raised rifles, and the door latched.

Emma sat them all in a circle and led breathing exercises. Then Dwayne righted the bed. Samantha straightened the printouts of various maps. Dorothy used paper towels to clean up the blood. Emma retrieved her notebook and pens and headed for her bed.

But Emma stopped and looked through the window straight at Isabel, who stood with both palms pressed flat to the glass. "Is that my blouse?" Emma asked.

Chapter 29

Patricia Maldonado met Isabel in the White House parking lot and escorted her to the Family Residence Dining Room through four successive Secret Service checkpoints. "It's just you and the First Family: Angela Stoddard; Bill Junior, sixteen; and Virginia, 'Ginnie,' who's fourteen."

"Is there any, you know, protocol I should follow?" Isabel asked.

One agent raised what Isabel thought was a gun to her forehead, but it was a non-contact thermometer, which beeped.

"Just stand when the president enters," Maldonado said.

The ornate dining room had curved, wallpapered, wainscoted walls hiding nearly invisible doors, presumably for servants. Atop gleaming hardwoods were an antique rug, Mahogany table and six upholstered chairs. A mature blaze in the fireplace added ambiance. Heroic portraits and landscapes reminded Isabel of an old-moneyed manor.

A butler in a white jacket seated Isabel before crystal goblets, dinner plates trimmed in gold and heavy silverware. A floral centerpiece dominated the table beneath a glimmering chandelier. "Just like the breakfast nook in my sister's place."

Maldonado managed to curl one corner of her mouth. Her wedding band barely fit over doubled, flesh-colored bandages. "I'll wait outside," she said, heading for the door.

"Patricia?" The aide halted. "Are you making plans? Personal plans?"

Maldonado knew what she meant. She checked the closed doorways before answering. "My husband is in the air force. A pilot. He's getting things ready."

After she left, a butler arrived with ice water and asked if she would like wine. Isabel very much did, but awaited the president and First Lady's lead. When alone, she extracted her cell phone, turned so the table was the backdrop and took a grinning selfie.

The doors opened. Children's voices filled the room. "You're so lame!" a boy said to a girl. The Spaniel that Isabel remembered from campaign commercials did figure eights at their feet. Both kids straightened when they saw they had company. Bill Junior was tall and reedy with keen eyes. Ginnie had long, shining hair with a gentle, natural wave, and braces. A woman—their nanny?—introduced her charges and disappeared with the energetic dog. The kids took apparently familiar seats in silence. The butler served Ginnie ice water with a slice of lemon and a straw. She used the straw to spear the donut-shaped ice, which she chewed noisily. Bill Junior got what appeared to be a negotiated half-glass of Coke, which he guzzled. Both glanced Isabel's way repeatedly but said nothing.

"Nice place you got here," Isabel said, smiling.

Bill Junior said, "This isn't ours. All *our* stuff is in storage in Maryland."

"Our real house wasn't like this," Ginnie explained. "It was just . . . regular."

"It must've been a big change," Isabel said, "to go from your family home, in Denver, right, to the White House?"

"That wasn't our house either," Bill Junior said. "Boettcher Mansion? The governor's residence? We haven't lived in *our* house for a long time."

"I don't even *remember* it," Ginnie said, "except for the Christmas tree smell."

The door opened. The president entered talking to an aide with the First Lady listening intently. "No big stir. I just wanna see who's on what evac list." The First Lady touched his arm and nodded at Isabel. They approached the table with a public smile.

The First Lady introduced herself and took Isabel's hand in both of hers, but said, "I guess we really shouldn't be shaking hands, right? People aren't doing that anymore?"

"Dr. Miller," her husband said, smiling warmly and actually giving Isabel a brief hug. "We're so glad you could make it." As Isabel tried to think of some appropriate pleasantry, the president hugged and kissed his children.

"Hey!" Ginnie said, straightening her perfect hair.

"Squirt!" he said, mussing Bill Junior's head. "How was soccer practice?"

"Cold as hell," his son replied. "Last one. Season's canceled."

"Hell is *hot*," his little sister pointed out, "not cold."

The instant the adults settled into their seats, bread, butter, soup, and wine arrived.

"I got it." The president waved off the butler and laid a white napkin across his own lap. A waiter placed the First Lady's black napkin on her dark pants unnoticed.

"So you're a doctor?" Bill Junior asked.

"Not a medical doctor. A scientist. A professor."

"Are you working on the plague?" Ginnie inquired.

The First Lady said, "Is that what they're calling it at Sidwell Friends?"

"*No!*" Ginnie whined defensively, as if she'd said something wrong. "Ma'am," she added when she saw her mother's expression. "Most kids call it the Chinese flu or the *P*. But that stands for plague, right?"

Bill Junior said, "It stands for *Pandoravirus*, dummy. But they did hand out supplemental reading in all the history classes about The Black Death and stuff like that."

"And in English," Ginnie added, "we started reading a book called *The Plague.*"

"By Camus?" President Stoddard said good-naturedly. "*Great* book."

"Uh-*huh*," Virginia said, face contorted as she poked at her braces with her tongue.

"Well, Ginnie," her mother said, "it's really called SED or *Pandoravirus.*"

The president added, "Dr. Miller is one of the world's leading neuroscientists." Isabel was shocked by that description, as would be the tenured professors back at UCSB. "And yes, she's working on SED. Your mother and I thought you're hearing rumors at school, on TV, and here, and might want to get the real science from Dr. Miller."

The girl lowered her voice. "I hear it turns you into a *zombie* with black eyeballs."

The First Lady opened her mouth, but the president raised his hand. "Well," Isabel said, "zombies aren't real. And their eyeballs don't turn black. Their pupils widen, like when the optometrist dilates your eyes. But that goes away after a couple of weeks."

"So . . . what *does* SED do that's so bad?" Bill Junior asked.

Isabel looked at the president. "They need to hear the truth," he said . . . to his wife.

Only in Washington did you call in an outside specialist for things like the truth, Isabel thought as she described the flu-like symptoms. "The virus damages your brain. That's why some people call them zombies. But they don't bite, or eat brains or anything."

She took a sip of wine. Bill Junior said, "So why's everybody so scared of them?"

"Every*one*," his mother corrected.

"Well," Isabel replied, "they're highly contagious for a couple of weeks. Plus," she drank again, "some are kinda violent. They can't control their emotions."

The First Lady said, "I didn't think they *had* emotions."

The waiters replaced their soup bowls and pristine dinner plates with new plates, then laid on them, in unison, an *amuse bouche*. They also refilled Isabel's wine glass.

"True. Sorry, I oversimplified. They can't control their fight-or-flight responses. The part of their brain that inhibits adrenaline production is damaged. They perceive a threat, their sympathetic nervous system fires, the adrenal medulla produces a hormone that triggers secretion of catecholamines—norepinephrine and epinephrine . . ."

"I think you overcorrected on the simplicity," the president interrupted, smiling. "They're smart." He winked at Ginnie. "So give them details, but . . . in simpler words."

Isabel knew she masked, in science, her own turbulent emotions, which lay in a shallow grave, threatening to reveal an elbow, a knee, a skull. "So, a big gush of adrenaline makes their hearts beat faster, breathing pick up, blood vessels dilate to carry more oxygen, digestion slow to preserve energy, sphincter muscles tighten and blood vessels constrict to reduce . . . fluid loss. Fat is liberated for energy, tunnel vision aids focus, spinal reflexes are disinhibited, allowing for faster-twitch responses. That's when they're primed to run . . . or to fight."

"I heard you can't kill 'em," Ginnie said meekly in her still childish high pitch. Everyone objected. "I heard you can't *hurt* them!" she said, defending herself.

"They're talking about pain," Isabel replied. "If you pinched them, they would know it, but it wouldn't hurt. They wouldn't say, '*Ow.*' Feeling hurt is an emotion."

The head butler spurred eavesdropping waiters to serve the pheasant, mixed vegetables, and caramelized risotto. This *so* beat the food at the NIH cafeteria! Isabel drained her second glass of wine and nodded when offered more. The First Lady genteelly patted her lips with a napkin.

Ginnie said, "I heard they come back to life, and the government is covering it up."

"*L'etat, c'est moi*," her father said with another wink.

Bill Junior translated. "The state, it's me. Dad's saying he *is* the government." He looked at Isabel. "So, do they, technically, die and come back to life?"

"No, of course not," Isabel replied, feeling warm from the silky wine, which went down like water. She kept forgetting to pull up the front of Emma's revealing blouse until Bill Junior noticed. "And it doesn't take anything special to kill them either. No head shots, silver bullets, wooden stakes, crucifixes, or garlic." She took another long draw of the deliciously full-bodied Malbec, then caught the First Lady's eye and put the glass down.

"Then what *is* different about them?" little Ginnie asked.

"Let's see. *Hmm*. Well, they can concentrate for hours without getting distracted. And they appear to have a total lack of empathy, which prevents social bonding."

"What's empathy?" Ginnie asked, turning to her big brother.

"*Uhm*, it's like, *caring*? About other *people*?" The First Lady nodded. The attending waiter refilled Isabel's wine glass, but the First Lady declined.

"What I don't get," young Bill said, "is, if they've lost consciousness, if *that's* true, how they can still walk around and talk and stuff. Is it like sleepwalking?"

"Oh," Isabel said, chewing in a hurry to reply. The president had obviously discussed SED with or in front of them before. "It's a different meaning of the word conscious." She defined it, then said, "They don't understand the concept of *you*, Bill Stoddard, being inside *your* body, at the controls, making all the decisions like the Great Oz."

The children were baffled by Isabel's hopelessly outdated cultural reference.

The president's son thought for a moment, then asked, "Do they have a soul?"

"That's a religious question," his father replied, "not a scientific one."

"But if they don't have a soul, the kids at Sidwell say it's okay to kill them."

"William!" his mother exclaimed.

"That's what they're *saying*! *Are* you?" he asked his father. "Gonna kill them?"

It seemed to Isabel like a straightforward question with a simple answer. But the president's delay in responding presaged a more significant reply. "I don't know," he said.

Isabel was shocked. But scrubbed, wide-eyed little Ginnie said, "I saw a YouTube video of a mom throwing her baby off a bridge." Everyone looked at her. "In China."

The president tapped the rim of his empty wine glass, which was instantly refilled. He motioned hospitably toward Isabel's, which was also filled without her objection. No one made any comment at all on Ginnie's horrible story.

"Are the people who turned," the boy asked, "like, robots or cyborgs? I mean, do they act like, you know, machines? Or, like, those people who had . . . lobo-ectomies?"

"Lobotomies," his mother said. "And we talked to you about filler words."

They awaited Isabel's reply. She washed the pheasant down with wine and smacked her lips. "Well, so . . ." *Were those filler words?* "They have brain damage. But they don't drool, or shamble, or moan. And they would share our perceptions of events we both experience. In fact, they have much more accurate recollections of traumatic events than *un*infected people. D'ya know why?"

Bill Junior looked around before saying, "'Cause they don't freak out in a disaster?"

"Th-tha'ss *right!*" Isabel replied. She had to pull Emma's blouse up again, this time because Mrs. Stoddard followed her son's gaze. "Most have no problem learning, thinking, and reasoning just like us. They're just . . . *different.*" That last bit was addressed to the president, who avoided her gaze.

"And a threat," Mrs. Stoddard noted.

Isabel considered several replies, but her silence ended up just being a long pause.

"Have you ever known anybody who turned Infected?" Ginnie asked.

"Any*one*," the First Lady said. "And Dr. Miller, you don't have to . . ."

"It's okay," Isabel said, clearing her throat. "My sister turned. My twin sister."

"Oh." Ginnie shot a look at her brother, who must have kicked her under the table. Ginnie then asked, timidly, "What does your sister do all day?"

"Most recently, before the incident yesterday, she had a map of the four quadrants of the United States: northeast, southeast, northwest and southwest. A little Infected twelve-year-old girl colored the maps with green for arable land, blue for freshwater supplies, purple for industrial base. In the margins they noted the length of growing seasons, climate extremes, sources of energy, military equipment, preexisting population, susceptibility to natural disasters. They seem to be focusing on the southeastern quadrant from Texas to D.C."

"Planning on seceding again, are they?" the First Lady joked.

Isabel wondered how close that might be to the truth.

"What incident yesterday?" the attentive young Bill Stoddard asked Isabel.

"Oh, an infected man at the hospital got shot and killed when he attacked a Marine."

"And the Marine died too," Angela Stoddard said.

"What?" Isabel replied, shocked.

"You hadn't heard?" The First Lady looked at her husband.

President Stoddard said, "His headgear was displaced. He caught it from blood spatter through fresh nicks on his neck from shaving. They used to require shaving because masks seal better. Now, the new rule is no shaving. Anywhere. Women too."

Isabel was appalled. *That* was all it took? A nick from shaving? Poor, poor man.

President Stoddard said, "Also, just so you know, they noticed that your sister had folded the pieces of paper before she tore them up, but they still can't make sense of them."

In the silence that followed, Ginnie lowered her voice. "Does your sister go to the *bathroom*?"

The other Stoddards broke out laughing. Ginnie blushed. Isabel attempted a save by turning it into a real question. "Her autonomic responses—the automatic ones—are intact. Respiratory rate, heart rate, pupillary response—*finally*—urination, sexual response. They're all normal."

The table fell quiet, but Bill Junior's eyes darted about. Isabel tugged her blouse up. Angela Stoddard turned to her son as if he'd spoken and said, "Yes, William?"

"I heard they," he hesitated, "Infecteds, rape people?"

Before Isabel could disabuse him of that falsehood, the president said, "Unfortunately that may be true." *What?* Isabel thought in distress. *His kids find that out at the same time as me?* "At least anecdotally," the president concluded.

Ginnie asked what anecdotally meant. The First Lady said it was an SAT word and had Bill Junior define it, then suggested it was time for homework and SAT prep.

"Dad said I could watch the *Pretty Little Liars* marathon!" Ginnie whined. "*Remember?*" Angela Stoddard shot a look at her husband, who could only shrug.

"And why study for SATs?" their son challenged. "Nobody's going to college. No Harvard. No Yale Law. No Congress. No Senate. Ginnie isn't marrying some prince she meets at St. Andrews." A stricken Ginnie, lips quivering over braces, shook crystal goblets when she pushed back from the table and ran from the room. Bill Junior, arms braced stiffly against his chair's back, said, "You should tell everybody the truth," and left.

Isabel motioned for a wine refill. "Thank you!" The waiter served dessert and, at the First Lady's direction, coffee. But Isabel clung to her wineglass. The First Lady thanked the butler for the meal, which appeared to be a signal. The room emptied.

When the door closed, Isabel said, "*Rape?*"

Bill Stoddard leaned forward. "It truly *is* anecdotal. The only evidence is drone footage. And how do we know the sex isn't consensual? It's in public, but we don't see men chasing down women. Just brief glimpses during flyovers, and . . ." He hesitated.

After a moment, his wife, herself curious, asked, "And what?"

"In one video, *one*, the woman was on top, okay? In a park. That's all we know."

Isabel downed her wine, which seemed to help. She'd never tried drugs. Now seemed like a good time.

The First Lady cleared her throat, switched to a businesslike tone, and changed topics. "I understand your brother went to federal court and the judge ruled that your sister is still a person under the Constitution?" Isabel remembered now that Angela Stoddard had been a partner at a big law firm before becoming homemaker-in-chief. "And you were certified an expert?" Isabel nodded. "And if you were asked again to testify, someday, whether a *Pandoravirus* survivor is a person under the US Constitution, understanding that your prior testimony was under oath and is in the record, what would you say?"

"Angela," the president said. "I'm sure there's really no reason to . . ."

"I'd like to hear her answer," his wife interrupted.

They waited. "My professional opinion hasn't changed," Isabel said.

"She's means me," explained the president. "If *I* get sick and turn. One of my wife's aides overheard Browner asking the Chief Justice, *hypothetically*, whether I'd still be commander-in-chief." He looked at his wife and tilted his head. "It was just *talk*."

"Fucking Browner," Angela said, refilling her own wineglass from a crystal decanter.

The president said to Isabel, "He wants to use nukes . . . in *America*. All his maps show outbreak simulations in red. They look like . . . *tumors* to be excised. An irregularly shaped blob sprouting little crimson veins extending outward along roads and rivers. But after a surgical strike, *poof,* the blob is gone, and its edges are all rosy. One showed the effects of hitting a city that was obviously Miami, you could tell from the bays, with twenty-*two*, dialed-down warheads. Little bitty twenty-kiloton strikes, not big, bad multi-megaton detonations. And great news! We've got enough warheads to service *all* our medium to large cities, with plenty to spare! And the best news? It buys us another few miserable years of existence, according to 'The Model.'"

Isabel stared at the table in silence. What could she possibly say?

"Dr. Miller," President Stoddard said, "Isabel, the security council decided today it's time to come clean about *Pandoravirus* with a coordinated, worldwide public information campaign while communications are still intact. I'd like you to go on television and tell the American people what you told our kids. My press office will set up the interviews."

Despite the alcohol, Isabel felt ice coat her veins. "Not Dr. Stavros or Aggarwal?"

The president shook his head. "The docs are punch lines these days. Their credibility is shot. Focus groups viewed video of you from Bethesda. You've got a high 'Q-Rating.' Plus, there's the human interest angle. Your sister. Just keep it sub-apocalyptic, please. They'll try to get you to say *Armageddon* or *extinction* or whatever. Stick to what we know. That's scary enough. And try to use simple language."

"Can someone brief me?" Isabel asked. "I hadn't heard about rape."

"What *you* know," said the First Lady, cryptically, from the opposite end of the table, "is what we want the American people to hear."

Isabel turned to the president. Petrified, she could only manage a nod of agreement.

"And we'll stay in touch on the other thing," the First Lady said, rising.

What other thing? Isabel wondered. She shook hands with the departing power couple, hearing fucking-Browner-this and fucking-Browner-that from the First Lady.

Maldonado paced the corridor in spike heels and returned her phone to her purse.

"Have you been waiting out here this whole *time*?" Isabel asked gushingly.

"So, you enjoyed dinner," Maldonado said, linking arms with the wobbly Isabel.

"That was *really* nice of them to invite me," Isabel said. "To get to meet their *kids*!"

Maldonado snorted. "Nobody does anything just to be nice in this town. Everybody always wants something, especially her."

Whoa! Isabel thought. *Me*-ow. Outside, Isabel took a deep, refreshing breath of the brisk night air. On the walk to Isabel's car, Maldonado stopped. "Have you heard the latest?" Isabel shook her head. "It's in Vietnam now. They think, you know, this is it."

"Oh, sh-shit," Isabel replied, slurring.

"The Vietnamese aren't even treating the sick," Maldonado almost whispered. "Their military went through wards not only shooting people in their beds, but in *waiting* rooms. Even family members who brought the sick *in*. Now, no one's going to hospitals. Everything is leaking, my husband got sent to fucking North Dakota, my housekeeper just walked out!" *The final straw.* Maldonado checked her phone again but found no new messages.

"So you're alone, with your kids!" Isabel realized and simultaneously said.

"Can I ask an off-the-wall question?" Maldonado said. "If you ever, God forbid, got caught by a mob of them and just went fetal, would they maybe leave you alone?"

"That's not the way . . ." Isabel tried to say.

"Don't antagonize them. *Talk* to them. Calm them down, like your sister does."

"Sorry, but no. Mobs feed off each *other's* agitation, not their victims'."

Maldonado heaved a sigh. "You should know, I'm walking back in and quitting."

"Quitting? Your *job*?"

The bright illumination of the White House left half of Maldonado's worried face in shadow. To Isabel's surprise, Maldonado hugged her. Her hard back heaved with sobs as she whispered, "You don't know what I've heard! You should get out while you can!" With those words, Maldonado did just that, heels clicking all the way back inside.

Chapter 30

Isabel shivered in CNN's freezing Washington studio despite the bright lights around the large vanity mirror. The special's host in the chair next to Isabel had her make-up tech bring Isabel a pashmina. "They keep it like a meat locker in here. Helps prevent flop sweats."

A man with a headset said, "Ten minutes," from the door.

Why am I here? Isabel kept thinking.

"You're gonna be famous," the woman said. "Atlanta's been promo'ing tonight heavily. You've got the whole hour. They're expecting record ratings. The White House asked us to go light on the doom and gloom." She took charge of her own eyelashes. "But how the hell do you do that?" When Isabel didn't risk betraying her nerves with an answer, the CNN reporter said, "You'll do fine. You're pretty. The camera will love you."

The momentary peace of mind following the compliment disappeared the instant a man arrived to lead them to the set. On the way, Isabel's handler from the White House communications office fell in alongside her and repeated, in whispers, "No apocalyptic shit. Just the facts. Don't *scare* everybody." *Right!* Isabel thought.

Time sped up. A CNN guy had Isabel remove the generic jacket from wardrobe, hastily pinned to fit her small waist, then clamped twin mics on the lapel of the silk blouse she'd borrowed from Emma's closet. Her jacket covered the wire to the transmitter they hooked onto the waistband of her jeans. The chair was awkwardly angled forward. She couldn't see anything in the blinding lights except the rectangular hood of the studio camera. When she inserted her earpiece, the director was telling her interviewer, "We've been talking all day about the infectious disease part. You do Zombies 101."

"Got it," the composed host said. Isabel feared she was shaking so badly she might fall out of her chair. "You *okay?*" the interviewer asked Isabel, which *really* didn't help. Isabel flashed a sickly smile.

The crew cleared the set as the audible countdown became a silent retraction of a stagehand's fingers. "Breaking news," the director said into their ears. "Dramatic music. Graphics." The stagehand's count hit zero and he pointed. Isabel smiled out of habit.

"Good evening," the grim-faced host said, and Isabel wiped the inappropriate grin from her face. "We have with us tonight Dr. Isabel Miller, one of the world's foremost neuroscientists," *oh God,* "who will give the American people their first definitive explanation of *Pandoravirus's* effects on survivors. Welcome, Dr. Miller."

"Pleasure to be here," Isabel said. Her voice sounded okay, but *pleasure?*

The woman went over Isabel's credentials—degrees, professorship, and work at the NIH. Isabel knit her hands together to keep them from going rogue. "So what *do* we know about the effects of *Pandoravirus* on its survivors?" The host nodded.

Got it. Talk. "There's been a lot of misinformation about SED given how new it is and how rapidly it's spreading. But all survivors, to varying degrees, suffer the same pattern of damage to the brain, which results in a range of altered behaviors." Isabel discussed the spectrum from low- to high-functioning, the latter with intellectual abilities undiminished and, in some cases, even enhanced by SED.

"What about the violence?" the host asked.

Isabel described the unregulated adrenal surges and fight-or-flight responses, and how not to agitate Infecteds. Then she described mob rampages.

"*Mmm,*" the host responded, wincing. "So, they attack in packs? Hordes? And what about pain? There was that awful video out of South Korea of an Infected man captured and tortured by a mob of uninfected people after an attack. His big black eyes just stared back, unblinking, as they did terrible things to him."

Isabel hadn't seen the video, but went over her now rote discussion of pain.

"So does the loss," the woman asked Isabel, "of their ability to understand what pain is account for the extreme levels of cruelty they reportedly show their victims?"

"Their lack of empathy," Isabel replied, "is the more profound issue. To put it simply, whatever bonds or relationships a *Pandoravirus* survivor had before infection are completely erased. Love, friendship, even simple virtues like kindness—they're all gone. The point everyone needs to understand, to *believe*, is that an Infected is no longer your parent, spouse, or child in any emotional sense, and there is a *great* risk that they will rise from their sick bed and do you and the rest of your family grievous harm."

The newswoman drew a deep breath and said, "Wow. We'll come right back after this brief commercial break. Don't go anywhere," she said to the camera.

"*Aaand* break," came the director's voice. "We're off-air. Three minutes."

A hand gripped Isabel's arm painfully. The angry-looking White House communications woman dragged Isabel out of the lights while repeatedly snapping, "I *know!*" into her phone. She reached inside Isabel's short jacket and unplugged the microphone from its transmitter. "What the fuck!" she said. "Kids killing parents? Are you fuckin' *serious?* What part of 'Do not cause a panic' did you fail to understand?"

"So I'm supposed to make *Pandoravirus* sound like a *good* thing?" Isabel replied. The stagehand pried her away from the functionary, who returned to her telephonic beating.

* * * *

During an advertisement for an Internet company selling survival supplies, poorly filmed and looking out of place on a prime-time national news program, Chloe, Jake, and Natalie turned to Noah, who had no idea what to say. "*Dad,*" Chloe said in a trembling voice, "what if one of *us* gets it?" Natalie put her arm around their daughter. "I can't shoot you, or Mom, or even Jake. Would you shoot *me*?"

"Nobody's shooting anybody," Natalie said, "because nobody's getting *sick*."

"So," Chloe replied, "we're special because we had a coupla weeks' head start?"

"We had a month's head start," Noah said. "Everybody else is just getting going. We threw a ton of money at the problem and got out ahead of the shortages and the panic."

"Do you really think *money* is going to save us?" Chloe shot back. As was typical of children who grew up rich, Chloe was blind to the importance of wealth.

"No," he patiently replied. "But all the things we bought *with* that money might."

"She's on," Jacob said.

They turned to the TV—rapt, presumably like the rest of the country, who were getting a dump of the complete, unvarnished truth for the first time.

"We're back with Dr. Isabel Miller of the National Institutes of Health," the CNN anchorwoman said. "The responses to what you've been telling the nation, Dr. Miller, have lit up our switchboard and servers. Here's one question from a viewer." She read from her laptop. "Charlene Gibbons of DeKalb, Illinois, writes, 'The government can't expect us to abandon our sick children. What advice can the doctor give us to help with their violent tendencies?' Good question, Charlene. Dr. Miller, how would you respond?"

Noah could tell, from the puzzled look on Isabel's always transparent face and her brief delay in replying, that she wasn't prepared to offer highly practical solutions. *Come on, Izzy,* Noah thought. Even a guess would help. "Charlene," Isabel said, "I understand your fears. My own sister, my twin sister, an epidemiologist, was the first American to contract SED about a month ago while in Siberia, where it broke out."

"Atta girl," Noah said, drawing a scowl from Natalie. His wife was more of a pissed-off citizen, angered by the government's deception, than a sympathetic sister-in-law.

"Oh, my God," the news anchor said, resting her hand on Isabel's forearm, "I had no idea. I'm so, so sorry. How is she doing? Did she . . . ?"

Isabel nodded. "She survived. And turned. She's very high-functioning. But my point is, she nonetheless exhibits signs of unregulated adrenaline production." Isabel went through the list. Rapid, shallow breathing, tense muscles, churning stomachs, racing hearts, skyrocketing blood pressure, clenched teeth, twitchy eyes, cold hands and feet, pupils, if they've returned to normal, dilating again, hypervigilance, jumpiness, paranoia. "You should reduce the noise and commotion around them. No sudden moves. Don't crowd them. Give them a way out. Don't lock them up or tie them down unless you plan to keep them that way. And definitely no threats like brandishing a weapon, although I'd . . . I'd keep one handy."

"Anything else help?" the newswoman asked, her voice losing its professional tone.

"Interestingly, my sister—Emma—found that exercise helps. We gave her access to a treadmill, and the exertion helps metabolize her excess stress hormones."

Natalie scoffed. "You wanta kill me, but why not hop on this treadmill instead?"

"So what *does* work?" the CNN anchorwoman asked.

Deep breathing, progressive muscle relaxation techniques, and sedation. Otherwise, their physiological response overwhelms everything, including their survival instinct.

After a somber silence, the anchorwoman said, "Let's go to commercial. We'll be right back with Dr. Isabel Miller."

* * * *

Emma and her roommates watched a commercial for a walled development in Montana, whose security force tore across idyllic, fly-fishing country atop ATVs. A map showed platted lots as the narrator urged viewers to get in on pre-construction pricing. "That looks safe," Samantha said, not realizing they would never admit an Infected as a resident.

"We've been deluged with questions," the host said on returning. "This one is from Bill Strickland, a psychiatrist in Reno, Nevada, who writes, 'Please have your guest talk more about their lack of empathy.' You mentioned that earlier in the hour."

"When an Uninfected mother," Isabel said, "sees the face of her newborn, fMRI imaging shows her orbitofrontal cortex light up like a Christmas tree. She feels happy, warm, and motherly, reinforcing maternal attachment. But in an Infected mother, there's zero activation of the brain even when she holds her infant in her lap during imaging."

"That's so sad," the CNN reporter commented.

"Why is that sad?" Samantha asked. "And what is *sad*?"

Dorothy said, "With the first baby, the sadness was bad. Postpartum depression."

"Being sad is a sickness," Dwayne added. "There's medicine for it."

"*Shh*," Emma said, taking notes as Isabel continued.

"This question is from Harlan Arnold of Syracuse, New York." The journalist's tone had gone flat. "'Can she explain what she meant about Infecteds having no *self*?'"

Isabel nodded. "This change may be the most important of all." She again described a sense of self, but Emma couldn't come up with anything to write. "We don't just perceive our own consciousness. We see it in others. We know we are conscious, so we assume everyone else is too. That's what Infecteds have lost."

Samantha said to Emma, "That sounds made up. What's she talking about?"

The newswoman also struggled to get it. "I'm sorry," she said to Isabel. "I think I speak for our viewers when I say I have difficulty understanding what you're saying." Dwayne nodded.

Isabel said, "You may think that your conscious brain directs you to ask your questions in this interview. But what actually happens is that alternative questions compete behind the scenes until the winning option wells up from a layer of mental function—the *sub*conscious—into which consciousness has no insight. When that question pops into your head, consciousness then claims it as the fruits of its labor. But history is replete with examples of *sub*conscious mental breakthroughs. Carl Friedrich Gauss tried for years to solve a mathematical theorem before the answer came to him 'like a sudden flash of lightning.' Henri Poincaré made a major mathematical discovery with his mind blank just as his foot landed on the first step onto a bus. Albert Einstein had so many insights while shaving that he took special care each morning that he didn't cut himself from astonishment. And we all know about Isaac Newton and the apple."

Dorothy said, "She's making that up. Is this a real broadcast? I've seen her here."

"Do you trust her?" Samantha asked Emma.

"I don't trust anyone," Emma said. That also made sense to Dwayne, who nodded again.

But Isabel described thoughts coming to you like a voice out of nowhere, exactly as Emma had experienced. Maybe there was something to that.

"That woman," Dorothy said, "might be sick. A cousin was put into an institution because voices told her to cut herself."

"Do they all have that?" Dwayne asked. "Voices telling them things?"

"*Shh!*" Emma said, trying to find points that she could record in her notebook.

"Lots of ingrained habits won't be disrupted," Isabel said. "But over time, the direction their society takes is bound to diverge from the one we created."

"It sounds like you're talking about a whole new society, a different civilization, emerging in parallel to our own," the newswoman said.

"I didn't say in parallel."

"Are you suggesting, then, Dr. Miller, that *we* might end up living in *their* civilization?"

Emma ignored the uninteresting question and found her list of plans: (1) Complete research, (2) Publish results, (3) Find a man, (4) Get married, (5) Buy a house, and (6) Have children. Beneath each were numerous subsidiary milestones.

Something was missing. Research. Publish. Man. Marry. House. Children.

"If they're going to destroy our civilization," the reporter said, "shouldn't we . . . ? There's been a lot of talk that this is a fight for survival. People have proposed pretty," she struggled to find words, "*extreme* solutions, like either we kill them or they kill us."

"It's really not my place to express a view on that subject."

Emma finally found something to note: (7) Organize for survival. She scratched out '7' and wrote '1.' It was the single most important task to be accomplished.

* * * *

Following the broadcast, Isabel sought out her White House handler. "When's my next appearance?" she asked. Without removing the phone from her ear, the angry woman snapped, "That's it for you," and walked away.

That was fine with Isabel, but she nonetheless felt the sting of rejection.

Chapter 31

Isabel's first decent night of sleep in a week was ruined at four in the morning by loud pounding on the door of Emma's apartment. She assumed it was the FBI again, but she looked through the peephole and saw a well-coifed blond woman lit by bright camera lights. *Shit*! By the time she showered and dressed, dozens of vans with tall antennae filled the apartment grounds.

She could no longer call Maldonado or FBI Director Pearson. But through the bathroom window she saw a Bethesda cop wearing a surgical mask, who must have been attracted to the disturbance. She stood on the toilet, opened the small window and asked him to come up and help. She opened the front door to him. "Thanks *so* much for . . ."

The maelstrom outside engulfed them. "Dr. Miller! Where do you recommend our viewers go to escape the disease?" The cop hauled her through the crush. "Dr. Miller! Will the White House shut down international flights?" The cop barked at reporters, but they didn't part. "Dr. Miller! Does SED turn men into rapists?" The cop fended off microphones like branches on a jungle trek. As they passed 208C, Josh held an imaginary phone to his ear, still not realizing she wasn't Emma. Another of Emma's neighbors booed. A third gave Isabel the middle finger.

At Isabel's car, the cop shouted, "Good luck!" as she squeezed into the driver's seat. He did his best to clear a path through the mob, and she did her best not to hit anyone, driving one mile per hour and hoping that the banging sounds she heard were reporters pounding on her hood and not her car colliding with them. Finally, she pulled clear. The world had officially gone insane.

The traffic was heavier than she had ever seen it, and it wasn't even light out yet. Every parking lot looked full. There were lines to enter grocery and hardware stores, some even before they opened. Cars queued around the block at every gas station. Outside a big-box electronics retailer, two men fought over a box. Drivers stuck in traffic blew horns and craned necks. Some vehicles were piled high with belongings. *All this happened overnight?*

After an hour, she made it the short distance to the NIH hospital, which stood in starkly serene contrast. Its grounds were empty save for Marines patrolling in pairs. She parked in the nearly empty lot and, as an afterthought, confirmed her pistol was still in the bag in her trunk. In the hospital, she saw only Marines and an occasional exhausted nurse. At the last ID and pupil check, she told the guard she wanted to see Captain Ramirez.

He escorted her to a cramped office. Ramirez and two young enlisted men lounged at computer monitors jury-rigged atop tables. On most screens were empty stretches of wall pierced by a gate, or a building entrance, or a security check. But on several were hospital rooms with mostly motionless patients. On one were six views of Emma and her roommates from cameras that must have been replaced.

"First," Isabel said, "let me say how sorry I am about the loss of your man."

"Hendricks," Ramirez said. "Tony Hendricks."

"Oh!" *Jesus!* "I *met* him." That was the young Marine she had met on her visit to Emma's room. The incident had suddenly gone from casualty of war to personal tragedy. He was nineteen. *Just a boy.* "Did he," she asked, "ever get his beers?"

"Yes, ma'am," Ramirez said. All three Marines looked stricken.

How many people had already died in blacked-out regions of Asia? How many more deaths were soon to follow? "I'm *so*, so sorry," Isabel managed. Tears welled up. They didn't seem particularly interested in her level of sorrow. Plus, she was there for a different purpose. "Captain Ramirez, I want to take my sister for a walk around the grounds. She's far less contagious now. We can put her in PPE, and I'll personally . . ."

"Okay," Ramirez interrupted.

That's it? Isabel thought. *Just . . . okay?*

Ramirez's attention was focused on his gloomy young Marines. "Just watch out for paparazzi," he added, punching one of the tense boys on the arm. He was trying to change their mood—to force them beyond their loss. This was war. There would be more. "Tony Hendricks," he said in a reverent tone. "U-S-Fuckin'-M-C."

As the Marines pounded Ramirez's proffered fist, each belted out, "*Marine* Corps!" "*Marine* Corps!" in turn.

Isabel couldn't tell how long to wait after the obscure ritual ended. "*Uhm* . . . you said something about *paparazzi*?"

"You know your sister's a star, right?" Ramirez said. Isabel's face must have betrayed her confusion. Ramirez backhanded an enlisted man on the shoulder. The boy somehow knew exactly what he wanted and pulled up a YouTube video on his laptop.

Stirring patriotic music and a flag waving in the wind began a Homeland Security video, which Ramirez said aired on multiple networks last night after Isabel's CNN appearance. "Where you been at, ma'am?" Ramirez said. "Everybody saw this." He ordered the young Marine to, "Go to the part . . . Yeah, yeah."

The young Marine dragged the slider about a third of the way into the video. Flying by were Drs. Aggarwal and Stavros, a microscopic image of a *Pandoravirus* capsid, a cartoon figure exhaling particles that filled a room, a close-up of dilated pupils, brain autopsy cross-sections. "There!" Ramirez said, slapping the unfazed boy on the back of his shaved head.

The host, in the uniform of this war—a lab coat, N95 mask and Latex gloves—said, "Dr. Emma Miller contracted SED while investigating the initial outbreak in Siberia. Dr. Miller, how do you feel?" He tilted the stick mike, which had its own blue impermeable barrier fashioned over a foam bulb as if to protect viewers from infection via the mic's wires. Emma sat in an office wearing her hospital gown.

"What the *fuck*?" Isabel exclaimed. The Marines grinned at her apparently inexpert use of profanity.

"I'm fine," Emma replied, peering blankly into the camera.

The host said, "Notice that her eyes have regained their natural color, which typically happens after about two weeks and makes identifying SED carriers much more difficult. The safest method then is to look for behavioral cues." Isabel clamped her hand to her mouth as the camera zoomed in on Emma's face. "A flat emotional affect. Bland personality. Absence of reaction when emotions would be expected." The inscrutable Emma, sweet or sinister, who could tell, filled the screen. "No demonstrative gestures. No animation in facial expression or vocal inflection."

"This isn't right!" Isabel protested. It reminded her of old, uplit film of mental patients taken by the Nazis in the late thirties to justify beginning the Holocaust with them.

"Dr. Miller?" Emma turned to the off-screen questioner, but the camera remained on her. "When you were in Siberia, did you see anyone killed?"

"Yes." The picture zoomed in on her uncreased, un-made-up, uncaring face, devoid of the vibrance of the living. "When our helicopter landed, we were attacked. Most of the attackers were shot, but one was stabbed by a Russian soldier who caught SED. That night, I shot that soldier when he crawled into my tent." She used the same tone in which she would have read a grocery list: otherworldly, robotic, inhuman. "And Russian soldiers shot the infected oil workers." She pointed, her finger the barrel of a Russian pistol, at the center of her forehead. "And in the streets of a small Siberian town, and in boats crossing a river, and on the tarmac of the airport, they shot 100 to 150 people, maybe more. And at the airport in Khabarovsk, an infected man attacked my sister and was shot by Marines."

"Yeah, *baby*!" shouted one of the enlisted men, and got high fives in celebration. Isabel noted that Emma still had trouble with the word "see." She hadn't witnessed the shooting in Khabarovsk, but still thought it responsive.

The camera pulled back. As if Emma weren't even there, the host said, "Note that Dr. Miller's expressiveness isn't simply blunted or impoverished. It's entirely absent. And it's not only that she doesn't *express* emotions. Her ability to *feel* emotion has been robbed from her. She is no longer capable of enjoyment, happiness, fun, interest, or even simple satisfaction. And she feels no empathy, no compassion, for anyone else. Without empathy, Infecteds are very, very dangerous."

"*May* be dangerous!" Isabel said, her outrage growing.

The scene switched to video of a riot, which the young Marine froze on a screen overlaid with a warning about graphic images to follow.

"Those mother*fuckers*!" Isabel shouted to the further amusement of the Marines. "They don't have any right to put her in a video!"

"She signed a consent," Captain Ramirez said. "We monitored the whole thing."

"Who said she could sign a legally binding document in her condition?" Ramirez shrugged. Isabel now *really* wanted to speak to Emma alone. "I'm taking her for a walk. If you make me, I'll get my brother to go back to court. . . ."

"I said it's alright, ma'am," Ramirez replied. "Go get yourself kitted out and we'll meet you in the robing area." Isabel nodded, belatedly remembering she had already won. "Oh," Ramirez added, "and Poonhound says to tell you hello."

"Captain Townsend?" she replied. "Did he say anything else?" she asked. Ramirez shook his head as if it had been a difficult and confusing question. "Just, 'hello'?" Ramirez nodded. "Okay. Thanks."

Isabel went to the enrobing room dangerously distracted. What did "hello" mean? Was it a good thing, or a bad thing? Was it, *Hello, don't forget me*, or more, *Hello, who is she again*? She donned full personal protective gear, twice having to make herself concentrate on what she was doing, and waited in the corridor until three Marines with rifles, also in protective garb, joined her. On closer inspection, she saw it was Ramirez and the same two boys from the security station. This must be therapy after helplessly watching their comrade's slow-motion death in his sick room.

But this wasn't the touchy-feely kinder-and-gentler type of therapy. "Shut the fuck up! Pay attention. On your toes!" Ramirez snapped. The boys were excited to get out of their office. Too much time at screens, too little toting guns. *That's about to change.*

She asked Ramirez, "Why are you being so accommodating?"

"I'm accommodating by nature, ma'am," he replied. He then added, "Orders."

Browner had been true to his word.

The robing room door opened. Emma leaned out looking left and right as if someone might be waiting there to seize her. She had not showered on exiting her hospital room; she wore only a mask and gloves sealed to the long sleeves of her gown with tape. Her isolation protocols were being relaxed. "Alright," Isabel said. "Let's go for a walk."

Isabel linked her arm through Emma's and led her toward the exit, having to drag her wary sister to achieve a normal walking pace. The Marines trailed. The corridor had been cleared. The exit remained propped open with a chair to ventilate the building.

The sun was low beneath a layer of wispy clouds. It was cool, but Isabel felt clammy in her impermeable one-piece coverall and hood. Isabel asked if Emma was cold, but she shook her head. "Not exactly fresh air for me," Isabel said as she led Emma down the steps. "But it's better than that hospital room, right?"

The only people in sight were Marines. Emma felt rigid. Her head jerked this way and that. Her eyes were wide. She repeatedly peered over her shoulder at their armed escorts and seemed resistant to every change in direction or speed. Up ahead, two Marines on patrol, not in PPE, steered wide of the garbed procession, stepping off the concrete walk and leaving boot prints in dew-covered grass. Emma eyed them and clutched Isabel's arm so hard she feared it might puncture the fabric. "Are you okay?" Isabel asked, trying not to make any sudden moves.

"Where is everyone? This is a hospital, and a regular workday."

"Lots of people are, ya know, bailing. Fleeing for the hills seems to be a surprisingly, literally accurate expression these days."

Emma acted as if she sensed danger all around. "Where are we going?" she asked.

"Emmy, you don't think I'm taking you to . . . Sweetie, no one is going to hurt you. We're just going for a *walk*." Isabel realized that strolling for enjoyment made no sense to Emma. It had to be for some sensible purpose like her execution. "Look, *you* pick where we go, okay?" Isabel disentangled their arms.

Emma stepped uncertainly off the paved walk, looked at the Marines and held her hand out back to Isabel, who hesitated for reasons that eluded her. But her conscious self overrode her subconscious reluctance, and Emma snaked her arm back through Isabel's.

They headed for the wall arm-in-arm, like sisters. But Isabel felt like a prospective hostage. She twice tried to loosen Emma's grip unsuccessfully. At the wall, Emma measured its height and followed its length, inspecting seams, base, and barbed-wire top.

Every time Isabel shied away, Emma pulled her back and checked the Marines. Soon, Isabel was perspiring from nerves. Emma, cool and collected, was attentive to every detail. A closed but unguarded gate. A hole Marines were digging that turned out not to be her grave. The pattern and spacing of patrols. Emma stared through a manned gate at the long tank barrel that pointed down an empty road toward a pair of police cars diverting traffic away from the NIH lab.

"*So*," Isabel said in a breezy voice intended to calm not her sister, but herself, "I guess *I'm* the normal one now." Isabel's snort was only a passing attempt at laughter.

But her remark distracted Emma from mapping her escape route or whatever she was doing. "Do you mean you've become popular?" she asked.

"No," Isabel replied, her feelings a bit bruised, and her speech a bit hyper. "Just, you know, by comparison . . . Never mind. Was I really that unpopular? Don't answer that! Oh, but some guy in the parking garage at your apartment—tall, scraggly beard, hunky muscles—*did* ask me for a quickie when I was on my way to work this week."

"Woody?"

"No," Isabel replied. "No, uhm . . . 208C."

Emma nodded. "Josh. He's dumb, but good in bed. Was it satisfying?"

"I—oh—I didn't have *sex* with him!"

"Why?" Emma asked. "Were you on your period?"

"*No*, I . . . We'd just *met*. We hadn't actually even met. He thought I was you. But that *is* pretty dumb. How fast does he think hair *grows*? So, you've . . . slept with him?"

Emma studied a recently erected metal pole festooned with cameras and lights pointing in multiple directions. "No. Just sex."

Right! Mental note on euphemisms. They walked on. "You know, I watched the recordings of you from Siberia," Isabel said. "They broke my heart. You were so scared, and got so sick." Emma was unmoved by the recollection. "And Dr. Lange's questions . . . I remember that lunch at the club after tennis. So, everybody at school thought I would die a virgin?"

Emma said, "Because you're so uptight."

Isabel's feelings were hurt further. She wasn't uptight. She was *discriminating*. "And mom and dad made you invite me?"

"Yes, because you didn't have any friends."

"I had *friends*!" Emma just looked at her. Why had she even brought it up? They circumnavigated the main hospital building, with Emma scrutinizing ground floor windows, brush that might obscure a run for it, and a service entrance with trash bins large enough to hide inside.

Emma made Isabel nervous. She had never felt that way around her before. "Can I ask," Isabel said mainly to break the tension, "what your Rules are in your notebook?"

Emma repeatedly tested a storm drain grate by stepping on it. "It's part of a plan," she explained. "Infected people won't show initiative or be motivated by long-term goals. It may be that missing voice not telling them what to do. When they get hungry, they'll look for food. When they get horny, they'll look for sex. But when their urges are sated, they won't do anything. They need plans and rules, or they'll kill for food and rape for sex."

"Jesus. *Really*?" Isabel finally wriggled free of Emma's grasp.

"Yes," Emma replied, turning toward Ramirez as if to confirm she would now obviously be shot.

"And so that's why you put *order* number one on your list of requirements? I mean, water was number two. Food number three."

"Air would be my number one," Emma replied, "if it became unavailable. Order is next most important. Without it, like without air, people die quickly."

When they came to the parking lot, Emma paused to look at each of the dozen or so cars they passed. Isabel finally concluded she was checking to see if they were locked.

"This is *my* really fly ride," Isabel said on reaching her gray, no-frills, midsized American-made sedan. "Zero-to-sixty in, like, twenty minutes."

"There's something wrong with the engine," Emma commented. *Why bother?* "Do you keep your keys in your pocket?" Emma asked.

Isabel froze. This time, she was the one who glanced back at the Marines several cars away. Her keys were in her right front pocket. She made no move to reach for or look down at them for fear Emma might tear through Isabel's coverall to get at them. It did Isabel's nerves no good to see Emma survey Isabel's headgear.

With her heart pounding, Isabel headed away from the parking lot. Emma followed her human shield. Isabel wanted to share with Emma all the frightening details in Browner's models urging impulsive eradication. Who better to double-check the math? But a voice cautioned against it. *It'll agitate her,* came a rationalization. *It's a secret,* came a thought closer to the truth. *It'll put ideas in her head,* came the real answer. "Emma, everybody noticed that you capitalized the words 'nuclear weapons.'"

Emma turned to watch a bird fly by, then said, "Nuclear weapons could win a war. But they and their delivery systems are too complex for Infecteds to maintain for long."

"So you highlighted nuclear weapons because you fear their use *against* you?"

Emma said, "Yes."

"And you're planning for some organized society after SED gets here?"

"Organization is the best way to maintain order, which is the top priority. Nature yields *dis*order. It has to be imposed by society. That requires planning."

"And infected people will just . . . do what you tell them?"

"The high-functioning will if they're fed, housed, and given safety and sex."

Isabel said, "So that's *it*? Take care of the basics and they're loyal patriots?"

"Yes."

"Okay. But what if, say, they're so damaged they can't follow rules?"

"Society is a collection of individuals," Emma said, looking at Isabel as if for signs of concurrence or disagreement. "Each, over a lifetime, contributes to and draws from society's resources." Again she waited. She was seeking feedback. Testing her ideas like she tested storm grates. "The net of contributions made less resources consumed is either positive or negative. Society needs members who are net positives."

"Yeah, okay. You *want* that, sure. Hardworking, self-denying Puritans, not freeloading hedonists and gluttons. The question is how do you get there?"

Emma seemed to think the answer was simple. "You eliminate the drags on society."

Isabel turned to her. "Eliminate *how*?"

"Border controls and immigration standards." Isabel heaved a sigh of relief. "And weeding out the unfit."

"*What?* How are you gonna do *that*?"

"Execution, or euthanasia, which are basically the same thing."

Isabel's mind reeled. "Emma, *Jesus*! That's . . . *eugenics*!"

"But not racial eugenics, which got a bad name. It should be meritocratic."

"I don't think you've thought this through. You're talking *millions* of people, in this country alone, who won't be able to function in the orderly society you're describing."

"My estimate is 35 million," Emma replied.

"*Christ*! So, you'd, somehow, *kill* 35 million *people*?"

"Do you have a better alternative?" Emma's question wasn't rhetorical. "If you expel them, they'll come back. They can't work, won't follow rules and will consume food, housing, clothing, medicine, mates. They'll murder, rape, and steal with no prospect of rehabilitation. A bullet only costs around a dollar."

Isabel felt disoriented. Not only would Emma presumably kill Isabel if the situation demanded, but she'd also decided that a Final Solution for the unfit was rational. Would Uninfecteds be far behind? She began to wonder whether the president's opposition to genocide was enlightened, or foolish and naive. She now knew Emma's answer to that question. And Browner's, and apparently the vice president's, too.

So long as Emma was opening up, Isabel decided, on a hunch, to ask, "Emmy, sweetie, what happens when the military takes you out of your room?"

Emma glanced over her shoulder. Ramirez, *et al.,* were out of earshot. "They asked me questions about SED for a video. Dwayne watched it and said Uninfecteds think Infecteds are monsters. And, as a general rule, you kill monsters."

"They're just scared of you," Isabel said. "You frighten them."

It felt like a real conversation until Isabel realized Emma was pacing off steps between two junctions in the sidewalk. "They *should* be afraid," Emma said upon completion. "I saw *you* on TV." Isabel should have asked about the first comment, but focused on the second. She wanted to ask, *How'd I sound? How'd I look?* But in addition to being bloodthirsty murderers, Infecteds were brutally honest critics. Better not to expose her brittle self-confidence. "They also shocked my arms with electrodes until my skin sizzled."

"*What?*" Isabel shouted, stopping in front of her sister.

"They wanted to see if I felt pain," Emma explained, as if defending them. "Those sons-of-bitches! *That* caused those marks on your arm?" Emma nodded. Isabel's outrage grew. "They put you in long sleeves to cover them up!"

"No," Emma said. "I asked for long sleeves."

A voice in Isabel's head said, *You could've known what they were doing to her if you wanted! You could have asked or demanded to know! You just didn't wanta piss off people like Browner, who made you feel important!* "Show me," Isabel said.

Emma unpeeled the tape that sealed her sleeve to her glove. "Hold on!" Ramirez called out. "Stop-stop-stop!" The Marines raised their rifles to their shoulders and aimed straight at them. Isabel stood between them and her sister, who finished unrolling the tape.

Emma raised her sleeve. Five inch-wide marks, fading and turning from red to brown, one scabbed over, ran across her right arm from the inside of her wrist up to the crook of her elbow. Tears of anger filled Isabel's eyes. First and foremost, she cursed her own fucking miserable, *worthless* self. She stepped aside and held Emma's arm up to Ramirez like a winning prizefighter. He ordered his Marines, who cast troubled looks toward their officer at the sight of Emma's wounds, to lower their already drifting aims. "Just following orders, ma'am," Ramirez said.

"Surely you heard that didn't work at Nuremburg!"

Ramirez stepped forward. "Look, *personally*, I'm sorry. Okay? It wasn't me and I don't agree with it. But . . . *Christ*, I also had to shoot an Infected last night. And as you know, I lost a man and had to call his parents yesterday and lie about how he died. Now where's the fucking fairness in any of *that*?"

"Who'd you shoot?" Isabel asked.

"I missed this crazy-ass lady doctor with a Taser, but hit her four times with my Beretta." He stared down, rifle held one-handed by its pistol grip and pointing at the ground, seemingly torn up by the experience.

"It wasn't him," Emma confirmed, re-taping her sleeve. "A heavyset general had them keep applying more and more power until the electrodes got too hot, then he stopped and said he was sorry. He was crying."

"Was his name 'Browner'?" Isabel asked. Emma nodded. Isabel jammed her eyes shut. *Oh-my-God. Oh-my-*God! That bastard! That fucking *bastard*!

Marines used almost an entire roll of tape to reseal Emma's sleeve. Ramirez said, "Let's head back inside." He stayed closer to them this time.

"Hey Emma," said Isabel, trying a normal, conversational tone. "Do you remember that time when we hiked up to that old stone house on a hill? How Noah threw rocks and broke a window, and dad got mad and said we shouldn't treat the place that way?"

"Yes," Emma replied, "it was down in the . . ."

Isabel grabbed Emma's arm, causing her to jump and cutting off her reply. After a moment, Emma looked at Isabel and nodded. "I understand."

Chapter 32

"Americans the world over," said the reporter over the radio in Noah's SUV, "are searching for a way home following the FAA's surprise suspension yesterday of all foreign flights inbound to the United States as a temporary public health measure. Mexico also imposed a national flight ban, and the Canadian Parliament is voting on a similar step later tonight."

"Will that stop it from getting here?" Chloe asked.

She'd said nothing for an hour but was now sprawled in the passenger seat—melting from boredom. "Probably not," Noah said. Isabel had called to warn Noah that this might be the exponential "boom" that Emma's math predicted. The end of the phony war.

"Reactions grew more heated to the long-delayed, worldwide release two days ago of a report on *Pandoravirus's* effects. The ruling coalition in Italy collapsed under pressure from street protests over a cover-up that benefited the connected and the powerful."

"That's us," Chloe said, her attention to the news surprising Noah.

"Overnight there was rioting in Amsterdam, Marseilles, Caracas, and Jakarta. In the US, members of Congress from both parties have called for an investigation once their suspended sessions are reconvened, and opinion polls show unprecedented anger over what many call official government deception. President Stoddard's popularity has now fallen to single digits, 8 percent, from what had been a robust 54 percent approval rating."

"Kids *hate* him," a distracted Chloe said, typing on her phone. "Didn't he . . . ? What'd he do?" But she was so uninterested she barely knew she'd asked a question.

"In New York City, seven were injured in a stampede onto the street following rumors that an office worker was infected with *Pandoravirus*. Police in HazMat gear found that the forty-six-year-old accountant in question instead suffered from seasonal allergies and bouts of sneezing."

Noah turned off the highway and unlocked the gate. He returned the waves of Natalie and Jacob, who followed in the second SUV, then relocked the gate behind them.

They began the drive up the one-and-a-half lane ridge road. In places, the mound of earth along the cliff's edge had eroded. "In Chicago, five were arrested for beating an elderly man attempting to board an elevator wearing wraparound, disposable sunglasses from the ophthalmologist. The accused claimed the man 'shambled' when he walked, and that he seemed confused and non-responsive."

"Peoples gone *cray*-cray," Chloe said, before chuckling at some text she got.

"That's why we're gonna get away from everybody," Noah said, "Infected or not."

After she hit Send, Chloe said, "Can you imagine, like, next Halloween? Maybe I should go as a slutty *Infected*. Everybody would *freak!*"

Noah had to look over at his daughter to remember just how much of a child she still was at fifteen. How sheltered they had made her life. He gave her jean-covered thigh a squeeze, but she jerked it away while checking Instagram.

"Grocery stores, hardware stores and especially gun and medical equipment stores report huge lines following the long-awaited release of the government report on *Pandoravirus*. Many businesses are adopting telecommuting policies to allow employees to work from home. We have no figures on workplace absenteeism, but school districts report a dramatic reduction in attendance, in some places falling below 50 percent."

Noah glanced over again. Chloe was the most beautiful, most perfect creature who had ever graced the Earth. Until she spoke. "Justin said there's, like, *nobody* at school today. Just him and Lucy *Fong!*" She laughed as if that were a punch line. "They're in the auditorium watching that CNN interview about the P from TV." Her phone vibrated again. She guffawed. "Oh! Justin said he shouted out, 'That's Chloe's aunt!' when Aunt Izzy came on. So I'm, like, *fa*-mous!"

Chloe tilted her head back and tossed, but nothing happened. Fabulous long locks no longer danced across her shoulders. As if watching a car wreck in slow motion, Noah saw her reach up. *No.* Her hand found bare neck, not blond tresses. *Oh no.* She lowered the vanity mirror. *No, no, no!* She ducked her head, peered at her hair and burst out crying. Again.

"Sweetie. Sweetie! Honey!" The road grew narrower and more perilous. "You look . . . You look . . ."

"Hideous!"

"Beautiful." He tried to focus on not driving over the edge.

"Like a *boy*!"

"No, no. Very . . . *Chic*, yeah chic, like your mother said." She, too, had cried.

"Justin's gonna *hate* it!"

"No he's not. I'm sure . . . I'm *pretty* sure . . ."

"He just *invited* me over for *dinner* so I'd talk his *parents* into *prepping*!"

"Honey, I . . . I'm sorry, but I don't know what you're talking about."

"When he sees my hair he's gonna *dump* me and go back to *Janie*!"

"*Noooo*, no! I'm sure that's probably not . . . Wait. Janie that really pretty girl?"

"I don't wanta *talk* about it!" She slammed the visor closed. She was probably right. Best leave it alone. "You have no *idea*!" Chloe added for good measure.

The road was easier the rest of the way. Noah checked on Chloe, who stared out across the valley. In the reflection, he could see that she had calmed, and was as beautiful as her mother. Almost ethereal; too perfect for this world. Tears welled in his eyes. He rested his hand on her head. Chloe recoiled. "Dad!" The moment passed.

When they arrived at the house, Noah was amazed at how many men still worked. But the contractor came to the gate to greet them, and workers began gathering on the wraparound porch. "Stay in the car," Noah told Chloe, "and keep your pistol handy."

"Dad?" Chloe responded. But she lifted her oversized handbag onto her lap.

Noah held a hand up to Natalie and Jacob to stay in their SUV. He wore his pistol on his hip and carried a backpack with half a million dollars in cash. He pulled out five thick envelopes and thanked the bleary-eyed and ill-humored contractor, who returned to the porch to divide the money. Most workers took their cash, bedrolls, and duffels straight to their trucks and drove off. Only five remained.

"We don't need 'em," the contractor said. "My best guys stayed. We'll git 'er done."

Noah, Natalie, and the kids unloaded the SUVs. This latest and possibly final haul had been all the goods they could find on store shelves picked clean, and it was of dubious value. Paper towels. An entire display rack of Mentos. Lighter fluid. Trampled boxes of Cheerios. Noxious orange drink in gallon jugs. Random baseball caps. And lots of lip balm. Then, on the side of the road, Noah had stopped at a fireworks stand, which was legal in the boonies, and bought out almost the entire inventory. Jacob had been thrilled, but Natalie had thought it was stupid. Noah had no idea what it was for, but the firecrackers, rockets, and mortars had really stunk up the car, so he decided to store them in the barn along with the lighter fluid, ammo reloading equipment, gunpowder, and gasoline.

Chloe tried to lift a box. It was heavy and she looked inside. "What's this?"

Natalie extracted a paperback. "These are called *books*, sweetie." Noah grinned.

"I *know* that," Chloe replied, rolling her eyes. "But why are they *here*?"

"*War and Peace!*" Natalie said. Chloe made a face at its thousand-plus pages. "And *Crime and Punishment*. And *Don Quixote*. Maybe I'll give it another try. Chloe?"

"*Hm*? Oh, yeah? Looks . . . *long*."

"Here's a shorter one," her mother said. "*Catcher in the Rye*."

"Already-read-it!" Chloe instantly replied.

"For school," Natalie said, "not pleasure. Your dad must've bought these for you and Jake. *Anna Karenina*! Oh, Chloe, I was your age when I read that. I cried and cried."

"From a *book?*"

"*Yes* from a *book!*"

"Weren't you, like, varsity head cheerleader, and popular and all?"

Natalie looked exasperated. "That doesn't mean I had to be ignorant. You and Jake need to keep your minds from rotting."

"Dad told me he didn't know how long we could stream, so he put me in charge of buying DVDs. He said don't worry about how much it cost. I got, like, twenty boxed sets." Her mother tilted her head, an eyebrow raised. "If I spend all my time reading, I'll be wasting Dad's money! And Jake downloaded, like, a lifetime supply of porn on his iPad, so . . ."

"Don't change the subject."

"So he can rot *his* brain with girl-on-girl humping, but I've gotta read," she picked up a random paperback, "*For Whom the Bell Tolls*? That's not fair!"

"Boys will do what boys will do," her mother said, repeating for the hundredth time her catchall explanation of the masculine sex. "But these are for him, too."

Noah took bags of cash withdrawn from his now nearly empty accounts down to the basement safe. He then rolled an incredibly heavy carry-on, filled with ninety-three pounds of gold, up the steps onto the porch bump by bump and, with grunts, down the stairs to the basement, with Natalie, on passing, warning him about scratching the hardwood floors. It took him fifteen minutes to stack the individual ingots in the safe.

Back at the SUV, Jacob asked, "What are these?" holding two identical Amazon boxes.

"Drones for patrolling the property." Jacob grinned. "And don't forget those."

Noah pointed at perhaps their most prized treasure—bag after bag of seeds. Jacob grimaced as he read labels of hated vegetables. "My own personal nightmare," he mumbled.

"There's a smart man," the proprietor had said at the seed-and-feed store in rural Virginia while Natalie and Chloe picked over a crowded Safeway across the road. "I guess when everywhere else is outa everything," the farmer-looking guy said, "they'll head this way. We've had a few customers like you plannin' ahead. Not as many as you'd think."

Noah locked the seeds with the cash and gold in the safe. Maybe *they'll* be the new currency. Beets, broccoli, sweet peppers, lettuce, green peas, squash, spinach, tomatoes, eggplant, string beans, watermelon, cabbage, carrots, cucumbers, radishes, onions, sweet corn, cantaloupe, cauliflower, and zucchini.

Back upstairs, Noah went on a tour with the contractor. "We didn't get to mount the cell phone radio on the tower. Guy never showed, so you've got a lot of leftover cable stored in the barn. But we got TV, radio and satellite up and running, and Wi-Fi around the house. I lost about a third of my crew as soon as they heard the news. Didn't even wait to get paid. I used their shares to keep these five workin'." He turned to Noah. "We've sorta been cut off up here. How bad is it?"

"You won't have a problem getting home," Noah said. "But I hope somebody's out buying stuff for you." The man had every reason to hate Noah, who had who had outright lied to him at the front-end.

But the contractor betrayed no animus. "Shop is one thing my wife can do."

The electrical systems were up and running. The low-voltage fence was ready to be electrified with the pull of a big red lever mounted to the wall in the barn. The windmill, high on the hill behind the house, *whirred* steadily. A meter in the barn showed the needle jiggling to the plus side of its gauge. They were generating surplus electricity and charging huge batteries in the barn from a combination of the windmill and the solar panels, not consuming battery power as they would when the sun went down and the wind died.

The contractor donned a tool belt and joined his men in their dash to complete the job. Noah helped his family finish unloading, then told Natalie they should leave one car and all make a last run back to their house in McLean in the other SUV. "There's one more load we can bring up here, plus, you know, one last night in our own beds."

"We're really going back to pick up Isabel, aren't we?" Natalie asked. Noah girded himself for an argument, but none came. "That's okay, sweetie," Natalie said, rubbing his arm. Noah could only imagine her reaction if she knew about Emma's *habeas* hearing in the morning, and his plan to put her in the cabin. "Isabel can have one of the bunk beds in Chloe's room."

"Wait! That's *my* room?"

They stopped at the country store on the state highway to refill their tank. Noah was tempted to buy out all their remaining food, but restrained his family only to a few bags of things that might keep. "You're becoming one of my best customers," Margie said as she rang it up. She still took credit cards. "You been up in War-shington?"

"No," Noah replied. "You need a permit to go into D.C. now."

Margie's small television displayed scenes of the apocalypse. The A1 in North London was devoid of traffic after the UK shut down all travel, foreign *and* domestic. Rumors that Infecteds in Korea were cleaning up towns and villages after the violence subsides. Fighting in Ho Chi Minh City. The Kremlin, paranoid as ever, had vowed "terrible consequences" if its neighbors tried to take advantage of the crisis.

"So you settlin' in up at the old Miller place?" Margie asked.

Shit, Noah thought. He should've avoided the store. He flashed a smile and left.

Traffic was streaming south out of Metro D.C., so the trip north went quickly until they were diverted off the Interstate, forced to take surface streets. Many of the houses along the way were dark. In the driveways of others sat SUVs and station wagons, many with trailers, all piled high with belongings. Noah couldn't imagine where everyone was going.

Chapter 33

The world outside the NIH lab had gone insane, so Isabel had bunked in an empty hospital room in a sleeping bag Beth had borrowed from Ramirez. She had been up late the night before and had overslept, waking only when the door onto the brightly lit corridor opened. "There she is," Ramirez said.

Rick Townsend entered. Isabel squinted until the door closed, then combed fingers through her unruly hair in the darkness. "Dr. Miller," Rick said, sinking into one of the chairs being stored in the unused room. She was afraid to say anything and screw it up. The only light came from her glowing tablet, propped open on the nightstand. On it, Emma and her roommates were up early, eating breakfast and watching TV.

"You can call me Isabel," she said, rubbing her eyes, "if I can call you Rick." He didn't object. "So, what's goin' on . . . *Rick*?" *That felt good.*

"It's here," he said. "Yesterday, a French telecom executive took a private jet from Hanoi home to Paris and his pilots apparently crossed paths with a commercial crew, who late last night flew Air Canada Flight 871 from Paris to Montreal. An American couple, arriving on a different flight, were exposed and transported the virus from the Montreal airport to Vermont. The husband died in their bed, but first thing this morning the wife got up and went to the grocery store like nothing was wrong and exposed people in line. So, it's . . . happening."

"*Je*sus," Isabel said. But she thought, *And you came here?* "Are you visiting Captain Ramirez?" she asked, but Rick didn't answer. "He told me to tell you to," *what was it*, "'watch your five or your *six*' or something?" Rick snorted. "What does that mean?"

Rick said, "We were in this bar in San Diego, and this gorgeous girl was flirting with me, only she wasn't a girl. 'Watch your six'? Six o'clock? Never mind. It was a joke."

Isabel took his word for it and laughed. "And . . . *Poon*hound?"

"*Fuckin'* Ramirez. So, lemme explain. My family owns a dairy farm in Wisconsin. Ramirez built up this whole routine at the academy about me being some horny white-bread hick. You know, like, I practiced on animals before working my way up to a first cousin. That sorta thing. It got pretty elaborate. Like, we were on exercise summer before fourth year and bivouacked right next to a freaking *sheep* farm. All weekend long over the radio it was, 'Poonhound, two o'clock, four hundred meters, get a load of that fluffy one by the barn!'"

Isabel was grinning in inky anonymity. Rick was totally and completely perfect. A *dairy* farm! How sweet was that?

On her iPad, the Infecteds in Emma's room watched flickering aerial scenes of the newly arrived disaster. A man she'd never seen sat among them. They had replaced the dead Infected industrial engineer with a blank-faced Caucasian man in his late thirties.

The darkness emboldened Isabel. She wished she knew how Emma made it happen. It seemed easier, somehow, for most girls. She and Rick were alone. Her sleeping bag was warm. The end of the world was near. Should she just come out and . . . *offer*?

"I noticed that you completely ignored my advice," Rick said. "You're still here. But you know what's coming, right?" Isabel understood intellectually, but hadn't processed it emotionally. Some part of her had rationalized that they would stop SED from leaping the oceans, at least long enough to develop a vaccine. But they hadn't. "It happens incredibly fast," he said. "The sick come streaming into a hospital, every precaution taken. A coupla hours later, there's gunfire, people running. You don't even know who to shoot."

Isabel felt a chill come over her, and she hugged herself.

"That little girl there," Rick said, his finger illuminated by her tablet as he pointed, "doesn't *look* violent." Samantha sat primly watching a bonfire of bodies on the tarmac of the Montreal airport. "She's the Chinese ambassador's daughter, right? And that's the embassy guard?" He pointed at Dwayne. "Ramirez said during evac the girl spent hours secretly sharpening a fork then shoved it right through the eye socket of a Navy SEAL who'd just rescued them. He clawed at her arms till he died of shock. In the scuffle, with her parents screaming and the SEAL's buddies dragging him away, that guard dove on top of her and kept the SEALs from firing, but she managed to pull off his headgear."

Isabel looked at Samantha in horror. "Nobody told me any of that!"

Her incipient fear and anger dissolved, however, when Rick's hand found her shoulder. Without thinking, Isabel leaned forward and grabbed the back of his bristled head. Their mouths joined and rejoined again and again until, far too soon, Rick pulled away. With his forehead pressing warmly against hers, he said, "I don't have much time, but . . . neither do you. I'm serious. This time, you've gotta get yourself outa here."

"I'm joining my brother in the Shenandoah Valley. In Virginia. The Shenandoah Valley," she repeated. "Rick, I'm, I'm scared." He said he knew. "No, really, *really* scared!" Her voice shook. They rose into an embrace. His big arms wrapped around her. She began to cry. He squeezed her to his body. Amazingly, like magic, it helped. It may have been the one thing in the world right then that would. His arms, around her. His chest, pressed against hers.

They kissed once, then again, and again. She desperately wanted him, here, now. To wrap her arms, her legs around him. To cement the bond that they were only now forming. To create the irresistible force that would send him searching the four corners of the Earth until he finally found her, no matter where she was. She could tell that he wanted her, too, but he pulled away. "*Noooo!*" she begged.

"I've got to go." Rick was free of her grasp. "And so should you."

"You have to go right *now*?" she asked. "*Where*?" But she knew the answer.

"Vermont," he confirmed.

"Will you find me?" In the darkness, she jammed her eyes shut in fervent prayer.

"Where, exactly, in the Shenandoah Valley?" She gushed directions through drying tears and gave him kisses like treats to reinforce his memory. Once, they both grinned, their teeth collided, and they laughed. They kissed, and kissed, and kissed again until Rick tore himself from her arms and stood in the open doorway. Fully backlit, he was tall, strong, square-jawed, broad-shouldered, U-S-fuckin'-M-C. *Please, please, please, please, please,* please *come and find me!* As if he'd heard her silent plea, Rick nodded before he left.

* * * *

Emma sat on a bench on the NIH hospital grounds beside her overwrought sister. They spent the first ten minutes with Isabel asking, in essence, how to get a man to have sex with her, then reacting bizarrely—grabbing her head, plugging her ears, pedaling her feet, chanting, "No-no-no-no!"—in response to Emma's rather obvious and explicit suggestions. Now, Isabel was sobbing about something inside her PPE. The guards stood twenty meters away. From there, any rounds that missed Emma would harmlessly strike the new concrete wall.

"It was all just a stupid fucking *experiment*!" she cried, now on to the next subject. "They hired me because I'm your twin! They asked my opinion for *show*! They probably burst out laughing as soon as I left the room after going on and on about consciousness or whatever! Emmy, I'm *so* humiliated! I'm sorry. I know you've got your own troubles and this is hard for your to understand. But I miss talking to you. And I feel like . . . like digging a hole and crawling in."

Emma was at a total loss. Why was Isabel saying these things? Of *course* she should have made the first move with that Marine. Of course Rosenbaum was doing a twins study. "What time," Emma finally asked, "is the habeas corpus hearing?"

The rustling noise made by Isabel's gear drew Emma's notice. "Jesus," her sister said. "Emma, when someone's pouring their *heart* out to you . . ." But Emma was left wondering what she meant when she didn't finish the sentence. Isabel sighed. "Never mind. Hearing's at eleven thirty." She sounded tired.

Emma asked, "Does Noah think the judge will let Emma . . . let *me* out?"

Another sigh. "He said it could go either way now that SED's here. The judge may think why hold you? Or he might freak out and say no to everything."

"It's going to spread quickly now," Emma said.

"They shut down all the roads and highways in northern Vermont."

"That won't help much."

There was silence until Isabel said, "Can I ask you something? Those pieces of paper that you had Samantha copy . . . what were they?"

"I was teaching them about deception," Emma said, studying Isabel's reaction.

"Deception?" Isabel repeated. "Lying?" Emma couldn't tell if Isabel believed her. "Meaning the drawings were nonsense? Well, if your plan was to drive the military nuts, it's working, but . . . is that the *truth*?"

Emma scrutinized her sister. Did Isabel believe her? How could she tell?

Isabel broke the stare first, squinting as the sun peeked through the trees. She grabbed her hood with her gloved hands and mumbled something.

Emma asked her to repeat what she had said. "Emma, why are you so put together, even *now*, and I'm a total mess?"

"Because when mom and dad died, you moved in with Noah rather than make a life for yourself." Emma tried to recall more of her now decade-old analysis. For some reason she couldn't today understand, Emma had worried for years about Isabel. "Because you never gained your independence. Never grew up or stood on your own two feet." Emma remembered the phrase but couldn't recall exactly what it meant. It was, however, key to understanding Isabel.

"Wha . . . ?" Isabel said in a thin whisper. "You didn't tell me this *before? Why?*"

"I don't know," Emma replied. "Do they help?"

"Yes. *No.* But . . . Wait. *They?*" she asked. "What do you mean—*they?*"

"The words. When I said them, you stopped crying. Ready to talk about the plan?"

"You were just saying *words*? Words you remember from before that might calm me down? Do you even understand what I'm going through? How I'm hurting because . . . because I feel like such a *loser?* I thought I was, you know, coming into my *own* and, and doing really important *work*, but then I find out . . ." *Find out what?* Emma waited. "And there's this whole *other* thing, with Rick, who I really, really, *really* like." She grunted and pounded her thighs. "*Ahhhh!* Why *now?*"

"If it wasn't now," Emma said, "you wouldn't even have met Rick. You wouldn't have been looking for someone like him, and you wouldn't have felt insecure enough to have sex with a stranger."

Isabel stared at her in silence. "Wow, Emmy. That. . . . You actually made sense."

"Good. Did you bring clothes?" Isabel had no idea what she meant. "Do you have clothes for me to change into today if I'm released?"

"Oh. Yeah. They're in the trunk. But I thought we were, you know, starting to talk. Like we used to." She began to cry again.

Emma lightly tapped her back until she quit. "Will Noah take his car, or will you drive me?"

"*What?*" Isabel's voice was far too loud.

The Marines edged closer, possibly to eavesdrop. Emma turned to Captain Ramirez and said, "I'm getting *agitated!*" He used hand signals to pull his men back.

Isabel whispered, "You're *agitated?*"

"No. So, if Noah drives to the NIH hospital for the hearing, he will have his car. But your slow, probably defective car will also be here. My question is, in which car will you take me home and will you and Noah ride together or separately?" Surely that was clear enough.

"It won't happen like that. They'll probably have to seal up your apartment, cover whichever car we use in plastic, that kind of thing."

Emma said, "Get the NIH to prepare the apartment and the car today."

Isabel laughed. "Emma, things take time. They don't just," she tried to snap her fingers, but her gloved hands made no sound, "*happen*."

"Make them happen," Emma replied.

Isabel shook her head. "So I just walk into Nielsen's office and say, '*Do* it, bitch'?"

"Yes. Minus the insult. You attend NSC meetings. You had dinner with the President. You went on national TV. She isn't powerful anymore. You are."

* * * *

Isabel felt exhausted. Weeks of worry, days with little sleep, hours spent angry, terrified, depressed, and defeated, and then minutes teased by the ecstasy she surely would've felt being with Rick, but now probably never would. It would be *so* much easier to be Emma. Care about nothing. Fear nothing. Endure no humiliating failures. Just live. Isabel tried to hug her sister goodbye, but Emma simply returned to her hospital room.

Isabel found Nielsen and Beth in Emma's observation room. Nielsen said, "Planning trips to the mall, are we? You know you'll never be able to take her out. One look at her in PPE and people will run screaming."

"I want the NIH to prepare my car to transport Emma out of here, and Emma's apartment to isolate her, and I want that all done today, before the judge releases her."

"Ha. Ha. Ha-ha-ha." Nielsen's amusement wasn't shared by Beth, who was tensed up at witnessing the confrontation.

Isabel extracted her cell phone and dialed. "White House operator," came from its speaker. "How may I help you today, Dr. Miller?"

"Could you please get me Dr. Rakesh Aggarwal."

Nielsen interrupted. "*Okay.* Jeez. I'll get it done." Isabel politely thanked the operator and hung up. "What's the point, really," Nielsen said, "now that our new friend here brought it to America?" She looked through the observation window at the new man, who sat beside Samantha watching helicopter video of panic-stricken Vermonters fighting each other over the few remaining spots on a flatbed rail car. "He was the Air Canada co-pilot on what ended up being the last flight out of Paris. He woke up covered in vomit, his pilot dead, so he took over from the autopilot and landed just before they ran out of fuel. He parked, stepped over the bodies in the galley, and headed up the Jetway. The gate agent got sick. A reporter there to interview Paris arrivals got sick. Two dozen people in the terminal got sick."

"Why is he *here*?" Isabel asked.

"He's American, so they shipped him down here. But he's our last. We're not taking any more patients. I'm being sent to the Pfizer Lab in Pearl River, New York, to oversee their work on a vaccine. They say it's showing promise, so there's *some* hope."

Beth, in scrubs, but wearing a prim sweater meant for someone thirty years her senior and wearing more make-up than normal, timidly tapped the paper logbook in her lap.

Nielsen said, "Oh, yeah. We just finished our last experiment. See that laptop?" It sat on a table in the hospital room. "The Pentagon had us give Zero One Four in there that laptop with a flight simulator on it. He flew a Boeing 777 from JFK to Rome, flawlessly. Requested altitude changes from the simulated air traffic control. Routed them around a storm in the Atlantic but still made an on-time arrival by re-plotting his course and burning more fuel. The program rated him ninety-nine out of one hundred: Master Flight Instructor. We checked his employment history. He seems to be an even better pilot now than before infection."

"Another skills improvement after brain damage," Isabel commented.

"And marvelous bladder control. Nine hours straight with no potty break. Barely scratched his nose. Then he set the brakes at the gate in Rome, used the bathroom, and ate his by then cold breakfast. He never mentioned the simulation. Never touched the laptop again. Zero curiosity about the test. About anything. How weird is that?"

Beth seemed to want to be heard. When Nielsen and Isabel turned to her, Beth raised her logbook and said, "That wasn't what I meant. I meant . . . the other thing."

"Oh!" Nielsen replied. "Right." She turned to Isabel. "Last night, just before Zero One Four did the flight simulator, he did your sister. They had sex."

"Wha*aat?*"

Nielsen chuckled. "Yeah. How long did it take?" she asked Beth.

"For him?" she replied. "Or for her, and which one?"

"Oh-for-God's-sake!" Isabel said. She doubled over and dropped her head into her lap so her hair fell forward to hide her. Nielsen clearly thought it was hilarious. From her hirsute fortress, Isabel said, "In there? In a room full of people? A *twelve*-year-old?"

262   Eric L. Harry

"Everyone was asleep!" Beth said before consulting her log. "We introduced him at 2214. They turned the TV off and all went to bed at 2232. I . . . I lowered the lights. One Four didn't go over to Emma's bed until 2258. Samantha and Dorothy were out cold. Dwayne was snoring. One Four asked if she would have sex. Emma said yes. She had *her* first orgasm at . . ."

"Okay," Isabel replied, sitting up. "I get it."

Nielsen shrugged. "What more could a guy want? Sex and then a video game." Isabel had to cover her blushing face again. "I guess we could've ordered him a *pizza*. But hey," Nielsen patted Isabel's back, "sex is an urge, right? With no inhibition, what'd you *expect*? And they've all been in there, using the same bathroom, no door, showering, with zero privacy but also zero issues. Emma's no reflection on you. She's not even a reflection on her*self.* But don't worry. We tested him for STDs on intake. He's clean. And, how should I put this, the way it ended there's *zero* chance she got pregnant."

"*Aaaah!*" Isabel exclaimed before hurrying out of the observation room. Emma had omitted that little tidbit despite Isabel's intensely personal description of her own failed sexual conquest. Even with brain damage, Emma had no problem getting laid. Twenty-eight and counting, to Isabel's one. *It's me. I'm pathetic!*

She went through the motions of getting breakfast in the cafeteria—dry cereal and black coffee was all they had—and sat at her table in the corner of the large, empty room eating corn flakes like popcorn. She called Noah and told him about the NIH preparing the apartment and car. But he missed the point—her triumph of assertiveness. "*Forget* that. We're not going to Emma's apartment. We're going to McLean, then we'll caravan down to the Old Place, okay? We'll put Emmy up in the hunting cabin. It's almost a mile from the main house."

"I've got a *job* to do, Noah," Isabel said, then wondered if that was still true. The NIH lab was barely functioning. The White House no longer called. And *Browner . . . !*

"*What* job? Working for liar-in-chief *Stoddard?* And you had me quit my job!"

"But *my* job matters. And I can't keep running back to you! I need my *own* life."

"*What?* Iz, we're not talking about where to spend summer breaks and holidays. We're talking about surviving the end of the world as a family! Together! I made all the preparations you told me to. You *promised*. We go straight to McLean, then down to the Shenandoah. No arguments. No delays. No bullshit. We're a family. We stick together."

Isabel hung up and felt, more than saw, Brandon behind her. "Has Browner called?"

"*Fuck* him!" she replied. "Evil bastard." She told him about the pain experiments.

He wasn't as distressed as he should've been. "But she couldn't feel the pain, right?" he replied. She also confronted Brandon about the twins study. "I had no idea," he said. "I swear. Plus maybe it started off that way, but that's not the way it ended up. You were a *huge* part of the science. You're highly respected." She snorted, but appreciated the remark. Brandon said, "General Browner is sending me up to Vermont, and he wants you to go too. To give orientation briefings to the troops."

"I *told* you! *Fuck* Browner!" But she couldn't help being pleased. She *was* still wanted and still *had* a job, or at least a job *offer*. Her reaction distressed her even more.

"This is his aide's direct line," Brandon said as he picked up her phone and input numbers. "It's listed under *Ensign Somebody*. Call her. He said they'd come pick you up wherever you are. Just *call*." Brandon clearly wanted her to say that she would.

"Good luck, Brandon." She kissed his cheek. Anything more wouldn't have been honest. Still, his pained reaction stabbed her in the heart. It was the reaction she had avoided ten years earlier when she left the note on his windshield.

* * * *

Noah had prepared for the legal fight of his life, brainstorming every imaginable government argument and Emma's successive fallback positions. She could wear an ankle bracelet or have an RFID chip, like a child or pet locator, inserted under her skin.

The same US District Court judge and three taciturn Justice Department lawyers as before crowded the same observation room in the radically changed NIH hospital. Doctors and nurses in scrubs had noticeably been replaced by soldiers in body armor.

Before following the others in, Isabel told Noah about Emma's request that he get her roommates released, and about her "tryst" with one of them. "With all her roommates there?" Noah asked, appalled. Isabel shrugged. Inside the observation room, the court reporter now had numerous Infecteds to ogle.

"Your Honor," Noah said, "it has come to my attention that the government has conducted experiments on Petitioner that can only be described as cruel and unusual." He had Emma sworn in, as useless as an oath ending in "so help me God" would be for an Infected, and testify about the pain test. The judge had Emma roll up her sleeve, and both he and the court reporter winced. It helped, Noah thought, that Emma's eyes now appeared human. If only some expression would cross her blank face.

"It has also come to my attention," Noah said, "that the government is considering a policy of impulsive eradication: extra-judicial execution of all sufferers of the *Pandoravirus* epidemic. Needless to say, their abuse of Petitioner while in medical detention and any such policy of extermination would both be in direct violation of your order in Petitioner's prior habeas proceeding. I would, therefore, request that this Court order the immediate release of Petitioner, whose apartment is being prepared for . . ."

"Is there any truth to this?" the judge angrily asked the government lawyers.

"Your Honor," said the assistant US attorney, "the United States does not oppose Petitioner's request for release from detention."

The judge glared at him for a moment, then rocked back in his chair. "So you're dropping this to keep it quiet? These policies of torture and mass murder?"

"I'm sorry, Your Honor," replied the government lawyer, "but I'm not privy to matters of national security. The United States will, however, stipulate that Petitioner is no more infectious now than the carriers of numerous other diseases, and therefore there is no need for her continued detention at the NIH."

The unhappy judge shook his head. "I see right through this. Fair warning—if a justiciable issue ever reaches this Court regarding the torture or extrajudicial killing of the sick, there's going to be hell to pay. For the record! But, there being no dispute, this is your lucky day, counselor." He raised his gavel.

"Your Honor!" Noah said quickly, rising. "Would you consider ordering the release of all the infected people in Petitioner's room? While I'm not technically their counsel, it would follow that their release would also be in order."

The judge got on the hospital room's microphone and had the four other Infecteds line up. "Please state your names, and how long ago you were infected." One by one they spoke. "Dorothy Adams. Seventeen days ago." "Samantha Brown. Seventeen days ago." "Dwayne Bullock. Sixteen days ago." "David Conners. Two days ago."

Everyone's pupils but Conners's looked normal. Noah wasn't sure, he realized with mounting concern, that if he met them on the street he could tell that they had turned.

The judge asked Dr. Nielsen how long it took for their contagiousness to fall to relatively safe levels. "In every case we've studied," she replied, "the airborne viral shedding fell to low, steady-state levels before the end of two weeks."

"The United States will so stipulate," the Justice Department lawyer said.

The judge ordered everyone released except the airline pilot, who was to be held for twelve more days and paid a per diem of "not less than thirty dollars until release." Noah understood what he was doing. The money meant nothing in one detainee's case. But multiplied by millions, the precedent was a powerful economic disincentive to mass detention of the sick.

"No objections, Your Honor," said the man from the Justice Department.

Down came the judge's gavel.

Chapter 34

On the way to Emma's hospital room, Isabel and Noah each donned only a single pair of Latex gloves, but even that was probably unnecessary. "By the way," Isabel said with her mask dangling beneath her chin, "good job, you legal genius you." She rose onto tiptoes and kissed her brother's cheek, then rubbed her nose. "Scratchy! Preparing for life as an outdoorsman, Grizzly?" Her good humor faded when they reached the corridor to Emma's room. The robing room door was wide open.

Noah didn't know enough to be nervous. "What's gonna happen with the others?"

Isabel, on guard, said, "I dunno. Mask on."

Noah fumbled with his mask's straps as they peered into the enrobing room. Emma's hospital room doors were also open. There was no nurse in the glass-enclosed decontamination workstation. No Marine guard with pistol drawn. The streamers above the open doorway hung limply. The buzzer was quiet and red warning light dark.

In Emma's room, the beds were stripped of linens. Isabel stuck her head inside.

Nielson, her back to the door, held Emma's shoulders. Emma had changed into the clothes Isabel had brought. They both wore only gloves and masks. Nielsen reached up to tuck a loose strand of Emma's messy hair behind her mask's strap.

"I hope you understand it was all necessary," Nielsen was saying. "Scientifically, medically, given what we're facing. You understand, don't you?" Emma saw Isabel and Noah and pulled free. "Oh!" Nielsen said. "She's ready."

It felt strange, and dangerous, to enter that room so casually. Nielson handed Emma a small, white plastic bag, closed with a drawstring, containing, she said, a comb, toothbrush, toothpaste, and floss. Emma held the bag, her eyes fixed on the open door. A wary Isabel subtly maneuvered Noah so they didn't stand between their sister and freedom.

On the desk lay Emma's four notebooks and a fifth, off to the side, open to the last page containing notes. Emma had studied scans of the first four notebooks, but hadn't seen the fifth. "What about those?" Isabel asked.

"Sorry," Nielsen said. "Property of the US government. I would let you have them. But General Browner made a special point of telling Ramirez that he wanted them sent over to the Pentagon. After, that is, they spend the day in some hydrogen peroxide vapor."

"You have copies," Isabel argued. "Why keep the originals?" But as soon as Isabel asked, she knew the answer. They weren't keeping the notebooks so that Browner could have them. They were keeping them so that Emma could not. "Noah, this isn't fair."

"It doesn't matter," Emma said.

"But Emma," Isabel said, "you put so much effort into . . ."

"I remember everything," her sister interrupted.

"All those calculations, observations, rules?"

"I remember everything," Emma repeated, looking at, yearning for, the hallway.

Nielsen shrugged, put her arm through Emma's and walked her toward the door.

Emma halted. "Where's the bird's nest?" she asked, looking up at the empty sill.

"They're boarding up the windows today," Nielsen replied. "They must have hosed it off." Emma caught Isabel's eye before Nielsen hauled her away saying, "I kept getting voicemails forwarded to me from some friend of yours. Amanda Davis? About lunch?"

What had Emma's look meant? Quiet condemnation of Uninfecteds' disrespect for other species? An unspoken commentary on the inhumanity of the supposedly humane? Or was it absolutely nothing at all?

"Are we going?" Noah asked. She could hear Nielsen chattering away in the robing room.

The light from the high window lit the cover of the notebook at the top of the stack of four. Indentations in its leather seemed to form a pattern. Isabel raised it to the light, tilting it so that the rays struck it just so. The indentations formed the letter 'S,' followed by three other letters. She instantly recognized the word. It was the same on the covers of the next notebook, and the next. All four! On the fifth, just begun, there was barely two-thirds of an 'S' carved into the cover by Emma's fingernails.

"Oh-my-God." Isabel doubled over and stooped all the way down to a squat.

"Hey!" Noah said. "What's wrong. You okay?"

"The notebooks." Isabel felt dizzy. "The covers!"

Noah tilted a cover to the light. "Yeah. Looks like she dug her fingernails into the leather or something. I see it. S-E-L-F. Self. Yeah?"

Isabel grew pissed at how dense he was, and stood. "That's her *Self*, Noah! Don't you get it? Jesus! I kept describing to her how she had lost this thing called a self that came up with ideas. So when she got a new idea, she wrote it down in those notebooks. What the voice in her head kept telling her. *Ideas!*" Noah kept waiting for Isabel to get to the important point. "Oh, forget it!"

Nielsen's laughter came from the corridor. Emma had only just begun taking notes in the fifth notebook. Isabel had seen no scans of it. She looked up at the cameras. Everything seemed shut down. She quickly tore out the pages with writing on them from Emma's fifth notebook, folded them and stuffed them into the back pocket of her jeans. Noah silently objected with an arched brow and stare.

At the exit at the end of the corridor, Ramirez and Beth stood, arms touching. Beth startled Emma by hugging her as she passed. Emma's gaze remained fixed on the sunlit outdoors.

Isabel had to say quick goodbyes and good lucks to Ramirez and Beth in order to keep up with Emma. Beth hugged her. Ramirez saluted her with his index finger. "Take care of Poonhound," he said. "He's the real deal." Isabel grinned and headed out.

Nielsen pointed in the direction of the parking lot. Emma took off at a fast walk. Nielsen, Noah, and Isabel hurried to follow. At the fortified main gate, Emma unceremoniously climbed into the back of Isabel's new NIH car with seats and paneling covered in crinkly plastic, her toiletry sack on the seat beside her. Isabel transferred her overnight and gun bags from her old NIH car to the trunk of her new car, then held her hand out to shake Nielsen's.

Nielsen hugged her. "Goodbye, Dr. Miller," she said, squeezing her. "I wish you, your sister, and your family the best of luck. Maybe we'll meet again on the other side."

Isabel got into the front passenger seat without a word. As Noah drove them off, he let his sarcasm fly. "Boy, you were *so* right about her! What a total bitch!" Isabel felt guilty for the chilly farewell. Nielsen was doing enormously important work during impossibly trying times. Isabel waved at her last sight of the woman, who waved back.

Outside the gate, two lines of trenches were dotted with helmeted heads. Interspersed were tanks, dug in up to their turrets. *What the hell is coming?* "We'll have to take the long way around D.C.," Noah said. Isabel kept turning to look at Emma, who stared, motionless, out the window. Noah ascended onto the Beltway.

"Does it feel good to be outa there?" Isabel asked Emma, who said nothing. "Noah got your favorite food group," Isabel continued nervously. "Mac and cheese, right?" She kept filling the silence. "Look at *that*," she said as cars slowed to ogle a strip center's parking lot filled with tank-like vehicles arrayed in a circle like a wagon train in the old West. Try as she might, Isabel couldn't engage Emma. Noah glanced repeatedly through the rearview mirror at their mute sister.

They crossed the Potomac to the Virginia side. As they descended the bridge, Emma suddenly said, "Could you stop?"

"You feeling sick?" Noah asked, slowing.

"Stop the car," Emma repeated. "I'm feeling agitated. I'm feeling *agitated!*"

Noah pulled over onto the shoulder of the busy, four-lane highway. At the last instant, Isabel, looking back at Emma, called out, "Don't stop! Noah . . . !"

But it was too late. The seat belt *clacked* and Emma's door flew open. "What the fuck?" Noah cursed.

Emma ran down the embankment. Both siblings climbed out and called her name. Isabel's last sight of Emma was of her tearing off her mask and disappearing into the thick woods carrying only the plastic bag with her hospital-provided toiletries. Noah craned his neck over the roof. "Did she have to go to the bathroom?"

"*No*, Noah!" *God, he was dense!* "She's gone! She just . . . She *used* us."

"I can't believe this," Noah said. "What do we do? Should we call somebody?"

As cars whizzed by, Isabel said, "No. They'll hunt her down. Should I go after her?"

"No," Noah decided. "We go on. Without her. If this is what she wants, at least we did this much for her. Let's get down to the Old Place before someone spots Emma and they start closing roads."

"Or she kills somebody," Isabel said.

"Iz! Jesus." They got back into the car and merged into traffic.

"I'm *serious*, Noah. They'll rape, kill, cook, and eat you. What do you think has been happening in Asia, for God's sake! You cannot trust an Infected. You're more at risk from Emma than from any random ex-con you meet in an alley. Do *not* trust them."

"Then what the *fuck* were we just doing with her in this *car?* Heading to meet up with my *family?*"

"I don't know!" Isabel replied. "She's still our sister. I guess. And it's not like I thought this all the way through! It's very confusing! But . . . you may not have seen the last of her."

"What?" Noah asked. "What does that mean?"

"I mean I kinda may have told her, you know, where we'd be."

"You *what?*"

"Well, it *was* our plan!"

"So she's just gonna, what? Skulk around the fence until she gets hungry, then slit our throats in our sleep? Great! Thanks for that, Isabel!" She couldn't come up with a good enough defense. Noah finally said, "Don't tell Natalie, whatever you do."

But Isabel couldn't stop thinking about it. "Emma probably already planned to go there. That's my guess as to what her drawings were." Isabel told him about the mysterious tracings. "I think Emma lied, and if you tear, fold and overlay the sheets a certain way that only Emma and her roommates know, they were, like, directions to the Old Place."

"Wait. Wait a minute! You think they all have *maps*! To my family's *hideout*! That whole freaking horror show you just had me get released! *Isabel!*"

"I could be *wrong,* okay? I don't know! And the military confiscated all of the drawings after the shooting. Plus she made those maps or whatever before I ever told her the plan! She probably came up with the idea to go there on her own!"

Noah's expression was a fixed grimace. He slammed his palms on the steering wheel every so often, but his subvocal cursing finally died down.

"What I don't understand," Noah began again, "is if she wants to go to the Old Place, and we were gonna *drive* her to the Old Place, why'd she jump out of the freaking car?"

"She doesn't trust *us,* Noah. She thinks *we're* dangerous."

That quieted him for a few minutes. Then he said, "She could be a fucking seasoned serial killer by the time she murders her way down to the Shenandoah. She'd make short work of us, I suppose. I did *everything* I could, Izzy! Thought of almost everything! But miss even one, little, stinking, miserable detail, and my entire family could *die!*"

"Jesus, Noah, *okay*! I get it now. You're freaked because everybody is depending on you. I understand." She rested her hand on his shoulder. "All those fears. Poor Noah. Did you get 'em out of your system? Are you good now?" He nodded. *"Then shut the fuck up and don't ever complain again until this whole apocalypse is over!"* He looked taken aback. "John Wayne didn't *bitch*, okay? 'Oh this isn't fair! Look how many Indians there are!' Get your shit together, Noah! It is what it is. Toughen the fuck up and *grow* a pair!"

Isabel's little pep talk did double duty: stiffening Noah's spine, maybe, and getting Isabel off the hook for the Emma thing. After driving for a while in silence, a calmer Noah asked, "Did you ever get a look at what she was writing in those notebooks?"

"Yeah! It's, like, a treasure trove. Didn't I tell you? I guess it was secret. It's like a fascinating road map. Her *self* gets ideas—*ping, ping, ping*—and she writes them down in those notebooks that she called her *Self*. You can follow her daily cycle in her notes. 'Birds build nests near materials.' Then in comes breakfast and it's, 'Preexisting infrastructure for bacon and eggs' or whatever. Then, it's like, 'Manned space program unnecessary.' And she gets smarter over time. She synthesizes discrete observations into generalizations. 'Need Uninfecteds for intellectual spark. Uninfecteds loathe violence. Order reduces violence. Rules impose order.'"

"Can I have a copy?" Noah asked. Isabel shrugged and texted the scans to Noah's phone.

They took a roundabout route to avoid D.C.'s *cordon sanitaire*. There was military everywhere. "I hope the NSA didn't just see me do that," Isabel said.

Noah looked over. "Do what? Send me Emma's notes?"

"Yeah. They're classified Top Secret or something."

"What? Why'd you *send* them to me? To my *Gmail* account? Isabel!"

"You asked me to!" They then alternated between Noah's aggravated silence, and Isabel's spates of concerned speculation about Emma, in the woods, on the run. She was worried about her sister. But left unspoken was her worry about the people who would run into her sister.

Noah finally spoke calmly of his plans in a way that might reassure Emma, but not Isabel. Eying her with sidelong glances, Noah delivered comforting descriptions of Isabel's eternal place in his family, trying to find the right words to manage her feelings in a manner slightly less adept than brain-damaged Emma's. "We'll make space for you in the SUV and only take one vehicle. We set up your room to share bunk beds with Chloe."

"Bunk beds?" Isabel muttered. Noah fell into uncertain silence.

On the Beltway, panicked civilians headed away from the city in bumper-to-bumper traffic, while military convoys cruised at highway speeds in the opposite direction. Noah surprised Isabel when, out of nowhere, he said, "You know mom and dad were always so proud of you and Emma."

"*You* were the one they admired," she said. "Going to law school, making money."

"Bullshit!"

"Emma and I just did well on tests," Isabel said.

"I *know*! You don't think I heard about every test score you two ever got? Co-freaking-Valedictorians!" He sounded annoyed. "I did well enough, but whatever it was, both of you always aced it! SAT. ACT. APs. I dunno, Pap smear!"

"*Pap* smear? Jeez, Noah. That's pretty misogynistic of you."

"Oh go fuck yourself."

"You see? You have tendencies." He looked over. They both broke out laughing. "Seriously, Noah," she said. "Your family? Amazing job there. Mom and dad really *would* be proud of them. And I'd give my right arm to have a family like yours right now."

"I'm not sure you would. Not right now."

When they got to McLean, they opened the windows to flush out the car before removing their masks and gloves so they wouldn't freak out Natalie. In front of Noah's suburban manse stood his new, giant SUV with a huge, tarp-covered heap on top. It wouldn't fit in the garage so Jake stood guard in the shadows by the house holding a rifle.

In reply to Isabel's look, Noah said, "He knows what he's doing. We took a course."

Chloe and Natalie came out to meet them. Noah ordered Chloe and Jake to clear a spot in the back of the SUV. "Right now! We're in a hurry."

"Izzy, I made you a PB and J sandwich for the road!" Natalie called out.

"Un-fucking-believable," came Isabel's nearly silent response.

Noah led Natalie toward the front door, out of Izzy's earshot. "I think she's getting sensitive about us treating her like our third child."

"She *is* our third child, Noah."

"But let's not rub it in. She *wants* to have her own life. Her own family."

Inside, Natalie said, "Then maybe she should stop clinging to *us*. I love her, Noah. But you know you're not helping her by always making a place for her with *our* family."

"Is this really the best time for this conversation? Do you want me to march out there and say, 'Sorry, Isabel. You'll be better off going it alone. But thanks for the heads-up about the apocalypse and all! Here's a sandwich'?"

"That's *so* unfair!" Natalie replied. Before Noah could apologize, she said, "Have I *ever* been anything but welcoming to your sister? And *this* is what I get? You *quit* your job, *sell* our things, *spend* our money, and then accuse me of kicking your *sister* to the *curb?* I've treated her like a *daughter!* How can you think so little of me? You have *no* respect for me! I'm just your *arm* candy! Your *cheerleader* you show off at parties!"

"Nat," he said calmly, "you haven't been a cheerleader in a *looong* time."

"Oh!" she shouted, slamming the master bedroom door in Noah's face.

Noah was beginning to think this might not all be about Isabel. He looked out the upstairs hall window. Instead of unloading the SUV like they were supposed to, the kids stood around doing absolutely nothing! *Why can't they ever just do what they're told?* But before he could fix that mess, he had to deal with the Natalie thing. *Christ!*

* * * *

Isabel ended her phone call and joined Chloe and Jake at the open rear tailgate of their SUV. "Did you hear all that?" Isabel asked. The two kids looked at each other before nodding. Neither knew what to say. Chloe checked her phone. Jake, holding his rifle, kicked at the gravel.

Chloe glanced at Isabel several times as if she wanted to talk, but just sat on the tailgate swinging her leg. A pistol holster protruded from under her short jeans jacket.

"I've got a gun too," Isabel said.

"Oh, yeah?" Chloe seemed almost interested. Isabel retrieved her bags from the car and her pistol from the gun bag.

Chloe slid off the SUV, took Isabel's pistol, held it over the tailgate, ejected the magazine, and pulled the slide back. A bullet bounced to a stop on the SUV's carpet.

"You keep a round chambered?" Chloe asked.

"I guess," Isabel said. "Am I not supposed to?"

Chloe thumbed a lever. The slide *clacked* forward. She pointed the pistol at the ground and pulled the trigger repeatedly. The hammer *clicked* each time. "It's double-action," Chloe said. "Amazing it didn't go off in your bag."

"Oh, Jeeze. I didn't realize."

Chloe pressed the bullet back into the magazine and the magazine into the pistol.

Isabel returned it to the bag, and they backslid into awkward silence. Chloe swung her foot. Jake kicked at pebbles. Isabel finally said, "I love you two." As soon the words left her mouth, she began to cry. Chloe slid off the rocking car to hug her. Jake even found a way to put his arm around Isabel's shoulders.

"We love you too, Aunt Izzy!" Chloe said, in tears, tucking her sweet-smelling head under Isabel's chin even though they were now the same height. "I'm afraid!" Chloe whispered. "Like, really, really *afraid*!" It was now Isabel who wrapped Chloe in her arms.

A tear ran down Jake's cheek. Isabel reached up and grabbed the back of his head. "Sweetheart," she said. "Come here." He held his rifle aside so she could pull Jake's head down onto her shoulder. "We're gonna see each other again. I swear!"

From the house came Noah's shout. "I told you to clear a goddamn space for Aunt Isabel!" He and Natalie carried out the last of their stuff—Noah's dopp kit, Natalie's plyometric resistance bands. "You two never listen!" he shouted before noticing the tears. "What's goin' on?"

"Noah." Distant engine noise rose. "You've done an amazing job!" The *chop* grew louder. "I love you! You're the best big brother I could imagine having! I . . . Thank you!" She could no longer get the words out.

Noah clearly had no idea what was happening until the roar of the helicopter grew loud. He searched the heavens, but the roar seemed to come from everywhere. "*Isabel?*"

She grabbed his arms. "Noah, you're gonna make it!" A stupendous downdraft preceded the huge aircraft, which blotted out the sun as it passed low and slow overhead.

"You're not *coming*, are you?" he shouted. She shook her head as everyone turned away from the dust. Noah began to cry.

She held his face and kissed his scratchy cheek. The giant helicopter landed in the expansive center of the circular drive, pressing the now overgrown grass flat in the gale. Isabel pulled Noah's forehead down to hers. "I've got a job to do, Noah! I'm going to Vermont to brief the military! I'll join you at the Old Place! I *will!* You keep everyone safe! But for right now . . . I have to go!"

She hugged Natalie, who shoved the sandwich into her hand, squeezed the kids tight, and got her two bags. The helicopter wasn't like any she'd ever seen. Bulging tanks above the wheels must be filled with fuel. A long tube stuck out of its nose. Six-barreled guns with giant ammunition boxes filled its doors, each manned by a helmeted, visored crewman.

"Isabel!" Noah shouted. "Goddammit you *promised*!"

For reasons initially lost on Isabel, she was grinning. As if a weight had been lifted. A test passed. "Be *happy* for me, Noah!" She took two steps, then wheeled back around. "I have a *life* now! My *own* life!" She ran to the helicopter and tossed inside her overnight bag from Santa Barbara and her range bag from the FBI. A tall soldier in full combat gear and sunglasses pulled her aboard. The patch sewn over his heart read: Townsend.

"Rick!" He grabbed her tightly.

"We were leaving when your call came in!" he shouted over the roaring engines. "I guess you're not very good at taking advice!" Isabel shook her head apologetically.

Rick's arm held her as the helicopter lurched skyward. On a big, swooping turn, she exchanged last waves with her family before the gunners slid their doors shut. In the sudden, relative quiet, Rick led her to two empty jump seats along the bulkhead amid over a dozen somber, heavily armed troops.

Everyone in the noisy aircraft was silent, which was fine with Isabel. She was content. She never wanted this moment to end. She almost, in fact, drifted off, warm at Rick's side, as the engine *thrummed* through the bulkhead into her back. But the minutes wore on. The smile had drained from Rick's face. She asked, "Wanta share a sandwich?" Rick's eyes lit up when he saw it was peanut butter and jelly. They passed it back and forth until it was gone, and she savored the warm, plasticky water from Rick's canteen.

"When we land," Rick said, looking at the pistol from Isabel's pistol bag as he transferred all her stuff into his bulky camouflaged backpack, "we'll get you proper kit. Helmet, body armor, a real weapon."

"Is it gonna be bad?" she asked. "I mean, I know it's bad, but . . ."

He looked ill with worry, and couldn't seem to find the words to answer. He fished a tiny white cloth from a pouch and obsessively ran its edge through the grooves, nooks, and crannies of his seemingly immaculate black rifle, which bristled with attachments.

She leaned her head onto his shoulder, then remembered. "Sorry." But none of the crewmen or soldiers paid them any attention. All looked to have concerns of their own. As she shifted in her seat, the paper in her back pocket crackled and she extracted it.

"What's that?" Rick asked, glancing down at the folded pages she had torn from Emma's fifth notebook. Isabel unfolded and pressed the wrinkled paper flat on her lap.

"Notes my sister took," Isabel replied. They read together. More random thoughts about "The Social Contract," and transition plans like "Temporarily enforce prior laws," both in red.

On the last page, however, Emma had switched to black ink, her security color, under the cryptic heading, Phases. What followed had just two lines. Number one, "Outbreak," was checked: *Complete.*

And the last thing Emma had written in her notebook, the phase into which they all now headed, was number two, which Emma had named "Contagion."

PANDORA: CONTAGION

Don't miss the next exciting novel in the Pandora series

Coming soon from Rebel Base, an imprint of Kensington Publishing Corp.

Keep reading to enjoy an intriguing sample chapter . . .

Contagion

"Turning and turning in the widening gyre
The falcon cannot hear the falconer;
Things fall apart; the centre cannot hold;
Mere anarchy is loosed upon the world . . ."
–W.B. Yeats, "The Second Coming"

Chapter 1

The sound of the zipper was Emma Miller's cue. She leaned over the trucker's lap and reached into her boot for the rusty screwdriver she had found on the side of the highway. "That's a good girl," said the man—fat, ugly, and missing a front tooth—who had given Emma a ride in exchange for a promise. She looked up, and attempted a smile. He seemed to sense something was amiss. She drove the rusty screwdriver through his neck up to its handle. It sank into the voids of his mouth and sinuses with surprising ease.

She extracted her crude weapon before his hands found the spurting wound. He gurgled more than screamed, bug-eyed in shock. She dried the screwdriver and her hand on his tattered cloth upholstery. The driver made animal sounds and thrashed from side to side. His gaze never left Emma, but his hands remained clutched on his neck.

Emma's stomach rumbled. It was time for lunch. When the trucker finally slumped, inert, onto the steering wheel, she searched the filthy cab. The only thing of value was the man's wallet. "Bert Walker," his driver's license read. Age forty-seven. From the lone photo, with its shopping-mall quality backdrop of lazy palm trees and thatched huts, she gleaned he was married to a similarly unattractive woman and had two overweight children. She took the roughly hundred dollars he had in cash.

Emma considered trying to drive his truck, but grinding through gears would raise too many questions. She was a petite, five-foot-four epidemiologist trying not to attract attention, spark calls to 9-1-1, and trigger a manhunt. She climbed down and headed back to the state highway from the secluded parking spot. Bert had made a mistake, she noted and committed to memory. He shouldn't have performed his side of the bargain before her turn came. Contracts are tricky, Emma thought. She needed to discuss them with her brother Noah, who was a lawyer.

After leaving the NIH lab hours earlier, Emma had abandoned her blue mask and gloves in the woods but still carried her hospital-provided white plastic bag and its toiletries by the loops of its drawstring. She knew she would have trouble passing for uninfected. Several times, the trucker had cast sidelong glances her way after replies that he must have found odd. And Emma also wasn't sure just how contagious she remained. If she left a trail of infected people along the way, someone might plot her route and zero in on her location. And she would have at most two hours until first symptoms appeared in her wake. She had to stay ahead of any outbreak she caused and the violence that inevitably ensued.

On reaching the highway, she walked down its shoulder but didn't hold out her thumb. The traffic was heavy, but not bumper-to-bumper like on the Interstate out of D.C. Cars and trucks flew by without stopping. Did Emma appear strange and out-of-place? It wouldn't take much of an incongruity for someone to phone the police. Everyone would be paranoid now that the disease had broken out in Vermont.

A large, older car, windows rolled down, passed slowly. A woman and her three kids scrutinized Emma before pulling off onto the roadside ahead. When Isabel reached them, the African-American woman asked, "Did your car break down, hon?" Emma dared only a nod, not a verbal reply. "Well, hop in, then," the woman said.

The kids were young; they'd be easy. She needed to worry mainly about killing the mother.

Emma climbed into the front passenger seat, displacing a long-legged girl of about ten who could probably run fast. "Where you headed?" the girl's mother asked as they drove off.

"South," Emma dared reply.

"I understand. Tryin' to get . . . away?" She glanced at her children through the rearview mirror, then at Emma, who thought better of trying to smile and just nodded again.

Wind rushed through the open windows. They probably wouldn't catch the virus, diluted as the air was in the car. Maybe Emma could avoid the hassles and risk of killing them all. Four was a large number to do all at the same time. It highlighted her need for a better weapon to make these things go more smoothly.

"What's your name?" the woman asked.

"Dorothy," Emma lied in case she didn't kill them. The assumed name had popped into her head, along with the image of a yellow brick road leading south. The origin of these mysterious thoughts, which hinted at some deeper mental processes that pondered questions not yet even posed, was increasingly curious. Where did they come from, and to whom did they occur? Were they, as proposed at the NIH lab by her twin sister Isabel, a neuroscientist, the product of unconscious reasoning? And if so, to whom were those solutions given if not some mystical, conscious *self*?

"I'm Francine. And that's Wanda, Marcus, and Brandon."

The woman glanced over as if it were Emma's turn to say something. "My sister's ex-boyfriend is named Brandon," came the thought out of nowhere. To Emma's ear, it sounded like suitable small talk. A semblance of a conversation.

"Where ya from?" Francine asked.

"Connecticut," Emma said, not lying where she didn't have to. That would help minimize later slipups and give her greater flexibility in choosing the time and place of their end.

"That's close," Francine replied. "To Vermont, I mean. How long do you guess it'll take for the *P* to get down there?"

"Eight days," Emma replied. When Francine shot her a look, Emma appended, "More or less. I would guess." At least she hadn't said, *"Per my calculations."*

"Whatta you do up there in Connecticut?"

"I'm . . . in between jobs," Emma replied, which was true. But something seemed off about the conversation. Emma would have to get Francine to pull over before aiming one jab at Francine's face, then taking down the girl, then grabbing whichever boy was closest. She would probably have to chase the last one, hopefully into the woods and not down the public roadway. Or maybe she should attempt to salvage the conversation by asking a question, but what? Emma wasn't interested in anything Francine had to say. "What, *uhm*, . . . ? Where are you headed?" Emma asked. *That sounded good*, came the silent pat on the back from the enigmatic hidden voice.

Francine shot Emma another look. Something in what Emma had said, or how she had said it, sounded off. "To Atlanta," Francine replied. "I got a cousin there with a big house. Takin' us all in."

"You shouldn't go to a city," Emma commented. When Francine asked why not, Emma said, "When SED arrives, cities will turn quickly." Again, not a lie.

"He's all stocked up and everything," Francine said, but her brow was now furrowed and she gripped and re-gripped the steering wheel. Emma's hand edged closer to her boot. "It's gettin' kinda chilly," Francine said. "Let's close these windows up."

"No," Isabel said, too sharply. Too abruptly. "I mean, can we keep them cracked?"

"Sure." They all adjusted their respective windows, alternately raising them above a howl from rushing airflow and lowering them below a squeal until the noise was tolerable. Isabel was now somewhat less certain whether the pathogen she exhaled with every breath would build in the car to levels dangerous for the susceptible family. If they got sick, the authorities would do contact tracing, inquiring about anyone they had met in the last few hours. The strange white girl, Dorothy, would sit at the top of their suspect list. But the relevant quotation, *dead men tell no tales*, arose from somewhere deep in her mind.

"What's in that plastic bag?" Francine asked Emma.

They're toiletries I was given upon my release from the National Institutes of Health after being studied for a month in their Bethesda laboratory. That was a bad answer. "It's my toothbrush and stuff," Emma said instead. There. That was better. Francine seemed calmer and smiled at her.

But the woman kept stealing looks at Emma. "I'm sorry, but you just look so *familiar*." Francine must have seen the Homeland Security video explaining the effects of *Pandoravirus horribilis* by reference to its first American victim.

"I'm fairly common looking," Emma replied, trying to avoid having to begin the killing right here and right now.

"Oh, no. You're *very* pretty! Don't ever sell yourself short, Dorothy. A girl has to have confidence, I always say. And don't worry about losing your job. Ever'body's gettin' laid off these days."

Isabel surveyed Francine, then looked over her shoulder at the children. No one seemed particularly suspicious of her. "Are any of you sick?" Isabel asked Francine.

"We ain't been anywhere near Vermont!"

"No, I mean regular sick," Isabel explained.

"Oh. No. We all got good health."

That militated in favor of not killing them. Their immune systems might successfully fight off a low-level exposure to *Pandoravirus*. Their odds of survival rose even higher when Marcus passed gas, Wanda berated and punched him, Brandon and Marcus shared a laugh, and Francine had everyone lower their windows before apologizing to Emma/Dorothy. The now doubly tainted miasma was quickly swept out by the gale.

When they reached the junction with the Interstate, which looked like a parking lot, Francine pulled over. "We gotta head west from here," she told Isabel.

It was now or never. If they were infected, how far away could Emma get before the dots connected back to her and every cop and sheriff for a hundred miles was given her description? She would have to try to do Francine with one jab, probably in through the eye socket. But if Francine flinched, it may take multiple stabs during which the kids would probably throw open their doors and scatter. There was a crowded gas station and convenience store a hundred yards away. Killing them here was not a good plan. Emma would just have to hope they hadn't contracted the virus.

"Thank you," Emma said, climbing out.

"Good luck!" said Francine.

"Good luck to all of you," replied Emma.

Emma was thirsty and hungry, so she went to the convenience store, which was busy despite its nearly empty shelves. Emma got in line with a large bottle of sports drink—the only consumable liquid she could find—and a package of miniature donuts dusted with confectionary sugar. On the small TV beside the cash register, a news helicopter filmed a large, angry crowd at a Vermont blockade formed by army Humvees. The people were loud, their gestures animated. They were clearly uninfected, presumably protesting their quarantine.

"Those poor people," said the woman in line ahead of Emma, who nodded in reply. The woman kept eyeing her warily. Could she, too, possibly have recognized Emma from the DHS video? On impulse, Emma took a knit cap from a rack and put it on. She needed to avoid interacting with people she couldn't kill.

Emma resumed her march down the highway, eating her donuts and passing car after car waiting to ascend the ramp onto the Interstate. The shelter of the overpass was occupied not by the old and weathered homeless, but by the new homeless: clean-cut families and couples whose cars had died or run out of gas or money to buy gas. One tall man about her age, skinny, unwashed and unkempt, fell in alongside her and said he liked her cap. "Thank you." He then asked if she had any money. "Yes," Emma replied.

"Can I have enough to put some gas in my van?"

"No," she answered.

He grabbed her arm to slow her up and said, "Hey!" When she looked down at his grasp, he released her. "Why so unfriendly?" he said. "A perty girl like you, I woulda thought you'd be lookin' for somebody to hook up with. Maybe we help each other out."

"A contract?" she asked.

He shrugged. "Yeah, I guess. You give me gas money, and I give you a ride."

The order was again wrong. Emma would be making the same mistake as Bert: paying her price of the bargain at the front end and relying on the counterparty to honor the trade they had made. But then again, he would probably expect sex from her at some point. And she could always kill him and take his van then. *Good plan*, came to her out of nowhere just like the silent voices Isabel said Uninfecteds heard in their heads.

"Okay," she said. "Where's your van?"

Meet the Author

Raised in a small town in Mississippi, **Eric L. Harry** graduated from the Marine Military Academy in Texas and studied Russian and Economics at Vanderbilt University, where he also got a J.D. and M.B.A. In addition, he studied in Moscow and Leningrad in the USSR, and at the University of Virginia Law School. He began his legal career in private practice in Houston, negotiated complex multinational mergers and acquisitions around the world, and rose to be general counsel of a Fortune 500 company. He left to raise a private equity fund and co-found a successful oil company. His previous thrillers include Arc Light, Society of the Mind, Protect and Defend and Invasion. His books have been published in eight countries. He and his wife have three children and divide their time between Houston and San Diego.

Contact him on Facebook or visit him online at www.ericlharry.com.

Chan...
Balance.

You saved £91.02 ...

Please keep this ... for ...

You were served by Chris
No. Lines: 1
24/10/14 14:55

M O W P O S - 0 1 0 1 0 8 3 3 0 9 1
MOW POS 9.0.109 (263:347)

Thank you for shopping with us

Have you visited our website?
www.ianallanpublishing.co.uk

bcc@ianallanpublishing.co.uk
VAT No. GB 207 5323 87